Kate Forsyth

SCHOLASTIC

First published in 2009 by Scholastic Children's Books
An imprint of Scholastic Ltd
Euston House, 24 Eversholt Street
London, NW1 1DB, UK
Registered office: Westfield Road, Southam, Warwickshire, CV47 0RA
SCHOLASTIC and associated logos are trademarks and/or
registered trademarks of Scholastic Inc.

ISBN 978 1407 10284 9

A CIP catalogue record for this book is available
from the British Library.

Printed in the UK by CPI Bookmarque, Croydon, CR0 4TD
Papers used by Scholastic Children's Books are made from
wood grown in sustainable forests.

1 3 5 7 9 10 8 6 4 2

www.scholastic.co.uk/zone

www.kateforsyth.com.au

In loving memory
of Nonnie, Aunty Clarice and Aunty Gwen –
my grandmother and great-aunts,
women of the Mackenzie Clan –
who first told me the story of the bloodstains on
Mary, Queen of Scots', floor –
which no amount of scrubbing can remove

The Thin Days

Scotland in the Sixteenth Century

PART ONE

THE HAG-STONE

The Curse of Wintersloe Castle

Hannah Rose Brown was not quite thirteen years old when she discovered her family was cursed.

The day she first heard of the Curse of Wintersloe Castle was the day her life was slashed in two, as if by a silver sword. Behind her was an ordinary life, just like any other girl's. Ahead was a life shadowed with mystery and menace and magic.

Hannah had not known the world could change so swiftly. For the rest of her life, she would never forget that brightness – and darkness – can break upon you at any moment.

Hannah had no way of knowing that the letter she found stuffed in their postbox was going to change her life for ever. She only found it because she had been sent home early from school in disgrace. If Hannah's mother, Roz, had found it instead, she would have destroyed it, and so Hannah would never have found out about the curse, or the puzzle ring, or her father's mysterious past.

The envelope was of thick parchment, with a row of golden stamps depicting a red heraldic lion. It was addressed to:

The Right Honourable Viscountess of Fairknowe

On the back was printed a brilliantly coloured crest. It showed a thorn tree with stars above and roses below. The word "*Audacia*" was inscribed on a scroll above it. Underneath the crest was printed:

The Countess of Wintersloe
Wintersloe Castle
Fairknowe
Loch Lomond
Scotland

Hannah wondered how such an unusual-looking letter could possibly have ended up in their letter box. She had been born at Loch Lomond, but did not remember anything about it, since her mother had brought her from Scotland to Australia when she was only a tiny baby. Hannah thought the letter was most intriguing.

She laid it on the table, made some cinnamon toast and carried it to her bedroom. Hannah's room was very different from the rest of the apartment. Her light was swathed in crimson silk, giving the room an exotic gloom, a guitar was propped up against the chair, and her bedside table was crammed with books.

More books filled the bookcase. Books about wizards, witches, fairies, mermaids, dragons, sea-serpents, ogres, trolls, goblins, boggarts, vampires, werewolves, winged horses, unicorns, magic swords, rings of invisibility, flying carpets, talking mice, frog princes, feisty princesses and vengeful gods.

Hannah refused to read anything else. This troubled her mother, who was a science teacher at Hannah's school. Roz believed in logic and reason and proof. She tried many times to persuade Hannah to read nice books about girls who set up babysitting groups, or went to pony club, or dreamt of being ballerinas. Hannah rejected them all scornfully. So Roz reluctantly bought Hannah the books she wanted, worrying in case she was feeding an unhealthy desire to escape from real life.

Hannah was picking out a sad song on her guitar when she heard the sound of her mother's key in the lock. Her stomach twisted. She knew her mother would already have been hauled to the principal's office and told about Hannah's suspension from school. She got up and went out to face Roz, her arms crossed, her face as stony as she could make it.

"Hannah, why on earth would you rub mud into the face of the principal's daughter?" Roz sounded bewildered. Hannah wished she would get angry and shout like other people's mothers. Roz never did, though. She thought Hannah's bad behaviour was because her daughter had no male role model in her life – and this was a source of perpetual grief to Roz.

5

"She deserved it," Hannah said coldly.

"But what did she say?" Roz took off her glasses and pressed her fingers to the red indentations on either side of her nose.

Hannah shrugged.

"I just don't understand, Hannah. It's not rational! You should be trying to make friends, not throwing mud into people's faces. Won't you tell me what she said?"

Hannah answered unwillingly. "She said I was such a loser, it was no wonder my dad walked out."

Roz closed her hand around the wedding ring she wore on a chain about her neck.

"I'm not saying sorry," Hannah said. "She deserved it."

"It's me who's sorry. So sorry, darling. Your father . . . he loved you very much . . . you know he would never have left us."

"So why did she say he did?" Hannah demanded.

"Well, it's just, when people's bodies aren't found, there are legal problems . . . and people talk. . ." Roz's voice grew choked.

Hannah thought of the photo of her father that she kept hidden in her diary. It was the only photo of the two of them together. Robert had been looking down at his newborn baby with a tired and tender smile. He had the same wild, copper-coloured curls and blue-grey eyes as Hannah herself, and the same long, straight nose. He had disappeared the very next day, three days before Christmas. Roz said that he had walked into the village to

6

visit a friend, and had never returned. She thought he had probably fallen into Loch Lomond and drowned. Except his body had never been found.

Hannah did not know if her father really had died that cold winter's evening, or whether her mother just refused to admit the truth of his disappearance. Sometimes, in that dark floating space between waking and sleeping, Hannah would make up stories to explain his absence. Perhaps he had fallen and knocked his head and forgotten who he was. One day he'd receive another blow to his head and remember, and then he would come to Australia looking for them. . .

Or perhaps he had witnessed a crime, and the bad guys had kidnapped him and kept him locked up in a dark prison from which he would one day escape and come looking for them. . .

"So, are they going to expel me?" Hannah asked.

"Maybe. Mr Devine was very angry."

Hannah set her jaw. "I hate that school anyway."

"But, Hannah, I have to work there! It'll be very uncomfortable for me if you're expelled. And it was so convenient . . . we could catch the bus together. . ." Suddenly she stopped, her hand flying up to her mouth. She had seen the letter.

"I forgot to tell you about that," Hannah said. "Look, it comes from a castle in Scotland, near where we used to live. I wonder what it's doing in our letter box. It's got our address on it. But no viscountesses live here!" She smiled at the absurdity of the thought.

Her mother sat down limply at the table, staring at the letter.

"I wonder if the old lady who used to live here was really a viscountess who lost all her money. But none of her other mail calls her that. Isn't it mysterious?"

There was no response. Her mother stared at the letter with a strange, fixed expression on her face.

"Mum? Are you listening?"

"It's for me," Roz said. "The letter. It's addressed to me."

"What do you mean?" Hannah stared at her mother in utter surprise. "You aren't a viscountess!"

Roz looked at her apologetically. "Well, technically speaking, I am, I suppose."

"What? But your dad was a butcher, not a count!"

"You mean an earl," Roz said absently. "And, no, of course he wasn't an earl. But your father . . . well, he was a viscount, and so when I married him, I did become a viscountess, ludicrous as it seems. Your great-grandmother is a stickler for etiquette. In her eyes, I'm still your father's wife, and so that's how she would address any letter to me."

"My father was a viscount?"

"Uh-huh."

"And I have a great-grandmother? Who's a countess? How could you not tell me that?" Hannah was white with rage, her hands clenched by her side.

"I left all that behind me when I left Scotland," Roz said

wearily, picking up the letter and turning it over in her hand. "It meant nothing to me, and it should mean nothing to you either, Hannah. We make our own destinies."

"Surely I have a right to know something like that!"

"Hannah, please, don't be angry. You must try and understand. I was brought up to scorn that kind of old-fashioned nonsense, and your father . . . he never used his title. He'd have been embarrassed if anyone did. It's only old fossils like your great-grandmother who still care about that kind of thing. . ."

"I care!" Hannah shouted. "Of course I care! You've never told me anything about my father."

"I'm sorry," Roz said. "It's not that I deliberately left you in ignorance. . . I always meant to tell you one day . . . it's just that . . . I wanted to leave all that behind me. Make a fresh start, where no one knew about my past. I was only a viscountess for such a short time, and it never defined who I was. Can't you understand?"

Hannah could only understand that her mother had lied to her. She folded her arms, and stared at her mother accusingly.

"Hannah, darling, please don't be angry." Roz crumpled the letter in her hand. "I never even changed my name when we got married. Your father's last name was Rose, and Rosamund Rose was a bit much, don't you think? Lady Wintersloe did not approve, though. In her day, a wife always took her husband's name."

"So, my name's not even really my name! I'm not really

9

Hannah Brown?" She felt stupefied, as if she had knocked her head hard in a fall.

"I changed your name when I left Scotland. It seemed simpler if we had the same last name. . ."

Hannah snatched the letter away from her. "But . . . it's from a castle! My great-grandmother lives in a castle? In Scotland?"

"It's not really a castle." Roz sounded tired. "The castle burnt down in the sixteenth century. It's really just a house. A big house."

"My great-grandmother lives in a castle in Scotland and you never told me?" Hannah was so angry, her words tumbled out over each other.

"Your great-grandmother and I didn't really see eye to eye," Roz said. "After . . . after your father died . . . we argued . . . she didn't want me to take you away but I couldn't bear to stay. I wanted to get as far away as I could. That's why I came here to Australia."

"So my great-grandmother is really a *countess*?"

Roz nodded and shrugged, her lips quirking into a wry smile. "She's the Countess of Wintersloe. Your father was Lord Robert Rose, Viscount of Fairknowe."

"Does that make me a lady too? Lady Hannah Rose?"

"I guess it does, now that your father is dead. I mean, you are your great-grandmother's only heir. If your father were alive, you would be the Honourable Hannah Rose, but since he's gone, I guess that means you're a lady too."

"Lady Hannah Rose," she repeated wonderingly. "Heir to a castle in Scotland. . . It must be a joke! It can't be true."

"It's true enough."

"Why did you never tell me?" Hannah demanded.

Roz flushed. "I've put all that behind me, Hannah. Lady Wintersloe never thought I was good enough for her grandson. I was nothing but a butcher's daughter! And your father and I were married only a month or so before you were born. Lady Wintersloe always thought I was out to get what I could. I saw no reason to stay."

"So why is she writing to you now?"

"I don't know," Roz said.

"Well, let's open it, find out!" Hannah's anger was replaced by a fizzy excitement. She tore the envelope open.

Dear Rosamund,

I know that you must be surprised to hear from me now, after so many years. I can only say that I am sorry. I should never have spoken so cruelly to you after Robert died. I think we were both half mad with shock and grief.

I am writing to you now to beg you to come home to Wintersloe, and to bring Hannah. I would very much like to see Robert's child before I die. Do not think me maudlin; I have not been well this past year. I fell and broke my femur and have not healed well, I'm afraid. Sitting here day after day, thinking about how the

11

curse has destroyed all that I love, and worrying about the shadow it must cast over Robert's child too, has not helped.

Please come home to Wintersloe, and let me make my peace with you, and meet the little one again. It would make an old lady very happy.

Yours sincerely,

Isabelle, Countess of Wintersloe

Hannah had wanted to ask her mother what a femur was, thinking it sounded like some kind of animal, but the very next sentence in the letter drove the question right out of her mind. "What does she mean, 'the curse'?"

Roz looked uncomfortable. "She's an old lady now, and not quite all there, I think."

"Does she think she's been cursed?"

"Lots of Scottish families have strange old stories attached to them. It's just superstitious nonsense."

"But what's the story, Mum? Don't you think you've kept enough secrets from me?" Hannah spoke with mock severity.

Roz sighed. "It's completely irrational, like all those old tales. Apparently some ancestor of your father's married a fairy princess, they quarrelled, he cast her out, and so she cursed him. I don't really remember the details. Your father knew it all; he was brought up on it."

12

"So Dad's family was cursed? By a fairy princess?" Hannah gave a little snort of laughter. She had read old fairy stories where such things happened, but had never heard of anyone who actually believed it had happened to one of their ancestors.

"I know! Isn't it ridiculous? Yet your father told me all about it quite seriously when we first fell in love, in case I wanted to have nothing to do with him."

"Is that why he just disappeared like that? Because he was cursed?"

Roz moved restlessly. "People die all the time, Hannah. It's got nothing to do with some old story about a curse."

"His body was never found."

"It was Christmas. It was freezing. There was snow everywhere. And Loch Lomond is very deep in parts. Almost two hundred metres deep. He could've fallen in the loch, and got caught in something under the water . . . it means nothing that his body wasn't found!"

It still sounds like cursed bad luck, Hannah thought, but she did not say so. Instead she said, "I've always wanted to go to Scotland. When can we leave?"

Roz looked surprised. "What do you mean? We can't go to Scotland! What about my job? What about school?"

"I'm going to be expelled anyway, and you hate that school just as much as I do. Why shouldn't we go to Scotland?"

"But. . ." Roz looked harassed.

"My great-grandmother says she's sick. She wants to see me before she dies. Well, I want to see her too! I never

1 3

even knew I had a great-grandmother. Let alone a castle in Scotland."

"It's not a castle," Roz said. "More of a house."

"A big house! I know. With a curse on it. I want to see it, Mum."

There was a long pause. "I swore I would never go back," Roz said quietly.

"Are you upset because the old lady was mean to you? But she's said sorry now, hasn't she? You're always telling me not to hold grudges. You should go and make it up with her."

"It's not just that. I don't think I can bear to be there again. At Wintersloe, I mean. Where your father. . ." She turned away to hide her tears.

Hannah frowned. "It was a long time ago, Mum. Almost thirteen years. Don't you think it's time you got over it?"

Roz smiled weakly. "Always so brutally frank, aren't you, Hannah?"

"Well, you're the one always telling *me* not to brood over things."

"Yes, I know, but. . ."

"Besides, if there's a curse on me, I need to find out all about it so I can break it."

"Oh, Hannah, it's just an old story. Curses don't really exist. It's completely irrational."

"So is keeping my great-grandmother secret all these years. Why shouldn't I go and meet her before she dies? If she's really so old, it might be my last chance."

14

"But it would cost a fortune."

"No, it won't. Only the air tickets. We can give up the rental on this apartment; that'd save us heaps."

"But what about all our stuff?"

Hannah grinned, scenting a weakening in her mother's resolve. "What about it? We don't have much. We'll have a garage sale and sell it all."

"But we'll need it when we come back."

"Maybe we won't come back," Hannah said. "Surely I'm meant to get the castle when my great-grandmother dies? It must be full of stuff."

"Full of debts, no doubt," Roz said.

"Well, at least I'll get to see it – a castle in Scotland! Oh, you couldn't be so mean to say we can't go." Hannah clenched her hands into fists. "I'll never forgive you if we don't go, never!"

Roz made a small, helpless gesture. "Maybe, just for a while . . . but only if we take all your worksheets with us. You can't start falling behind with your school work."

Hannah flung her arms about her mother. "Thank you! Oh, what an adventure!"

Roz tried to press her close, but Hannah had already broken free and was marching to her room to look up curses in her *Encyclopedia of Secret Knowledge*. Her mother might not believe in curses, but Hannah most certainly did. If there was any truth to the old story, it seemed clear to Hannah that she must be the one to break the curse – the sooner, the better.

15

Fairknowe

"Mum, what does maudlin mean?" Hannah was reading her great-grandmother's letter again.

Roz sighed. "Oh, I don't know, Hannah. Sad and sentimental."

"It's a good word. I like it. It sounds like someone's name. Maudlin." Hannah imagined a sad little girl with drooping black hair, sitting on a chair with her feet turned inwards and her shoulders slumped.

"Put that letter away, it's going to fall to pieces if you keep poring over it."

Hannah carefully stowed the letter away and turned to look eagerly out the bus window again. Almost a month had passed since the arrival of her great-grandmother's letter. Roz had had to give notice to leave her job, apply for passports, and have their furniture put in storage. Even the flight had taken a day and a night, for there were nearly ten thousand miles between Australia and Scotland.

Now they were on a bus heading north into the Scottish

Highlands. Undulating green hills rolled past, each field contained within old mossy walls overgrown with brambles and thorns. The bright autumn leaves of birch trees fluttered in the wind, brilliant against the moody grey sky. Every now and again Hannah saw a grand house with turrets and battlements, and she would cry out in delight and point them out to her mother. Most of the houses, though, were small and grey.

Gradually the gentle rounded hills humped higher against the horizon, showing bare brown flanks where nothing seemed to grow except heather and the occasional patch of a brilliant golden flower that Roz said was gorse. Then the bus bumped its way through a small village, past tiny cottages with flowering boxes at the windows and past an inn built of slate and timber. Then at last Hannah got her first glimpse of Loch Lomond.

It had been drizzling that morning, but over the loch the skies had cleared so the wide stretch of water was a soft blue. Islands floated here and there, the still water reflecting a blurred mirror image. Then the road took them back into the forest, the silver trunks of the birch trees hanging with silvery-green moss as if they were thousands of years old. In the distance, Hannah saw a glimpse of a gloomy mountain peak towering above the other high peaks.

"That's Ben Lomond," Roz said. "I climbed it once with your father. It was a beautiful warm spring day when we left, and by the time we got to the top, it was snowing. Lucky your father had packed a fleecy jacket in his backpack, else I might've frozen to death." She sighed. "To think we've come in October! I swore I'd never live through another Scottish winter."

"It can't be that bad," Hannah said.

Roz shot her a wry look. "Just you wait, you little Aussie."

"Well, I'm looking forward to having a white Christmas."

"A dark and gloomy Christmas," Roz retorted. "It doesn't always snow this low down."

"It will for me!"

"I hope so, honey."

The bus rumbled into another small village, built close on the shores of the loch. Dinghies bobbed on the swell only a few metres away from the bus stop. Hills rose on the far side of the loch, purple laid upon brown. Here and there clumps of trees blazed gold and red.

Roz pulled her make-up compact out of her handbag and squinted at herself anxiously, then outlined her lips with a soft brown lipstick that hardly changed the colour of her lips at all. Hannah thought that she would wear fire-engine red when she was allowed to wear make-up.

The bus came to a halt and they clambered out, Hannah lugging her guitar, her backpack heavy on her shoulders. Roz heaved out their two enormous suitcases, saying, "How are we to get all our stuff to Wintersloe without a car? There must be a cab. Let's go into the general store and ask."

Dragging their suitcases, they crossed the road and went

18

inside Shaw's Store, a small shop built of grey stone with tiny windows whose frames had been painted a dazzling white.

A pretty girl about Hannah's age was reading a magazine behind the shop counter. Her blonde hair was tied back in a ponytail, her eyes were blue as forget-me-nots, and she wore tight jeans and a baby-doll top with red and blue embroidery. She made Hannah feel taller and gawkier than ever. She was dressed in a navy-blue smock with a white Peter Pan collar. Hannah hated it, but Roz thought she looked sweet.

"Can I help you?" the blonde girl asked in a bored voice, not looking up from her magazine.

"I was wondering if we could call a cab? We need to get up to Wintersloe, and it's a bit far, what with all our bags. . ." Roz waved an apologetic hand at their suitcases.

The girl stared at them in open curiosity. "No cabs round here. Why do you want to go up to the big house?"

"We're staying there," Roz said.

"We're going to stay with my great-grandmother," Hannah put in proudly.

The girl flashed Hannah an unfriendly look. "Mum! Need you!" she called.

"What's wrong? Can't you manage it, Scarlett? The boys have run me off my feet, and I've only just sat down for a cuppa," a woman's voice grumbled down the stairs.

"People here wanting to get to the big house."

"Really? Is it Lady Wintersloe's great-granddaughter?

19

Linnet said she was expected today." A short, round woman with a mass of dark, curly hair hurried down the stairs. Her hazel eyes were bright with interest. "Why, Roz! I mean, Lady Fairknowe. How lovely to see you again after such a long time. Is this your little girl?"

Roz smiled awkwardly, as if she didn't really remember who the woman was. "Oh, yes. This is Hannah," she said.

"My, but you're the vision of your great-grandmother!" Scarlett's mother said to Hannah, smiling broadly. "Welcome home!"

"Lady Wintersloe doesn't have orange hair!" Scarlett shot a hostile glance at Hannah.

"She did when she was a lass," Scarlett's mother replied. "All the Roses have red hair."

Scarlett snorted. "Her hair's not red, it's orange as anything."

Roz leapt to her daughter's defence. "We normally call it copper-coloured. It's beautiful."

Hannah just stared at Scarlett with her stoniest expression.

Scarlett looked away. She twirled her blonde ponytail round and round her finger.

"Best go over to Allan's place," Scarlett's mother said, frowning in thought. "He's got a van, with plenty of room for all your bags."

"Allan?" Roz cried in surprise. "Not Allan MacEwan?"

"Yes, that's right," she said.

"That's amazing. Allan is still here? Allan was your

father's best friend," Roz said to Hannah. "They grew up together. Yes, let's go and ask Allan."

"Do you remember the way? Scarlett, best show them."

Scarlett screwed up her nose as if she had smelled something disgusting, and reluctantly came out from behind the counter. "Great way to spend the first day of the holidays," she muttered.

"Leave your bags," her mother said, ignoring her. "Allan can pick them up for you. My, but Lady Wintersloe will be pleased to see you, lassie. It's a bit lonely up there, that big old pile. A young thing like you will liven it up no end."

Hannah nodded as the two mothers exchanged a rather stilted farewell, and followed Scarlett as she led the way outside. The shops were all lined up along one side of the road, facing the loch. Most of them were built of the same grey stone as the general store, with white-painted window frames. There was a hairdresser, a pharmacy, a butcher, and an inn called The Green Man. At the very end of the row was a shop with its door and window frames painted candyfloss pink. A sign hung above the street, depicting a green hill with a flowering tree upon it. The sign read *The Fäerie Knowe*. Crammed in the window were fairy dresses, sparkly wands, glittering tiaras, books on fairies, and fairy dolls sitting on toadstools. Hannah paused to look in the window. Her eye was caught by a small booklet in one corner. It was called *The Curse of Wintersloe Castle*. A chill ran down her body.

"That's new," Roz said, catching up with them. "It used to be a baker's shop."

21

"I work there on Saturdays," Scarlett said. "They run parties in a little room upstairs. It's all painted to look like a fairy forest. I dress up as a fairy princess; I have the best outfit!"

"What fun that would be!" Roz said. "Maybe Hannah could come and help out sometimes."

Scarlett looked less than enthusiastic. "I guess. Though Miss Underhill won't let just *anyone* work for her. They have to be able to sing and dance and do face-painting."

"I can sing," Hannah said.

"They've got to look like a fairy princess too." Scarlett's voice made it clear she thought Hannah would not be at all acceptable.

"Hannah would make a perfectly beautiful fairy princess," Roz said.

"Fairy princesses don't have red hair," Scarlett said flatly.

"Of course they do." A voice spoke behind them. "Legends say that anything red and white is fairy-born. They used to believe that a glance from a red-haired girl could kill a man."

Hannah looked around. A woman stood on the doorstep of the fairy shop. She had grey hair pulled back from her face, and wore a shapeless cardigan over beige slacks. Big glasses obscured her eyes.

"Well, that's just nonsense, isn't it, darling," Roz said.

"Maybe," Hannah said, and shot Scarlett her best glare. Scarlett glared back.

"You're the Rose girl, aren't you?" the woman asked.

22

"I'm Morgana Underhill. I own The Fäerie Knowe. I'm very interested in fairy lore. Are you? You should be, with your heritage."

"I like fairies. I mean, I used to, when I was little."

"You don't have to be little to believe in fairies," Miss Underhill said. "Not real fairies, anyway."

Roz looked exasperated. "Come on, Hannah, let's keep going, shall we? We said we'd be at Wintersloe in time for afternoon tea."

"Come and see me if you'd like to earn a little extra pocket money," Miss Underhill said. "I'm always interested in red-haired girls that can sing."

Hannah nodded, and followed Scarlett and her mother along the street. Scarlett was walking quickly, looking cross. Roz gave Hannah a little smile and a shrug. As Scarlett led them into a crowded mechanic's yard, a motorized bicycle whizzed past at top speed, spraying them with gravel. Crouched on its back was a boy with long black hair whipping around his face.

"That Donovan!" Scarlett cried. "He'll kill somebody one day."

The boy looked back over his shoulder at them. Hannah went scarlet and looked away, embarrassed to be caught staring.

A thin, crooked-looking man limped after the boy, shaking an oily rag and looking furious. "Come back here, you little brat! Did I say you could go?"

He stopped shouting at the sight of Roz and the two

girls, and rather self-consciously shoved the oily rag in his back pocket. He wore a torn blue singlet under a dirty flannelette shirt. "Sorry about that. That boy would enrage a saint! What can I do for you?"

"Allan? Is that you?" Roz stared at him.

He stared back. "Roz?"

She nodded. "I've come back. Just for a little while. This is Hannah. My daughter." She put her hands on Hannah's shoulders.

"My God. Bob's daughter? Bob's little girl?"

With difficulty, Hannah stopped herself from rolling her eyes.

Allan huffed out a great breath and limped towards them. He didn't seem to know whether to embrace Roz, or shake her hand, or just nod and smile at her. He settled for the latter, perhaps because of the dirt and grease on his hands, which he wiped on his shirt. Hannah then saw, with a shock, that one of his hands was badly scarred. "Welcome home, Roz. It's been a long time."

Roz nodded and smiled too, and said, "Yes, indeed."

"Where have you been all this time?"

While Roz answered politely, Hannah looked around her with curiosity. They were standing in a yard crowded with cars and motorbikes and trucks, all in various stages of dismemberment or decay. A big shed had its doors thrown open. Inside were a dirty white van and a bench littered with tools.

Roz was explaining about their bags. "I think we may

just walk up to Wintersloe, it's such a lovely day, and it's not far from here, really. If you wouldn't mind bringing up the bags for us later."

"Of course, not at all. Good to have you back."

Hannah picked up her backpack and her guitar. She was not leaving *them* in the care of this dirty-looking man. She followed her mum out into the street.

"I warn you, the castle is haunted," Scarlett said, close to Hannah's ear. "A witch was burnt to death near there. You'd better be careful."

"Really?" Hannah asked, but Scarlett just called "See you!" and went back down the hill towards the village with a casual wave of her hand.

"I cannot believe how much Allan has changed!" Roz was saying. "I guess thirteen years is a long time. I would not have recognized him if I'd passed him in the street. He's got so. . ." She groped for a word.

"Old?" Hannah suggested.

"Older, of course. We're all older." Roz sounded irritated. "I mean we were only quite young when I saw him last. No, I don't mean that. I mean . . . he was just so. . ."

"Dirty?"

Roz flashed her a look. "Yes, I guess that's what I mean. He's changed an awful lot."

"Oh, well, I bet you've changed heaps too," Hannah said cheerfully. "Lots more grey hair now."

Roz smiled wryly. "Thanks, darling."

25

Blackthorn Twigs

The road ran through close-growing trees. Glimpses of the loch could be seen to the west. To the north rose a high green hill, crowned by a great mass of twisted black twigs and thorns. A shadow hung over the hill, as clouds gathered before the sun. Hannah gave a little shiver and pulled her cardigan closer.

"That hill is called Fairknowe," Roz said. "See how the landscape changes? That's the Highland Boundary Fault. A collision of tectonic plates about four million years ago caused the Midland Valley to fall by, oh, I don't know, several thousand metres. That's why the highlands are so much higher than. . ."

"Let me guess, the lowlands. Thanks, Mrs Science Teacher."

Roz grinned. "Well, I thought you'd be interested. It's very dramatic, geographically speaking. It's the fault that causes Fairknowe Hill to rise up so steeply from the land all around it, and made all those islands across the loch. The fault crosses Scotland all the way to Arran."

"It certainly makes pretty scenery." Hannah paused to catch her breath at the top of the hill. From here, they had an uninterrupted view of the loch and its scattered islands, which looked like the beads of a broken necklace.

"The view is even better from Wintersloe. Come on! Just round this corner."

Hefting her guitar higher, Hannah followed the curve of the road and found herself standing before a wide set of iron gates. Stone gargoyles were crouched on top of the massive pillars, each holding a twig. One looked merry, the other sad.

High walls curved away from either side, with trees hanging over the capstones. Beside the gate was a tiny stone house, gabled and turreted, surrounded by tall spires of foxgloves and a spilling profusion of alyssum. A boy's bicycle lay abandoned on the drive outside the small wooden gate. It had a ramshackle motor attached to the back, and Hannah recognized it as the one ridden by the black-haired boy in the village.

"That little house was practically a ruin last time I was here," Roz said. "It looks like someone lives there now. And the gates are shut. Should we ring the bell, I wonder?"

"Of course we should." Hannah seized the chain attached to the clapper and rang it vigorously. A magpie flew down to investigate. Head cocked, it perched on the gate, regarding her with a black beady eye.

"One for sorrow," Hannah said.

"Superstitious nonsense," Roz replied automatically,

her fingers playing with the ring hanging about her neck. The magpie gave a shriek and flew at her, as if trying to seize the ring with its beak. Roz ducked, hastily pushing the chain back inside her shirt and waving her arms to frighten the bird away. "Magpies are such thieves! They'll steal anything bright."

"It's much smaller than the magpies in Australia," Hannah said.

The magpie fluttered to the top of the sad gargoyle, which was holding a twig with berries on it. The happy gargoyle was holding a twig with flowers. "I wonder what plant that is," Hannah said.

"Blackthorn," a woman's voice replied. "*Prunus spinosa.* It's part of the rose family. It has flowers in spring and sloe berries in autumn. At least, most blackthorns do. The one on top of Fairknowe Hill has not bloomed in living memory. The castle is named after it, you know."

Hannah and Roz looked round, and saw a woman with very short black hair and a dirt-streaked face standing in the middle of the foxgloves. She was dressed in a khaki shirt and trousers, and wore heavy-duty gardening gloves. She was carrying a little spade in one hand.

"You must be Lady Fairknowe." She stripped off her gloves and came forward with a warm smile. "You won't remember me, though we did meet, many years ago. I'm Evangeline Lombardi, the gardener here. Come on in." She swiftly unlocked a little gate set on one side of the main gates and held it open for them.

"Please, call me Roz." Hannah's mother looked at the other woman with interest. Although she was only small, she looked wiry and strong, and her hands were brown and hard. Her eyes were a clear blue, startling in her brown face, and her teeth were charmingly crooked.

"OK, Roz. You can call me Genie, most people do. You go on up to the house. Lady Wintersloe is so looking forward to seeing you."

Roz nodded, smiling.

"You look like you could do with some help," Genie said to Hannah as she heaved her backpack up on to her shoulder again. She turned her head and yelled, "Max!"

"What?" a distant boy's voice yelled back.

"Come and help out, OK?"

"But, Mum, Donovan's here."

"He can come and help too. And then I want you two out in the garden."

"But, Mum, I'm just reading an article on anthrax! It's really cool."

"You've had enough time on that computer, young man! It's a beautiful day. And I need you to come and carry Lady Hannah's bags."

Hannah felt a little shock of surprise. No one had ever called her Lady Hannah before. She considered it, and decided she quite liked it.

"Please, just Hannah," Roz said. "No need to call a twelve-year-old girl 'lady'!"

"But, Mum, I'm almost thirteen," Hannah protested.

"Still no reason to get all lah-di-dah on me," Roz said firmly.

The upstairs window was flung open and a boy around Hannah's age put his head out. He was thin and dark like his mother, and wore round, gold-rimmed glasses. He stared at Hannah in open curiosity.

"Come on, Max, can you do what I ask for a change?" Genie put her hands on her hips, staring up at her son.

"All right, all right, I'm coming," he answered, sounding very put-out.

Hannah raised her chin. "I'm fine. I don't need help. I'd rather carry my own stuff."

"Are you sure?" Genie looked troubled, but then smiled and shrugged. "All right then. I'll be seeing you around. Come down and have a cup of tea whenever you like."

"Thanks, I'd like that," Roz said.

Mother and daughter walked past the gatehouse and up the curving drive towards the house. Hannah was so excited she felt as if she had springs attached to her boots. Even her backpack and guitar didn't seem so heavy any more. The drive came out of the shadow of the trees into sunshine, turning a giant circle around a garden where crimson roses, heavy-headed, filled the air with sweet fragrance.

"They call that the Queen's Garden. Mary, Queen of Scots, is meant to have planted the first red rose there. Personally I always thought that very unlikely. If she had slept in all the beds and visited all the houses she's meant to have visited, she can't have spent many nights under her own roof! She only lived in Scotland for six years or so."

Hannah gazed at the garden in awe. "Imagine if she did, though. I wonder which rose it was?"

"She died hundreds of years ago, Hannah. Roses do not live that long! It's not reasonable to think any one of those roses is more than ten or twenty years old."

"They could be the descendant of the rose planted by Mary, Queen of Scots," Hannah argued. "Just like I'm the descendant of the people who lived here then."

"I suppose that may be possible," Roz conceded. "Though I still think it's very unlikely she ever came near this place!"

Hannah was not listening. She stood still, staring up at Wintersloe Castle, which had just come into view behind the trees. Built of warm golden-grey stone, the house basked in the sunshine, surrounded by a tangled profusion of flowers. At one end was a tall pepper-pot tower, its bronze roof turquoise blue with age. At the other end was a small turret crowned with a pointed roof on which stood an ornate weathervane. In between was a tall house with large bay windows, tall chimneys, crow-stepped gables and steeply pitched slate roofs that sported stone gargoyles and heraldic beasts.

"Wow!" Hannah said.

"See, I told you it wasn't a castle. Built in the 1860s, I think."

"It looks like a castle."

31

"Believe me, real castles were never so pretty. It'd take a marauding army about ten seconds to breach this place's defences."

"It's gorgeous!"

"If you like that sort of thing. I must say, *I* think it's the most impractical house I've ever seen. All it needs is a folly in the garden."

"What's a folly? I thought that meant doing something stupid."

"Yes, exactly. In this case, architecturally speaking." Seeing Hannah's look, Roz smiled. "It means when you build something in your garden that has no use. You build it just for the look of it. Rich people in Victorian times used to build fake ruins in their garden, for example. Too much money!"

"Not everything has to be practical or useful, you know."

"Why not? What's the point of it if it's not useful?"

"I don't know. Fun, perhaps? Or maybe just because it's beautiful?" This was an old argument between mother and daughter, and so was conducted lazily, without rancour.

"Does it really have a ghost?" Hannah wanted to know.

"Of course not. The whole concept of ghosts is completely irrational, you know that."

"I wish it did."

Roz cast her a look, half amused, half irritated. "The only scary thing in this house is your great-grandmother, you can trust me on that. Come on, let's get it over with."

Together they walked up the broad stone steps to the

front door. Roz smoothed down her skirt with both hands, took a deep breath, and then put her finger to the bell. They heard a shrill ringing somewhere inside the house.

She was just ringing it again when the door was flung open.

A very old, very small woman stood in the doorway. Her back was so stooped she had to twist her head sideways to see. A cloud of short white curls covered her head, and her skin was as creased and spotted as ancient linen. Her green eyes were dim and clouded. At the sight of Hannah, her whole face lit up. She reached out two trembling, clawlike hands and seized Hannah's shoulders, drawing her down into a close embrace.

"My darling girl, it's so very good to see you!" she said in a soft, husky voice. "Let me have a look at you! Are you not the very picture of your father? Red as any Rose, we always say round these parts! Just look at you, my lamb!"

Hannah normally disliked being kissed and hugged by strangers, but this little old woman was so soft and gentle and sweetly scented Hannah hugged her back just as naturally as if she had known her all her life. She was conscious of a sense of relief. Her great-grandmother did not seem so scary!

But Roz was exclaiming in surprise, "Linnet! How lovely! I wasn't expecting to see you."

The old woman smiled broadly, her eyes disappearing into a net of wrinkles. "No doubt you thought I'd be dead and gone long ago."

"No, no, I just meant. . ."

"No harm done, my lady. I was very old last time you saw me, and now I'm even older. Sometimes I surprise myself that I'm still tottering around!"

"Hannah, this is Linnet. She has been the cook here at Wintersloe for . . . well, for as long as your father could ever remember. He always used to say she cooked the best marmalade cake in the world!"

"Aye, Bobby loved his marmalade cake. I wondered if you'd remember. I made it for the wee one to have for her tea." She smiled at Hannah, who bit back a grin at the idea of this tiny woman calling her "the wee one".

"Her ladyship is so pleased you've come. She's been that cranky since she broke her leg. Come in! Where's all your bags?"

"Allan MacEwan is going to bring them up from the village for us," Roz replied.

Linnet shook her head sadly. "Och, the poor man. That Donovan leads him a merry dance, I can tell you. But come in, what am I doing leaving you on the doorstep? We can talk just as well in the house."

She flung wide the arched door, and let Hannah and her mother into a vast hall, its domed ceiling far above them. Light poured in through the great windows, illuminating the golden colour of the panelling and the gilded frames of immense pastoral paintings, so vast and lifelike it seemed they were windows into another time. Hannah looked about her in amazement. Antlers were hung on the wall above

34

the great stone fireplace, and shields and daggers lined the wide wooden staircase that led in a great swoop up to the upper floor. Hannah hugged herself in secret delight.

"But how's all with you, Lady Fairknowe?" the old cook said. "You're too thin! I'll have to be doing what I can to fatten you up! We're having a feast tonight to celebrate your homecoming. I've made game soup, and roast grouse with skirlie, and bramble crumble, all your favourites, my lamb." Linnet pinched Hannah's cheek affectionately. Hannah could only stare at her in amazement, having never heard of any such dishes. Game soup sounded very odd, while Hannah had always thought "grouse" meant to complain. And bramble crumble sounded positively dangerous!

"Let me take you in to see her ladyship, then I'll bring you a nice cup of tea and a wee bite to eat. You must be starving." The old cook led them down a wide hallway, every spare inch of the walls decorated with paintings of mountains and moors and stags and stormy seascapes.

Hannah barely had time to glance about her before Linnet was knocking on a panelled door. Without waiting for an answer, she opened the door and led Hannah and her mother into a large drawing room that looked out over the garden. Hannah received a confused impression of warmth and colour and richness, but all her attention was concentrated on the woman who sat upright in a wheelchair by the fire.

Lady Wintersloe

Lady Wintersloe was long and thin and very elegant, dressed in a green woollen suit with a cameo brooch pinned to one lapel. A newspaper was folded on the table beside her and she held a fountain pen in one long, manicured hand. Unlike most old ladies Hannah had seen, her hair was not cut short, but smoothly coiled into a knot at the back of her head and secured with a tortoiseshell comb. It was a silvery-gold colour. High cheekbones gave the impression of hollowed cheeks on either side of a long, patrician nose. Her eyebrows had been carefully drawn in with a pencil, and she wore powder, blusher and lipstick, very bright against her withered skin. A tartan rug was laid over her knees, but Hannah could see one leg was enclosed in a cast.

"Ah, Rosamund, Hannah. Do come in, please." Lady Wintersloe laid down her pen upon the newspaper and removed her glasses, letting them hang from a gold chain around her neck. "How lovely to see you both. Forgive me for not rising. I broke my femur, you may remember, and I'm afraid it is not healing as it ought. The ravages of age, I'm afraid. Come, draw up a chair, sit down."

Hannah looked around for somewhere to sit. The seat closest to her great-grandmother had a smoke-grey cat curled up on it. Hannah went to pick her up, thinking to hold the cat on her lap, but her grandmother held up a warning hand. "Watch out!"

It was too late. The cat had lashed out, scratching Hannah on the hand.

"Ow!" she cried, and sucked her hand. The cat leapt down and stalked over to the window, where she sat, back to the room, tail lashing.

"That nasty bogey-cat!" Linnet said.

"I'm so sorry," Lady Wintersloe said. "Are you all right?"

Hannah nodded, looking down at the line of red beading where the cat's sharp claws had drawn blood, then sat in the chair the cat had vacated, sucking her hand. Her mother sat nearby, looking harassed.

"She's really not a very friendly cat, I'm afraid. Your father called her Jinx, which sadly proved to be prophetic. It was because of Jinx that I fell down the stairs and broke my femur. She has a way of always being underfoot when you least want her."

"Which is always," Linnet muttered, as she went out and shut the door behind her.

"So what did you break? Is that why you're in a

wheelchair?" Hannah saw her mother grimace at her to be more tactful, but ignored her. Hannah could never see how being good and polite helped you find out the things you wanted to know.

"I broke my femur. That's your thigh bone." Lady Wintersloe indicated her right leg. "It is such a nuisance! The doctor says I need a rod put in, but I must wait until a bed becomes available, which could be a long time."

"So your leg is still broken?" Hannah cried.

Her great-grandmother nodded.

"Doesn't it hurt?" Hannah asked.

"I'm afraid so."

"That's terrible."

"Oh, well. Nothing I can do about it. I can't afford private care. I've already sold nearly all I have of value, just to keep the house from falling apart. I'm reluctant to sell any more paintings, because about the only income I have is from the open days, and no one will come if the house is bare." She sighed. "I do hate to sell what has been in the family for generations. I'd like to be able to pass it down to you, my dear."

"Oh, that's all right," Hannah said. "Better to sell it and fix your leg. We can always buy it back again later."

"You'll have to set about restoring the family's fortunes," Lady Wintersloe said with a strained smile.

"I want to be a great soul singer! I'll sing all over the world and sell millions of records, and then I'll be able to buy anything I want."

"You like singing? I see you have a guitar. Your father was musical too, did you know? He played double bass very well."

"He called her Mary-Lou," Roz broke in. "He said she was the only other woman in his life."

"His double bass? He had a name for it?" Hannah realized just how little she knew about her own father. It made her angry at her mother, for not telling her things she should know.

"For her," Roz corrected. "He always called his double bass 'her'."

"Can I see it . . . I mean, her? Mary-Lou?"

"Of course," her great-grandmother replied. "The double bass is in the music room. There are quite a few musical instruments there; our family has always loved music. You must ask Linnet to show you where it is."

"OK. I'd like that."

"So let me look at you. Red as any Rose, I see. You'll grow very tired of people saying that to you around here. I know I did. And tall! The Roses are always tall."

Hannah smiled and Lady Wintersloe smiled back. "I am so very glad to see you, Hannah. Thank you for coming all this way."

"Hannah was very keen to meet you," Roz said stiffly. Hannah wondered if she was annoyed at being left out of the conversation for so long, since Roz made it sound as if she had not been very keen to meet Lady Wintersloe again herself.

"I am pleased to meet you too, Hannah. I'm only sorry I left it so long to write. I had not altogether realized how much you would have grown. It was only as my own birthday approached, and I remembered how old I was, that I realized."

"So how old are you?" Hannah asked.

Her mother exclaimed in horror, but Lady Wintersloe smiled. "I'm eighty-eight, Hannah. A magic number, your father would have said."

"Why?"

"Because it's a palindrome, just like your name, Hannah."

"Oh. That means the same forwards and backwards, doesn't it. Did you know my father called me 'Hannah' because my birth date is like that? It's the twenty-first of December." Lady Wintersloe nodded to show she knew the date. Hannah seized her pen and scribbled *21/12* on the edge of her great-grandmother's newspaper. "See? It's the same backwards as forwards. Apparently Dad said it was a mathematically perfect date."

"Your father liked palindromes," Lady Wintersloe said. "He thought they were magic. The Fair Folk are either drawn to them or repelled by them, according to their nature. The Seelie Court love order and symmetry, but the Unseelie Court hate it and are confounded by it."

Hannah was puzzled, and her great-grandmother smiled wearily. "You do not know the terms? The Seelies are spirits of a benevolent nature, while the Unseelies are cruel and malicious. Unfortunately it is the Unseelie Court which now rules the hollow hills."

"Fairies, do you mean?" Hannah was not sure she had understood her great-grandmother properly.

Lady Wintersloe's eyebrows drew together. She leant forward, laying one thin hand on Hannah's arm. "I am speaking of the Sidhe, Hannah. Pronounced 'shee' but spelled S-I-D-H-E. We call them the Fair Folk, or the Good Neighbours, because it is not safe to call them by name. They are not pretty little fluttery things like the fairies you see drawn in books and cards. They are as tall as you or I, or even taller, and powerful indeed."

"Like elves?" Hannah asked, thinking of Legolas in the movie of *The Lord of the Rings*.

Lady Wintersloe's face relaxed, and she sat back. "Yes, Hannah, very like elves, though they are German in origin and we are talking about the Sidhe, who are Scottish and Irish. They have always been here, or rather, living alongside us in their own realm. Some think they are ancient nature-spirits, maybe even the old gods and goddesses, who withdrew from this world when they were no longer worshipped. Others think they are just another race of people, more in touch with the natural magic of the world than us humans, who withdrew into the hollow hills and mounds when they were defeated in battle. *Sidhe* is Gaelic for 'people of the mounds'."

"They say that up to ninety-five per cent of Scots continued to believe in fairies right up to the end of the

41

nineteenth century. Isn't it incredible?" Roz shook her head in disbelief.

Lady Wintersloe said sharply, "The Sidhe have been known in Scotland for centuries, Rosamund. There are endless stories and poems and ballads describing their deeds."

"Well, yes, fairy stories," Roz replied. "Every culture has its myths and legends. That is how primitive people try to explain natural phenomena like thunder and lightning and the moon waxing and waning. We know better now. We have science to explain such things."

"Science cannot explain everything, Rosamund," Lady Wintersloe said austerely.

Roz huffed out her breath in exasperation. "Perhaps not, Lady Wintersloe. . ."

"Please, Roz! You're my grandson's wife; it is ridiculous to stand on ceremony with me," Lady Wintersloe said sharply. Roz flushed scarlet, and Hannah looked from one to the other in dismay. "Why do you not both call me Belle? It sounds much nicer," Lady Wintersloe said, trying to speak more gently.

"Then you must call me Roz," Hannah's mother replied coolly. "No one calls me Rosamund."

"But it is such a pretty name. . ." Lady Wintersloe said, then paused. "Very well, then, Roz. Don't you sometimes think, like Hamlet, that there are more things in heaven and earth than you can dream of in your philosophy?"

"Perhaps, though I cannot imagine that fairies are one of them," Roz answered drily.

"It is not wise to underestimate the Fair Folk," Lady Wintersloe said, sitting as stiffly as she could, with her cast held out awkwardly before her.

Hannah glanced at her mother, and saw Roz surreptitiously roll her eyes. She obviously thought the old lady was wandering in her wits. Hannah was a little surprised too, she had to admit, even though it was not so long since she had been leaving letters to the fairies at the bottom of the garden.

Lady Wintersloe turned pointedly to Hannah. "But we were speaking of palindromes, weren't we? Do you know this one? 'Did Hannah say as Hannah did?' Write it down; you can't get it otherwise."

Hannah took her great-grandmother's pen and wrote the sentence down, and Lady Wintersloe leant forward to run her finger backwards over the sentence. "See? It's the same forwards or backwards."

Hannah laughed in surprise. "So it is!"

Lady Wintersloe nodded. "Your father told me that one. He knew lots. Let me see. There's one about 'rats' and 'star', I don't remember that one. Oh, here's one! Write down: 'Do geese see God?'"

Hannah had to turn the newspaper round to find a piece of margin free from scribbles. She wrote the sentence down, and then read it backwards. "It's a palindrome too."

"Your father's favourite was always, 'Draw, O coward!' He and Allan used to have pretend sword fights in the old castle, and shout that all the time." Lady Wintersloe sighed.

A soft knock on the door made Roz look up from the magazine she was rather noisily riffling through, and caught Lady Wintersloe's attention. "Ah, Linnet! Tea? Lovely." As Lady Wintersloe moved, a twinge of pain crossed her face and was sternly repressed.

Linnet came trotting into the room, pushing a wheeled trolley. It was laden with delicate china plates and cups, painted with a design of blackthorn blossoms and sloe berries, and a two-tier cake stand heaped with goodies. A tall, elegant teapot, bearing the shield of the Rose family, steamed enticingly.

Hannah jumped up to investigate. She saw scones, a bowl of whipped cream and another of dark purple jam, sugar-dusted shortbread, and a huge sticky cake crowned with curls of orange peel.

"I hope you're hungry!" The tiny old woman beamed round at them as she pushed the trolley next to Lady Wintersloe's left hand.

Lady Wintersloe poured two cups of tea, her hands trembling visibly, then paused and looked at Hannah. "Tea, or would you prefer milk?"

"I'll have tea, please." Hannah cast a quick look at her mother to see if she objected, but Roz gave a little nod. Her great-grandmother carefully poured her a cup, added quite a lot of milk and two sugar lumps, and gave it to Hannah, who drank it thirstily, feeling very grown-up. No one had ever offered her tea before.

"What a spread! You've done us proud, Linnet," Roz

44

said, sitting forward in her chair. "I think I'll try your famous marmalade cake. Thank you."

"And you, my lamb?" Linnet twisted her head up to look at Hannah, her green eyes shining. "I know you'd like some marmalade cake!"

Hannah hesitated. She did not like marmalade. She could feel her mother willing her to be polite, and so said reluctantly, "All right. Just a little bit."

She took a tiny fragment of cake into her mouth, and was surprised by the explosion of taste. "Mmmm!" She took another, larger bite. The cake was one of the most delicious things she had ever tasted: tangy and yet sweet, moist and yet not too sticky.

"More?" Linnet asked, cutting another huge slice.

"Yes, please!"

Linnet did not eat with them, trotting out as soon as everyone was served. The comfortable ritual of food eased some of the tension that had risen between Roz and Lady Wintersloe, much to Hannah's relief. She did want them all to be friends.

"So what do you think of Scotland so far, my dear?" Lady Wintersloe asked, pouring milk into her saucer and putting it down on the floor. The movement obviously cost her some pain, for she grimaced as she straightened and put her hand to her leg. The cat stalked over, orange eyes disdainful, and lapped at the milk delicately.

Hannah had to swallow down a huge mouthful before she could answer. "I like it! It's so pretty. I love all the castles."

"There are some very fine ones. We must organize some day trips for you both now that you are here. You won't want to spend all your time entertaining an old lady."

"No," Hannah agreed.

Roz frowned at her, but a sudden smile lit up Lady Wintersloe's gaunt face. Hannah suddenly wondered if her great-grandmother had once been beautiful.

"You must meet Max, my gardener's boy. He is only a couple of days younger than you. You would remember the night he was born, Roz. It was that dreadful winter, the year we lost Robert. His mother's car broke down in the snowstorm, and she saw our lights."

"Oh yes," Roz said blankly. "Of course."

"Genie had nowhere to go, and so I offered her a job. You would've seen the garden? She does a wonderful job. It's about our only source of income now, people coming to see the house and the garden. I don't know what I would've done without her."

Roz said nothing. Like always, she had frozen at the mention of her dead husband and seemed hardly to hear what Lady Wintersloe was saying.

"There are quite a few children your age roundabouts, Hannah," Lady Wintersloe went on. "The little Shaw girl from the general store, and Donovan, of course. Donovan is Allan's boy, Roz."

"But . . . Bob never told me Allan was going to have a baby too. . ." Roz was startled out of her reverie.

"I think it was rather a surprise for Allan as well,"

46

Lady Wintersloe admitted. "He and Donovan's mother weren't married. I don't think they even knew each other that well. I certainly had never heard Allan mention her, and I've known him all his life. It was all very sad. She came to him for help, when the baby was on its way, but there was a car accident and she died. It was the same night Robert went missing. You remember how thick the snow was? Allan tried to get her to the hospital, but went too fast on a corner and went over the cliff. The van burst into flame, but he managed to get her out in time. She gave birth to Donovan there in the snow, and died before the ambulance could get to her. Two nights before Christmas Eve."

"So Donovan's birthday's the day after mine?" Hannah asked in quick interest. "We're practically twins."

"Two nights before Christmas Eve," Roz repeated. One hand went up to clutch the wedding ring she wore hanging on its chain inside her shirt.

"Yes. An odd coincidence, don't you think, that he should be born the very same night Robert died? I've taken an interest in the boy as a consequence. He's rather wild, as you would expect of a boy growing up without a mother, but very talented." Lady Wintersloe sipped her tea and set her cup back in its saucer. "Have you had enough, Hannah? Would you ring the bell and ask Linnet to come and clear?"

"There's no need for that," Roz said. "Hannah and I can clear everything away." She nodded at Hannah, who obediently got up and began to stack the cups and saucers back on the trolley.

"Really, Roz, there's no need. Linnet. . ."

"Linnet is probably enjoying a nice sit-down and a cup of tea herself," Roz said firmly. "Come on, Hannah."

Carrying the teapot and a dirty plate, Roz sailed out of the room. Hannah pushed the trolley after her.

"I know she means well," Lady Wintersloe murmured, "but Linnet hates having her kitchen invaded."

Hannah was trying to manoeuvre the trolley out the door. She glanced back. "How come?"

Lady Wintersloe shrugged elegantly. "I suppose she does not like anyone to see her work her magic."

The Queen's Garden

Hannah thought about her great-grandmother's words as she pushed the trolley down the hallway. Had Lady Wintersloe meant that Linnet's cooking was so good as to seem like magic, or something more mysterious? Was Linnet some kind of witch? Hannah couldn't help feeling excited at the thought.

Jinx promenaded down the hall before her, tail crooked like a question mark. Roz was waiting for her by a swing door, teapot held high.

"She has got to be the worst snob I have ever met! She hardly even looked at me, let alone asked me how I was. Did you notice? And the way she treats poor Linnet, who must be nearly as old as she is. Wanting to be waited on hand and foot. . ."

"She does have a broken leg," Hannah said.

"Well, yes, but still!"

"I liked her. I didn't think she was a snob. I mean, she is a countess."

"So? A lucky accident of birth. Doesn't make her any better than anyone else."

Hannah gazed at her mother in surprise. "I don't think she meant to ignore you. I mean, I am her great-granddaughter and she'd never met me before."

Roz huffed out her breath. "Sure. Of course. It's just. . ." She bit her lip. "It was just the same with Bob!" she burst out. Hannah looked enquiringly at her mother, but Roz would not look at her, and instead opened the low oaken door into the kitchen.

It was like stepping back in time. A fire smouldered in an immense black cavity in the wall. The carcass of a large bird hung on a copper spit above it, its juices dripping down on to the coals and making them spit with yellow flame. An ancient table ran down the middle of the room, copper saucepans and ladles and bags of onions and bunches of herbs hanging on hooks from a long copper grate above. Three oaken dressers, all mismatched in size and style and colour, were crowded with pots, bowls, plates, platters, colanders, egg cups, glass bottles of cloudy liquids, and jars of marmalade and jam. A one-legged bird was perched on the sill of the open window, eating from a flowerpot of snails.

Linnet was stirring something in a big orange pot on the ancient cooking range. She was so small she had to stand on a three-legged wooden stool. She turned in surprise, and hopped nimbly down. "Oh, you shouldn't have worried! I'd have been there in just a moment!"

"It's no trouble," Roz said. She went to pour the leftover tea down the huge old porcelain sink, but stopped in surprise. There was a basket of baby squirrels sleeping on the draining board, all curled up together on a baby blanket. They were tiny hairless things with curling tails and fast-shut eyes. "Look, Hannah!"

"Oh, aren't they gorgeous!" Hannah hung over the basket. "Can I pat them?"

"Best not," Linnet said. "They're only here until the Wildlife Trust can come and get them. Donovan found them out on the hills this morning. Their mother was killed by a stoat, he thinks. He has to come back every two hours to feed them, so I hope they're collected before bedtime else he'll be sleeping over again."

"He's rescued hurt animals before?" Hannah asked. She liked the sound of a boy who rescued baby squirrels.

"Oh, yes! All the time. Last year it was a baby fawn who had been hit by a car, and another time it was an injured hedgehog. There's been lots of bunnies and birds – he even brought home a peregrine once, with a broken wing. He rescued old Hoppy the jackdaw there too." She nodded at the one-legged bird, which cocked its head and stared at them with a silvery-white eye. "He loves his animals, that boy does."

"So why doesn't he keep them all at his place?" Roz asked.

"His dad won't let him," Linnet said. "Allan doesn't think it's right for a boy to be mooning around over a load of baby animals. Besides, half the time Donovan found the animals when he was out on the hills instead of being at school, and Allan doesn't want to encourage him to run wild."

Roz frowned. "He does sound rather wild."

Linnet smiled fondly. "Oh, he's been a handful since the day he was born, that boy. Whizzing all over the place on that bike of his, and playing his trumpet loud enough to wake the dead. But he's a good lad."

Jinx leapt up on to the bench and crept along it, long and low, her glowing eyes fixed on the sleeping squirrels.

"Watch out for the bogey-cat!" Linnet shrieked and swept the yowling cat off the bench. "How did she get in here?"

"She came in with me," Hannah said guiltily.

"Watch out for that Jinx!" Linnet said grimly. "She'll kill every one of those baby squirrels just for the fun of it. Nasty, sneaky thing! I wish her ladyship was not so fond of the dratted thing, but she's fair taken in by her. Here, help me chase her out, else she'll drink all the cream and spit in my soup. Yah! Out of here, you old bogey!"

The old woman caught up a tiny broom that looked as if it had been made for a child and began to sweep under the table, whisking it into the corners and around the huge pantry. A grey streak flashed past and out the door, and Linnet slammed the door behind it. "That got rid of her!" she said with satisfaction, as Hoppy the jackdaw screeched and flapped its wings in surprise.

52

"Has Lady Wintersloe still not got you a dishwasher or a microwave, Linnet?" Roz said, looking around. "This kitchen is like something out of the Middle Ages!"

"If I wanted to be serving up food like soggy rubber, then I'd be getting one of those darned newfangled things, but I don't. My old cooker does the job just fine, thank you very much!"

"Well, let me help you wash up." Roz picked up the basket of squirrels and looked for somewhere to move it.

Linnet took the basket from her and put it back into the sink. "No need for that, Lady Fairknowe. I'd rather do it on my own, when I'm good and ready."

"Call me Roz, please."

Linnet ignored her. "Now why don't you go and have a walk about the garden, and enjoy the sun while it lasts? You've never seen the garden so pretty before."

"All right then, if you're sure."

"I'm sure." Linnet ushered Roz and Hannah out the door and into the garden.

There was a tall, slim tree growing right outside the door, bending delicate sprays of red leaves and berries over the lintel. Beyond was a long garden, bounded by tall stone walls, where fruit trees had been trained to grow flat against the stone like old wooden runes. Basking in the sunshine were rich mounds of black soil in which flourished herbs and vegetables of all kinds, grown in neat rows mulched with straw. The garden beds were divided by thick hedges of lavender, cut back hard in preparation for winter. In one corner, hens clucked in a small portable coop, while Jinx the cat stared at them with lashing tail and hungry golden eyes. In the other corner was a row of square white boxes, humming with bees. A small but very pretty glasshouse took pride of place in the centre.

"What a difference! This garden used to be half in ruins. I can remember Linnet out here, trying to turn the soil over with a spade near as big as herself, and Bob having to help her," Roz said.

They walked through an iron gate, Jinx deciding to leave the chickens in peace and follow them instead. A velvet lawn stretched towards a tumbledown grey wall at the far end of the garden. "That's the old castle," Roz said, pointing. "Not much of it left now. Your father used to have a kind of cubby house in it."

Together they wandered round the garden, Jinx following lazily. Roz had a story for every tree and glade. "We were married here," she told Hannah, as they walked down to a white summer house by the loch. "Your father fixed it all up for the day. We were so happy. . ." Her voice failed her and she stared out at the soft blue waters, clutching her wedding ring with one hand and hurriedly wiping away tears with the other. Hannah looked away. She always felt uncomfortable with her mother's grief, and wished she knew some way to make her happy again.

A white van revved up the drive. "There's Allan with our things. I'd better go and help, I suppose," Roz said, dabbing her eyes dry.

"I'll keep on looking round, OK?"

"Don't go too far, will you?"

Hannah ran away through the trees. She could hardly believe this whole garden was hers to explore. First she went to the rose garden, where crimson roses with golden hearts spread their thorny arms above grey-silver plants like woolly lambs' ears. *I wonder*, Hannah thought, *if it's true that Mary, Queen of Scots, walked here. . .*

Hannah had read about Scotland's most famous queen on the plane, and knew that Mary had inherited the throne when she was only six days old. She was sent to France as a child to marry the king's son, and became Queen of France at the age of sixteen, when her husband inherited the throne. She was widowed the very next year, and returned to Scotland, unable even to speak their language and knowing nothing about her native country. Queen Mary had loved to dance and sing and flirt, and had married again twice, before murder and scandal made the country rise against her, and she had fled to England. In the end she was executed by Queen Elizabeth the First.

Imagining she was that beautiful, doomed young queen, Hannah danced a few steps, lifting her skirt and swaying a curtsy, then bent her head to smell a rose. In the centre of the garden was a mossy old sundial, inscribed with the words *Now Is Yesterday's Tomorrow*. It sounded like a riddle, but Hannah was too excited to think about it for long. The rest of the garden beckoned.

The loch was dusky-purple now, the islands looking

more mysterious than ever. *They must have looked the same,* Hannah thought, *a thousand years ago. . .*

She walked down to a small wooden jetty with a rowboat bobbing at the end of a rope. It was a battered old thing, worn to grey by the elements, but Hannah was thrilled nonetheless. She imagined herself rowing about on the loch, fishing, exploring the islands and the wild shore. She wondered if the boat had belonged to her father once, and lay down on the jetty and trailed one hand in the water. It was shockingly cold. A narrow path went creeping away through the undergrowth, and Hannah followed it, damp leaves underfoot. Jinx slunk along behind her, and skittered away when Hannah tried to pat her.

"Donovan! Your father wants you!" Linnet's voice called from the house. Hannah parted the leaves and looked through. She saw Allan – freshly washed and combed – standing on the front steps, his arms crossed. Linnet and Roz stood beside him, both looking rather anxious.

"Donovan!" There was no answer, and Linnet shrugged. "He'll be back in his own good time," she said and disappeared back into the house.

"I'm at the end of my tether with that boy!" Allan growled. "Never does a thing he's told, always sneaking out to come up here. He might as well just move in!"

"Oh, well, he has his pets here, doesn't he?" Roz said. "Allan, you shouldn't have let Lady Wintersloe pay you for bringing our bags up, that's my responsibility. Tell me how much it was so I can repay her."

56

Allan flushed scarlet. "That's between me and Belle," he said. "You can pay me for bringing up the bags. It'll be ten quid."

"Oh! All right." Roz gave him a curious glance, then bent her head and rummaged in her handbag.

"Belle helps me out with the boy," Allan burst out, looking red and uncomfortable. "I've had a rough time since the accident. She knows that I . . . well, it's been hard, bringing up the boy on my own. She knows I've made sacrifices. . ." His voice trailed away, and he looked down at his scarred and crippled hand. Words burst out of him. "I wanted to help, you know . . . to do what Bob would have liked . . . but it's not what I expected to do with my life!"

"What do you mean, you wanted to do as Bob would have liked?" Roz asked after a long moment. Her face was very pale.

Allan went scarlet and looked away, shoving his hands in his pockets. "It doesn't matter. What's done is done. I have to go, I've still got work to do. If you see that boy, tell him he's in big trouble if he doesn't get home and do his chores right now!" He limped down the steps, clambered into his van, and drove off in a spray of gravel.

I don't blame that boy Donovan for skipping out, Hannah thought. *Mean old man!* She worried over Allan's words as she crept away through the undergrowth. What had he meant? His words had upset Roz too, she knew. Her mother had gone back into the house, gnawing on her lip,

57

the frown between her eyebrows deeper than ever.

The path led through a shadowy thicket of rhododendrons to a tall, spreading tree dressed all in golden leaves, growing tall beside the pepper-pot tower. It had scattered its leaves in a great circle around its trunk. Hannah ran and kicked and twirled, throwing up armfuls of shining yellow leaves that rained down upon her head. Then she ran on, across the lawn, and through an archway cut in a tall hedge to a knot garden of low hedges, with trees cut into the shape of rearing horses at each end. A dancing statue stood in the centre of the knot garden, lifting a set of pan pipes to his stone lips. He had the body of a man and the horns and hooves of a goat, and looked merry and wild and free. Beyond the statue was the ruined castle. All that was left were a few towering walls with arrow-slits and broken archways.

Hannah was enchanted. She roamed about, trying to imagine her father playing here as a boy, and found a room that was not nearly so ruined as the rest of the castle. It was furnished with a rickety wooden table, three mismatching chairs, and a shelf on which stood some battered tin plates and cups. Black ashes were in the fireplace, with an old kettle slung from a hook above. Shoved in one corner was a pile of plastic swords and daggers, and a bow with rubber-tipped arrows, and even a few light-sabres. Although they were all rather battered and discoloured, Hannah did not think they could have belonged to her father. *They must belong to the gardener's son*, she decided. *Obviously he*

58

and his friends played here. A pang of possessive jealousy surprised her. Already she was thinking of the ruined castle and the garden and the grand old house as being *hers.* She did not like the thought of people playing here without her permission. She realized they must have played here many, many times before, and felt a fresh stir of anger at her mother for depriving her of a childhood spent here instead of in a grungy flat.

In the inner courtyard there was an old crumbling stone seat over which grew a great bush of roses, its trunk as thick as a tree, its thorns as long as daggers. The petals of the few roses remaining were pink with a golden heart. When Hannah walked through an archway hung with the roses, she breathed in a faint, sweet fragrance.

Jinx the cat sat on the back wall, washing her paw. As Hannah walked along the wall, the cat slinked after her, but would not come when Hannah held out her hand, instead streaking over the wall and disappearing.

Halfway along the back of the garden, the wall was interrupted by an immense old tree. Its trunk was so thick that Hannah could not have hugged even half of it with both her arms spread wide. It towered overhead, its foliage black in the fading light. Needles were strewn underfoot, so that Hannah's footsteps were silent. She drew close, and put her hand on the scaly bark. A rift yawned under her hand. Hannah bent her head and stepped inside. It was a doorway that led straight through the very heart of the living wood. She could see long rays of sunlight striking

59

through the trees on the far side, and the steep cone of Fairknowe Hill rising behind. Hannah could hear a little tinkle of falling water as a spring trickled down into a dark green pool that lapped against the roots of the massive old tree on the other side of the wall. She could not walk through, though. An ancient iron gate was set deep into the wood, barring the way.

Hannah gave the rusty bars a little shake. They did not budge. Her eye was caught by the gleam of something metal. A chain was looped about the bars, secured with a modern padlock. Hannah picked it up to examine it, but it was so dark in the rift of the tree that she could see very little. She backed out, turned, and gave a yelp of surprise.

The Fairy Hill

A boy was standing right behind her. Dressed in black jeans and a long black coat, he was almost invisible in the shadows under the foliage.

"Hi!" he said.

"Hi," Hannah answered, her voice coming out too high. She took a deep breath, trying to calm her startled nerves.

"I'm Donovan MacEwan. I know who you are. You're Hannah Rose, the long-lost great-granddaughter."

"Your father's looking for you."

"Again? Oh, well, let him look."

"He said you'd be in big trouble if you don't go home now."

"I'm always in big trouble." He gave her a brief, crooked smile.

Hannah smiled back. "Me too."

"You like it here?"

She nodded. "You bet!"

"This yew tree's more than a thousand years old, they reckon." Donovan rubbed his hand on the bark.

"Really? How can it be? Trees don't grow that old!" Hannah looked up at the tree. Its roots and trunk and branches were so thick and gnarled that it seemed almost possible.

"Yew trees do. There's one at Fortingall, not far from here, that's meant to be five thousand years old. They say it could be the oldest tree in the world. Older even than the pyramids."

"That's amazing."

"Miss Underhill says people would have walked through the doorway in this yew tree for centuries, on their way to the fairy hill and the pool."

"Is that the fairy hill?" Hannah looked up at the high hill rising on the far side of the yew tree, with its crown of dark thorns.

Donovan nodded. "Knowe means hill. In the olden days, they thought the Fair Folk lived there. Fairies, you know."

Hannah nodded, thinking of what Lady Wintersloe had said.

"Why is the gate locked?"

Donovan hesitated. "Miss Underhill says that one of the ways into fairyland is to walk through a rift in a yew tree. So I think people used to come and run through it all the time. Just for fun, half the time, but also, who knows? Maybe it works. It's like the witch's pool over there." He pointed through the doorway in the yew tree to the shadowy gleam of water on the far side. "People still come and wish on the pool."

"I'd like to wish on it," Hannah said impulsively.

"What would you wish for?"

To stay here. . . For my father to come home. . . For a friend. . .

"You can't tell, else the wishes don't come true," she answered.

"OK. Let's go then."

"OK." She cast Donovan a shy glance. He was a striking-looking boy, with blue-grey eyes edged with thick, dark lashes, pale skin, and a thin, bony frame. He looked as if he did not smile much, let alone laugh out loud.

"It takes ages to go all the way round," Donovan said. "You need to go out the front gates, and then through the woods. I normally just climb the yew tree to get over. But maybe you'd rather. . ." He cast a dubious look at her prim and proper navy-blue dress.

"I'd rather climb the tree too," Hannah said at once. She looked up at its thick, spreading branches. "It looks easy enough."

"All right, then, come on." Donovan swiftly clambered up into the yew tree, then put down his hand to help Hannah up. She scorned his help. After hitching up the hated navy dress, she scrambled up after him with quick agility. Her hem caught in a twig, and tore, but she dragged it free rather than show any slowness in front of him. One branch extended over the wall. Hannah was halfway along it, precariously balanced, when suddenly a magpie came diving down from the sky, striking at her head with its sharp beak. She cried out and flung up her arm. Donovan caught her other arm, keeping her from falling. The magpie beat about their heads, shrieking, and Donovan struck out at it. The magpie darted away.

"I think it ripped a chunk of my hair out." Hannah touched her fingers to her scalp. They came away bloody. "I'm lucky I didn't fall!" Rather shakily she let herself down to the ground, touching her fingers to her scalp every now and again.

"Magpies are bad luck. Always raiding other birds' nests and stealing things. I wonder why it attacked you like that."

"Maybe it's got a nest nearby." Hannah looked up into the tree branches.

"Not in October," Donovan said. "They only nest in spring. Maybe it thought your hair was something valuable. They like flashy things."

"Oh, so my hair's flashy, is it?" Hannah was not altogether pleased.

He gave her a quick crooked grin. "It's certainly bright."

She tossed back her hair irritably. "All right, then, bring out all the old red-hair jokes."

"I don't really go in for jokes," Donovan said. "You want Max for that. Besides, I kind of like it."

To her dismay, Hannah felt heat rise in her cheeks. "So did that magpie." She turned to stare down into the pool, deep, green and mysterious. Faded ribbons and scraps of material had been tied to the yew branches overhanging the water, and Hannah could see a few coins shining in the murk at the bottom of the pool.

"Let's climb the hill first," Donovan said. "We can see the sun going down over the loch. Then you can make your wish at sunset. That's a good time for wishing."

As they walked up the path to the top of Fairknowe Hill, Donovan jerked his head towards a great boulder that half concealed a narrow cave in the hillside. "That's where they burnt the witch, you know. One of the first witches burnt in Scottish history."

"Where?"

"Just in front of that big rock. It's meant to guard the gateway to fairyland. Miss Underhill said she was really a fairy that had been locked out, and the locals caught her and burnt her for a witch. Miss Underhill wants to put a plaque there, but Lady Wintersloe won't let her."

"That girl at the shop. . ."

"Scarlett?"

"Yes, her. She said the witch haunts the castle."

Donovan gave a little snort. "Miss Underhill would have told her that. She's always telling ghost stories at Halloween. She's really into all that sort of stuff, ghosts and witches and fairies. I mean, really into it. Not just playing at it. Scarlett says Miss Underhill is really a witch herself. A modern-day witch. Wicca, it's called."

Hannah nodded to show she had heard of it, though she was much too puffed to speak. It was a steep climb to the top. To her chagrin, Donovan was not short of breath at all. He climbed with long easy strides, the wind blowing back his dark hair from his face.

They had a spectacular view over the countryside from the crown of the hill. Ben Lomond glowered from clouds to the north, and lights sparkled here and there on the far shore. The sun was spilling liquid flame on to the clouds along the horizon. It had grown so cold it hurt to breathe. Hannah shivered and hugged her arms about her.

They did not speak. Everything was too grand and beautiful for words. Once Donovan touched Hannah's arm, then pointed. An owl flew past on muffled wings. Hannah stepped back, turning her head to follow its flight. She gave a little cry as her arm brushed against the dagger-sharp barbs of the great twisted hulk of blackthorn behind her. "Ouch!" she said, and tried to pull her sleeve free. It was snagged on the thorns.

Donovan snapped the twig off, heedless of the sharp tips, and handed it to her.

"You know this bush has not bloomed in more than four hundred years?"

"The gardening lady said something about that."

"There's a prophecy that says it won't flower until the true king sits on the throne under the hill. The fairy king, you know."

"So I guess it won't be flowering any time soon," Hannah said, then regretted her cynicism. It seemed so magical up here, at the very edge of night, with the world spread out under their feet. The first star shone out over the mountains.

Donovan shrugged. "I guess not." There was a long pause. "It's a magical bush, though. Miss Underhill says witches make their wands out of its wood. And if you cast a blackthorn twig behind you it grows into an impenetrable hedge that nothing can cut through. She says the thorns around Sleeping Beauty's castle were probably grown that way."

He shrugged one shoulder, as if embarrassed to be caught talking about such things. "Come on! It'll be too dark in a sec."

Hannah thrust the blackthorn twig deep into her cardigan pocket, heedless of the thorns, and followed Donovan down the hill, laughing as they slipped and skidded on the damp earth. They ran through the trees to the pool, which was darker and more mysterious than ever.

"What do I do?" Hannah asked.

"I don't know. Drink some of the water. It's meant to be healing. Then you tie a clootie to the bush."

Hannah knelt by the pond and looked down into its gleaming black depths. The water was cold and sparkled on her tongue. She hesitated, not sure what to wish for. It seemed important that she choose wisely. *For us to be happy*, she thought. *Here at Wintersloe Castle.*

"What's a clootie?" she asked.

"A bit of rag. You've got to tear it, not cut it."

Hannah did not hesitate. She took the torn piece of hem

67

and ripped away a long strip of cloth. She tied it to the branch of the yew tree that hung over the pool.

"Done," he said. "I hope you made a good wish. It'll come true, you know."

"I hope so."

A sudden loud croak made her jump. An enormous brown toad sat right by her hand. She squealed and scrambled back, then, bitterly ashamed of herself, bent to look at it more closely.

It croaked again, then opened its wide mouth and spat out a small grey stone with a hole bored through it. Hannah looked at it in astonishment. The toad croaked again, urgently, then pushed the stone towards her with its head. Wonderingly Hannah bent and picked up the stone. It was rather sticky and unpleasant, so she rinsed it in the pool and then raised it high to look at it.

"It's a holey stone!" Donovan said. "Wow! I've only read about those."

"The toad gave it to me." Hannah was pleased and puzzled and intrigued all at once.

"They're meant to be magic." He stared at the toad in amazement.

"In what way?" Hannah had goosebumps all over her body. She stared at Donovan, wondering if he was mocking her with all his talk of magic and witches. He seemed serious, though, and she held in her hand a holey stone that a toad had spat at her feet. It was all too strange and uncanny.

"I don't know. Take it to Miss Underhill and ask her."

"At the fairy shop?"

Donovan nodded. "She calls them hag-stones, I don't know why. She asked me once if I'd ever found one here in the woods. You should show it to her. She might buy it from you." He shook his head slowly, in disbelief and awe. "A toad, of all things. It makes you wonder. . ."

"I don't know. I mean, it's a bit weird, isn't it?" Hannah looked down at the toad, which was sitting very still, regarding her with huge dark eyes.

Donovan shrugged. "Yeah. Weird things happen, though, especially round this hill. Maybe he likes you. Let's catch him! I'd like a pet toad."

As if understanding his words, the toad turned and quickly waddled away under a bush. In seconds, it had disappeared. Donovan laughed. "Well, he didn't want to be caught, did he?"

"He? How can you tell?"

"By his big thumbs. Also, I heard him calling before. Girl toads don't call like that."

"How come you know so much about toads?"

He shrugged. "I like animals. I'd like to be a vet, except you have to go to uni and stuff, and I can't stand school. So I might be a park ranger or something."

"I hate school too." Hannah got up, clutching the hag-stone in her hand. By now it was dark under the trees, too dark to climb the yew tree back into the garden. She could hardly see its thick, hulking shape any more, let alone where

69

to safely put her feet on its branches. She was shivering, both from the cold and from a sudden superstitious terror that made her wish she was somewhere warm and bright and ordinary.

On impulse Hannah lifted the hag-stone to her left eye, looking through it. To her amazement, Hannah could now see the path as clearly as if it were drenched in moonlight. She dropped the hag-stone. All was dark and cold. She lifted it to her eye again. All was clear and bright.

Beside her, Donovan stumbled through the bushes, swearing. She held out her right hand. "Here, take my hand. I can see the way."

"You must be able to see like a cat. I can't see anything," he grumbled.

Hannah did not say anything about the hag-stone. She was by nature reluctant to confide in anyone, let alone a boy she had only just met. She wanted to have time to think about what had just happened, and what it meant. *The less said, the better*, she thought, repeating one of her mother's favourite maxims.

She reached out and took his hand. He held her fingers as lightly as if he were holding some small hurt animal. Hannah led him along the path, the hag-stone held to her left eye, wondering at the clarity of her sight. She felt as if she had strayed into a fairy tale, as full of peril as of wonder, a place where anything could happen. She looked about her and saw odd shadows crouched under bushes, and small points of light like gleaming eyes, and her steps

70

quickened with her heart. Donovan kept pace with her, stumbling over snaking roots and stones that Hannah could see clearly.

When Hannah reached the road that led from the village, she dropped the hag-stone from her eye and was once again standing in darkness. Only the row of black and white striped posts, with their red shiny triangles of reflective metal, showed where the road ran. The tall gates of Wintersloe Castle were only a few steps away, and Hannah could see the lights of the tiny gatehouse and smell food cooking.

"I'd better head back. My dad'll be furious. See you tomorrow, hey?"

"OK." Hannah gave a wave of her hand and went in through the little gate. Donovan began to hurry away down the road, his shoulders hunched under his long black coat.

As she walked up the shadowy driveway to the house, Hannah lifted the hag-stone to her eye to see the landscape illuminated brightly, then dropped it to see the landscape dark and scary once more. It was a trick she thought she would never grow tired of. Her body fizzled with excitement and amazement and disbelief. All her life Hannah had longed for magical adventures – to ride a unicorn, to find a dragon's egg, to rub a lamp and conjure a genie. Never had she expected a toad would spit an enchanted stone at her feet. But then, she had never expected to discover she was the lost great-granddaughter of a countess either.

71

The Black Rose

"Where have you been?" Roz cried as soon as Hannah came through the front door. "We've been calling for you for hours!"

Hannah stiffened. "I went up the hill with that boy Donovan."

"Look at you! Your dress is torn, your hair's a mess! You are not to go wandering off with some strange boy!" Roz's voice was shrill. "It's dark out there, Hannah! When are you going to learn some sense?"

"She's right, my lamb." Linnet was standing in the shadows, her face creased with concern. "That hill is not a safe place at the best of times, but certainly not at dusk or dawn or midnight. You mustn't go round it, or climb it, and you must never, ever go inside the cave. Will you promise me?"

Hannah had no intention of promising any such thing. She glared at her mother. "I was just exploring. I didn't go very far. It's not my fault I didn't hear you. It's a big garden!"

Roz gave her a little shake. "Just stay where I can see you, all right?"

Hannah wrenched herself free. "Oh, don't fuss, Mum! I'm not a little kid any more. Nothing's going to happen to me."

"Your father was a grown man," Roz said through stiff lips, her hand clenched about the ring beneath her shirt. "Yet something happened to him, didn't it?"

"That doesn't mean I have to spend my whole life being treated like a little kid," Hannah flashed back. "It's not fair!"

Roz took a deep breath. "Just don't go wandering off with any more strange boys. Please!"

"Not up the fairy hill," Linnet murmured from the shadows. "It's a wicked place now, that green hill."

Hannah rolled her eyes as her mother stalked away.

"Come, my chick," Linnet said. "I've given you your father's old room, the tower room. It's only tiny, but I think you'll like it. There's not a child alive who would not like to sleep in that tower room. I've made up the bed for you, and put a hot-water bottle in it, 'cause you'll not be used to the cold. It was your father's hot-water bottle and you'll smile when you see it, for I knitted him a puppy dog cover for it because he so badly wanted a dog when he was a boy. . ."

Talking softly, the old woman led Hannah through a bewildering sequence of oak-panelled staircases, echoing corridors, and empty halls with faded tapestries and vast stone fireplaces, through which the icy wind whistled in a most mournful way. Hannah thought that she would never be able to find her way back down to the warm comfort of her great-grandmother's drawing room, with its gold-velvet drapes and gilded mirror.

"Don't you worry," Linnet said. "Give you a week and you'll know the place better than I do."

They came to a long hallway hung with massive portraits. The faces were all grim and stern and sad. "Are these all my ancestors? They look utterly miserable."

"A lot of sorrowing at Wintersloe," Linnet said. "It's the curse, you know."

"So there really is a curse? It's not just an old tale?"

"I wish it were," Linnet said. "But the curse is all too real. It was all due to him, the first of the Black Roses." She nodded her curly white head at the portrait of a tall, dark man with a pointed beard, a curled moustache and a sardonic expression.

"Who's he? And what's a Black Rose?"

"That's Lord Montgomery Rose, the first Earl of Wintersloe. Up till then, the Roses all had red hair, like you do yourself. But his mother was a Spanish lady. Lord Montgomery inherited her black looks and her black temper, and since then, it's said there's a Black Rose every few generations, all with a devilish temper."

"I always thought it was redheads who had bad tempers," Hannah said ruefully, tugging at her wild copper-coloured curls.

"Oh, yes, but with the Red Roses it's quickly lost and quickly regained. The Black Roses, though, they can brood over something for years."

Hannah stared up at the portrait. The young man was dressed in a doublet and ruff, with a wild rose in one hand. In the background was a castle with a hill behind it crowned with a flowering thorn.

"What did he do?"

"He lost his temper," Linnet said. "Then when he got it back again, he was too proud to admit he was in the wrong. It's a bad combination, temper and pride. He caused a lot of harm."

"I mean, what did he do to get himself cursed?"

Linnet sighed. "He married a lady from under the hill, one of the Fair Folk, but he didn't trust her. His jealousy drove him half mad, and he cast her out of the castle. The local folk burnt her as a witch."

Hannah felt a chill. She rubbed her arms. "So she cursed him?"

Linnet nodded.

"What happened to him?"

"Lord Montgomery had fought for Mary, Queen of Scots, and she made him an earl in thanks. But then when she fled to England – a few months after Lord Montgomery's wife was burnt as a witch – those who had supported the queen were all punished by the rebel lords. Lord Montgomery died defending the castle, and it was burnt down around his ears. It was what his wife had predicted. 'By fever, fire, storm and sword,' she said, and indeed we've had them all here at Wintersloe."

There was a long pause, and Hannah heard the wind moaning through the vast cold chimney. The curtains at the window stirred, and somewhere a board creaked.

"They say that one day a Red Rose will save a Black Rose, and solve the puzzle ring, and break the curse," Linnet said softly, tweaking one of Hannah's long red curls. "Who's to say it won't be you?"

Hannah nodded. "I mean to break it," she answered.

"But that's enough talk about curses and witches." Linnet smiled rather sadly. "We don't want you having nightmares your first night at Wintersloe. Come and I'll show you your room."

Linnet led Hannah up another staircase, so narrow and steep and twisty that only a child or a very small old woman could walk up it without having to go sideways. At the top was a low arched doorway of oak so old it was almost black. A star made of twigs hung above it.

"Rowan," Linnet said, pointing one gnarled finger. "Protect you from all harm. In we go. There's your things, all safe and sound, and look, I've hung your pyjamas on the radiator so they'll be nice and warm. I'll let you get settled, then I'll come back by and by to show you the way to the dining room. Och, but it's a feast I've cooked for you tonight!"

Hannah woke slowly. She lay for a moment, conscious of the warmth of her bed, listening to birdsong that was quite different to the hectic mocking laughter of the kookaburras greeting the dawn in Australia. She opened her eyes and looked around, curling her toes in joy.

Linnet was right. It was only a small room, but quite big enough for a skinny almost-thirteen-year-old girl. It had eight narrow walls, with the door taking up one side, and the windows another four. This left room for a tiny fireplace; a long, thin wardrobe painted blue with cream wheat sheaves on the doors; and a tiny dressing table with six shallow drawers. A plump stool covered in faded red velvet was just the right height for Hannah to sit down and look at her face in the mirror. A painting of a stag and a loch and a castle hung above the fireplace. To Hannah's disappointment, the fireplace had been bricked up and a radiator put in. She would have liked to lie in bed and watch flames flickering on the hearth.

Hannah leapt out of bed and ran to one diamond-paned window after another, looking out across the chimneys and gables towards Ben Lomond, at the sparkling loch, at the wych elm tree tossing its bright golden leaves in the wind, and over the garden to the ruined castle, Fairknowe Hill rising behind. Its crown of blackthorn looked more tangled and misshapen than ever in the early-morning sunshine.

As she leaned out of the window to look at the view to the north, Hannah noticed there was a gargoyle perched below her window sill. She hung out over the sill, and saw it had fronds of leaves curling from its brow. So at each window she bent over to see, and sure enough, there was a gargoyle for each direction of the compass. Westwards was a scaly merman with a triton shell to his mouth. South was a dragon with spread wings and a snarling mouth. Facing east, towards Fairknowe Hill, was a horned imp with wings and a wicked face.

A painted chest stood at the foot of the bed. Opening it, Hannah discovered it was full of old toys and books. She sat on the floor and looked through the books. Most of them had the name *Robert Rose* inscribed in them in a dashing, impatient hand, with a strange symbol drawn underneath. It looked like a heart on three legs, one straight and two curling. It was formed by two capital Rs drawn back to back, facing in either direction like Janus, the two-faced god who looked to both the past and the future.

The books were mainly Biggles and Hardy Boys, but there was one thick old volume called *A Child's Treasury of Verse*, which Hannah picked up, for she loved songs and poetry and often tried to write her own. As she opened it, Hannah was most surprised to find that all the pages in the book had been glued together and a hole had been cut in the centre. Inside was an old ornate iron key, red with rust.

Hannah stared in amazement. Who could have hidden the key? And what did the key open? Her mind flashed to the gate in the old yew tree, but that was a modern padlock and this key looked very old. Thoughtfully she weighed it in her hand, then, feeling shivery with cold, skipped back to bed and pulled out the hag-stone from under her pillow. It lay in her palm, rough and grey and ordinary, except for the hole worn through the centre. She lifted it to her left eye, but the room looked just the same. So she held it to her ear. She could hear the piteous sound of a dog howling. When she took it away from her ear, the howling stopped. Each time she held it to her ear, she heard the dog again.

Pondering this, Hannah tried slipping her fingers through the hole, as if the stone were a ring. It fitted perfectly on the ring finger of her left hand. She twisted it round and round her finger, wondering how she could find out more about the hag-stone. *I'll visit the Fäerie Knowe*, she thought. *Though I won't tell Miss Underhill I've got it.*

A soft knock came on the door. Hannah took the stone off her finger – to her relief, it came off without any trouble – and thrust it and the rusty old key under her pillow, just as Linnet came in, stooped over a tray.

"Morning, my lamb! I thought you'd like breakfast in bed your first day here. I know you don't like porridge, so I made you some cinnamon rolls. I know you like cinnamon."

How? Hannah thought. *How could she possibly know?*

Linnet put the tray down on the end of Hannah's bed. It had four little legs that folded down so Hannah could sit up in bed and eat as if at a tiny table. A crimson rose was tucked into her napkin. Hannah smelled the rose, then unfolded her napkin. She had never had breakfast in bed before.

Linnet smiled when Hannah told her. "Many new

79

things happening to you now. Oh, but it's good to see you, my chick." She surprised Hannah by seizing her face and kissing her warmly on both cheeks.

"I need you to tell me more about the curse," Hannah said, breaking a piece of warm cinnamon roll and tasting it cautiously. It was delicious, and she ate some more.

Linnet's face sobered. She sat down heavily on the red velvet stool, her feet dangling centimetres above the floor. "Did you have nightmares?" she asked anxiously. "My lady said I shouldn't have told you so soon."

"Why not? I need to know all about the curse, if I'm going to break it."

"Yes. . ." Linnet said doubtfully. "But you're still so young . . . and my lady is so happy to have you here. She's afraid your mother will want to leave once she realizes how very bad things are."

"So how bad are things? I mean, what does the curse *do*?" Hannah asked.

> *"By fever, fire, storm and sword,*
> *your blood shall suffer this bane.*
> *No joy or peace for Wintersloe's lord,*
> *till the puzzle ring is whole again."*

Linnet was silent a moment, then went on: "That's what she said, and so it's been. Year after year, generation after generation, no peace and no joy, no matter how deeply in love they are, no matter how fiercely they swear to resist the curse."

80

Hannah put down the cinnamon roll. Suddenly it tasted like cardboard in her mouth.

"Your great-grandmother, now," Linnet said. "My lady was a young thing in the Second World War. Fell in love and married, but her husband died fighting the Nazis and she was left to raise a child alone, as her mother had done. Then her son and his wife – that's your grandparents – they were killed in a car crash, and she was left to bring up your father too. Then one night he goes missing and is never heard from again. . ."

Linnet sighed and pressed her gnarled fingers against her eyes. "So it's been, ever since the time of Lord Montgomery. It's been very hard to stand by and watch it happen."

Hannah felt as if a heavy cat was crouched on her chest, making it difficult to breathe. "What . . . what's the puzzle ring?"

Linnet stared at her in surprise, then suddenly smiled. "I keep forgetting you don't know all about it already. Sometimes the past seems so much clearer to me than the present." She saw Hannah's roll lying in pieces and jumped nimbly to her feet. "But you're not eating! Breakfast time is no time to be talking about such sad things, and you'll need to keep up your strength. Eat up, my lamb, and we'll talk later, hey?" The little old lady trotted out the door, leaving Hannah to tear her utterly delicious breakfast to pieces and worry.

Bloodstains

After a while Hannah got out of bed and rummaged through her bag until she found her favourite skirt, which she had bought for five dollars at a garage sale. It was long and made of crushed green velvet, and she wore it with black stockings and black boots and a black beret, which made her feel like some kind of romantic and tragic figure. Very appropriate for a girl who was cursed. She wore her favourite T-shirt with it – one with a picture of Nina Simone on it – and a black cardigan with a belt and deep pockets. She put the hag-stone in her left pocket and the old key in her right pocket, and went out her door.

Jinx the cat was sitting halfway down the narrow twisty stairs, washing her ear. At the sight of Hannah she leapt up, hissing, all her fur standing on end, her tail swollen to three times its usual size. Her round orange eyes blazed with fury. Hannah stopped in her tracks, suddenly frightened. The cat yowled and leapt for her, claws raking. They caught in Hannah's cardigan, almost ripping off the

82

left pocket. Hannah swept the cat away with her arm, and the cat twisted, yowling like a banshee, and raked her claws viciously. Hannah shrieked with pain as Jinx yowled again and turned and fled. Hannah scowled and rolled back the sleeve of her cardigan, to see a nasty scratch welling blood. She lifted her arm and sucked the cut, then went on down the stairs, her left hand fingering the hag-stone hidden in the torn pocket of her cardigan. It was all very curious and troubling.

She found Roz sitting with her great-grandmother in the big drawing room, chatting politely over steaming cups of tea. At the sight of Hannah, she frowned and gave her daughter a cool look. *She's still angry with me for climbing the hill in the dark with a strange boy*, Hannah thought.

"Mum, can I have some money?" she demanded.

"What on earth for?"

"I want to go down to that fairy shop and buy something I saw there. Please? I haven't had any pocket money for ages."

"Neither have I," Roz said drily. "Since I left my job."

"You didn't like that job anyway, Mum, admit it!" Hannah said.

"Are you speaking of that dreadful shop in the village, the one that sells plastic wands and tiaras and pretends to know all about fairy lore? You must not go there, Hannah, I will not allow it!" Lady Wintersloe spoke sharply.

"But why not? It's just the sort of shop a little girl would love," Roz said.

Hannah rolled her eyes. "Mum! I'm not a little girl, and I'm not into pink tutus and tiaras, you know that. It just looked as if it had some interesting stuff in there. I wouldn't mind taking a look."

"That woman is a ghoul!" Lady Wintersloe cried. "She said she was researching a paper on fairy lore and asked me all sorts of impertinent questions, and then she wrote a book about Wintersloe Castle. I was never more mortified. She wants to turn Fairknowe into some kind of tourist attraction. She had some strange woman up on the hill, playing a harp and singing last May Day! I will not allow you to have anything to do with her, Hannah."

Hannah glared at her great-grandmother. She was just opening her mouth to say, "I will if I want to!" when her mother hurriedly said, "Of course Hannah will respect your wishes, if you feel so strongly about it. There's plenty of things we can do without going to a fairy shop!"

"But I want to go," Hannah said obstinately. "They have all sorts of interesting books there, and besides, she offered me a job. Singing at fairy parties. I have to have some way of earning pocket money if you won't give me any, Mum."

Lady Wintersloe looked agitated. "We have many books here, Hannah; you can look at them any time you choose."

"And of course you can have some pocket money!" Roz hurriedly opened her purse and thrust some notes into Hannah's hand, grimacing at her in a familiar expression that was half begging Hannah not to say anything and half warning her of dire consequences if she did speak.

The obstinate look did not leave Hannah's face.

"Hannah, my dear, I beg you. Do not tell that woman anything. She will try to worm information out of you so she can add it to that book of hers, but our family is none of her business. Will you promise me that?" Lady Wintersloe leant forward, wincing with pain at the movement.

"All right. I promise I won't tell her anything about our family. Not that I know anything to tell!"

Lady Wintersloe sat back, looking exhausted. "You've only been here a day. I know there's so much I need to tell you, about the fairy hill and the curse. . ."

"Please, Belle!" Roz said sharply. "I don't want you filling Hannah's head with any of that nonsense. She's only twelve years old."

"I'm almost thirteen, Mum!"

"But, Roz . . . my dear . . . she needs to know sometime . . . she'll hear talk in the village . . . and I have to explain. . ." Lady Wintersloe's voice was wavering, and her face was white and drawn.

Roz stood up. "Belle, please, there's no need. . ."

Lady Wintersloe leant forward, saying sharply, "But, Roz, there is a need! Hannah must know. . ." Then she gasped and fell back, grimacing in pain.

"Are you all right? Can I get you anything?"

"My pills are on the sideboard . . . but I didn't want to take them until I'd talked to Hannah . . . they make me so drowsy."

Roz went over to the sideboard and brought the old lady the pills and a glass of water.

"Hannah, I'm sorry. . ." Lady Wintersloe fumbled to open the little bottle, her face drawn. "I've had a bad night . . . I fear the castle is being watched. . ."

"Here, let me." Roz took the bottle, opened it deftly and shook out two small pills, which she dropped into Lady Wintersloe's trembling hand. "You'll feel much better when you've had your medicine. You should be in hospital."

Lady Wintersloe shook her head. "But who would be left to guard the house? And I must find the child of true blood . . . if only I knew for sure. . ."

Roz lifted the glass to Lady Wintersloe's mouth and helped her wash down the pills. "There, all done. We'll leave you to rest now. Don't you worry. All is well now."

Lady Wintersloe leant her head back against the cushion, her eyes closed. She looked gaunt and grey.

Roz led the way out into the corridor. "I'm worried about her. She seems a little . . . non compos mentis."

"I know what that means!" Hannah said hotly. "It means you think she's losing her marbles! You just think that because she keeps talking about the curse and stuff. But she obviously believes it's all true, Mum."

"The things people believe." Roz shook her head in wonder.

"I bet you would have said that in the olden days when someone tried to tell you the world wasn't really flat."

"I would not! I would have observed the curvature of

the horizon and deduced that the world must be round," her mother replied indignantly.

"All right, Mrs Science Teacher, bad example. But you know what I mean."

"No, I don't. You're saying that I'm close-minded just because I don't believe in curses. Forgive me, but your deductions are completely unsound. The fact that I don't believe in fairies and ogres and giants is a sign that I'm an intelligent and rational human being."

Roz was still lecturing when mother and daughter came into the kitchen, where Donovan was sitting on a stool by the fire, patiently feeding one of the tiny squirrels with a dropper. Dressed all in black again, he was hard to see in the gloom of the unlit kitchen, and Roz did not notice him. Hannah did, though.

"OK, Mum, I get the point." Hannah's cheeks burnt with embarrassment. "Can we just leave it?"

"Well, I think it's important that we try to understand the universe as it really is, not as we wish it to be," Roz said, taking a plastic bottle to the sink to fill it with water. "Clinging to a delusion simply because it is reassuring is totally irrational. We all need to. . ."

"All right, Mum!"

Her mother stopped and smiled ruefully. "All right, then. Lecture over for now. So what do you want to do today? Shall we go to Edinburgh? I think you'll love it."

"OK." Hannah snuck a look at Donovan, who was gently mopping the baby squirrel's nose with a tissue.

"We should enjoy the sunshine while it lasts," Roz said, taking two apples from the bowl on the table. "Make sure you pack your raincoat, though, darling; the weather can change pretty fast."

"If you're going to Holyrood Palace, make sure you look for the bloodstains on the floor of Queen Mary's bedchamber," Donovan said, looking up. Roz turned in surprise.

"Bloodstains?" Hannah demanded.

"Yes. Her secretary, David Rizzio, was murdered there, right in front of her. By her husband and his friends. They stabbed him about a hundred times and he fell on the floor, and his blood spread everywhere. No one's ever been able to get rid of the stain."

"Really?"

"It must be some kind of natural discolouration in the wood," Roz said coolly.

"That just happens to be in the exact same spot where David Rizzio fell," Donovan said, making his voice deep and ghoulish. Hannah laughed.

"Shouldn't you be in school?" Roz asked.

He gestured with the milk dropper. "It's the holidays. I can do what I like. Besides, I have to feed the squirrels. I've been here all night." He yawned ostentatiously, hiding his mouth behind his hand. Hannah couldn't help yawning too, and he flickered a smile at her.

"I'm surprised your father lets you," Roz said.

"He doesn't know I'm gone," Donovan said. "I climbed out the window. He'll be furious when he finds out."

"So he should be," Roz said austerely, and swung her backpack on to her shoulder. "Come on, Hannah."

"See you later, then," Donovan said, and Hannah waved in farewell.

Roz and Hannah had to walk to the village, catch a bus to Balmaha, and then a train to Edinburgh. "I might have to see about hiring us a car," Roz said. "Scotland is the most difficult country in the world to get around. If it's not a mountain in the way, it's a loch!"

"And I want to see everything!" Hannah said.

They spent a happy day exploring the Royal Mile and the labyrinth of wynds and closes around it. They began at Edinburgh Castle, towering high above the Old Town on its steep rock, then headed down the hill, stopping to look at the Witches' Well, where a bronze fountain commemorated the thousands of witches killed in Edinburgh during the Burning Times, when the witch-hunts of the sixteenth century reached a frenzy of fear and hatred.

In St Giles' Cathedral, Roz showed Hannah the bagpipe-playing angel in the Thistle Chapel, and then they museum-hopped all the way down the Royal Mile to Holyrood Palace. Hannah was particularly interested in the rooms of Mary, Queen of Scots, and not just because of the bloodstains. She knew her ancestor, Lord Montgomery, had fought for the young queen, and that the Curse of Wintersloe Castle had been cast during her reign. She was thrilled to find the large reddish stain beneath one of the windows.

"Can you imagine how awful that would be?" she

exclaimed to her mother. "To have someone killed right in front of you? He was stabbed fifty-seven times. And Queen Mary was held prisoner here by the murderers. She knotted her sheets together and climbed out the window and escaped, even though she was about to have a baby."

"Really?" her mother asked, examining a tiny high-heeled shoe in one of the cabinets. "That was brave of her."

"Yes. And look, the stain is still here, four hundred and forty years later, just like Donovan said."

"It's not really a bloodstain, Hannah. How could it be? They must scrub that floor every day! And would have done so for hundreds of years."

"No, it's definitely blood," Hannah argued. "It's red as anything!"

Roz sighed.

I Put a Spell on You

By the time Hannah and her mother got home, it was dusk and rain had begun to fall. The looming mountains were wreathed in mist, and a cold wind blew curtains of rain across the loch. Donovan's bicycle was thrown down on the grass outside Wintersloe Castle. Music poured in a golden blast from the ground-floor window of the smaller tower. It was just the sort of music Hannah liked, with a sweet voice and a saxophone and the blue note of soul.

Then she heard a trumpet join in, not quite so smooth but played with unmistakable passion and verve. Through the window Hannah glimpsed Donovan playing, his head bent back, his hair tossed away from his face. Hannah turned away, afraid he would see her watching him and know she had seen the look on his face. It was both joy and misery, it was both longing and loss. She felt she had seen a glimpse of something he would rather have kept hidden and she understood this, having the same hunger for privacy herself.

"Run on upstairs and get changed," Roz said as they came dripping into the front hall. "Here, give me your raincoat, I'll hang it up for you."

Instead, Hannah followed the sound of horns to the far end of the house. Soul music was her great passion. She knocked on the door, waited a moment, then went in. Donovan put down his horn and turned towards her, scowling.

"I love this song," Hannah said. "Nina Simone."

"Yeah." He sounded surprised.

She showed him her T-shirt. "I love Nina. Play it again and I'll sing with you."

So Donovan started the CD again, and Hannah began to sing along with the words. Donovan nodded his head once or twice, then lifted his horn and began to play. It was an old-fashioned instrument, with a large flared bell and only three valves, and a beautiful, deep tone.

When they had finished there was a pause. "I like your horn," Hannah said shyly. "I've never seen one like it before. Is it some kind of trumpet?"

"It's a flugelhorn," Donovan said. "It's very old. It belongs here, but Lady Wintersloe lets me play it. It's got a darker, lower tone than a trumpet. I like that."

"Me too," Hannah said. "You're pretty good."

"You're good too. You should join our band. You're a much better singer than Scarlett."

Hannah's heart sank. "Scarlett's in your band?"

"Yeah."

92

"What sort of music do you play?"

"Whatever we like, really. Scarlett's into pop, while I like jazz and blues, anything that's got horns. Max plays the keyboard and the recorder, though not that well."

"I play the guitar. Mostly I like to sing, though."

"What else can you sing?" he asked.

Jubilant, she said, "Anything, really. Play me what you've got."

They mucked about, playing and singing snatches of songs, talking about who they liked and why. In one corner of the room was a grand piano (out of tune, as Hannah discovered when she tried it); in another an old electric organ that must have been state-of-the-art thirty years earlier. There were also bongo drums, tambourines, flutes, and tin whistles in cases so old their velvet had almost rubbed bare, and a beautiful big double-bass which Hannah guessed must be Mary-Lou. She opened the case to have a look at it and plucked a few strings, wondering about her father.

It was cold in the music room, and Hannah was still damp from the rain. She shivered and glanced at the streaming window. It was dark outside. Donovan's eyes followed hers. At once he leapt up and started throwing all his things together.

"I've got to go! Dad said he'd give me the belting of my life if I was late again."

"But it's pouring!" Hannah followed him out into the hall.

"So? A little rain won't melt me. I'll see you later. We

practise on Saturday afternoons. So we'll see you tomorrow, if not before!"

He rushed out the door into the rain and Hannah heard the sound of his motor *putt-putt-putt*ing into life. She was left alone, standing in the cold, dark hall. Hannah looked around her with interest. Behind her was a narrow, twisty staircase leading up into darkness. Otherwise everything was bare. There were lighter patches on the walls, as if showing where furniture and paintings had once been. It was in stark contrast to the richly furnished and decorated front hall.

On an impulse, Hannah pulled out the hag-stone and put it to her left eye. At once the hall looked quite different. It was filled with warm light, and there were bright rugs on the floor and paintings on the wall, and a sideboard with gilded candlesticks and Chinese urns. When Hannah dropped her hand, the hallway was once again bare, cold and dark. Experimenting, Hannah lifted the hag-stone to her ear. She heard music, laughter, chatter; yet when she moved the hag-stone away, all was quiet.

Next Hannah put the stone ring on her finger. At first, everything seemed the same. Then she noticed something dark and squat on the steps, watching her with huge gleaming eyes. It was the toad.

Hannah's heart began to beat faster. The hairs on her arms stood up. For a moment she hesitated, then slowly she moved forward. At once the toad began to hop up the stairs. Hannah followed it. The narrow steps wound tightly upon themselves in a spiral. Hannah could both see and hear the toad, hopping a few steps ahead of her. It gave a moist plopping sound each time it landed.

Something hissed in the darkness behind her. Hannah jumped and spun round. A grey shadow streaked past, tripping her up so she fell on her hands and knees. It was Jinx the cat, leaping upon the toad. Hannah scrambled forward, but was too late to stop the cat closing her sharp teeth upon the toad's neck. To Hannah's surprise, Jinx yowled and took off like a flash, leaving streamers of saliva behind her. The toad sat stolidly, eyes gleaming.

Hannah looked at it doubtfully. The toad turned and began to once again hoppity-hop-hop up the steps. Hannah followed.

At the top of the stairs was a low oaken door. Hanging above its lintel was a rough star made of three twigs strapped together. Its door handle was made of iron, forged into a spiral. There was a keyhole below it, thick with cobwebs. With a feeling of inevitability, Hannah put her hand into her right pocket and brought out the old key. It slid into the lock and, with a screeching sound, unlocked the door. Hannah stepped into a small, round room. Groping automatically, her hand found the light switch. She flicked it on. A dim light filled the room.

The tower room was a miniature version of her bedroom, with four long, narrow windows, one with a telescope set up at it. Between the windows were bookcases overflowing with dusty books. More books were spread across a wooden table.

Hannah sat down at the table. Before her lay a notebook with a battered red-leather cover. She drew it towards her and opened it. Drawn on the first page was the symbol that looked like a heart with three legs. Inside was page after page written in the same quick, vigorous handwriting. At the top of each entry was the date. They were the only thing that made sense in the book. Everything else sounded like the ramblings of a madman. The first entry read: *Pestis must be infractus, but the baffled moon is lost in the mists of time.* The last entry read:

> *Back through the winter gate I must go*
> *to the time of two hornet queens*
> *flying around the one great chair.*
> *Cut free sweetbriar from thorny tower,*
> *find the waxing gibbous moon,*
> *its bewildered quarter I left safe*
> *with the rose of the world, my double rose.*

It was dated the day after Hannah's birth. The day Hannah's father had disappeared.

Outside, the rain swished through the trees, so it sounded as if the tower was afloat on a stormy sea. Hannah shivered with cold. Or perhaps she shivered with sorrow and fear and a creeping sense of horror. For Hannah had no doubt that this room had been her father's, and this notebook filled with mad scribbling was his too.

She covered her face with her hands. *Audacia*, she told

herself. It was the motto that had been on Lady Wintersloe's letter – Hannah's family motto. It meant courage.

Hannah had always prided herself on her boldness, but now she felt her courage failing her in this old, dusty room with her father's last words so strange and mad on the page before her. She felt as if a gulf of black water had opened below her and her foot could no longer touch the sand.

It was all too strange. The curse, the toad, the hag-stone, the hidden key, the locked tower room with its crazy scribblings, the feeling that she had opened a door that could never be shut again. Hannah pushed her father's diary away from her violently and ran out of the room, locking the door behind her.

Toad Poison

When Hannah entered the warm, firelit drawing room Lady Wintersloe was bent over Jinx, who was lying on her lap, shivering and meowing piteously. Long strings of saliva dripped from the cat's mouth.

"Something's happened to Jinx," Roz said. "We think she's been poisoned."

"It's just like Eglantyne and her dog all over again." Lady Wintersloe's voice quivered. "There's something evil at work here!"

"Jinx bit a toad," Hannah said.

"Toads are poisonous, aren't they?" Roz cried. "We'd better take her to the vet."

"I called Genie to stop Donovan on his way out," Linnet said. "He'll be here in just a minute."

"Donovan? What could he do?" Roz was surprised.

"He's very good with animals," Lady Wintersloe said.

Just then the door opened and two boys raced in. Donovan was in the lead. Behind him charged Max. He was dressed in camouflage trousers, and his gold-rimmed glasses were fogged up from the rain. The enormous boots he wore on his feet made his legs look really skinny.

"Where's the poor old thing? Let me have a look at her." Donovan lifted the cat gently from Lady Wintersloe's lap and sat down, laying Jinx on her back so he could feel all over her distended belly with gentle fingers. The cat hissed and struck out with her claws, but Donovan was waiting and caught her attacking paw with his hand.

"Hannah says she tried to bite a toad." Lady Wintersloe twisted her thin hands together in anxiety.

Donovan shot Hannah a quick look. "How long ago?"

Hannah shrugged. "Not so long ago. Just after you left."

Donovan looked worried. "We need to get Jinx to the vet as soon as we can."

"I'll take you if you like," Genie said, standing just inside the door.

"I'll just rinse out the poison first. Do you have any water?" Donovan said.

Lady Wintersloe indicated the jug of water by her elbow. Hannah passed it to Donovan, who thanked her with a quick crooked smile before bending over the distressed cat again. He rinsed out her mouth, wrapped her in a towel and gently lifted her to his shoulder as he hurried towards the door.

"Don't you worry, Lady Wintersloe," he said. "She's a tough old puss, she'll be fine."

"As a matter of fact, toad poison is pretty toxic," Max said. "Did you know. . ."

99

"Max! Not now," his mother cried. "Come on!"

Linnet followed them all out, adroitly catching a vase Max would have knocked over with the end of his long striped hand-knitted scarf.

The room seemed much quieter once they were all gone. Hannah could hear the clock tick-tock-ticking.

"Where were you all that time?" Roz asked in exasperation. "Look at you! You're still in your damp clothes. Where did you get to?"

"I was in the music room," Hannah said. "With Donovan. He's asked me to be in their band."

Roz was torn between pleasure that Hannah was making friends and disapproval over whom she was making friends with.

Lady Wintersloe, however, was delighted.

"Oh, that's wonderful! I'm so pleased you're making friends. You're all so close in age."

"You don't make friends with people just because you're the same age," Hannah said, thinking of old Mr Wheeler, her music teacher back in Australia, who had been just about the only person she had liked. "I hate most girls my age."

"Don't say 'hate', Hannah," Roz said.

"I'm sure you won't hate any of the midwinter bairns. I call them that because they were all born in midwinter, just like you, Hannah dear. Strange, isn't it? Is it any wonder I don't know which is the one?" Lady Wintersloe leant her head back against her chair and closed her eyes.

"The one what?" Hannah asked.

100

Her great-grandmother opened her eyes. "The one of true blood."

"What does that mean?"

"It's part of the curse," Lady Wintersloe said wearily. Roz made a small movement, as if to try to stop her speaking, but the old woman went on, in a faint but steady voice:

> "By fever, fire, storm and sword,
> your blood shall suffer this bane.
> No joy or peace for Wintersloe's lord,
> till the puzzle ring is whole again.
> The thorn tree shall not bud,
> the green throne shall not sing,
> until the child of true blood
> is crowned the rightful king."

Her voice broke at the end.

"Don't tire yourself out," Roz said. "There's no need to distress yourself."

"Hannah needs to know," Lady Wintersloe said gently. "It's her heritage."

"Does that mean the blackthorn on the hill?" Hannah asked. "The one that hasn't blossomed in so many years?"

"Yes, though it means the family too." Lady Wintersloe's voice was very weak. "Wintersloe Castle is named for the blackthorn, remember, and our family arms bear the symbol of the thorn tree. Eglantyne spoke both curse and prophecy – they are entwined."

101

"Who's Eglantyne?" Hannah demanded.

"She was the eldest daughter of the king of the hollow hill," her great-grandmother replied. "The king of the fairy realm. Our ancestor Lord Montgomery saw her ride out one May Day and fell in love with her. He wooed her and won her, and took her away from fairyland to be his bride. Except she was betrayed."

Roz stood up. "Please, Belle," she said sharply. "I don't see what can be gained by dwelling on this silly old story."

"She needs to understand," Lady Wintersloe said.

"You filled Bob's head with all this nonsense when he was a child too, and he became obsessed with the idea of breaking this stupid so-called curse," Roz said angrily. "Even after we were married, and when Hannah was just a newborn, he was always worrying about it and thinking about ways he could break it. He would never have gone out that night if he hadn't thought he had found a way to break it!"

"You mean the night he disappeared?" Hannah cried. "He went out to try and break the curse . . . and ended up dead?"

She was remembering the diary with its strange, incoherent messages. *Back through the winter gate I must go. . .*

"It was an obsession with him," Roz said tightly. "And I won't have you infecting Hannah with the same nonsense! I knew I should never have come back."

Just then the door opened and Linnet came trotting in, pushing her tea trolley. It had a steaming silver punchbowl

102

and a bottle of whisky instead of the usual gilt-edged teapot. "I've brought you all a nice hot posset to drink. It's a nasty cold night and you've all had a bit of a shock, seeing Jinx like that."

"What's in it?" Hannah sniffed the steaming bowl suspiciously.

"For you, my lamb, sweet apple cider, rosehip syrup, and some heather honey." Linnet doled out a cup for Hannah, who sipped it carefully before deciding she liked it, and swallowing more bravely. "I made the syrup from our own sweetbriar roses, which grow in the castle."

"Sweetbriar?" Hannah cried. "That old rose in the castle, it's called a sweetbriar?"

"Yes. Sweet for its fragrance, and briar for its thorns. Though Genie would call it *Rosa eglanteria*. She always likes to give plants their proper name."

"Eglantyne," Hannah breathed. She remembered the last verse in her father's book:

> *Back through the winter gate I must go*
> *to the time of two hornet queens*
> *flying around the one great chair.*
> *Cut free sweetbriar from thorny tower,*
> *find the waxing gibbous moon,*
> *its bewildered quarter I left safe*
> *with the rose of the world, my double rose.*

As a final message from her father, it left a lot to answer

for, but suddenly some of it seemed to make a kind of sense. *Cut free sweetbriar from the thorny tower* must be a reference to Eglantyne, and surely the thorny tower meant some kind of prison or cage. Her father had meant to rescue Eglantyne!

But Eglantyne had died in the time of Mary, Queen of Scots, more than four hundred and forty years ago. . .

Hannah's heart fell in disappointment. Maybe her father had been mad after all.

Linnet went on chatting genially, though her eyes were bright and curious on Hannah's face. "But for Lady Wintersloe and Lady Fairknowe, I'll add a nice shot of whisky." She poured a generous splash of whisky into the teacup and passed it to Lady Wintersloe. "Lady Fairknowe?"

"Please, call me Roz," Hannah's mother said, her arms folded tight across her chest. "Lady Fairknowe just doesn't sound like me."

"Oh, I couldn't be doing that," Linnet said, sounding shocked. "It wouldn't be right."

Roz shrugged, exasperated, and let Linnet splash some whisky into the cup.

"Now then, that's better, hey?" the old cook said. "Shall we get you away to bed early tonight, my lady? You could have a nice sup of soup in bed."

"That would be lovely, thank you," Lady Wintersloe said.

"Can I help?" Hannah suddenly wondered how Linnet

104

was going to manage by herself, but both old women shook their heads.

"Let me preserve my dignity a while longer," Lady Wintersloe said. "Besides, Linnet has been looking after me since I was just a baby. She knows what to do better than anyone."

Hannah nodded. It was only once Linnet had wheeled her great-grandmother from the room that this comment struck her as nonsense. How could Linnet have looked after Lady Wintersloe when she was just a baby? Hannah's great-grandmother was eighty-eight years old. That meant Linnet would have to be at least a hundred, if not even older. Hannah frowned. Maybe her mother was right. Maybe Lady Wintersloe really was losing her marbles.

Roz and Hannah ate a solitary meal, listening to the rain beat against the windows. As usual, the food was delicious, but neither much noticed what they were eating. Hannah was thinking of Donovan and the music, and the toad and the cat, and the tower room with its cryptic notebook, and the curse. She did not know what her mother was thinking about, but the anxious frown between her brows was deeper than ever.

"I think we should go home," Roz said abruptly, laying down her spoon.

"Go home? But why? We've only just got here!"

"Your great-grandmother's not well."

"Which is why we should stay and look after her."

"I'm worried. . ." Roz's voice trailed away.

Hannah got to her feet and said very firmly, "Surely you're not letting the stories of an old sick woman spook you, are you, Mum? Why, it's just not rational!" She kissed her mother and went out of the room, saying, "Night, Mum! See you in the morning."

Suffer This Bane

Hannah did not go up to her room, but went quietly down the hall to the dining hall that had been turned into her great-grandmother's bedroom, since she could no longer climb the stairs to the upper floors. She knocked quietly.

"Yes?" called Lady Wintersloe drowsily.

"It's me," Hannah said. "Can I come in?"

"Of course, dear."

Hannah opened the door and went in. Her great-grandmother was lying in a low bed covered with a pale pink satin quilt. She was dressed in an old-fashioned nightgown with a high neck and long sleeves, and her silver hair had been unpinned and plaited into a thin braid. Her face was clean of make-up, and looked very old and haggard. The newspaper lay beside her, open to the crossword.

"I thought you'd best tell me the whole story," Hannah said.

Lady Wintersloe nodded. "Come sit near me, Hannah, my dear, so I don't need to raise my voice. I'm very tired."

Hannah sat down and took her great-grandmother's thin hand. "So, what happened? Why did the fairy princess curse us?"

"She was betrayed," Lady Wintersloe said. "She had a cousin, you see, who was jealous of her. Her name was. . ." She hesitated, and then drew the newspaper towards her and wrote quickly, in the margin, the name *Irata*. When Hannah would have read it aloud, she shushed her and said, "Careful! Names have power. We do not want to call her attention here. Her spies watch the castle."

"Spies?" Hannah wondered if her great-grandmother was indeed more than half mad. "Like who?"

"There's a magpie that behaves very oddly," her great-grandmother said slowly. "In all my long life I've never seen it with a mate, and it kills the little songbirds and attacks strangers. It was fluttering at the window of the drawing room the night Robert told me he planned to save Eglantyne, and then . . . he never came back. And my grandmother always told me magpies could speak to witches."

Hannah remembered the magpie that had plucked one of her hairs, and felt a cold shiver down her skin.

"There are other creatures too, otherworldly creatures that come out of the cave in Fairknowe Hill. Linnet says she has warned you never to go into that cave. It's not safe. That's where Eglantyne came from, you see, but the Unseelie Court has power now under the hill, and so it is creatures of evil that walk the woods."

Her great-grandmother's voice was so faint Hannah

worried she might grow too weary to speak any more. "Tell me about the curse," she urged. "Tell me everything."

"Eglantyne left the fairy realm to marry Lord Montgomery. Her father was furious, and so she left with nothing but the clothes she stood up in, and her faithful maid and her dog. The little hound was white with red ears and tail, and refused ever to be parted from Eglantyne, sitting at her feet during meal times and sleeping on her bed at night. When Lord Montgomery locked it out of her room, it howled so piteously that he was forced to let it back in again, much to his disgust."

Hannah slid her hand into her pocket and fingered the hag-stone wonderingly, remembering the howls she had heard.

"Lord Montgomery was very jealous of his beautiful wife, and had a ring forged for her, a puzzle ring which would fall apart when removed."

"A puzzle ring! Linnet said something about that. What is it?"

Lady Wintersloe sighed and pressed her fingers to her temples. "It's a ring very cleverly constructed from four interlocking bands. When it is fitted together by someone who knows the secret, it looks just like a normal ring, with a golden rose in place of a gem. However, as soon as you take the ring off, it falls apart. You can only fit it back together again if you know the secret."

"And Eglantyne didn't know the secret?" Hannah guessed.

Her great-grandmother shook her snowy head. "No one knew, only Lord Montgomery and the goldsmith who made it."

"So what happened?"

"Well, at first Eglantyne was happy, but as the months passed she grew lonely. Lord Montgomery often left her to ride to the court of Queen Mary in Edinburgh. The young Queen of Scots was then not quite twenty-five years old and had recently married her cousin, Lord Darnley. In those days an ambitious man had to win the favour of his monarch if he was to prosper, yet Lord Montgomery dared not show his fairy bride at court. So he left Eglantyne behind, forbidding her to ride out for fear of those who muttered against her."

"That seems a bit mean," Hannah said.

"People in the sixteenth century were very superstitious," Lady Wintersloe said. "They feared anything that seemed otherworldly."

"But he didn't have to keep her locked up!"

"Maybe he did, given that Eglantyne was burnt to death as a witch only a short time later. These were dangerous times in Scotland."

"So tell me, what happened?"

"Eglantyne was bored and lonely. Her only consolation was to walk in the castle garden, the only spot of green in all that grey. She would take her little dog and go and play with it on the lawn, and smell the herbs and flowers, and sit in the sunshine. In time, she made friends with the young gardener who loved all green and growing things, as she did."

Lady Wintersloe's eyes were hooded with weariness. "It was not long before Eglantyne realized she was to have a child. She could not wait for Lord Montgomery to return so she could share her happiness with him. However, her cousin, whom we shall call the black witch, was furious to hear the news from the spies she had left at Wintersloe Castle. She had encouraged Eglantyne to elope with Lord Montgomery because she wanted to become queen of the fairy realm in Eglantyne's place."

"Oh," Hannah said with a sigh. "So was Eglantyne the heir to the throne?"

Her great-grandmother nodded. "She and her sisters after her. But the black witch had plans for them too. First, though, she had to dispose of Eglantyne and her unborn child. She had one of her spies poison Eglantyne's meals. Eglantyne, however, had a hag-stone she wore on a cord about her neck. It enabled her to see true, and she saw that certain dishes came to her tainted."

Hannah touched the hag-stone again, wondering. Surely it could not be the same stone? She almost pulled it out to show her great-grandmother, but Lady Wintersloe had continued with her story, a faraway expression on her face.

"Puzzled and afraid, Eglantyne refused to eat from those plates. So the black witch had to formulate another plan. She knew of the puzzle ring, for one of her spies

111

had watched the ring being made, and she knew of Lord Montgomery's jealousy. The black witch waited till the lord was almost home, then she took Eglantyne's little dog and she strangled it and hanged it from the archway into the garden."

"She didn't!"

"She did. And of course, when Eglantyne found it, she was beside herself with grief. She cut down her dog and cradled it in her arms, weeping bitterly. The young gardener found her there and, deeply troubled, fetched his spade and dug a grave at the spot where the little hound and his mistress had most loved to sit. Eglantyne had decided she must bury her dog herself, and so she took off her satin kirtle and laid it on the stone seat and then carefully took off her wedding ring, not wishing to clog it with earth. She didn't notice how the ring fell apart into four separate circles of gold. She was too busy cradling her beloved dog for the last time. She wrapped him in her kirtle, then laid him in the cold earth and, weeping all the while, buried him with her own hands."

Hannah listened, rapt with interest, thinking of Lady Wintersloe's distress when her cat had been found poisoned. No wonder she had said it was just like Eglantyne and her dog all over again!

"The gardener brought her a little bush of wild sweetbriar rose, and Eglantyne planted it upon her dog's grave, and then lay there sobbing a long time. At last the gardener raised her up and tried to comfort her. That was how Lord

Montgomery found her, in the young gardener's arms, her petticoats stained with dirt, her wedding ring discarded. Lord Montgomery was maddened with jealous rage. He shot the young gardener dead."

Hannah gasped in surprise. "Not really?"

"Yes, I'm afraid he did, though Eglantyne was screaming and trying to explain. And then he drove her out of the castle, still in her dirt-stained petticoat, and tossed the puzzle ring after her. Tradition has it that she caught the four loops of the ring, still hanging together, and chanted: 'Break, break, golden ring, like my heart, like his word, out, out, golden ring, to the four corners of the world.' And then the puzzle ring broke apart and was swept up into a whirlwind and flung in the four directions of the compass. And that was when Eglantyne cast the curse upon the house of Wintersloe."

"What was it again?" Hannah asked. "Something about fire and swords. . ."

> "By fever, fire, storm and sword,
> your blood shall suffer this bane.
> No joy or peace for Wintersloe's lord,
> till the puzzle ring is whole again.
> The thorn tree shall not bud,
> the green throne shall not sing,
> until the child of true blood,
> is crowned the rightful king."

113

Lady Wintersloe spoke slowly and heavily. Her face was deeply graven with lines.

Hannah was silent. The words tolled like a funeral bell in her imagination.

"It was Samhain Eve," Lady Wintersloe said. "Samhain marks one of the two great doorways of the Celtic year, for the Celts divided the year into two seasons: the light and the dark. Samhain, of course, was the dark doorway."

"Halloween," Hannah said, remembering what she had read in some of her books.

"Yes. Samhain is a dangerous and mysterious time. The gateways between the worlds are thrown open, so that the Fair Folk can roam freely through the night and the spirits of the dead can return to earth. It was a powerful time to be casting a curse."

There was a long silence, and then Hannah asked, "So what happened next?"

"Exhausted and in tears, Eglantyne stumbled towards the fairy knowe, hoping to cross through the gateway to her own world. But her cousin, the black witch, rode out on the Wild Hunt with her host of wicked fairies and drove her away. Eglantyne could not reach the gateway. She could only run, searching for shelter. She tore the hagstone from around her neck and flung it into the pool at the foot of the yew tree so the black witch could not steal it from her, and then ran to the village for help."

Lady Wintersloe sighed. "In the time of Mary, Queen of Scots, the country folk of Fairknowe believed Halloween was a time when all the witches of Scotland gathered together to cast their spells. So when the strange elfin wife of the Earl of Wintersloe came stumbling through the snowy darkness, they thought she must be a witch. They captured her and locked her up, and accused her of witchcraft."

"And they burnt her," Hannah said sadly, remembering the tales she had heard.

"It was the beginning of the Burning Times in Scotland," her great-grandmother said. "Mary, Queen of Scots, had passed the first Witchcraft Act only three years earlier. Eglantyne was one of the first witches to be burnt alive. Lord Montgomery did not know. He had ridden out that very same evening, to return to Queen Mary's court, and the black witch ensured no messengers reached him. By the time Lord Montgomery found out, it was too late. Eglantyne was burnt on the night of the winter solstice, near the spring they all call the witch's pool."

"That's so sad," Hannah said.

"Your father wanted to save her," Lady Wintersloe said. "He thought that perhaps the cave in the fairy hill could be used as a gateway to another time, as well as another world. He thought if he could just work out how to go back to that midwinter night, he could save her from the pyre, and save her unborn child, and maybe find the lost parts of the puzzle ring. He had found the magical hag-stone, you see, in the witch's pool, soon after he brought your mother home to meet us. He thought it was the key that would unlock the fairy gateway. He dared not tell your mother; she does not believe in such things, and he was afraid she'd think him mad or a fool. But he told me . . . he told me everything."

Lady Wintersloe's thin fingers plucked at her coverlet, and a tear slid down from under the heavy hoods of her eyelids. She dashed it away impatiently.

"So he went through the gateway," she continued in a low voice, "and he found one part of the puzzle ring, and he came back determined to save Eglantyne and her baby. He had a plan. . ."

"What? What was he going to do?"

"I don't know. He would not tell me. Too many eyes, too many ears. . ." Her voice trailed away.

"Belle! Tell me, what happened?"

Her great-grandmother heaved a deep sigh. When she spoke, her voice was so faint Hannah could hardly hear it.

"He went to the fairy hill that night. . ."

"The night after I was born?" Hannah demanded.

"Yes. You were born on the twenty-first of December, and the midwinter solstice is the twenty-second. He went . . . and he never came back." Lady Wintersloe leant her head back on her pillow and shut her eyes.

"But . . . you think maybe he did save her . . . somehow . . . and her baby is alive here and now." Hannah spoke very slowly, trying to make sense of her great-grandmother's words.

"All the old tales say that when Eglantyne was burnt, there was a great flash, and when the smoke cleared, nothing was left but ashes. No kind of remains at all, not even bones. Nothing but the twisted and melted remains of the iron chains they had used to bind her. Those of fairy kind cannot bear iron, you know, and so she had been kept chained the whole time to stop her from working her magic. It was always said the white flash of fire, the fact that nothing but ashes remained, was proof that she was not human . . . but now I wonder . . . three children as well as you were born that week, here in Fairknowe. Donovan, Max, and Scarlett Shaw. And your father always said he didn't believe in coincidences." Lady Wintersloe's voice was very faint and she did not open her eyes.

"But surely . . . surely it's impossible," Hannah whispered. "You can't go back in time, it's just not. . ."

"Logical?" Lady Wintersloe smiled wearily. "When is magic logical, Hannah?"

Hannah left her great-grandmother to sleep, and crept back to her room through the cold, dark, shadowy house, her breath short in her chest. The only sound was the wind and the rain. She changed in the darkness and crept into her bed, glad to find the hot-water bottle had taken the chill off the sheets. Hannah lay quietly for a long time, and then groped under her pillow till she found the hag-stone. She held it to her ear and heard, far away, the ghostly howling of a dog.

Cryptic Clues

Hannah did not sleep well. All night in her dreams she heard the sobbing of the wind about her tower room, carrying words of pleading, and mocking laughter, and the pitiful howl of a long-dead dog. She woke early, jerked out of sleep by the flapping of wings and a staccato rapping on her window. The magpie was fluttering outside, banging against the glass as if trying to get in. Hannah clutched her eiderdown to her, staring in bemusement at the bird. She had seen birds fling themselves against windows before, but never trying to get *in*. Again and again it banged against the glass, staring at Hannah with beady black eyes. She got up and ran to the windows, dragging the curtains across, and at last the fluttering and banging stopped.

It was bitterly cold. Hannah dressed in jeans – the warmest clothing she owned – and put the old key and the hag-stone in her cardigan pockets. As she passed the spot where Jinx had attacked her yesterday, she wondered if the cat had survived the night. It was very strange the way she had behaved. As strange as that magpie banging against the glass. It was all very mysterious and unsettling, and Hannah was all too aware that she was meddling with dangerous things.

She no longer thought that her father's notebook was the scribbling of a madman, or that her great-grandmother was losing her marbles. Too many uncanny and unaccountable things had happened. So Hannah had decided she must somehow decipher her father's notebook, which must, she thought, have been written in some kind of code.

She would have liked to have spoken to her great-grandmother about the curse, and the hag-stone, and her father's notebook, but Roz was in the drawing room too, and Hannah knew she must not talk about the curse in front of her mother any more in case Roz wanted to leave Wintersloe Castle.

Lady Wintersloe was drinking tea and frowning over the cryptic crossword, as she did every morning. An idea came to Hannah. She sat down and said, "Belle, did my dad ever help you with the crossword?"

"He did indeed, my dear," Lady Wintersloe answered.

"Could you teach me how to do it too?" Hannah asked. Roz looked up from her newspaper and frowned, but did not protest as the two heads – one silver and elegantly coiffured, the other copper-red and wild – bent over the newspaper.

"Now, the first thing you need to know is that, unlike normal crosswords, the clues to the cryptic crosswords are actually hidden inside the sentence, which is why it can often sound a little strange," Lady Wintersloe said. "Usually a cryptic clue has two pointers, or hints, one of which is fairly understandable and the other one that is hidden. 'Cryptic' means 'hidden', you see. So, here, this clue says 'Oddball manages to break a saucepan'. What do you think the answer is? It's got eight letters."

Hannah had no idea.

"Well, lots of cryptic crosswords use synonyms. Can you think of any other word for 'oddball'?"

"Ummm. Weirdo? Strange? Not quite right in the head? Ummm. Flaky? Crackpot?" As soon as she said the last word, a favourite expression of her mother's, something clicked in Hannah's brain. She looked again at the clue. 'Saucepan' was another word for 'pot' and a cracked pot could conceivably be a broken pot. "That's it, isn't it? The answer is crackpot." She quickly counted the letters on her fingers.

"Well done! See, it's not so hard when you get the knack of it. There are lots of other kinds of wordplay, though, apart from synonyms. Sometimes the hidden clue is an anagram, which means the letters of the word have been rearranged. Usually you're given a clue like 'mixed up' or 'rearranged'. Let me see if I can find one for you. All right. Try this one. 'The young girl in distress will mix medals'. You can tell the answer is an anagram because of 'mix'."

Hannah stared at the newspaper for ages, but she could not make any sense of the clue. Her great-grandmother picked up her fountain pen and wrote *medals* on the edge of the newspaper. Then underneath it she wrote *damsel*.

"See? Isn't it clever? A 'damsel' is a young girl, and an anagram of 'medals'." She smiled at Hannah's chagrined face. "I know, it seems easy when it's explained to you, but it's never so easy when you're trying to figure it out on your own. Some of these cryptics are fiendishly clever."

She went through the crossword with Hannah, explaining each clue. Many of them still seemed like garbled nonsense to Hannah, but she began to see why her great-grandmother found cryptic crosswords so fascinating.

It was pouring with rain again, and so Roz was easily persuaded to have a morning at home. Hannah took a thermos of hot chocolate and some warm cinnamon rolls up to her father's tower room, and set herself to break her father's code.

She made some progress. Not all of the writing in the notebook was in code. Some pages were hastily scribbled notes, with references to the other books. There was a page of notes on hag-stones, which Hannah read with great interest.

Hag-stones are curious pebbles that have naturally formed holes running right through them. The holes were created by the friction of running water over many centuries, which may explain why they are such a powerful protection against dark witchcraft and the forces of evil, as it is well known that such forces cannot cross running water.

Hag-stones are also linked with faeries, and are often regarded as keys into the Faery Realm. They allow the owner to see faeries and the Faery Realm, and have the power to bind a faery to the owner's service. Hag-stones are used for healing and to make healing water.

Hag-stones can help you be understood when you speak, and understand when you listen. When tied to a cord and swung above the head, hag-stones can chase away storms. Hag-stones will bring a person to you, or send them away. They are also used to bring luck and wealth to you, or to send it away. Hag-stones have the power to reveal the truth from lies when held as pledge stones, and reveal the true nature of any person or creature viewed through the stone's hole. As wish-stones, they are held in the palm of the left hand and rubbed with the right thumb while wishing.

Hag-stones can only be found or given with love, never bought or stolen.

Putting her hand in her pocket, Hannah touched the hag-stone in wonder. She drank the rest of her hot chocolate – now only lukewarm – and flicked through the pages until she found another section that was not written in code. There were descriptions of fairies – banshees and hobgoblins and kelpies and selkies; a recipe for a smoke bomb – sugar and saltpetre cooked together and then allowed to cool in a mould made from aluminium foil; and an account of the Wild Hunt, which rode out at the beginning of each quarter of the year and would often steal humans away to fairyland.

On one page, her father had written:

Ley lines are ancient paths that led in straight lines from places of power, like Stonehenge. These ley lines cross the earth like a mathematical grid, intersecting at circles of stones, ancient monuments, high hills and sacred sites. Experiments show these ley lines – and the points of power – are imbued with higher than usual magnetic force. The folk traditions of the Scottish Highlands believe that such sites are "thin places", places where the membrane between the worlds is insubstantial, where time stands still and two worlds meet. People who have a heightened psychic awareness can often "sense" such vortex points, and many legends attest to the possibility of these points being gateways to the Faery Realm or even, perhaps, to different times.

Her father had scribbled in his notebook, under this reference, "Fairknowe a thin place?"

Hannah felt a surge of excitement. She pushed her chair back and went to look out the window at Fairknowe Hill. Could it really be a "thin place", a gateway to another world, or even another time? It seemed impossible.

Hannah sighed and rested her elbows on the window sill, looking at the green cone of hill with its black, thorny crown. It had stopped raining, and the mist on the hills had lifted. A ray of sunlight pierced the clouds and reflected brightly off something on the hill. Hannah squinted, then bent and looked through the telescope. Someone was lying on the top of Fairknowe Hill, watching Wintersloe Castle through binoculars. A woman, short and dumpy, dressed in nondescript clothes and large glasses. Miss Underhill!

Hannah quickly stepped away from the window. Her heart was beating uncomfortably fast. She did not like the idea that their house was being spied on. Suddenly the tower room seemed too small and dark. Hannah ran out, locking the door behind her, and raced down to the kitchen, her boot heels rapping urgently on the floorboards.

The kitchen was toasty warm and smelled deliciously of soup. Linnet was stooped over the table, pounding something in her mortar and pestle.

"That woman from the fairy shop is spying on us," Hannah burst out.

"Miss Underhill?" Linnet looked up and smiled. "Och, don't you worry about her, she's all right."

"Belle says she's a ghoul."

"Oh, well, my lady didn't like that wee book of hers. She thinks the curse is family business." Linnet hopped down from her stool and began to sweep the floor with her tiny broom.

Hannah sat on the edge of the table and swung her foot. She was so full of questions that she did not know where to start. She looked up and saw Linnet's cloudy green eyes fixed on her enquiringly.

"Linnet . . . do you believe in magic?" she burst out.

Linnet smiled. "Of course! Why, there's a flame of magic inside everything, in every stone and every flower, every bird that sings and every frog that croaks. There's magic in the trees and the hills and the river and the rocks, in the sea and the stars and the wind, a deep, wild magic that's as old as the world itself. It's in you too, my darling girl, and in me, and in every living creature, be it ever so small. Even the dirt I'm sweeping up now is really stardust. In fact, all of us are made from the stuff of stars. Ask your mother. She's the one who first told me that."

"Really?"

"Yes, indeed."

"But Mum doesn't believe in magic."

"No, I know she doesn't. But she has a great feel for the wonder and mystery of the world, don't you think? That's why your father loved her so."

Hannah felt a sudden and most unexpected sting of tears in her eyes. She blinked them away grimly, telling herself she was tired after her disturbed night.

"So hasn't anyone tried to break the curse?" she asked.

"Many people. They've brought in all sorts of folk over the years, with holy water and who knows what else. And then, of course, many people tried to find the broken parts of the puzzle ring."

"My father found one part, though, didn't he?" Hannah demanded. She thought her great-grandmother had told her so last night, although there was so much else to remember, Hannah was not completely sure.

Linnet went to open the door, looking all round outside, then came back to stand very close to Hannah, taking her hand in one of her own, bony and age-spotted and trembling. "Yes," she whispered. "He wouldn't tell me how or where, he said it was too dangerous. He hid it somewhere safe. With the rose of the world, he said."

Hannah nodded eagerly, recognizing the phrase from the final entry in her father's notebook. *Its bewildered quarter I left safe, with the rose of the world, my double rose. . .*

"He was so happy. He said he knew where the others were too, and that he would go and find them. But he never came back." Tears swam in the old green eyes. "That black-hearted witch got him, that's what I think."

"Irata?"

Linnet looked round anxiously. "Don't go saying her name, my chick. Names have power. Names are for calling."

Hannah gave a superstitious shiver. She sat in silence for a while, thinking. It thrilled her to think her father may have found one quarter of the puzzle ring, for it proved to her that his notebook was not just nonsense, that it did indeed have the secret to breaking the curse hidden within it. She wondered where he might have hidden the quarter of the puzzle ring that he had found. Somewhere here at the castle? She would have to start hunting in earnest.

Linnet busied herself washing up and Hannah went off

into a dream where she found the missing loops of the puzzle ring, joined it together again and broke the curse. After a while she asked: "Linnet, do you ever hear a dog howling?"

The stooped old woman tilted her face up to stare at Hannah. "You can hear the dog? Howling as if its heart were breaking?"

Hannah nodded, and on an impulse slipped her hand into her pocket and brought out the hag-stone. Linnet took it from her with trembling fingers. "Glory be, where did you find this?"

"A toad gave it to me."

Hannah felt a flush of embarrassment burning her cheeks, but Linnet seemed to find nothing odd in her words. "But where, my lamb?"

"At the witch's pool."

Linnet sat down on the stool as if her legs had suddenly grown too weak to hold her up any longer. "But that is how your father found it, not long before you were born. He said the toad brought it to him at the witch's pool. It had been gone so many, many years . . . I had thought it gone for ever."

"Eglantyne threw it in the pool, didn't she?" Hannah asked, remembering what her great-grandmother had told her.

"Yes. The night of the Wild Hunt . . . the night she cast the curse." Linnet gently rubbed her thumb over the hag-stone. "More than four hundred and forty years ago."

"And so the toad gave it to my father, before I was

127

born?" Hannah felt a sharp thrill of excitement. "When was that?"

"It was late October," Linnet said. "Bobby had brought your mother home, to meet my lady and me. He went walking one evening by the pool, and the toad brought him the hag-stone. Your father had always declared he would be the Red Rose to break the curse, and spent a lot of time in his teens studying all the old folklore and fairy tales, looking for clues. He'd stopped by the time he was in his late teens, but finding the hag-stone brought all his old dreams back to life. And I suppose he wanted to make sure the curse would not hurt your mother or you, once you were born."

"So he went through the gateway then, and found one quarter of the puzzle ring," Hannah said slowly.

"Yes. He went through at sunset on Halloween. I was that worried about him! He came back safely the next morning, though, and told me that he'd had a grand adventure, and that the hag-stone had even greater powers than he'd imagined. He said he'd found one of the quarters of the puzzle ring, but would not show me, or tell me where he'd hidden it. He said he wanted to go back, to try and save Eglantyne, and to find the other three parts of the ring. Six weeks later he went again, but this time he didn't come back."

Linnet looked down at the hag-stone in her hand. "So I would like to know where that old toad found the hag-stone. For your father took it with him that night. I thought it had gone missing with him."

"What happened that night? What happened to my dad?" Hannah spoke fiercely.

"I don't know. It was Midwinter's Eve, a time when the walls are thin. He said he was going to break the curse once and for all, and undo all the harm that had been done. Something went wrong. I don't know what. It's an evil place now, that green hill. You mustn't go there, my chick, not on your own, and not at noon or midnight, or dawn or dusk, and definitely not on any of the thin days. You. . ."

"Thin days? What do you mean by that?"

"The days when the gateway opens, my lamb. You should know those days. Midwinter and midsummer; the midpoints of spring and autumn; and the days that mark the halfway points between – May Day and Candlemas, Lammas and Halloween." Linnet drew a circle on the tabletop, quartering it once and then again so it looked like a wheel with eight spokes. "It's on those days that you can cross the threshold. . ."

". . .and go where?" Hannah demanded.

"To the Otherworld, of course."

Jinx

Hannah could not keep still. She put on her raincoat and went out into the garden. First she went to the ruined castle and looked at the rosebush growing upon the wall, marking the grave of a long-dead fairy hound. When she put the hag-stone to her ear, she could hear howling. When she put it to her eye, she saw the limp corpse of a little white and red dog dangling from the archway, twisting slightly in the breeze. She caught her breath in horror and quickly dropped her hand.

She went next to the yew tree, black in the rain and smelling of graveyards. She hid within its hollow heart and closed her hands about the hag-stone, not daring to look through it or listen. Some of its magic seemed to have taught her ears, however, for she could hear yelling and taunting laughter and the sound of a woman weeping and pleading for her life. Hannah wanted to jam her fingers in her ears. *Audacia*, she thought, and slowly lifted the stone to her left eye.

Hannah saw a crowd of people in old-fashioned clothes, shouting and shaking their fists, their faces distorted with hatred. A young woman wearing a filthy white shift, with long dark hair knotted and snarled down her back, was chained to a stake in the midst of a great pile of firewood. She was heavily pregnant. Snow flurried down from a leaden sky, weighing down the branches of the yew tree. The pool was filmed over with ice. It was dusk, and the woods were filled with swaying shadows.

A tall, stern-looking man in a long dark robe, with a white ruff pushing up his pointed beard, raised high a flaming torch, the only colour in all that cold, dark landscape. He pointed at the distraught young woman and intoned words of damnation and hellfire. She lifted her voice and screamed for her father.

As if seeking to drown her voice, the man in black robes flung the torch into the pyre. Flames at once shot high, and thick smoke billowed. Eglantyne screamed. Hannah gasped and dropped the stone, and found herself back inside the yew tree, damp and shivering, the hag-stone at her feet.

I need to know what happened, she told herself. *I need to know the truth.*

Slowly she lifted the hag-stone to her eyes again. "Show me true," she whispered.

Once again Hannah saw the snowy scene by the dark pool, but this time she saw a young man creeping out from the cleft in the hill. He was dressed in modern clothes –

131

jeans and a dark hooded parka. His tangled curls were red, and he had the long nose that Hannah had inherited. It was her father!

The man in the black robes shouted and raised high his flaming torch. He did not see Hannah's father crouched behind the boulder a few metres away, drawing something out of his parka pocket. It was shaped roughly like a squat brown candle. Robert waited till the man had flung his torch on to the pyre, then he hastily lit a match and applied the flame to the wick of the candle.

At once thick smoke began to pour out, billowing across the clearing. As the onlookers coughed and turned away, Robert ran forward and leapt on to the pyre. He held a long pair of bolt cutters in his hand, which cut through the iron chains as if they were made of paper. Eglantyne collapsed into his arms. Robert carried her behind the boulder, then turned and flung a handful of powder on to the fire. At once, there was a giant flash, blindingly bright. Women screamed, and the crowd all cringed back, shielding their faces as smoke poured out once more.

A magpie screeched and darted frantically overhead, but everyone was coughing and shielding their eyes from the smoke and so did not notice. Robert lifted Eglantyne and carried her through the long, dark crack in the rock, and out of sight. The magpie swooped after them.

Hannah's hand dropped. Her heart was pounding and her mouth was dry. She thrust the hag-stone into her pocket and ran back towards the house. For the first time in her life she longed for things to be ordinary.

Haddock and potato soup, and playing Scrabble with her mother and great-grandmother by the fire all afternoon, helped make the world seem stable again. Lady Wintersloe won every game, which pleased her enormously, and made Roz rather cross. Hannah was just happy to be warm and comfortable again.

Around four o'clock Linnet came in pushing the tea trolley, laden with freshly made scones and sticky marmalade cake. Behind her came Donovan, dressed as usual in the colours of a bruise. His T-shirt was too small for him, showing a pale line of his thin, hollow stomach above his studded belt. He was carrying Jinx wrapped up in a towel.

"Jinx!" Lady Wintersloe held out her arms.

Donovan laid Jinx on her lap and she stroked the cat's plush fur.

"She should be fine. She was lucky. Toads are pretty venomous."

Hannah surreptitiously slid her hand into her pocket and pulled out the hag-stone. *Hag-stones reveal the true nature of any person or creature viewed through the stone's hole*, the book had said. Hannah lifted it to her eye and looked at the sleeping cat.

Hannah saw a small grey winged imp-like creature with stubby horns, scaly skin and sharp claws. The imp opened her round orange eyes and blinked once or twice, then saw Hannah observing her through the hole in the stone.

133

At once, she arched her back like a cat, hissed in rage, and leapt from Lady Wintersloe's lap, racing away through the half-open door.

Hannah put the stone back in her pocket.

"Looks like Jinx is back to her old self." Lady Wintersloe ruefully examined her scratched hand.

"Bogey-cat," Linnet said with feeling. She and Hannah shared a meaningful glance. Hannah knew without a doubt that Linnet could see the true nature of the cat as clearly as she had. "I'll get you a sticking-plaster for that. You're bleeding." The tiny old woman went hurrying out of the room, leaving Roz to pass Lady Wintersloe a napkin and a cup of tea.

"Did you see the bloodstains on the palace floor?" Donovan asked Hannah.

She nodded. "Clear as anything! It's amazing, isn't it? Why do you think they're still there after so many years?"

"My dad says it's a fake. He says they must paint it there every morning, so the tourists have something to gawk at."

"My mum says it's just a natural discolouration in the wood."

They looked at each other and shook their heads, both saying "Parents" at the exact same time, and then laughing.

"So do you like Scotland?" Donovan asked.

"I love it, what I've seen so far," Hannah said.

"You've got to go out into the wild places," Donovan

said. "You should climb Ben Lomond, or go into the woods, where all the wild creatures are. Or go out on the loch. Do you like fishing?" Donovan flicked his hair out of his face, his blue-grey eyes glowing.

"I love it," Hannah lied.

"What about birds? You have some amazing birds in Australia. All those parrots and . . . what are they called? Those laughing jackasses?"

"Kookaburras."

"Yeah. I'd like to hear them laugh."

"Not at five-thirty in the morning you wouldn't."

"Yeah, I would. I don't mind getting up early. I often get up before dawn and go out bird spotting, or looking for foxes and badgers. You should come out with me one morning and see if we can spot any pink-footed geese flying in from Iceland. They come in their tens of thousands at this time of year, honking away. It's amazing. Or we might see some stags fighting, if we go into the forest."

"I'd like that. I've never seen a stag before."

"Never seen a stag! We'll have to go find one for you then. They come down to the lower ground in winter, so they're easier to find."

"OK. When?"

"Tomorrow. I'll meet you at the gates at six o'clock. It'll be dark, though, and cold, I warn you. The sun doesn't rise till after seven."

"I'll wrap up warm then."

"Let's go set up the music room," he said. "Max is

135

already there, his mum took me to pick Jinx up from the vet. Scarlett will be along any minute."

"I'll just get my guitar," she said.

Hannah went slowly through the dark, cold, silent house to her room, and came back just as slowly, carrying her guitar. She felt a knot of nerves in her stomach, but raised her chin and reminded herself that this was *her* great-grandmother's house and she had more right to be here than any of the others.

She could hear laughter and talking as she came through the music room door. It died away with her appearance. Donovan nodded and gave his crooked smile, but Max and Scarlett stared at her in open curiosity. Hannah stared back. She wondered if her grandmother was right and one of these three was really the long-lost child of a fairy princess. It seemed impossible. They all looked too normal.

Max was dressed in baggy khaki trousers and an old army jacket, and was sitting sideways at the keyboard, kicking at the stool with his heels. Scarlett was wearing a cream suede jacket with fringed sleeves and skinny jeans pushed into knee-high boots. Her blonde hair swung loose and shiny, and she had pink lipgloss on. Immediately Hannah felt too tall, too plain and far too unfashionable.

"Hi!" Max said. "Sorry I didn't help you carry your stuff the other day. My mum was cross with me."

"I can carry my own stuff, I don't need help," Hannah replied stiffly.

"Donovan says you think you can sing," Scarlett said, in a decidedly unfriendly tone. "I'll just have you know that *I'm* the singer in this band." She tossed her blonde hair.

"We can have more than one singer," Donovan said. "Besides, she plays the guitar."

"Mmphf," Scarlett said, clearly not impressed.

"So what can you play?" Max said.

Hannah wanted to impress them, so she chose a song that needed a tricky change between the G and C chords. She picked up her guitar and strummed it lightly, listening to see if it needed to be tuned.

Scarlett snorted in disgust. "She doesn't even know how to hold the stupid guitar!"

Hannah looked at her coldly. "I'm left-handed, you idiot."

"You can't play a guitar left-handed!"

"Why not? Paul McCartney's left-handed, and so were Jimi Hendrix *and* Kurt Cobain." Hannah had had this argument a few times before.

"Just let her play, Scarlett," Donovan said.

Hannah began to play "Ain't No Sunshine". There was silence while she played and sang, then Max and Donovan clapped their hands. Scarlett kept hers on her hips, her head tilted crossly.

"Not bad," Max said. "I think I've got the music for that somewhere." He found it, and began to play the tune on the keyboard and sing. He played for laughs, drawing out the vowels, throwing back his head and wailing the sad

137

parts, and banging up and down the keys dramatically, not always hitting the right note.

Donovan said his name, once, quietly, and Max grinned and began to play it straight, singing along. After a moment's listening, Donovan began to improvise on his flugelhorn, and Hannah played along, singing too. Only Scarlett didn't join in. She looked cross and sulky.

"Come on, Scarlett," Max said coaxingly. "It's a good song. You must know the chorus."

After a while Scarlett joined in too. She had a sweet voice, though it was not very strong. Hannah found it easy to dominate and drown her out, to her secret satisfaction. Scarlett sang louder. Hannah sang deeper, stronger, longer. With the two striving to outdo each other, they sang up quite a storm, and Hannah saw by the glow in Donovan's eyes that he was glad he had asked her to come along.

They mucked around for a while longer, trying to work out how to play songs they all knew from the radio or from their school choirs, or flicking through the piles of old sheet music on top of the piano, looking for things that were not too difficult. Scarlett was not happy at having Hannah there, and sneered at the music she chose, saying, "Can't we play something written this century? This is all so *boring*!"

"Well, bring us something new to play then," Donovan snapped. "I bet Hannah can play it, if you bring us the music."

Hannah concentrated on her guitar, trying to hide the

138

little glow his words gave her. Scarlett just tossed her head, and banged the old tambourine against her hip irritably.

All too soon the light began to dim outside, and Donovan packed away his flugelhorn. "I've got to get home. Dad said no more getting in after dark."

"Mum too. She doesn't like me walking past the fairy hill in the dark." Scarlett pulled on her suede jacket. She glanced slyly at Hannah. "It's haunted, you know."

"I know. By the witch who was burnt to death there. At night you can hear her dog howling and, sometimes, the sound of her screaming."

Scarlett stared at Hannah with round eyes. Hannah smiled. "Have a good walk home."

Scarlett Spry, Super Spy

The next few days were fine, and Roz hired an old rattletrap from Allan so she and Hannah could go and see some of Scotland. Since no one mentioned the curse, or Hannah's father, she seemed to relax a little and her small frown eased away. When they came in from the cold, Linnet always had the kettle boiling and they would sit with Lady Wintersloe in her warm, firelit drawing room and drink tea and talk over their day in such a cosy and comfortable way that Roz lost some of her stiff politeness and began to smile and chatter in a way Hannah had never seen before.

The following Friday, it was pouring with rain.

"Not really the weather for driving," Roz said, standing at the window and looking out at a world of grey.

"We could have a quiet day at home. Catch up on some reading," Hannah said.

"Or on some maths worksheets," Roz retorted. She had insisted Hannah must keep up with her schooling, and had brought a pile of worksheets for her to do, which Hannah had nimbly managed to avoid till now.

"All right," Hannah said. "I'll help Belle with the crossword first, OK?"

Lady Wintersloe was bent over the newspaper, her glasses perched on her nose. "Boggle? That could fit. But no, that can't be right. Roz, what's another word for puzzle? Beginning with 'B'."

"I don't know; Hannah's our wordsmith, not me. Bewilder?"

"Too many letters."

"So it can't be bamboozle. What about baffle?" Hannah suggested.

"Baffle! Of course. Clever girl. Thank you." Lady Wintersloe scribbled down the word with her gold pen, while Hannah tried to remember where she had seen that word recently. Suddenly she remembered. It appeared in her father's book, in the very first entry: *Pestis must be infractus, but the baffled moon is lost in the mists of time.*

It suddenly occurred to her that her father must be talking about the puzzle ring. "Baffle" meant, of course, "puzzle"; and both "ring" and "moon" were round. It all began to make a strange sort of sense.

"Belle, what does 'pestis' mean?" Hannah asked.

"What, darling? 'Pestis'? Oh, it means to curse, I think, in Latin. Like a pestilence."

"So what does 'infractus' mean?"

"My word. I have no idea. There's an infraction of the

141

rules. That sounds like it might be related. But I couldn't tell you what it means, exactly. I didn't ever learn Latin, not like your father, who thought it might be useful for his medical degree."

Breaking the rules, Hannah thought. *Breaking the curse*.

When Roz and Lady Wintersloe were both absorbed in the newspaper, Hannah very quietly got up from her maths worksheet and crept from the room. Jinx had been curled by the fire, but got up to follow Hannah. She quickly closed the door on the bogey-cat's nose, shutting her into the room, then, feeling very pleased with herself, ran to the little tower room, unlocking the door with the key she always carried in her cardigan pocket.

Hannah sat and opened the first page of the notebook, staring at the first line: *Pestis must be infractus, but the baffled moon is lost in the mists of time.*

If she translated it, it read: *The curse must be broken, but the puzzle ring is lost in the mists of time.*

She sat back, smiling to herself. She had been right. The odd, disconnected sentences were not the ramblings of a madman but a careful and deliberate attempt by her father to conceal his efforts to break the Curse of Wintersloe Castle.

Hannah began to go systematically through the cryptic verses, translating what she knew, or guessing at their meanings. But so little of it seemed to make sense. *Gate is guarded, stone eyes are watching*, he wrote, and on the next page:

Why does the black witch watch us, why does she care?
She rules the hollow hills, she sits in the green chair.
Does she fear the child of true blood, the lost heir?
But why and who and when and where?

Next came long pages of notes about Einstein, and space curvature, and time dilation, and wormholes, and warp drives, and black holes, and cosmic strings, none of which Hannah understood, and then another page of verse:

Sing a song of spells, there's reason in rhyme,
like ringing the bells, to unlock the gate in time.
Sing a song of spells, three times is the charm,
like ringing the bells, to help keep you from harm.

It was like a riddle, but Hannah could not work out the answer. By late afternoon, her head was aching and she was feeling frustrated and angry. She wished she was not cursed. Taking out the hag-stone, she slowly rubbed it with her thumb, and wished she could just be a normal girl, hanging out with her friends, talking about the things normal girls talked about, whatever they were.

Then Hannah sighed, stretched her arms above her head and, putting the hag-stone back in her cardigan pocket, went moodily down to the kitchen. She sat on the edge of the table, swinging her legs. Linnet was chopping onions so fast her knife was practically a blur, while various soups and sauces bubbled on the stove top. The kitchen smelled of baking.

143

"Why don't you go down to Scarlett's place?" Linnet suggested. "She'll be home from school by now, and a girl your age needs girlfriends."

"Scarlett doesn't like me," Hannah said, feeling only faint surprise that Linnet should know what she had been thinking without needing to be told.

"Scarlett doesn't know you yet, does she? It's clearing up, so it'll be a nice walk for you. I've made you some marmalade cake to take. It's her favourite."

Carrying the warm cake tin, Hannah walked slowly down to Fairknowe, enjoying the late-afternoon gleam of the loch. She paused as she passed *The Fäerie Knowe* and looked in the window, then on impulse pushed open the door and went inside. Miss Underhill was serving a mother with a little girl dressed in a white tutu over a long-sleeved T-shirt and striped stockings, a thick cardigan tied over the top. Hannah browsed among the shelves, examining the crystals, looking at the books. Many of them she recognized from her father's tower room.

"We are always *fairy* happy to help," Miss Underhill said as she passed over a plastic bag with gold, sparkly fairies on it. The mother and daughter went out and Miss Underhill looked across the counter at Hannah. The overhead light glinted on her big glasses so Hannah could not see her eyes.

"You need my help." It was a statement, not a question.

"Yes. I . . ." Hannah's voice faltered. She did not know what to ask.

144

"There are some things you should know." Miss Underhill spoke quickly. "You must be very careful. The Fair Folk are not pretty little things that give wishes and flutter their tiny wings. They're strange and dangerous. Their world is very different from ours, and they do not care much for mortals. You need to know that they do not like cold iron. It does not matter what form it comes in. A sword or a knife, a pair of scissors, a needle or nail, a fish hook, yes, even a key. Keep it in your pocket at all times."

Hannah tried not to let her surprise show on her face. It was as if Miss Underhill knew she carried an old iron key in her pocket.

"If you should be taken against your will to the fairy realm, a nail or pin stuck in the door will stop them from closing it again, so you can escape. Do not eat or drink while you are there. Do not think to stay to watch the dancing or the feasting, for time moves at a different pace in the Otherworld and you may find yourself there for a hundred years when you thought it only half an hour."

Hannah nodded. She had read that before.

"Halloween is coming. That will be the most dangerous time. You must protect yourself. Rowan is one of the best protections against evil. You have a rowan tree planted outside your kitchen door. It has bright red berries that last all winter. Cut yourself some twigs from it and tie them together, either in the shape of a cross or a star, whichever you prefer. Hang them above every door and window in your bedroom."

Hannah thought about the star made of silvery twigs

145

that was nailed above the lintels of the two tower rooms. She wondered if her father had made them.

Miss Underhill took a deep breath. She had been talking so quickly, so urgently, her cheeks had grown flushed. "The best thing, though, the very best protection is a hag-stone. This is a stone that has had a hole worn through it naturally by running water."

She leant forward, staring at Hannah intently. "Have you seen any stone like that, Hannah? I'd . . . I'd very much like to see it if you have."

Hannah shook her head, making a little grimace with her mouth. She had to clench her hands by her side to stop them sneaking into her pocket and closing around the hag-stone.

Miss Underhill looked disappointed. She moved away, her hands mechanically tidying the counter. "Well, they are very rare. I had heard there was one in your family, passed down through the generations. I did hope the tale was true. A real hag-stone! Never mind. Was there anything else I can help you with?"

The colour in her cheeks had faded, and her voice sounded quite normal again.

"No. I'm fine." As Hannah spoke, she realized these were the first words she had uttered since she had come into the shop. It was all very strange. She did not know whether to trust Miss Underhill. She was so intense, it was unnerving. As Hannah left, she was conscious of Miss Underhill's eyes boring into her back.

The village store was busy, with women gossiping in a queue to buy bread and milk and the newspaper. A man Hannah had never seen before was behind the counter. He was a big, broad man with a red face, straw-coloured eyebrows and a shining bald head. He saw Hannah hesitating at the back of the queue, the tin of marmalade cake in her hands, and nodded at her. "Come to see Scarlett, hey? Go on up."

He indicated the half-open door behind him with a jerk of his head. All too aware of the many curious eyes, Hannah sidled through the queue and went up the steps to the apartment above.

In a small, crowded, noisy living room strewn with toys and paper and crayons, three small, plump, sticky-faced boys were jumping up and down and shrieking as they watched some cartoon on television. They had mops of dark curly hair and hazel eyes like their mother, who was frowning over an account book at the table.

Mrs Shaw smiled as Hannah came through the door. "Why, it's Hannah, isn't it? You've come to see Scarlett? How nice! She's in her room. Just down the hall. You can't miss it."

Hannah gave Mrs Shaw the marmalade cake and went hesitantly down the hall. It was easy to guess which one was Scarlett's room. It had her name on it in teddy-bear letters, with a poster of a gorgeous, moody-looking singer in ripped denim and chains sticky-taped above it. Hannah knocked.

"What?" Scarlett yelled.

"It's me. Hannah."

"Oh." There was a moment's silence before Scarlett opened the door. The two girls looked at each other. Hannah thought how different Scarlett was from the rest of her family, with her blonde hair and blue eyes and slender figure. She was a lot older than her brothers, who must all have been under the age of six. She was wearing a school uniform, which made her seem less grown up, and somehow more approachable, than usual.

It was in Hannah's mind that she should say something to Scarlett about the last time they met. Something like sorry. Hannah was never very good at apologizing, though, and besides, it was Scarlett who had tried to scare her with her story about the castle being haunted.

So instead she said, "Your dad told me to come up and say hi."

Scarlett pushed out her bottom lip, then shrugged. "You want to hang out? I'm not doing anything much."

"OK." Hannah came into the room, looking about her with interest. It was incredibly messy, with clothes and shoes and magazines all over the floor. Every wall was covered with posters of pop stars. The small bookshelf above the desk was crowded with trophies. Hannah went over to examine them.

"You do judo?"

"Karate," Scarlett replied. She flopped down on the bed again and began flicking through a magazine. "And gymnastics."

"You must be pretty good."

"Yeah."

"You must practise a lot." Hannah looked around for somewhere to sit, feeling as awkward as a giraffe in this tiny room.

"I try to. It's hard, though. There's not much room here and the boys always have their stuff all over the place. Hey, don't touch that!"

It was too late. Hannah had bumped her hip against the chair, and a pile of paper cascaded over the floor. "Sorry!" she cried, and went down on her knees to gather the papers together again. Scarlett bounced up crossly and came to help her.

The papers were covered with drawings. They all featured a girl with huge eyes and a blonde ponytail, doing karate leaps and chops against a succession of monsters and villains.

"Wow! These are fantastic! Did you do them?"

"Yeah." Scarlett shuffled the pages together, her cheeks turning red.

"Are you making a comic book?" Hannah looked through the pages. "What are you going to call it?"

Scarlett shrugged. "I dunno. Can't think of a name for her."

"Scarlett's a good name for a spy," Hannah said. "It's a shame your last name isn't Spry. Then it would rhyme. Scarlett Spry, Super Spy," Hannah said.

"Scarlett Spry, Super Spy." Scarlett rolled it round on

her tongue. "Wow, that's amazing. Did you just come up with that, just like that? I've been trying to think of a good name for ages!"

Hannah felt pleased. "I like making up rhymes like that. I try and write songs sometimes. I've been writing one since I got here."

"Really? Can I hear it?"

Hannah hesitated. "It's not very good yet."

"So? You saw my drawings."

"Oh, all right. It starts like this. . ." Hannah took a deep breath, then sang:

> *"I'm coming home, I'm coming home, to a place I've*
>   *never been,*
> *my feet know the road, my eyes know the scene,*
> *although this is a place that I've never seen.*
> *I'm coming home, I'm coming home, to a place I've*
>   *never been,*
> *my ears know the song, my heart knows the green,*
> *never have I felt so safe and serene."*

"That's really good," Scarlett said. "I wish I could write stuff like that."

"I wish I could draw like you. You want to be an artist when you grow up?"

Scarlett's cheeks went pink again. "Nah. No money in art. I want to be a famous actress. I do acting lessons too, you know."

"As well as music and karate and gymnastics?" Hannah asked.

"And horse-riding, and singing lessons," Scarlett said. "Well, it's tough breaking into acting these days. I figure the more I can do, the better chance I have."

Just then, Mrs Shaw knocked on the door. "Hungry, girls? This marmalade cake smells good."

"Marmalade cake?" Scarlett cried. "My favourite!"

"Me too," Hannah said, and together the two girls jumped up and raced out to the living room, where Mrs Shaw had made them hot chocolate and cut them slices of cake, still steaming gently and smelling delicious.

The Blue-Faced Hag

It was Halloween that weekend. Miss Underhill organized a street party in Fairknowe for all the children. There were prizes for the best costume and the best pumpkin lantern, dooking for apples, ghost stories and a walk to the witch's pool.

"What about trick or treating?" Hannah asked, in the music room that Saturday afternoon.

"We don't really do that here," Scarlett said. "I mean, not the tricking anyway."

"That's so American," Max said scornfully.

"Here we go guising," Scarlett explained. "You go from door to door, and you've got to sing or tell a joke or tap-dance or something to get the treat."

"Let's all go together," Donovan said. "We'll sing 'Loch Lomond'. That's a good one for Halloween."

"Oh, spare me!" Scarlett rolled her eyes.

"Why? I mean, why is it a good one for Halloween?" Hannah could only vaguely remember the chorus of the song, which went:

You'll take the high road
And I'll take the low road
And I'll be in Scotland afore you
But me and my true love will never meet again
On the bonny bonny banks of Loch Lomond.

"Because it's about death," Donovan said with his usual intensity. "The low road is the spirit road that the dead travel home on. It was written by a guy who'd been condemned to death for fighting against the English . . ."

"In the time of Bonnie Prince Charlie," Max put in.

". . . but his friend has been set free. So the friend gets to take the high road, you know, like the highway, but the other guy, the one that's being hanged, will take the low road, the spirit road, and he'll get to Scotland. . ."

"*Afore you!*" Max sang, with a broad dramatic gesture, knocking his music sheets off the stand so they cascaded to the floor.

"People always sing it wrong," Donovan said with passion. "They do it all happy, but it's a sad song, a lament."

"I guess we could really ham it up," Max said, on his knees to pick up the music sheets. "It could be fun."

The Fäerie Knowe did a roaring trade, selling skeleton suits and witches' hats and fright masks. Hannah put her own outfit together, with a black velvet skirt and her beret and lots of her mother's powder and black eyeliner, but Scarlett turned up in the most expensive witch's outfit the

153

shop sold. Donovan dressed just as usual, with the addition of some black lipstick and nail polish, while Max wore his most tattered combat gear with a gory, red-splashed plastic axe stuck to his head.

"Don't be late coming home, my chick," Linnet said to Hannah, looking worried. "It's not a night to be out wandering about in the dark."

"But the sun sets so early! It's practically dark by four o'clock! Besides, I'll be with the others."

"Don't worry, Linnet, I'll go with the kids," Roz said. She had only given her permission for Hannah to go after her daughter had begged her, and only because she was so glad Hannah was finally making a few friends. "I don't like the idea of them being out alone on Halloween either. All sorts of crackpots come out on Halloween."

"It's not the people I'm worried about," Linnet muttered. Only Hannah – whose ears seemed preternaturally sharp these days – heard her.

The four friends had great fun roaming up and down the streets, singing "Loch Lomond" in the most mournful and heart-rending way, and collecting bags of lollies and chocolates, which they gave to Roz to carry.

Then, at dusk, Miss Underhill led an expedition up the hill and into the woods, everyone carrying plastic Halloween lanterns that Miss Underhill sold in the fairy shop for five pounds each.

She was dressed all in blue, with blue paint on her skin and a blue wig, and she carried a tall wooden staff and an enormous moon-shaped orange lantern. "I am the Cailleach Bheur, the blue-faced hag of winter," she intoned in a deep, scary voice. "I was worshipped here in Scotland for centuries before the missionaries came. I carry hailstones in my pockets to blight the crops, and with every strike of my staff I freeze the ground beneath me." *Bam, bam!* She struck the ground with each step.

"One touch of my staff knocks all the leaves off the trees." *Swish, swish!* She swiped her staff through the twigs of a tree, bringing the leaves showering down. Everyone giggled. "The ocean's whirlpool is my washtub. . ."

Hannah followed the swinging moon of her lantern, her breath puffing white before her.

"Did you know you can find out who you're going to marry tonight?" Scarlett said. "You've got to sit by a mirror, with a candle burning and an apple in your hand. . ."

"Don't you know not to look in mirrors at night?" Donovan said. "That's how you see ghosts."

"That's so not true!"

"Yes it is. Everyone knows that."

"I tell you what you're meant to do on Halloween," Max said. "You light two candles and you sit in the dark in front of the mirror, and then you say 'Bloody Mary' nine times, louder and louder and louder. . . 'Bloody Mary . . . BLOODY MARY . . . **BLOODY MARY**. . .' and then she reaches through the mirror and scratches your eyes out!"

"Why on earth would I want to do that?" Hannah said.

"I don't know . . . for fun?"

"Doesn't sound like much fun."

"It's better than sitting around and staring into a mirror waiting for your one true love to appear," Donovan said scornfully.

They came to the witch's pool, black as ink under the yew tree, and everyone grew silent. The trees bent and swayed in a cold wind, and only the blackthorn tree that crowned the high hill was still irradiated with the last blood-red streaks of light.

Out of the corner of her eye, Hannah saw shadows leaning over them and thought she could feel eyes watching them from the darkness. She remembered what Linnet had said. *It's an evil place now, that green hill. You mustn't go there, my chick, not on your own, and not at noon or midnight, or dawn or dusk, and definitely not on any of the thin days.*

Halloween was a thin day. Hannah pressed closer to her mother, who slung her arm about her shoulders protectively.

Miss Underhill sat on one of the yew tree's thick, contorted roots, holding the moon-lantern under her chin so it shone upwards on to her face, blue and hollowed, with strange glittering eyes. She began to tell the story of Eglantyne, who was burnt to death here, and whose ghost was thought to haunt the clearing.

But it can't, Hannah thought. *Not if my father rescued her from the fire.*

She had been thinking a lot about her great-grandmother's story, and whether it could possibly be true. In the hag-stone vision she had seen her father and Eglantyne escape

156

into the cave in the hill. What had happened to them then? If her father had the hag-stone with him, how had it ended up with a toad in the pond? She looked at the black water and shivered.

"It's much too cold to be out this late, listening to this nonsense," Roz said. She got to her feet, drawing Hannah with her and giving Miss Underhill a hostile glance. "Come on, let's get home."

Hannah waved to her friends, who glanced up in surprise; then she walked in silence back through the night-haunted trees. Roz walked in silence too, hands shoved into her pockets.

"You mustn't listen to those old stories," she said gruffly. "There's no ghost here at Wintersloe, and no curse either."

Hannah knew that her mother was wrong. Magic existed, both benevolent and baneful, and she was stalked by the shadow of a centuries-old tragedy. She did not say anything, though, just slipped her hand through her mother's arm and walked home with her in silence.

That night the wind moaned around the tower, rattling the bare branches of the wych elm and banging a loose shutter somewhere. Hannah lay and listened. She was sure she could hear high eerie cries, and the beat of wings and the drum of hooves. *It's only geese flying over*, she told herself. *Donovan's pink-footed geese. . .*

But her scalp was crawling and her skin was raised in

goosebumps. There was a tight knot of fear in her stomach. *Audacia*, she told herself, and groped under her pillow for her hag-stone. She got out of bed and padded across to the east window, pressing her nose against the glass and looking towards Fairknowe Hill. All she could see was racing clouds and tossing branches. Hannah lifted the hag-stone to her eye.

And screamed.

Across the sky galloped a horde of strange beasts, ridden by tall beings with flashing eyes and streaming hair and whips of lightning, all speed and cruelty and darkness. And on Hannah's window sill crouched the winged gargoyle with the horns, its wicked face turning to glare at her with eyes burning red as embers.

Hannah dragged the curtains shut and ran round the room. At every single window crouched a gargoyle come to life. Their eyes glowed red as they snarled with the most blood-curdling sound. Hannah drew shut every curtain, then ran back to bed, her heart pounding with terror. She burrowed under the bedclothes, the hag-stone and the key clutched against her chest, and listened with all her might. She heard jeers and catcalls, and the scrape of claws against stone, and then the rattling of the windows in their frames as the gargoyles tried to get in. Hannah thought of the stars of rowan twigs she had nailed above each window and door, and hoped it was true they protected against evil. The rattling and snarling continued for a few long minutes; then she heard howls of frustration and the flap of leathery wings as the gargoyles flew off to join the Wild Hunt. Gradually the gibbering and shrieking faded away. But Hannah did not sleep until she heard the first calls of the birds' dawn chorus.

Two Hornet Queens

As the days grew shrunken and silvered with cold, Hannah's life fell into a natural rhythm. She breakfasted every morning with her mother and great-grandmother, helping Lady Wintersloe with the cryptic crossword while Roz pored over the guidebook and planned their day. Then Hannah and Roz drove out in the rattletrap to see Scotland. They explored ancient castles, saw baby seals playing off the icy beaches, visited ancient battlegrounds and climbed snow-dusted hills, before coming home in the chilly dusk for Linnet's famous afternoon tea.

Hannah spent the rest of the time hanging out with whichever of her friends were free. Max and Scarlett rarely had the time during the week, for their afternoons were filled with homework and music lessons, or in Scarlett's case, karate, drama, singing and horse-riding lessons. Donovan turned up most afternoons, however, the roar of his motorized bicycle destroying the peace of the silent old house. The two of them would go tramping through the woods in the chilly dusk, looking for badgers or stags. Evenings were spent reluctantly in home schooling, and, less reluctantly, reading by the fire.

Every Saturday afternoon the band would get together in the music room and practise. After Hannah said she thought Scarlett had fantastic rhythm and should take up drums, Scarlett was a little less sore about not being the lead singer any more. She began to muck around with the tambourine and the little hand-drum and found she had a real flair for it.

Otherwise, Hannah spent every free moment decoding her father's notebook, or searching the house and the old castle for some kind of double rose, tapping on walls, twisting carved roses, examining tapestries and cushions, even digging under rose bushes in the garden, all to no avail. Her father had hidden the recovered loop of the puzzle ring too well.

One afternoon she came out of the tower room, locked the door behind her, and turned to head down the steep, narrow steps. Suddenly Jinx darted forward right under her feet. Hannah tripped and fell heavily. The old iron key was flung out of her hand. Jinx launched herself into the air, caught the key in her mouth and, with a lithe twist, landed halfway down the steps and began racing away.

Hannah scrambled to her feet, ignoring the pain in her bruised knees, and raced after the bogey-cat. Jinx was quick and nimble, but Hannah was driven by fury and desperation. She flung herself on the grey cat, wrestled her to the ground and wrenched the key away. Jinx scratched her viciously, but Hannah fended her off, exultant to have the key back in her hand. She shoved it deep into her pocket again and limped down the hall to the drawing room, where Lady Wintersloe and Roz were reading companionably together, while Linnet built up the fire.

"Jinx just tripped me up *on purpose*!" Hannah said furiously. "On the stairs! I could've broken my neck."

"Are you all right?" Roz asked anxiously. "Let me see."

"On the stairs coming down from the old tower room?" Lady Wintersloe asked. "Why, that's where she tripped me up!"

"She's a wicked creature," Linnet said with intense feeling.

"She likes to lurk around on those steps," Lady Wintersloe said. "I don't know why. Maybe because your father spent so much time up in that room."

Hannah rolled up her jeans to show her mother her red, bruised knees. "I hit my shoulder too."

"I'll get you some cabbage leaves from the garden," Linnet said. "Nothing better for bruises!"

"I think an ice pack might do more good," Roz said. "They do look sore!"

She followed Linnet out, and Hannah sat down stiffly, putting her feet up on the footstool. "So was that where you broke your leg?" she asked her great-grandmother with interest. "On those twisty stairs coming down from the tower room?"

Lady Wintersloe nodded. "Oh, it was silly of me, I know,

162

going up those steps at my age. I thought I would have one more go at opening up that door. I was sure, you know . . . well, that your father had found the way to break the curse. He told me he was close. But then he disappeared. . . He'd always kept that door locked and I didn't know where he'd hidden the key. I watched some show where the detective picked a lock with her hairpin, and so I thought I'd give it a try. But Jinx tripped me up before I even got to the door." She sighed.

Hannah slid her hand into her pocket and brought out the key. "I found it in my bedroom."

"But I looked everywhere! Where was it?"

Hannah told her, and Lady Wintersloe threw up her hands. "I never thought to look through those old books. So you've been in your father's secret room?" She leant forward anxiously. "Any clues? I mean. . ."

"On how to break the curse?" Hannah gave a little nod. "I think so, though it's hard to understand. It's all in code."

"Be careful, my dear," Lady Wintersloe said. "Really, maybe it would be best to leave it alone. Your father. . ." She dabbed her eyes. "Maybe it's best not to meddle with such things."

"But don't you want the curse to be broken?" Hannah demanded.

Lady Wintersloe shrugged elegantly. "Of course! But not if it means risking yourself, Hannah. I don't want to lose you too!"

Hannah scowled. She had no intention of giving up.

"Won't you help me, Belle? To at least decipher his code? Then we could maybe find out what happened to him?"

Her great-grandmother hesitated. "But what can I do?" She indicated her broken leg with a graceful wave of her long, thin hand.

"Well, he wrote cryptic clues . . . what do you think this one could mean?" Hannah wrote on a piece of paper: *two hornet queens flying around the one great chair.*

"Well, let's see. Could be an anagram with 'flying around' in it. Great chair. Mmmmm. I know! 'Hornet' is an anagram of 'throne'! Am I right? But why the two queens?"

"Was there ever a time when there were two queens fighting over the throne?" Hannah asked.

Lady Wintersloe nodded. "I guess that would be Elizabeth the First and Mary, Queen of Scots."

Of course, Hannah thought.

Lady Wintersloe went on musingly. "Mary declared herself queen of England as well as of Scotland when Elizabeth first inherited the throne. That was because in the eyes of the Catholics Mary had a better claim than Elizabeth, who had been declared illegitimate by her father, Henry the Eighth. You could say that was why Elizabeth cut off her cousin's head all those years later – to make sure of the crown on her own head."

"Elizabeth and Mary were cousins? I didn't know that. And did Elizabeth really cut off Mary's head?"

"Oh, yes, poor Queen Mary. She was nine years younger than Elizabeth, and far prettier. Her English cousin was

164

always jealous of her. They had very different childhoods, of course. Elizabeth's mother, Anne Boleyn, was beheaded when Elizabeth was only three, and Elizabeth lived the next twenty-odd years of her life in and out of prison, in fear for her life."

Hannah listened intently. She had been reading about the history of the Tudors and Stuarts, but her great-grandmother had a way of bringing dry facts alive.

Lady Wintersloe was pleased to see her so interested. "Mary had inherited her throne when she was only six days old, and then she was sent over to France as a little girl to marry the French prince. She was petted and spoiled all her life, and made Queen of France when she was only sixteen or so. For a few years Mary was one of the richest and most powerful women in the world."

Hannah wondered what it must have been like for Elizabeth, motherless at such a young age and having Henry the Eighth as her father. Hadn't he had six wives, and chopped off the heads of two of them? Along with the heads of lots of other people. It must have been lonely and terrifying. Seeing her young and pretty cousin as queen of both Scotland and France must have been a bitter pill for Elizabeth to swallow.

"Then Elizabeth inherited the throne when she was twenty-five, and ended up rich and powerful and loved by all," Lady Wintersloe continued. "While poor Mary lost her throne when she was twenty-five and ended up living the next twenty-odd years as Elizabeth's prisoner, poor and afraid. Really, their lives are like reverse images of each other. I've often thought it was uncanny."

"But there was a time when they were both queens together?"

Her great-grandmother nodded. "Only a few years. When her first husband died, Mary was queen of France no more and so came back to Scotland. I can't remember how old she was then. Maybe eighteen or nineteen. She only ruled here for five years. She stayed here once, did you know? In the castle before it was burnt. And Lord Montgomery fought for her when the lords rebelled, and was with her when she was defeated at Carberry Hill. Our family seems always to fight for lost causes."

"So when did the castle get burnt down?" Hannah asked.

"The summer of 1567," her grandmother replied promptly. "The same year Mary abdicated. After the battle, Lord Montgomery fled back here but the lords who had fought against Mary did not want anyone trying to rescue her. So they came and burnt the castle down."

Hannah wondered when Eglantyne had been burnt as a witch. It had been in winter, she remembered, just before Christmas. It must have been 1566 then.

Hannah sat, hand on her chin, watching the flames flicker and dance, thinking about her father's clues. She knew most of them off by heart now.

"Belle, what does 'gibbous' mean?" she asked.

"Do you know, I have no idea. Something to do with the moon."

Roz came in just at that moment, carrying two ice packs wrapped in tea towels. She laid them tenderly on Hannah's knees.

"Mum, do you know what 'gibbous' means?" Hannah asked.

"It means when the moon is waxing. You know, halfway between the half moon and the full moon."

"So when the moon is three-quarters full," Hannah said, half to herself.

"That's right."

Hannah sat back, her brain so busy she hardly noticed Linnet bringing in cabbage leaves or her mother trying hard not to roll her eyes. She doodled with Lady Wintersloe's fountain pen on the margin of the newspaper. She drew a tree, and a gate, and a hill with a thick criss-cross of pen strokes upon its peak, and then she drew circles within circles. As she doodled, she thought.

She remembered Lady Wintersloe telling her that her father had believed the cave in Fairknowe Hill could be used as a gateway to another world, and another time. Donovan had told her that the rift in the yew tree had been barred and padlocked to stop people from running through it on their way to the fairy hill. *Through the winter gate I must go*, her father had written. And Linnet had told her to beware of the green hill at the quarter points of the year, at midwinter and midsummer, and the spring and autumn equinoxes, and the cross-quarter days between, for they were the days when the gateway opened. She remembered her father's notes and how they had said there were "thin places" where two worlds meet and time stands still.

As Hannah doodled and daydreamed, the conviction that her father really had gone back in time to the days of Mary, Queen of Scots, grew upon her strongly, until she could not bear to sit still any longer. She got up, despite her sore, stiff knees, and began to pace back and forth. Questions whirled through her mind. Was it even possible? And if she was to break the curse, as she had vowed, must she too go back in time? Which brought her again to the biggest question of all. How?

"Mum, is it possible to travel back in time? Scientifically speaking, I mean?" Hannah asked, as they sat in the drawing room after dinner.

Roz looked surprised. "Do you know, your father once asked me exactly the same question! How like him you are, darling." Her hand briefly touched the wedding ring about her neck.

"So what did you tell him?"

"Well, theoretically, it is possible. One of the consequences of Einstein's special law of relativity was that it changed the whole way we understand time and space." Roz leant forward, her face beginning to glow with eagerness. "Once upon a time people used to think time and space were separate forces, but now we know they're a single entity, like a piece of fabric." Roz showed Hannah the cloth of her skirt. "See how the fabric is made from threads weaving in and out of each other? That's what space-time might look like."

"So it is possible?" Hannah was excited.

Roz smiled. "Only theoretically. We haven't got the technology to build a time-travel machine, and I doubt that we ever will. Though when you think of the leaps we've made just in the past ten years. . ."

Hannah interrupted her. "But what if there was some way of travelling back in time without having to build a machine. Something . . . natural." She had wanted to say "magical" but knew her mother would immediately become scornful.

"Again, just like your father! It's really quite uncanny. I guess the answer is yes, Hannah, it's possible. Some scientists have worked out that there are things called wormholes, which *could* connect different parts of the space-time continuum. If you could find a way to travel through a wormhole, you'd find yourself in quite another time or place."

Hannah listened intently, her face rapt.

"What's amazing about this is that scientists now think wormholes could be found anywhere, at any time. One could be a mere millimetre away from us right now, only we can't see it because it's in a different dimension." Roz was speaking rapidly now, waving her hands about, her cheeks pink. The permanent line between her brows had almost smoothed away.

"So time-travel tunnels could be anywhere?" Hannah asked.

"Yes! Isn't it amazing? Though, of course, we don't know how to access them."

Hannah thought of the dark cave in the side of the fairy hill. She had explored the passageway one afternoon, with Donovan, and found nothing but graffiti-scrawled rock. But that had not been at any of the thin times, the turning points of the year. Hannah was determined to explore it the next time a thin time came along, which was the upcoming midwinter solstice, the day after her birthday.

Dreamily Lady Wintersloe said, "You know, T S Eliot said, 'The moment of the rose and the moment of the yew tree are of equal duration.' Even though one lives such a short time, and the other for so long." She was often vague and faraway in the evenings, after Linnet had given her her medicine.

Roz burst into words again. "It's such an exciting time we live in! We're so lucky! So many mysteries being cleared up, so many misunderstandings. Did you know that they may have discovered the theory of everything, which so many scientists have dreamt of for so long? They're calling it M-theory."

Hannah thought it sounded like the name of a band. "Why?" she asked.

Roz laughed. "Who knows? M could stand for master or mother or mystery or even music. . ."

Or magic? Hannah asked herself silently. She yawned. It had been another long and busy day, and she was very tired.

"But the idea is that at the very heart of everything is a tiny vibrating string, like a guitar string. It's the very stuff of the universe, and it's in everything," Roz said.

So, Hannah thought, *music lies at the very heart of all things, like Linnet's flame of magic.* And, half asleep, she suddenly began to *see how* her father had managed to cross the threshold between times. *Sing a song of spells, there is a reason in rhyme, like ringing the bells, to unlock the gate in time. . .*

Midwinter Bairns

For Hannah's birthday, Lady Wintersloe invited all of her friends over for dinner. She had given Hannah an antique topaz ring, which glowed golden on her finger like captured sunlight.

"It comes from the Cairngorms, not far from here," Lady Wintersloe said.

"Cairngorm stones drive away darkness and evil," Linnet said. "It'll help keep you safe and well, my chick."

Roz lifted up her eyes in silent exasperation. She hated any of what she called superstitious nonsense, though she was too polite to let Linnet see.

Roz had given Hannah a new winter coat, for her old raincoat was far too thin for the Scottish winter, and a book about the human body which showed all the nerves and muscles and bones. Hannah, who had wanted an electric guitar, took this as a sign her mother thought she was spending too much time reading fairy stories. She tried to look grateful, and thought she could always lend it to Max. He would adore it.

Linnet had made Hannah a new strap for her guitar, embroidering it beautifully with flowers and leaves and thistledown heads. She pointed her gnarled finger at one flower after another, saying, "Elderflowers, for protection from evil; and rue, the herb of grace; and carnations, to keep you safe; and thistledown, to help lighten your load."

Rather oddly, Linnet had also given Hannah an old walking stick. It had a most beautiful handle made from deer antler, and the wood glowed a soft golden colour with a mottled effect that made it look like snakeskin.

"Why, that's my father's old stick," Lady Wintersloe said in surprise. "I haven't seen it for a while."

"Hannah is spending so much time out tramping the hills with Donovan that I thought she needed a good stick," Linnet said.

Lady Wintersloe nodded her elegant white head. "Of course. I remember her father always liked that stick. Don't go losing it, Hannah, it's very old and very precious."

Linnet winked one cloudy green eye. "It's made of rowan," she said. "Cut from the tree outside my kitchen door. If you're ever in any trouble, twist the handle three times." No one but Hannah seemed to hear her. Sometimes it was as if Linnet had the ability to speak straight into Hannah's mind, with no one else the wiser. Or perhaps Hannah's hearing was growing sharper because of all the time she spent with the hag-stone pressed up against her ear.

Max bought her a new guitar songbook, Scarlett gave her some shiny lipgloss (which Hannah thought might have been an unsubtle hint), and Donovan gave her an encyclopedia of witches and fairies which she found absolutely fascinating and much easier to read than most of her father's heavy tomes.

Linnet had cooked a feast of all Hannah's favourite foods and, after dinner, the four friends lay in front of the fire and talked.

"The twenty-first of the twelfth," Max said, poking a twig into the fire and watching its tip turn translucent gold. "Cool birthdate."

"Yeah. The same forwards as backwards. It's called a palindrome. That's why Dad called me Hannah. It's a palindrome too. See?" She wrote her name on a piece of scrap paper.

The others at once began to write their own names backwards.

"I'm Xam!" Max shouted. "How cool is that? Xam! Bam! Pow!"

"I'm N-A-V-O-N-O-D," Donovan spelled out. "That doesn't mean anything."

"You're N-O-D if we just call you Don," Max said. "We could call you Noddy."

"No thanks," he replied.

"Let's try yours," Max said to Scarlett. He wrote it out carefully and at once began to laugh. "Ttelracs. That is so weird. It sounds like some kind of computer virus."

"It does not!" Scarlett flushed red with annoyance.

They wrote the names of everyone they knew backwards, shrieking with laughter at the results. Then, as the fire began to die down and shadows bent over the library, the talk turned back to their birthdates.

"Did you know that means we four kids were all born within four days and four kilometres of each other?" Donovan said dreamily. He had his chin propped in his hand and was staring into the fire as if he saw strange and beautiful things there.

Hannah nodded, thinking of Lady Wintersloe and her belief that one of these three was really the child of true blood, heir to the realm under the hill. "Yes. Belle told me. It's an amazing coincidence, isn't it? I didn't realize that all our birthdays were quite so close, though. Were we really born within four days of each other?"

"It's my birthday tomorrow. The twenty-second of December. Then Max was born on the twenty-third, and Scarlett a day later, on Christmas Eve."

"That is so weird," Hannah said. "And only four kilometres apart?"

"Well, you were born here, weren't you?" Scarlett said. "Lady Wintersloe has often told us the story."

"I was?"

"You came early, and so fast your dad only had time to bring the car round," Max said. The twig he was poking in the fire suddenly flared into life, and he yelped and dropped it, sucking his finger where he'd burnt it.

175

"You were born in the front hall," Donovan said. "Your mum didn't even have time to get into the car."

"Linnet delivered you," Scarlett said.

Hannah scowled and looked away. Why had she never heard this story?

"You never heard any of that?" Max was flabbergasted.

"Mum doesn't like to talk about my dad. You know."

The other three nodded.

"Linnet delivered me too," Max said. At Hannah's exclamation, he went on, "Yeah, it's true. I was born here too. My mum's car broke down out on the road, and she came looking for shelter. It was snowing like anything, and the house was all lit up because everyone was still sitting around waiting to see if your dad came home, and Mum went into labour right here on your doorstep."

"And you were born here and never left," Scarlett said.

"Where was I then? I was only two days old."

"I guess you must've still been here then," Max said. "I know your mum packed you up and left, once they declared your dad dead or gone or whatever they do, but that must've been later."

"You'd have been here together as babies," Scarlett said. "You probably had baths together."

"Ewwww!" Hannah and Max said together.

"So what about you?" Hannah asked Scarlett. "Where were you born?"

"Oh, nothing so dramatic," Scarlett said rather peevishly. "I was born at home, at the shop. Mum doesn't

176

like hospitals. She had me in the bath. Disgusting. It was on Christmas Eve. Don't you think that's so inconsiderate? To have me in the bath, on Christmas Eve? I never get as many pressies, and I have to think about it every time I go to the bathroom."

"Well, we were all born at Christmas-time too," Max pointed out.

"Yes, but *I* was born on Christmas *Eve!*" Scarlett said. "Anyway, I've always wondered. . ."

"What?" Hannah asked.

"Well, it just seems so odd. I can't imagine really giving birth to someone in a bath. And I'm so much older than the boys. Six years between me and Cooper. And they're all brown-haired and brown-eyed and I'm so fair." She twirled her blonde ponytail. "*And* Mum always says what a great Christmas pressie I was, because she'd never thought she could have babies."

"So?" Max demanded.

"Well, I always wondered if I was, you know, adopted."

There was a little silence. "Could be, I guess," Donovan said cautiously. "But wouldn't they tell you?"

"Not necessarily." Scarlett heaved a dramatic sigh. "I've heard of people who only found out they were adopted when their parents died and left them out of their will."

Max gave a little snort of derision. "Well, your parents spoil you rotten so I can't see that happening."

Scarlett tossed her head.

"Four of us, born within four days and four kilometres

of each other . . . it feels somehow fateful. . ." Hannah stared round at her friends, all rosy in the soft flicker of the fire.

"Statistically speaking, there were probably a hundred kids born in this area during that period," Max said.

"But so close?" Donovan asked. "I've got to admit, it feels a bit eerie."

"And you were born the same day my father disappeared." Hannah stared at Donovan, who turned his head so she could not see his face. "Tomorrow."

There was a short silence. Somehow Hannah found the courage to say, "It was the curse, you know, that made him disappear. The Curse of Wintersloe Castle."

No one said a word.

"He was trying to break it. He was trying to find the broken bits of the puzzle ring. He said he found one part, but I don't know what he did with it. I've searched everywhere."

Donovan gazed at her with serious, blue-grey eyes. "What do you mean, *he said*?"

"I found his notebook, hidden in the little tower room, you know, the one with the weathervane on top. It's been locked up since the day he disappeared, but I found the key. The room is filled with books on curses and fairies and time travel. He's made a real study of it. He was determined to break the curse."

"So he really believed in it?" Max was torn between scorn and scepticism.

178

Hannah ignored him. "There's this one book of his which says there are places where the membrane between the worlds is thin, and different worlds and different times meet. Wouldn't it be amazing to think it was true? Just imagine if you could travel back in time!"

"It's impossible," Max said. "You just can't do it. Yesterday is gone for ever. A minute ago is gone for ever."

"But you're thinking of time as if it was a river, all running in one direction," Hannah said. "You're meant to be the scientist; you should know that it's not like that at all."

Max went red. "Well, that may be so, but you still can't turn time back."

"I didn't say it was easy," Hannah said. "I just said it was possible . . . theoretically speaking."

"Well, maybe theoretically," Max said. "But what is the use of that?"

"I've been thinking about what the sundial in the rose garden means. It says *Now Is Yesterday's Tomorrow*. I thought it meant we have to do what we want *now*, else the moment is gone."

"Seize the day," Scarlett said. Everyone looked at her in surprise and she made a face. "My English teacher says it all the time."

"Exactly," Hannah said. "But I think it means more than that. I think it means time is all around us, all time. Yesterday and tomorrow and now."

There was a long silence.

"So what would you do, if you could go back in time?" Donovan asked.

"I'd try and break the curse, of course. I'd find the lost quarters of the puzzle ring and put it back together again. I think that's what my dad was trying to do."

"You think your dad went back in time?" Max was openly sceptical now.

"Maybe. I mean, if it's true that Fairknowe Hill is a gateway to other worlds and other times, who knows, maybe he worked out the secret. Maybe he went back in time and got trapped there. And that's why he disappeared."

"Delusional," Max said in a friendly way. "It must be the colour of her hair. Heats the brains up, you know."

"Do you really think that's what happened to your dad?" Scarlett wanted to know.

Hannah moved restlessly. "I don't know. Maybe. But just imagine going back in time. What an adventure!"

"You'd probably catch the plague," Max said caustically. "They'd nail the door shut so you couldn't get out and then, when you were dead, bring round the plague cart." He pretended to ring a bell, intoning mournfully, "Bring out the dead! Bring out the dead!"

"I'd risk it, if it meant finding the puzzle ring," Hannah said fiercely. "It's all right for you lot, your family isn't cursed!"

"I'm the one with three little brothers," Scarlett pointed out. "Believe me, I feel cursed!"

Everyone laughed.

180

"But let's say you did manage to travel back in time . . . theoretically speaking . . . how would you manage?" Donovan asked. "I mean, Max is right, there was the plague and all sorts of other horrible diseases. And people used to carry knives and swords everywhere, and stab each other at dinner. And you wouldn't have any money. They didn't have pounds back then."

"And what would you wear?" Scarlett demanded. "Everyone wore long gowns and corsets and ruffs and things. And how would you get around? No cars or buses or trains back then."

"You could pretend to be a leper," Max suggested. "You could wear a long robe with a hood, and carry one of those clapper things, and go about begging. Though they might stone you, of course, or lock you up in a leper hospital."

"I'd be a travelling minstrel," Hannah said. "I'd take my guitar and I'd wander the roads and play and sing."

"A thirteen-year-old girl on her own? Sounds dangerous to me," Donovan said.

"You could dress up like a boy," Scarlett said. "Sing love serenades to Mary, Queen of Scots, and all her ladies-in-waiting. Maybe she'd fall in love with you. She was always falling in love with people."

"Anyway, I'm going to give it a go," Hannah said determinedly. "Tomorrow night. It's Midwinter's Eve, the night of the winter solstice, which means it's a thin time. I'm going to pack up some food and my guitar and go and have a midnight feast at the fairy hill."

"You're joking." Scarlett's blue eyes were round. "It'll be freezing! And spooky!"

"I'll wrap up warm," Hannah said.

"Do you really mean it?" Donovan said in a low, serious voice. "But what if it's true? What if you find yourself back in the past?"

"Well, then I'll find the lost quarters of the puzzle ring and come home again."

Max laughed. "You are crazy."

Just then, Linnet came in to say everyone's parents had come to pick them up and take them home. As Hannah scrambled to her feet, she saw a slinky grey shape slip out the library door. She scowled, not at all liking the idea that the bogey-cat had been listening to their conversation.

The Wild Hunt

The next morning was the thirteenth anniversary of Robert Rose's disappearance. Linnet lit a fire in the drawing room, as if to comfort them, but it only served to show how dark it was outside, with an icy rain hammering against the windows. Everyone tried to be cheerful, for Hannah's sake, but it was a false charade. Roz barely managed to eat a thing, while Lady Wintersloe was white and drawn. Jinx prowled the room, spitting at anyone who came near and sharpening her claws on Lady Wintersloe's cherry-wood antique chair. Even Hannah found it hard to swallow down more than a mouthful of Linnet's delicious hot cinnamon roll.

The phone shrilling made everyone jump as if stuck with a pin. Then Linnet came trotting in, a wide smile on her face. "It's Genie," she announced. "She says she's taking Max and Donovan and Scarlett to the Winter Wonderland in Edinburgh for their birthdays, and do you and Hannah want to go too, Roz?"

"It's freezing cold outside," Roz said doubtfully.

"I'll wear my new coat. Come on, Mum. It'll be fun. Please?"

The sun was setting over the loch as they drove home along the winding road. The pine trees stood up stiff and black, casting elongated shadows, while above the mountains a spectacular stack of clouds was lit to an incandescent rose.

"Do you think there's snow in those clouds?" Hannah was huddled under a thick warm rug, happy and tired after the long day in Edinburgh.

"Maybe," Max said. "It feels cold enough."

"I'd love a white Christmas," Hannah said wistfully. "I've never even seen snow."

"Never seen snow?" Scarlett sat upright. "You're kidding!"

"What's Christmas like in Australia?" Max asked.

"Hot. Boiling hot. We usually go to the beach."

"Going to the beach on Christmas Day." Scarlett was incredulous.

"It's funny, though," Hannah said. "Everyone still has snowmen and reindeers and fake snow on their Christmas trees, even though it's stinking hot. And some people have baked turkey too."

"Traditions can persist a very long time, even when people no longer understand the meaning behind them," Roz said from the front seat. "Things like decorating the

Christmas tree and hanging Christmas lights – these all come from pagan traditions."

"I'll never forget my first Christmas here in Scotland," Genie said. "I'd never seen snow before either, Hannah, and that year there were the worst blizzards. Fairknowe was snowed in, and we were all stranded."

"That was the year I was born, wasn't it?" Max said. His mother made a noise of agreement, leaning forward to study the road. Mist was rolling down from the hills, like a grey flannel curtain drawn by a giant hand. They drove into it, and within seconds the loch and trees and stone walls were gone, and all the world was mist.

"And me too. Thirteen years today since I was born, and my mother died." Donovan's voice was very low and quiet. "It would have been somewhere around here that she died too."

There was a long moment of silence. Hannah could almost hear the way everyone's hearts grew heavy. She would have liked to have put out her hand and touched Donovan, offering comfort, but she did not dare. The silence dragged on.

"So don't they have snow where you came from, Genie?" she asked, trying to shield Donovan's grief.

"No, never. It was always warm and sunny there. We used to swim all year round. There was a grotto, a cave under the sea, which we used to swim down to, called the Blue Hole, and the most amazing pillars and towers of rock. Figs and grapes grew everywhere, so we could pluck

185

a handful whenever we wanted, and it was so safe no one locked their houses and we children could run quite free, exploring wherever we liked."

"It sounds like paradise," Roz said. "Why did you ever leave?"

Genie shrugged. "Oh, the same old story. You know, fell in love, thought it'd last for ever. But he turned out to be not so kind. Ancient history now."

"And you've never gone back?"

Genie shook her head. "Can't go back." She didn't say any more. They drove in silence for a little while, the only light coming from the glowing dashboard.

It's dusk, Hannah thought. *The thin time.* And she wondered to herself whether she really would go to the fairy hill tonight, at midnight, and try to cross through the doorway in the yew tree, the winter gate.

I have to go, she thought. *If it doesn't work, I'll just have a cold and rather creepy walk through the woods at night. No harm done. But I bet it will work. . .*

She fell again into the familiar daydream of finding the puzzle ring and breaking the curse, and returning peace and joy to Wintersloe, and began to think about what she must take with her to the fairy hill. Her guitar, a blanket and some food, her walking stick, and maybe a dagger from the downstairs hall. . .

A few lights prickled out of the mist ahead. Genie sighed as if in relief. The old truck began to labour up the hill. Suddenly the engine died. They came to a halt on the verge of the road. Genie exclaimed in dismay and wrenched the key in the ignition again and again. Nothing happened.

"Heap of junk." Genie slammed her hand on the steering wheel.

"Do you want me to take a look under the bonnet?" Donovan said. An offer like this from any other thirteen-year-old boy would have had most adults snorting in amusement, but Donovan had to help out in his father's workshop all the time, and had built the motor for his bicycle all by himself.

"That'd be great," Genie said.

Everyone clambered out and stood, shivering and stamping their feet, on the side of the road, watching as Donovan peered under the bonnet with the help of the torch in Genie's mobile phone. Mist swirled around them. It was so thick that Hannah could barely see Scarlett standing next to her, or the shape of the truck. Hannah turned to stare out across the loch. Slowly the string of lights that marked the village on the far shore was engulfed by the mist. Everything was deathly quiet. Hannah turned back, and could see nothing on either side of her. No dark hunched figures muffled in parkas and hats and scarves. No truck with its bonnet propped open. No narrow beam of light probing the engine. The mist had swallowed everything.

Hannah started forward a few steps. "Mum!" Her voice was weirdly muffled, as if she were shouting through a gag. "Mum! Donovan!"

No one answered.

Hannah stood still, her heart beating frantically. She strained her eyes to see, but it was as if she were blindfolded as well as gagged. A slow creeping horror stole over her. She stretched out her hands and carefully felt forward with her feet. There was rough ground under her feet, not the smooth, hard tarmac of the road. She could scarcely breathe for panic. *Don't be silly*, she told herself. *It's just the mist. Of course everyone's still here. You only turned away for a second. They're just a few more steps away.*

Hannah stumbled forward, feeling her way like a blind person. The silence and the darkness were terrifying. Then she heard, distinctly, the flap of leathery wings right above her head. She ducked, and felt giant claws rake her back, as if seeking to wrest her off her feet. Hannah fell to her knees and crawled hastily away. She heard again the swoop of huge wings, and then a long, drawn-out, high-pitched shriek that seemed to drill through her ears and into her brain. She cowered, covering her ears, and rolled away, feeling the cold breeze of movement past her head. The mist swirled and eddied.

Shakily Hannah thrust her hands into her pockets, searching for the comforting shape of key and stone, but realized with a sharp drop of her heart that she had left them in the pockets of her cardigan.

Another screech sounded to her left. Behind her Hannah heard the drumming of hooves. Panting, terrified, she scuttled away, rocks and thorns tearing at her knees and

188

the soft palms of her hands. The wings swept down above her. She glanced up and caught a glimpse of some giant bat-like creature with a fanged mouth and huge black eyes. Someone crouched on its back, amongst a tatter of black draperies and flying hair. Hannah caught her lip in her teeth and scrambled away. A sharp-tipped spear thudded into the ground only centimetres beyond her leg. Hannah lurched to her feet and ran, ducking and weaving, stumbling in the darkness.

Shrieks and screams and hullaballoos filled the air all around her. Giant horses with flaming eyes galloped, massive hounds bounded, strange hunched figures ran and shouted and shook clubs and spears. No matter how Hannah ran and swerved, sobbing in exhausted terror, her pursuers were always panting and slavering on her heels.

The next moment the ground vanished under her feet. Hannah plunged into black, icy water. It closed over her head with a great green roar, thrusting her down, down, down. The cold penetrated to the very marrow of her bones, numbing every nerve in her body so that she could not move a muscle despite the screaming of her brain. She felt the weight of her heavy winter clothes and her boots dragging her downwards.

In a panic, Hannah wondered if this was how her father had died too. Chased into the loch by the Wild Hunt and left to drown.

The water was so cold. Cold as ice. Cold as death. Something was twining around her ankles, her wrists, her

189

knees, dragging her down. It felt like bony fingers. Hannah struggled, her hair suspended all about her, blinding her, choking her. She kicked hard, glancing down desperately. She saw pale ghostly faces, dark malevolent eyes, brackish-green draperies like floating water-weed.

Hannah sobbed involuntarily, and water burst through her mouth and down into her lungs. Instinctively she tried to gasp a mouthful of air, and swallowed only water. Head spinning, eyes blind and ears deaf, she flailed her arms and legs, fighting against the merciless cold hands dragging her ever deeper. It felt like she was climbing an endless staircase into darkness.

Suddenly the dark water convulsed with a great splash. A heavy body hurtled down past Hannah. She had a confused impression of a face, broad and white, searching through the gloom. Then her clothes were seized. A dark blade flashed out, sweeping through the floating, tangling draperies. Shrill cries pierced the water, and Hannah's ankles and wrists were released. She kicked feebly, trying to help as she was dragged swiftly to the surface.

Her head broke through the surface of the loch. At last Hannah was able to gulp oxygen. Almost at once she sank again, but her rescuer dragged her up once more, panting for breath. Hannah grasped rocks with her outstretched hands and dragged herself out on the stones of the shore, shivering violently, gasping and sobbing and vomiting. But alive.

"Are you all right?" a voice demanded. Hannah was

turned roughly on to her side, and hands squeezed her, causing a gush of loch water to come bursting out of her mouth. She coughed and coughed, her throat feeling like she had swallowed acid. Dimly she realized it was Morgana Underhill, the owner of the fairy shop, who had plunged into the water to save her.

"It's all right, I've got you now," Miss Underhill said, smoothing back Hannah's wet tangle of hair. "What was it? Who lured you away? Was it a water-wraith?" There was a peculiar eagerness in her voice.

"Something . . . they hunted me . . . drove me here. . ." Hannah could scarcely speak.

Miss Underhill nodded her head sharply. "Ah, the Wild Hunt. I thought I heard something. I was waiting and watching, but that damned mist, it came from nowhere."

"Hannah! Hannah!" Voices drifted towards her through the bitter night air. Hannah turned her head to look, unable to find the strength to lift herself from the ground.

"Here!" Miss Underhill cried.

Donovan ran out of the darkness and flung himself down beside her, crying her name. She clung to him with icy-cold hands. "What happened?" he cried. He saw Miss Underhill, kneeling beside her, her grey hair hanging in dripping rats' tails down her face. "What are you doing here? What did you do to her?" he demanded. He saw the knife that lay discarded on the stones beside Hannah. It was old and made of iron. He looked at it in horror and then glanced accusingly back at Miss Underhill, who spread her hands placatingly.

She had no time to try and explain, though, for Max came running through the trees, falling over his enormous boots to land on the ground right by her head.

"She was in the water? But how?" Max cried.

"They hunted me . . . drove me into the loch . . . didn't you see them?" Hannah could barely speak through the violent chattering of her teeth. "Their eyes, flaming red. . ."

Donovan snuggled his long, black coat round her, then unwound his scarf and tucked it under her head. He shouted into the darkness, "She's here! We've found her!"

She grasped his hand. "Watch out! Watch out! They were just here. They'll be hiding. . ."

"Who?" he whispered.

"The fairies. It's the thin time. They want to stop me . . ." She tried to find the words to frame her thoughts but her brain seemed to have frozen. ". . . stop me breaking the curse . . . my father. . ."

"She must be freezing. Maybe she's got hypothermia," Max said. "Do you hallucinate if you've got hypothermia? I'll have to look it up."

Miss Underhill made a sound of disgust, but before she could speak Roz came running, wild-eyed and white-faced, and flung herself on Hannah. Scarlett and Genie were close behind.

"Hannah! Hannah!" Roz cradled her daughter in her arms, rocking her.

"What happened?" Genie dropped down on one knee. "She's soaking wet! Did she fall in the loch?"

"But what is she doing all the way over here?" Scarlett said. "She was right beside me a minute ago!"

The clamour of their voices washed over Hannah in waves. "They chased me . . . there were hundreds of them . . . they want to stop me. . ."

"She's feverish," Roz said. "She must be half frozen! We've got to get her home. How could this have happened? I only took my eyes off her for a second. . ."

Her gaze fell on Miss Underhill, and she frowned, puzzled. The next moment she saw the knife, and her frown deepened. She cradled Hannah closer.

"I heard the splash as she fell in," Miss Underhill said, drawing the knife towards her and tucking it away in the pocket of her big coat, which lay discarded on the stones. She drew it around her, shivering. "I was not so far away. I jumped in, and was lucky enough to catch hold of her and drag her out."

"Thank you so much," Roz said, trying to smile. "But what were you doing out here, on such a cold night?"

"It's the winter solstice," Miss Underhill said. "I was casting circle for Yule. I like to do my rituals out in the open." She hunched her shoulders against the biting cold and got to her feet. "I'm glad I could help. I'd best get home before I get hypothermia." She bent and said to Hannah, "Did I not tell you? It's a dangerous night to be out wandering in the mist." Then she stumped away up the slope, hands thrust in her pockets.

Genie was pressing numbers on her phone desperately,

then she cried out in frustration. "Why won't my phone work? It's ridiculous! What's the point of having a mobile if it won't work in emergencies?" She shook her mobile phone furiously, as if that would help. "We need to call the ambulance!"

"It's the black witch," Hannah murmured, shivering uncontrollably under the damp coat. "Watch out!"

Donovan bent his head over hers. "You saw her? Really saw her?"

Hannah remembered that one glimpse of windswept hair and a cold, pale, pitiless face, and a white hand gripping a spear of polished jet. She nodded her head, though her neck felt as if it were in a vice of iron, and her temples pounded dreadfully. Chills ran all over her.

Somehow Donovan and her mother lifted her up, and supported her between them. With the others pressing close, shocked and afraid, they managed to stumble back towards the road.

Hannah barely remembered how they got her home. She saw pale beams of headlights, and faces hanging over her, and whirling trees, and then the march of walls hung with paintings and antlers, and then at last the soft blue walls of her own room. She was laid down on her own bed, and then Roz and Linnet fussed about her, drawing off her wet, stiff clothes, towelling her frozen limbs, dressing her in warm, dry pyjamas, and tucking her up in bed with a hot-water bottle. Genie came back with something hot for her to drink, and she was made to swallow some kind of medicine from a spoon.

Hannah cried out to Linnet, "My stone, my stone!"

"It's all right, darling, it's all right," Roz said, smoothing back her damp, tangled hair, but Linnet bent and searched rapidly through the pile of clothes Hannah had thrown on the chest that morning, and found the hag-stone and the key in the pockets of her cardigan. She thrust them into Hannah's outstretched hands.

With a groan of relief Hannah clutched them to her, rolled herself into a ball and fell fathoms deep into sleep.

PART TWO

THROUGH THE WINTER GATE

The Old Straight Way

At eleven minutes past eleven o'clock, on the second day of the second month of the new year, Hannah's alarm clock shrilled out into the dark, cold night.

It took a few seconds for the sound to penetrate Hannah's sleep stupor, but then she sat bolt upright and looked at the clock: 11.11. She smiled wryly. When she had set her alarm earlier that night, she had purposely chosen this palindromic time, remembering that the Unseelie Court was confounded by order and symmetry. Tonight of all nights Hannah wanted them confounded.

It was Imbolc, one of the thin days, the cross-quarter day poised halfway between the winter solstice and the spring equinox. Tonight, at midnight, the gateway between worlds and times would open, and Hannah intended to try to follow in her father's footsteps and go back to the days of Mary, Queen of Scots.

It was bitterly cold outside, for blizzards had swept Scotland all month, causing chaos on the roads and bringing down power lines so that Wintersloe had been without electricity for days. Hannah and her friends had built snowmen, had snowball fights, and slid down the slope towards the loch on flattened-out cardboard boxes. Hannah had even tried skiing with her mother at the Glenshee ski resort an hour or so to the north. Although she remembered, with a secret smile to herself, that Glenshee meant "valley of the fairies", she did not say so to her mother. Hannah was being very careful not to mention anything about curses or witches or fairies to her mother, who had very nearly packed Hannah up and taken her home to Australia after her midwinter swim in the loch.

Had Hannah not come down with a nasty cold afterwards, and had the roads not been so blocked with snow, Roz probably would not have given in to Hannah's begging and pleading to stay. Hannah's explanation that she had gone quietly into the forest to relieve herself behind a tree, and then got lost in the fog, did not seem at all satisfactory to her. However, Lady Wintersloe told many stories – both tragic and funny – of people who got lost in the Scottish mists, and Linnet worked her own subtle magic in the kitchen and the house, so that eventually Roz had promised Hannah they would stay just a little longer. The days turned into weeks, and then into more than a month, and all that time Hannah had quietly made her preparations to go back in time.

She was glad now that she had not tried to cross through

the gate on Midwinter's Eve. The extra six weeks had given her a chance to finish decoding her father's notes, read through his books on fairy lore, magic and history, and plan her journey. She had studied as hard as any scholar swotting for an exam, and now felt she was as expert on the subject as she could be.

Hannah had worn her warmest clothes to bed that night. All she had to do was drag on her new winter coat and slip her feet into her sturdy black boots, fumbling to do the laces up with fingers stiff with cold and apprehension. She slid her left hand under her pillow and took out the hag-stone and the iron key, and stowed them carefully in her pockets, then picked up her backpack. For weeks now, Hannah had been slowly filling it with all she thought she might need. She had packed an old blanket, a change of thermal underwear, two pairs of warm socks, a soft packet of tissues, a torch, a box of candles and two boxes of matches, a travelling sewing kit, a packet of crackers, a small jar of peanut butter, some cheese in blue wax, some muesli bars, the Santa chocolate she had got in her Christmas stocking, two plastic bottles of water, and a pair of stout wire cutters that she had taken from the garden shed.

She had taken down one of the antique daggers from the hallway and secretly sharpened it in the kitchen while Linnet was busy elsewhere, and hung it from her belt in its worn leather scabbard. She fumbled now in the darkness to strap it around her waist. The feel of it bumping against her hip made her feel, more than anything, as if she truly was living inside one of her books.

Lastly she picked up the sturdy walking stick that had once belonged to her great-great-grandfather, and hung her guitar over her shoulder. It was a strange thing, but the strap Linnet had given her made the guitar so much easier to carry. It hardly seemed to weigh a thing.

Hannah did all this in darkness, for she dared not turn on her light in case it should signal to any watcher that she was awake. She wanted nobody – or no thing – to know what she was planning.

She went silently through the dark, sleeping house, knowing what steps to avoid putting her weight on and being careful not to knock her hip against the old sideboard in the hall. Hannah knew where Linnet hid the key to the kitchen door. It was a matter of only a few moments to unlock it and look out into the snowy garden.

She paused and listened. All was quiet. Hannah raised the hag-stone to her left eye and looked all round, but nothing moved. Slowly, quietly, she pulled the kitchen door shut behind her, and stepped out into the snow.

The cold took her breath away. She huddled her chin into her scarf and slogged across the snow, glad of the help of the stick. As she walked, she ran over all she had learnt about Imbolc, the second day of February. Also called Candlemas because traditionally candles and lanterns were carried in procession, it was a day that honoured the Celtic goddess Brighid, spirit of poets and smiths, healing and the hearth. It seemed right to Hannah that this was the day that she would try to cross through the gateway.

The stars were like points of white fire in the frosty sky. Once or twice Hannah looked back at the dark shape of the house, sure she had heard something slipping along behind her. It made her stomach clench with anxiety, but she saw nothing except tree-shadows wavering over the snow.

The yew tree loomed above her. Hannah stepped inside its gaping belly and fumbled for torch and wire cutters. She wanted to go through the gate in the yew tree to reach Fairknowe Hill, as people had been doing for centuries in the hope it would help them cross into the Otherworld. *Back through the winter gate I must go. . .*

After a hard struggle, Hannah managed to cut through the padlock and chain with her wire cutters and ease open the gate. It squealed loudly, and she wished she had thought of oiling it first. She switched off her torch and stood listening, but heard nothing save the pounding of her heart.

So Hannah swung her backpack on again and glanced at her watch, hesitating. She could tell by the luminous glow that it was still ten minutes to midnight.

A rustle of branches behind her. A soft footfall. Hannah's pulse leapt erratically. She swung around, pulling out her dagger.

"I told you she'd be here!" Scarlett's voice came out of the darkness. "I knew she'd be crazy enough to try and do it."

"You don't really think you can go back in time, do you?" Max demanded. "Scientifically speaking, it's just not possible."

"It is so," Hannah protested, her heart filled with joy and relief. She slid the dagger back into its sheath. "You of all people should know that."

"Yeah, well, the special theory of relativity is all very good, but it's perfectly ridiculous to think that there's some kind of time tunnel here in Fairknowe. It's beyond the bounds of belief."

"Maybe so," Hannah said. "But I thought I'd find out anyway."

"Testing your hypothesis," Max said. "Yeah, that's why I came too. My scientific reputation would be secured for ever if I was the first to prove the wormhole theory. I could skip secondary school and go straight to uni. Get my PhD at the age of thirteen."

"It's *my* wormhole," Hannah said. "*I'd* be the one with the PhD."

"What use is a PhD to a soul singer? Very uncool. No, better leave it to me."

Hannah peered through the darkness at the third shadow, standing quietly to one side of the yew tree. He was almost invisible in his black jeans and coat. "I'm glad you came," she said to no one in particular.

"You should have told us what you planned," Donovan said in a low, angry voice. "We had to figure it all out by ourselves."

"Lucky Donovan remembered that Candlemas was one of the days that the gateway is meant to open," Scarlett said exuberantly. "We had to go and ask Miss Underhill when that was. Else we'd have missed you."

"Hopefully I'd have been back before anyone missed me," Hannah said.

"You should've known we'd have wanted to come too," Donovan said. He sounded like he was scowling.

"Yeah, fancy leaving us out of an adventure like this," Scarlett said. "It's just plain mean."

"It's *my* curse," Hannah said. "I have to be the one to break it."

Again she looked at Donovan, willing him to understand.

"No reason we can't help you," he said. "I brought my flugelhorn just in case."

"I brought the little pipe from the music room," Max said. "You know, the one that's like an old-fashioned recorder. I've been playing it heaps this winter."

"And I brought the tambourine," Scarlett said with satisfaction. "We'll be travelling minstrels."

"It may not work," Hannah said. "You might all be out here in the cold for nothing."

"Oh, well, it's still an adventure," Scarlett said. "I had to sneak past my parents' bedroom and then I dropped one of my boots, *bang!*, right outside their door. I just about had a heart attack."

"I had to walk here," Donovan said. "I couldn't risk Dad

hearing my bike. I haven't walked up that hill in ages. *And* I was carrying a really heavy backpack." By the tone of his voice, Hannah could tell he was smiling.

"Come on," Hannah said. "Let's give it a go. It's almost midnight. If it doesn't work then we can all go back to bed and get warm again."

"But if it does work. . ." Max said.

"We'll be going back in time," Donovan said dreamily.

"To the time of Mary, Queen of Scots," Scarlett cried in glee. "I hope we get to see her! Everyone always talks about how beautiful she was, but she looks plain as anything in her portraits."

"It's not a tourist trip," Hannah said sternly. "It'll be dangerous. That's why I didn't tell you."

"Danger is my middle name," Max said in what he obviously thought was a sinister voice.

"Come on, stop mucking about, this is serious," Donovan said.

"So what do you want us to do, noble leader?" Max said to Hannah.

She thought quickly. "Let's light a candle. I do have a torch, but I thought candles would be more suitable. It is Candlemas, after all." She rummaged in her bag and took out a candle, which she lit with some trouble, as a cold wind was blowing and her hands were shaky. Outside all was silver and black, but within the hollow yew tree warm golden candlelight flickered mysteriously over the cracks and fissures of the ancient wood and the solemn faces of her friends.

She saw they were all dressed for a hike in the mountains, in thick coats and jeans and boots, with heavy packs on their backs. Scarlett's parka was hot pink, with pink fluff lining the hood and cuffs. Max's was grey and black and olive, while Donovan wore his usual long black coat.

"We'd better all hold hands," Hannah said. "Girl, boy, girl, boy, so we're as symmetrical as possible. Four's a good number. Like the points of a compass or a cross. I'll go first."

Donovan seized her hand and held out his other for Scarlett, who took it, giggling.

"Aw, do I have to?" Max said as Scarlett held out her other hand. "All right. I guess sacrifices have to be made in the name of scientific research."

"I'm going to sing a song," Hannah explained, her cheeks growing hot. She did hate to look ridiculous. "In all the fairy stories they always say things in rhyme." *Sing a song of spells . . . there is reason in rhyme. . .*

Self-consciously, she half-spoke, half-sang:

> *"Open, open, high green hill,*
> *on this night of winter chill.*
> *Open, open, winter gateway,*
> *let us walk the old straight way,*
> *Back to the year fifteen sixty-seven,*
> *By tree and stone and stars in heaven."*

Hannah had rewritten her rhyme over and over again and learnt it off by heart, and now, as she spoke, she pushed open the iron gate in the yew tree and led her friends through.

Hand in hand, they marched past the dark, glimmering pool and through the tangle of shadowy trees, all too aware of the strangeness of the wood at night and the sense that unseen watchers lurked in the shadows. Hannah would have liked to scan the woods through the hag-stone, but both her hands were occupied. She turned her face from side to side, starting at every rustle and creak, and felt Donovan squeeze her hand in reassurance. She paused at the gaping crack in the hillside. Her frail little candlelight did nothing to penetrate its blackness. When she chanted her rhyme again, her voice trembled noticeably. She cleared her throat, gripped her candle tightly, and led her friends into the dark, gaping chasm in the side of the hill.

Her candle illuminated a narrow passageway that had formed naturally in the rock. Graffiti was scrawled all over the walls near the entrance, but disappeared the deeper they went within the hill. It was bitterly cold, and their breath smoked from their mouths. There was no sound but their rapid breathing and the scrape of their boots on the rock, which echoed behind them in a very spooky way. Hannah sang her rhyme for the third time. *Three times is the charm*, her father had written.

The passageway climbed and fell, twisted back on itself, opened into a little antechamber, then narrowed again into a mere crack that Hannah could barely squeeze through. Beyond was another long, crooked, narrow passageway that led them down in a series of rough steps and falls, back to the cave they had first entered. Weary and disappointed and baffled, Hannah stumbled out on to the hillside, her friends trailing along behind her. Her candle blew out, and they were left shivering in the moonlit darkness.

"Did it just go in a big circle?" Scarlett asked. "Or did we go the wrong way somehow?"

"Should we go through again?" Max said. "Maybe we took a wrong turn."

"I don't think we did," Donovan said in a low voice. "Look!"

They all turned and looked out over the valley.

The loch gleamed silver under the moon, with the familiar black shapes of islands floating like scattered lumps of ebony. They could see the snowy peak of Ben Lomond and the distant lines of hills to the west, just as they had seen them a thousand times before.

What was different was Wintersloe. There was no house with mismatching turrets and crow-stepped gables, no garden laid out in knots of green hedges. Where the ruin normally lay was a tall, grim castle of stone, with narrow slits instead of windows and a moat of dark, gleaming water.

"We did it," Hannah breathed. "I can't believe it."

A sudden gust of excitement overtook the four friends, and they danced and capered about madly, their packs banging on their backs. Just as suddenly, sobriety crashed down upon them. What had they done?

In that moment, all four realized that they had not truly believed it was possible to travel back in time. Now, though, now they knew it was not a game. The four of them had left their own lives and their own time behind them, and come into a world that played by far different rules. They could easily die here, or be trapped, unable to find their way home again. It was a terrifying thought, and one they all flinched from.

"Don't drink the water," Max said. "We'll have to make sure we boil everything."

"What shall we do about our clothes?" Scarlett cried. "They'll lock us up if we walk around looking like this!"

"We'll have to steal some," Donovan said. "But we'd better make sure we don't get caught. Didn't they cut off your hands or something for stealing?"

"I think thieves were . . . are . . . hanged," Hannah said soberly.

They stood in silence for a moment, completely overwhelmed by the enormity of what they had done. Hannah's mind was blank, and she found it hard to breathe. Thoughts and questions scrabbled through her mind. Instinctively she turned back to the crack in the hill, seeking to scramble back through to her own time. But she saw Jinx crouched behind the boulder, her orange eyes glowing. Behind her was a host of other strange and menacing shadows, with hooked wings and claws, and slitted, smouldering eyes.

Immediately Hannah panicked. "Run!" she cried.

"They've followed us through! Don't let them catch us!"

She plunged down the hillside, calling urgently to the others to follow. Uttering cries of alarm and terror, the other three crashed after her, racing towards the castle.

Backflips and Cartwheels

Hannah crashed straight into a man who was hiding in the blackness under the yew tree. All the breath was knocked out of her, and her nose was jammed hard against sour-smelling wool. She tried to leap away, but he seized her arms roughly and spoke in a deep, gruff voice which sounded like the guttural growl of an animal.

Hannah was so frightened she could not speak. She pointed wildly up the hill. The next instant the man was running, dragging Hannah along with him. She called shrilly to her friends, and they bolted after her, following the thin, pale, winding path away from the fairy hill and towards the forest. Behind them came a howl and a yowl, and the flap of feet, and the scratch of claws, and the whirr of leathery wings.

They came to a stream, water tumbling white and foamy over boulders and blocks of ice. The man turned and plunged into the stream, and Hannah was dragged willy-nilly after him. The water was cold and deep and strong. She was wet to the waist, but stumbled after the man, remembering that evil spirits could not cross running water. She could hear her name being called behind her, and turned and whispered, "Here! Hurry!"

The man hissed, "Wheesht!"

Donovan scrambled beside her, and Hannah could hear Scarlett's quick breaths just behind. Hannah looked back anxiously, checking to make sure Max was still following them. He trailed behind, hunched and gasping. Round the corner came a dismal ululation as the fairy host realized they had lost the trail. Max suddenly hastened his pace.

They splashed along the stream for another ten minutes or more, not daring to climb out on to the bank in case the fairy host picked up their scent again. At last the man clambered out, and Hannah crawled after him, lying gasping in the snow. Her feet in their drenched boots felt like blocks of ice, and she could not stop shivering. Her friends were all crouched beside her, as cold and exhausted as she was.

The man spoke to them again. Hannah could not understand a word. She bit her lip in consternation. It had not occurred to her that a completely different language would be spoken in Scotland in the mid-sixteenth century. Thinking quickly, she sat up and groped in her pocket for the hag-stone and lifted it to her mouth. "Let me hear true and speak true and all my friends too," she whispered through the hole.

At once the man's words began to make sense. "Who are

you? What are you doing coming through the fairy hill? Where's Lord Fairknowe?"

"Lord Fairknowe is my father," Hannah said, stiffening her back. "Were you expecting him?"

"Of course I was. He said if he did not return at the midwinter solstice, to expect him tonight. But . . . you can't be his daughter! He said he was soon to be a father, that his babe was due any day now."

Hannah nodded. "That was me. I've grown."

"But it's been only six weeks since he was here!"

Hannah was completely flabbergasted. She stared at him, open-mouthed, while her brain did backflips and cartwheels. She realized that he was, of course, right. Her father had made his first journey back to the time of Mary, Queen of Scots, at Halloween, when he had found – somehow – the first part of the ring. Then he had returned to 1566 on the midwinter solstice, the twenty-second of December, the day after she was born. It was now Candlemas, the second of February, 1567. Her father had been here, at this very spot, only six weeks ago.

"It's been thirteen years in our time," Hannah said.

The stranger uttered a sharp exclamation. "That can't be!" He bent towards her and examined her face closely in the uncertain light of the moon through leaves. She stared back at him, seeing only a great bush of beard and hair, and craggy brows bent close over shadowy eyes. "You have a look of him," the man said gruffly. "Your nose . . . your hair . . . but how can you be his bairn all grown?"

214

"I just am. More time has passed in . . . in our day than in yours." Hannah found it very hard to frame a sentence that made sense.

Luckily he seemed to understand, for he nodded. "Aye, I see. So you're his daughter. Where is my lord? Why is he not here with you?"

"He never made it home that night," Hannah said. "He died, or disappeared, we don't know what happened. So I came instead. With my friends." She waved her hand at the other three, who had all rolled and sat up, their panting breaths showing frostily in the night air.

"What of my Lady Eglantyne?" the man demanded, seizing her shoulder. "Lord Fairknowe was going to try and rescue her and take her back to his own time, where she would be safe. Did he succeed?"

She gave a little shake of her head. "We don't know for sure. I think . . . I think he might have . . . except we don't know what happened when they got back to their own time."

The man turned away. One hand went up to cover his face. "My poor lady. To think we were so glad she had got away from the witch-burners!"

"Who are you?" Max demanded. "What do you know of all this?"

"My name is Angus MacDonnell. My grandson was one of the gardeners here at the castle, but . . . Lord Montgomery killed him. Didn't wait for an explanation. Saw what he thought he saw and killed my poor boy because of it. That is one reason why, I think, my lady was in such a state. She had Ian's blood splashed all over her."

Hannah winced, and Scarlett said, "Urrghh."

"So the gardener . . . the one that helped Eglantyne bury her dog . . . was your grandson?" Donovan asked, and Angus nodded.

"So . . . you knew my father? You helped him?" Hannah asked.

"Let us get away from here and I'll tell you the tale. We'd best go quiet and quick; we do not want the Wild Hunt upon our heels."

Angus led them away into the forest, heading east into the hills. He moved at a swift jog that soon had Hannah panting and sweating, despite her damp clothes and the icy night air. The pack, her guitar and the walking stick all seemed very heavy and cumbrous, and she wished she had not brought them.

They heard a howling some distance away, and then something with immense black wings soared against the moon. Angus and the four friends crouched silently in the shadow of a bush. Hannah's limbs trembled so much with fear and cold she could barely stand up again, when at last Angus straightened and whispered, "Let's go on – quietly now."

As they plodded on, he spoke in a low voice: "I found your father at the fairy hill last Halloween, the night my lady Eglantyne was cast out of the castle. I was seeking to help her, but it was too late; they had locked her up in

216

the prison. I was angry at the death of my grandson, and worried about what would happen next. So I set up camp under the yew tree, to watch and learn what I could. Your father came creeping out of the fairy gate at midnight. I thought he was something evil, come to do more harm, and tackled him. I'd have killed him too, if he had not thrust my lady's hag-stone in my face."

"How did you know about the hag-stone?" Hannah asked.

"My grandson had often seen my lady Eglantyne with it. She would look through it, or hold it to her ear, or put it on her finger. She carried it with her always. Ian had asked me about it, and I told him it was a fairy stone, a thing of power. You hear stories about things like that, growing up in the shadow of the fairy hill like I did. Your father said it had been given to him so that he could break the curse. So I said I would help him, if he would try and help my lady Eglantyne. He agreed. It was no use trying to break her out of prison, it was impossible with just the two of us, so he decided to track down the first quarter of the puzzle ring, and try to save Eglantyne later. And so that is what we did."

"So Hannah's father really did find part of the puzzle ring?" Donovan asked.

"Aye," Angus said. "He found it, and he went back to his own time six weeks later, at noon on the day of the midwinter solstice. He was going to try to get back to his own time earlier, though, at dawn of the same night he went away, since he said he could not be away from home so long. He was afraid he would miss the birth of his baby." Angus turned and gave Hannah a long, hard stare, then shook his head in disbelief.

"So what night was that?" Max asked, trying to get the dates straight in his head.

"Halloween?" Hannah suggested. "He must've managed it, because no one missed him that night. It was the night of the midwinter solstice that he disappeared, six weeks later."

"That's useful to know," Donovan whispered. "That we can come back to any time we please."

"We wouldn't want to meet ourselves on the way," Hannah whispered, before turning her attention back to Angus, who was saying, "Aye, that's right. Lord Fairknowe told me to wait for him at the fairy hill, because he would come back at dusk to rescue Lady Eglantyne from the fire. So I waited and watched, though it was very hard to see them tie my lady to a stake and burn her."

"You watched them burn her?" Scarlett was horrified.

"I watched the crack in the hill, and I looked for smoke. Lord Fairknowe said he would conjure smoke to hide him while he cut Lady Eglantyne free. I was the only one to see him do it. Except, perhaps, for the witch's magpie."

Hannah was silent, trying to work out the sequence of events. Scarlett stamped her feet and rubbed her hands together, saying with a rising note in her voice, "All right then, but what about us? I'm freezing! I'll die if I have to stand out here in the cold any longer! What are we going to do?"

"We need to find the other three pieces of the puzzle ring, that's what we're here for!" Hannah replied sharply, to hide her own confusion and anxiety.

"But it's the mid-sixteenth century! They burn people as witches! They had the plague! They all wore codpieces, for heaven's sake! How are we going to survive?" Scarlett's voice was distinctly wobbly.

"Angus will help us, won't you, Angus?" Hannah was dismayed to hear how frightened her own voice was.

"The first thing to do is get you somewhere safe," Angus said, sounding distracted. "Then we'll see what can be done. Linnet will know what to do."

"*Linnet?*" The name was like an electric shock. Hannah stared at Angus in absolute disbelief. "No. Surely not. You can't mean . . . not my Linnet?"

"I don't know if she's yours or not," Angus said. "Linnet is Lady Eglantyne's maid. Or was, I should say." Grief thickened his voice. "My lord has let her stay on at the castle, for she has nowhere else to go. Besides, she's handy in the kitchen."

"Linnet was Eglantyne's maid? *Linnet?*" All four were astounded.

"But that would mean . . . she must be well over four hundred years old. Older. Four hundred and sixty years at least." Max calculated the numbers quickly.

"Don't be a fool!" Angus said scornfully. "Linnet's as young as a spring lamb."

"Linnet? Young?" A hysterical laugh bubbled out of Scarlett's mouth.

"Can we see her?" Hannah said eagerly.

"She's up at the castle. We'd better not go near there. Lord Montgomery's not happy with me, for I took off after my grandson died and so he lost his best gillie. Come, we'll go to the hut where I've been hiding out and decide what to do in the morning."

Feet leaden, breath harsh, bones aching, they plodded on through the frosty night. Hannah looked up at the night sky, swarming with more stars than she had ever seen, and felt a great sense of the enormity of time and space pressing down on her. *Will we ever get home?* she wondered.

At last Angus led them to a tiny cottage, built of rough stones and thatched with old heather. It was so low it seemed part of the hillside itself. There was no door, only a curtain made of ox hide. The fire was built in a hearth in the centre of the room, and there was no chimney, so that when Angus poked at the sods of peat, smoke erupted into the room, stinging their eyes and making them cough wretchedly.

Angus lit a crudely made iron lamp that stank abominably of old fish. By its flickering uncertain flame, Hannah saw the tiny room was furnished with only a clumsy three-legged stool, a shelf with a black pan and kettle, and a pile of straw with a few rough hides spread across it.

"You can sleep in here; I'll lay me down in the pen," Angus said, and went through another low door into what smelled like a pigsty. After a moment he stuck his head back through the doorway. "Don't be afraid. You're safe enough here for now."

The children were so exhausted they could only drag off their damp boots and their coats and crawl into the straw, to fall instantly asleep.

The First Day

Hannah woke stiff and aching the next morning. At first she did not know where she was, and then a dreadful cold realization spread through her, sinking like a lump of lead into the pit of her stomach. She leant up on one elbow and looked about her.

The bare earth beneath the straw was hard as rock. Although a fire glowered on the circular hearth, it did not throw out much heat. Angus was crouched on the three-legged stool, stirring something in an iron pot above the fire. By the drear light of day he was revealed as a thickset old man, with a weathered face, huge hard hands, grizzled hair and a silver beard. He wore a length of brown and grey wool, woven in checks, pleated about his body and secured with a broad leather belt. The remaining length was drawn up and over his shoulder against the morning chill, and tucked back through the belt.

"You awake now?" he said, showing a mouth full of

222

yellow crooked teeth and gaping holes. "You must be hungry. I've got some porridge on."

"Porridge?" Hannah asked in dismay. "I hate porridge. Isn't there anything else?"

He scowled. "No, there's not."

"But . . . porridge," she wailed, suddenly as homesick as she had ever been in her life.

"You should be glad for what you get," he snapped.

The children got up and trailed disconsolately to the fire, coughing in the smoke. They looked around for bowls, and some spoons, and maybe some sugar or honey, but there was nothing.

"What are we meant to eat with?" Scarlett demanded.

"Didn't you bring your own spoons?" Angus asked. The children shook their heads, surprised. "Och, well, you'll just have to share mine." He pulled out a black-stained wooden spoon from his sporran. The children stared at it in distaste.

"Could we boil it first?" Max asked.

Angus scowled, flung his spoon down on the ground and stamped outside.

"Ewww, yuck," Scarlett said. "Can you believe he expected us to share his spoon? Can you imagine the germs?"

"Did you see his teeth?" Max said. "Clearly not a big fan of dental hygiene."

"I'm not eating any," Hannah said. "I hate porridge!"

Donovan turned a cool look on her. "Well, they don't

223

have McDonald's back here," he said. "I wouldn't be too fussy."

But he did not pick up the stained wooden spoon from the dirt floor, nor try to eat any of the porridge. All four were snappish and irritable, and sniped at each other until Angus returned with a bucket of icy water. He was not pleased to find the porridge uneaten, cold and congealing in the pot. "Och, well, that's all there is till supper time," he said. "Happen you'll be hungry enough to eat it before I get back."

"But where are you going?" Hannah asked, her jaw aching with tension. "We need to get on our way!"

"You can't be going anywhere dressed like that," the old man replied. "I'll have to find you some decent clothes before you step foot outside. I'll be a while. Only the Lord knows where I'm to find clothes for the four of you, let alone the money to be paying for them!"

By the time Angus returned, in the cold dark of the evening, the four teenagers had almost driven each other crazy with anxiety and irritation. The old man had turned the free length of his plaid into a kind of sling in which he carried various supplies, and four sets of old, shabby clothes which he said he had purchased from a woman whose children had grown out of them.

"Have they been washed?" Max said, wrinkling his nose.

Angus scowled. "Of course!"

"I wish we could boil them," Max said, lifting one of the shirts and sniffing it. "Typhus was spread by the lice which nested in the seams of clothing."

None of the children were keen to try the clothes on after that, but the material smelled pleasantly enough of lavender and mint, and Angus scowled so fiercely and muttered so angrily that at last the children were persuaded to try them on.

"If you do get bitten by lice, don't scratch," Max instructed them. "It's not the louse's bite that gives you typhus, it's rubbing the louse's poo into the wound."

"Oh God," Scarlett said. "I think I'm going to be sick."

"We'll hang the clothes over the fire tonight," Max said. "The stench of that smoke will be enough to kill them!"

"You hope," Donovan muttered.

Angus had brought loose shirts of linen for the boys, which were worn over what looked like long woollen bloomers, with a rather embarrassing flap in the front so the boys could pee without having to undress.

The girls were given loose ankle-length smocks, which they wore under heavy woollen petticoats. A rough brown dress went over the top of that, lacing up the front, and an apron of unbleached linen with a deep pocket that could be tied close with a drawstring.

Angus had also brought four crudely made sheepskin jackets, with the woolly side inside; and four broad lengths of grey-brown plaid, which were to serve the children as blankets, slings, hoods or scarves; as well as four knitted tam o'shanters. All four had worn stout leather boots, so at least they did not have to go barefoot.

"Oh my God, what a hideous outfit!" Scarlett cried,

holding her coarse brown skirts out stiffly. "The poor girls, having to get around in this get-up all the time. I look like such a frump!"

"I thought everyone wore ruffs," Hannah said, remembering the book on Tudor costume in the library.

Angus looked disapproving. "Only the rich wear such fripperies. Do you know how much one of those costs?"

Giggling, the friends paraded up and down in their new clothes, bowing and curtsying to each other. It was odd how different they all looked. A shrill sort of hilarity possessed them, a reaction to the long hours of anxiety and dread. Angus glared at them and shook his shaggy head, but that only made them giggle harder.

It was by now growing dark outside again. Hannah thought she would never get used to how short the days were in Scotland in winter. It worried her that they had wasted a whole day, but she consoled herself thinking that it did not really matter, as she would make sure they returned to their own time on the same night as they had left. At dawn of the next day, instead of at midnight, she thought, so they did not meet themselves in the tunnels of the fairy hill. The very idea gave her the heebie-jeebies.

While they had been trying on their clothes and laughing at each other, Angus had been quietly preparing a meal for them. Thin vegetable soup with a dry oatcake. The children were all so hungry they ate obediently, even though they once again had to eat straight from the pot. At least they had cutlery this time, for Angus had brought them each a spoon carved from horn and a small but sharp knife. The old man wore his knife in his belt at all times, and used it to chop the carrots and turnips, to clean his fingernails, and to transfix a small mouse that scurried over the beaten-earth floor. He was most offended by Max's insistence on squirting antibacterial gel all over it before he returned to chopping turnips. Max had brought two big bottles of the gel, as well as a first-aid kit.

Hannah and her friends were lying sleepily in the straw, watching the strange muted glow of the peat fire, when a soft voice called from outside. Angus got up from the stool, where he had been mending an old leather satchel, and opened the curtain.

A young woman came in, unwinding a shawl from her head. She was small and slight and brown-haired, with eyes that looked too large in her wedge-shaped white face. She was dressed plainly in brown, with a long grey apron, and her feet were bare.

"Angus? How is it with you?" she asked. Her voice was very soft, and had a strange lilt to it, as if she had grown up speaking another language.

"I can't complain," Angus said in a tone of deep depression.

"What's wrong? Have you news of my lady?" she asked, noticing the four children in their bed of straw with a widening of her eyes, which Hannah noticed were a deep and vivid green.

"No good news, I'm afraid. Here, let me warm some ale

for you, you're freezing!" He poured her a cup from the barrel and thrust in the hot poker. She sank down on to the stool and held out her hands to the orange glow.

"Tell me, what news?" She fixed her anxious eyes upon his face.

"Lord Fairknowe failed. He was never seen again after that night, and no word of my lady either. I'm so sorry, Linnet."

She closed her eyes. Tears began to trickle down her white face. She lifted her arm to blot them away with her sleeve. "How do you know?"

"Lord Fairknowe's daughter is here. She came through the fairy gate." He waved one hand towards the pile of straw, where the four children sat, staring in amazement.

"Linnet?" Hannah asked uncertainly. This young woman looked and sounded so different from the old woman she knew and loved. Her figure was slim and straight as a willow wand. Her face was oddly shaped, like a cat's, with wide-spaced eyes set at a slight angle and wide cheekbones that narrowed to a pointed chin. If it was not for the green eyes, Hannah would not have thought it possible that they could be the same person.

"Yes?"

"Linnet!" Hannah leapt up and ran to embrace her. To her astonishment, Linnet did not hug her close but leant back, stiff and surprised.

"Of course! You don't know me yet." Hannah thought how odd she must sound. "I'm sorry. It's just so confusing.

You know me well, in my own time. You always put a hot-water bottle in my bed, and make me marmalade cake because I love it so. . ."

"What's marma . . . marma . . . what?" Linnet asked.

"Marmalade. I guess it's not invented yet." Hannah wondered how long it would be before she stopped getting tangled in these confusing loops of time and tenses. It made her brain hurt, just thinking of it all. "You are Linnet, aren't you? My Linnet?"

"I don't know. Am I?" Linnet sounded weary. "I was my lady's Linnet, but she's gone now. We thought she'd been rescued and taken to safety, but . . . you say she and Lord Fairknowe never made it back safely?"

"They made it back," Hannah said slowly. "Because I found my father's hag-stone, which he had brought back in time with him. . ." She bent to find the holey stone, which she had hidden in the pocket of her dress.

"My lady's hag-stone! You have it?"

Hannah nodded. "So my father must have made it back safely, else surely I could not have found it? But we don't know what happened after that. He disappeared. . ."

"And my lady?" Linnet spoke with fierce intensity.

"I don't know." Hannah hesitated, then looked towards the bed, where three sets of eyes were watching intently. "I think my father brought her to some kind of safety. I think . . . well, I wonder . . . if maybe she had her baby. These are my friends. They were all born that same week. I don't know. Maybe. . ."

"Maybe what?" Donovan demanded, his blue-grey eyes fixed on her intently.

"Belle . . . my great-grandmother . . . she was convinced that one of you was Eglantyne's child. That somehow my father did rescue her, and bring her back to our time, and that something happened. . ."

"Of course!" Scarlett sat bolt upright. "That explains everything! I must be Eglantyne's child. That's why I look so different from the rest of the family. That's why I always felt like I didn't belong! My father . . . I mean, my adopted father . . . he always calls me his fairy princess. Maybe they found me on their doorstep or something."

"That only happens in stories," Max said dismissively. "If they did find you on the doorstep, they'd have had to turn you over to the police or something."

"Not if they hid me, lied about how they got me," Scarlett said eagerly. "Mum is always saying how she thought she could never conceive, and how I was the best Christmas present ever."

"Well, I've always thought you look exactly like your father," Donovan said brutally.

"What do you mean? He's fat and bald and ugly!" Scarlett was horrified.

"He's got blue eyes just like yours."

"My lady had eyes as blue as the loch," Linnet said.

"See? It must be me. I'm the lost child." Scarlett clasped her hands together and gazed rapturously up at the smoke-blackened rafters.

"Well, it's not me," Max said gruffly. "No mystery about me and my mum. Just another sordid love story."

"Except that you were born at Wintersloe, at a time when all the roads were closed because of the snow," Hannah pointed out. "Where did your mum come from? There's only the one road. And she talks about her homeland as if it were the Otherworld."

His sallow cheeks reddened. "She's no fairy princess, my mum."

"And her name," Hannah went on. "Evangeline. It sounds a bit similar, don't you think? And her nickname is 'Genie' which is like a fairy. And she loves gardens, just like Eglantyne."

"So? Lots of people like to garden. Mum came to Scotland because of the gardens. She told me so."

"Doesn't it make you wonder, though?"

"No," Max said roughly.

Donovan, as always, had been silent. Now he said, with an edge to his voice, "And I, of course, have a mother who died giving birth to me. But her name was not Eglantyne. It was Rose. At least, I always thought it was."

"Eglantyne means 'rose', you know," Hannah said slowly.

Donovan stared at her, sudden hope on his face. "My father doesn't have one single photograph of my mother. And he'll never tell me anything about her. Do you think. . .?"

"Well, my mum says that's because he barely knew

231

her," Scarlett said unkindly. "He didn't even know she was pregnant."

Linnet looked from one face to another with eyes that blazed with eagerness. "I cannot tell. Oh, by the stars, I hope it is you." She stared at Max hungrily. "To know that my lady is alive and well, and growing a beautiful garden. . . It could be you. Lord Montgomery has eyes as dark as yours."

"It's not my mum," Max said, his arms crossed, his face obstinate.

"How can you be so sure?" Hannah asked, disappointed. She had had high hopes of Genie. "I thought you didn't know where she came from?"

Max went scarlet. He took off his glasses and polished them. "She comes from Gozo. All right? Satisfied?"

"Gozo?" Hannah repeated blankly.

"Yeah, Gozo. It's a small island near Malta, in the Mediterranean. I don't like to tell people because everyone always laughs, all right?"

"Gozo!" Scarlett repeated, then snorted with laughter.

"See?" Max cast Scarlett a furious look, and the blonde girl grinned back at him, drawling, "Oh, that explains so much! The gonzo from Gozo!"

"You see why I never tell anyone?" Max said in a long-suffering voice.

Donovan was sitting up, his arms crossed on his knees, his blue-grey eyes fixed questioningly on Hannah's face. "Does Lady Wintersloe really think one of us is the lost heir, the child of true blood?" When Hannah nodded, he whispered, "It'd explain so much. . ."

Scarlett snorted. "Sure. Much better than having to admit your dad is a mean old man. No, it's obviously me!"

Donovan glanced at her angrily, opened his mouth to say something, then thought better of it. "Whatever," he said, and rolled away to face the wall.

Looking Through the Hag-Stone

"So, what's the plan?" Scarlett asked next morning as they chewed their way through another pot of gluey porridge. It was early, so early it was still dark outside, and bitterly cold.

"Well, my great-grandmother says the four loops of the puzzle ring were flung in the four directions of the compass. We know my father found one . . . but we don't know which one or how."

"I went with him," Angus said. "We went south because it was winter still, and the travelling would be easier that way. He found the ring in Galloway, at some old standing stones near Drumtrodden."

"But how did he know to go there?" Donovan asked.

"He looked through the hole in his fairy stone," Angus said, "and chanted some spell."

Hannah nodded her head. "I wondered if that was how he did it." She did not mention that she had tried to locate the quarter of the ring her father had hidden at

Wintersloe using the same method, and had seen nothing more remarkable than her mother sitting across the room from her, reading the paper.

"It was an eerie place. Your dad told me it was very old. A local told us the stones marked the rising of the sun at midsummer and its setting in midwinter. We saw the sun set, a few weeks before the midwinter solstice, and it's true, if you stood with all the stones aligned, it almost blotted out the sun."

"And the ring was just lying there, at these standing stones?" Max asked.

Angus nodded. "There were three stones, just standing in some field. It was lying on the top of the middle stone. We had no trouble finding it at all, really, apart from the journey there."

Hannah and the other three exchanged quick glances of relief. They had all spent a good part of the night worrying about the difficulties of the task that lay before them.

"Drumtrodden is about a hundred miles south of here," Angus said. "Your dad said he thought the other quarters of the ring would be about the same distance, north, east and west."

"A hundred miles. . ." That was about a hundred and sixty kilometres. Hannah's heart quailed within her. From the cries of dismay and consternation from her friends, she could tell they felt the same. A hundred and sixty kilometres was a long way to travel without a car.

"Your father planned to go east to Edinburgh next. He

235

thought that was where another part of the ring had fallen. That's not so far," Linnet consoled them.

"That would be the best place to go next," Angus said. "There's a highway that runs to Edinburgh from Stirling, so it'll be easier walking. And it's not a good time of year to head north; the snow will still be deep."

"*Walking!*" Scarlett cried. "Couldn't you have got us some horses to ride? It'll take for ever if we have to *walk* across Scotland!"

Angus looked at her as if she were mad. "Do you know how much a horse *costs*? It's got to be ten pounds or more!"

"Is that all?" Scarlett began.

Angus cut across her. "I'm only paid four shillings a year! It cost me all my savings to buy you those clothes and some food for the road. I can't afford to mount us all."

Scarlett's eyes were round. "Four shillings a year? But that's practically nothing!"

"All too true, lassie," Angus said with feeling. "Luckily I do not work much in the winter, and so no one will miss me if I go with you to show you the way. We must be careful, though. Wandering beggars are not welcome anywhere, nor poachers. We'll have to travel light, and keep away from the villages as much as we can. Do not go killing any rabbits or birds unless I tell you to."

"We're not going to kill any rabbits," Scarlett cried, revolted.

Max grinned. "A week or two of light rations and I'll bet you're as eager for a bit of roast rabbit as anyone."

To their dismay, Angus made them sit down and sort through their packs, for he would not allow them to carry anything that was too modern or strange to his eyes.

"They'll be calling this a tool of the Devil," he said about their torches, fear and suspicion all over his face at the sight of the light-beam flicking on and off. He said the same about Max's spectacles, but let the boy keep them after Max promised to hide them in his pocket whenever they went anywhere near people.

Max had also brought a pile of books with titles like *The Black Death*, *Plagues and Poxes*, and *Medicine and Magic in Tudor England*. Angus went pale at the sight of them, and insisted on hiding them as deep in the thatch as he could thrust them.

"But they're library books and I haven't finished reading them!" Max protested. "How am I meant to be able to recognize the symptoms of bubonic plague without them?"

Scarlett shuddered theatrically. "Oh, God! I don't want to get the plague!"

"Just don't touch any dead rats," Max said.

"I'm not going to touch a dead rat!"

"And keep an eye out for fleas."

"Fleas!" she screeched. "Why did I ever come?"

Angus made Scarlett leave most of her backpack behind, since it consisted mainly of clothes and gossip magazines. The sight of these filled the old man with such disapproval that his eyes were almost completely hidden by his frowning grey eyebrows.

Of them all, Donovan had brought the least. He had his flugelhorn; a lightweight rain jacket which Angus fingered enviously but hid in the thatch anyway; his compass; a wind-up torch; and a travel mix of nuts, seeds and dried fruits that Angus approved of heartily. Since Angus would not let any of them carry their backpacks, Donovan was going to find the flugelhorn awkward to carry, so he and the old man contrived a carry strap with some old rope made of heather.

By this time, it was growing light outside. Max and Scarlett were arguing over whether anyone would find her pink Barbie sleeping bag peculiar, and Angus was packing his battered leather satchel while Linnet went out to wash the dishes in the fast-running burn. Hannah went outside too, her hag-stone in her hand. She wondered what she had done wrong when she had tried to find the loop that her father had hidden at Wintersloe.

The cottage was built low to the ground, and grass and heather grew on its roof so that it looked like a mossy boulder that had been there for ever. It was ridiculously easy to climb on to the roof, which gave her a clear view in all directions.

"Um," Hannah said, holding the hag-stone to her left eye. "Where's the puzzle ring?"

Hannah was whirled around, as if by an impatient hand playing blind-man's bluff. Her vision swam dizzyingly, as far-distant landscapes and people spun in and out of sight. She lost her balance, and tumbled down the roof and to the ground again. Luckily the roof was so low to the ground, she was only a little shaken and bruised.

"What happened?" Scarlett and Max came running outside, looking startled.

"You OK?" Donovan said, helping her up.

"Mmm-mmm," Hannah grunted, too winded to speak. She was scowling. First time she tried, she saw nothing. Second time, she saw too much. What was she doing wrong?

"You'd probably better be specific," Donovan said. "If the ring has been split in four and thrown in four different directions, the hag-stone won't be able to show you it all, will it? Try asking for just one direction at a time."

Hannah grunted again. It was good advice, but she was angry she had not thought of it herself.

"I need paper and pen," she said. "I'd better ask in rhyme. It seemed to work for the fairy gate." She found the little pad and pencil she had packed, and sat down again, scribbling on the paper. Every few seconds she would stop, squint up at the leaden sky, and mutter a few words. "Ring, sing, sling, king, bling."

"I think 'bling' is a bit modern," Scarlett said helpfully.

Hannah ignored her. "East, beast, feast, least. Sun, bun, fun, done. Oh, how can I say this?"

Eventually, she had something that satisfied her. She did not try to climb the roof, having no desire to fall off again, but walked up the gentle slope of the hill behind the house till she could see across the bare hillside to the east.

"Show me, show me, magic stone,
where one quarter of the ring was thrown,
east where the new sun does rise,
help me to find the golden prize."

It was not very good poetry, but it was the best Hannah could do on short notice. To her delight, looking through the hag-stone as she chanted the words, she saw the landscape rushing towards her as if she were flying over the moors in a helicopter. A walled grey town hurried towards her. Before it crouched a great hill, shaped like a sleeping lion. Closer she came, until she saw a spring of water bubbling down into a small carved bowl.

"Surely that was Arthur's Seat in Edinburgh?" she murmured. "Though the town was so small."

"Edinburgh would be much smaller then . . . I mean now," Max said.

When she described what she had seen, Angus nodded his grizzled head. "I've heard tell of that spring. They say it's got magical healing properties. It's called Saint Anthony's Well."

"If it's the spring of water I know, it's far older than your Saint Anthony," Linnet said, coming barefoot through the snow with the porridge pot on her hip.

"So you know the place I saw?" Hannah demanded.

Linnet nodded her head. "Aye, many's the time I've danced on that hill on May Day. Though not for many a long year." She handed Angus the pot, and he hung it to

240

his satchel, along with a big leather bottle of water – which Max had insisted he boil first – and a flat griddle pan.

"So are you going to come with us?" Hannah asked eagerly, the hag-stone in her hand. "You'll stay until we join the puzzle ring again, won't you, Linnet? And you too, Angus?"

There was a strange silence for a moment. Linnet was pale, her green eyes wide in her small, wedge-shaped face. Then she surprised them all by going down on her knees before Hannah, heedless of the mud on her skirt, and bowing low her head. "As you bid, so shall I do," she said, her voice husky. "However long it takes."

Angus glanced up. "For sure, lassie," he said irritably, slinging a tall bow over his shoulder and picking up a quiver of arrows. "Haven't I said so? Come on, let's be getting on the road! Plenty of time for blethering while we walk."

Hannah, standing astounded with Linnet kneeling in the mud before her, suddenly remembered what her father had written in his diary:

Hag-stones have the power to bind a faery to the owner's service.

What have I done? she wondered in dismay.

Arthur's Seat

All that day Hannah was haunted by the possibility that she had just bound Linnet to her service for the next four hundred and forty years. Was that why Linnet had grown so very old? She had spoken impulsively, but it was clear by Linnet's reaction that she took the pledge seriously. Hannah tried to apologize, but Linnet just said gently, "I was bound to my Lady Eglantyne, and now I am bound to you. I will serve you well, my lady."

Hannah was too cold and exhausted to worry for long. It was a long, hard day, following rough paths that wound through tangled forests, over boulders and rocky streams and patches of bog that oozed black mud. When Hannah stumbled and fell to her knees, she had to haul herself up and keep on walking, cold and muddy though she was, her guitar banging uncomfortably on her back. There was nothing to eat but cold leftover porridge, cut into slices they ate as they walked.

A magpie followed them for some distance, making

Hannah feel quite apprehensive, but then Linnet spat it at, crying "I defy thee" seven times. In a welter of feathers, the magpie somersaulted backwards as if flung by a sudden gust of wind, and flew away, squawking loudly. Hannah smiled faintly, and Linnet told her that if she ever saw a magpie again, she was to do the same thing.

"It is the black witch's spy, that bird," she told Hannah. "My lady's cousin slit its tongue with a silver knife and then trickled a drop of her own blood into the wound, so that the bird could speak to her. You must always beware of magpies."

Hannah nodded, remembering the black and white bird that had attacked her in the garden at Wintersloe, plucking a strand of hair.

Max and Scarlett were quiet and morose all day, only speaking to complain of the ache in their legs, or how cold they were, but Donovan walked with a long easy stride, his head held high, his eyes bright with pleasure.

"I wonder if we'll see any wolves," he said. "They weren't extinct nowadays."

"You've got to get your tenses sorted," Max said gruffly, taking off his glasses to wipe away the sweat. "They *aren't* extinct *these* days."

"Wolves. Just what we need," Scarlett said.

"I'd love to see a bear in the wild too," Donovan said. "And look out for beaver dams. Can you believe they hunted beavers to extinction?"

"All I want to see right now is a Pizza Express," Scarlett said tartly.

Donovan cast her a look of contempt. "Typical."

The forest was far thicker and darker and wilder than the woods Hannah had explored with Donovan back in their own time, and there was no distant sound of traffic, or the white trails of aeroplanes in the sky. If it had not been for the heavy confinement of her petticoats and skirt, she could have believed they were just out for a hike and would soon go back to Wintersloe for a cup of hot chocolate and some marmalade cake. It made her feel very frightened and alone to think the house, with its mismatching towers and crow-stepped gables, had not even been built yet.

When at last Angus called a halt, it was dark and bitterly cold. Hannah's hands and feet and face were frozen, and her whole body ached. Yet there was nowhere to sleep but on the ground. The children huddled together, too exhausted to even speak, as Angus cut fronds of brown bracken and heather with his knife, and Linnet gathered together kindling.

Angus scowled at them. "Do you expect to be waited on hand and foot? There's water to be got, and a meal to cook. And it'll be a cold night if you don't cut yourself some bracken to sleep on."

"Surely we're not sleeping here!" Scarlett said. "Out in the open!"

"We're still too close to Wintersloe Castle to risk finding shelter," Angus replied tersely. "Lord Montgomery will hang me if he finds me."

"Just for quitting your job?" Max demanded.

Angus was surprised. "Of course."

"It's not just Lord Montgomery we need to worry about, but the black witch's spies," Linnet said. "Luckily the gate is now closed again, which gives us another six weeks before the black witch can send her host against us. Her spies will still be watching for us, though, so we must try to keep you hidden, at least till we are well away from Fairknowe."

"I wouldn't be lighting a fire at all tonight if it wasn't that you look so cold," Angus said. "But if you want the fire to last more than an hour or two, I'd be gathering up some wood!"

As Hannah got up stiffly, she looked out at the dark, shadowy forest with a sense of misery approaching despair. There was still snow on the tops of the hills and in the furrows under the trees. Surely they would freeze to death?

Their dinner was little more than a mug of hot water in which a few turnips had been boiled and mashed. Cold and hungry, the children wrapped themselves in their plaids and lay down on piles of old bracken and heather, as close to the fire as they could. Their breath puffed white. Hannah could not stop shivering, so that the dry bracken beneath her rustled noisily, poking her through her clothes.

Linnet came and spread her own plaid over the two girls, and then heaped more bracken and heather upon them. "Sleep, my lambs," she whispered, gently touching Hannah's brow. Somehow, Hannah did.

The next day was the same. All day, they walked and walked and walked. At midday, they ate what Angus called "brose" – uncooked oats shaken up with water – and walked on till it was dark, when they shared a thin broth made with water and limp vegetables, and, hollow with hunger, rolled themselves in their plaids to sleep.

Hannah woke in the morning, stiff and sore and shivering, to find Angus once again stirring a pot of plain porridge flavoured with nothing more than a pinch of salt. She groaned loudly. "Not porridge again!"

Angus looked affronted. "Nothing better to stick to the sides of the stomach."

"What I wouldn't give for some bacon and eggs and sausages," Donovan said.

"I'd love a hot croissant," Scarlett said. "With lots of butter and strawberry jam."

"Cinnamon rolls with hot chocolate," Hannah said longingly.

Angus had been scowling ferociously all this time. At Hannah's words, he burst out, "The Lord preserve me! It's cinnamon they be wanting now! Where am I meant to be getting the gold for that? A king's ransom, it costs!"

Hannah stared at him in surprise as he got up, seized his bow and arrows, and stumped off into the forest.

"What's up with him?" Scarlett wondered.

Linnet knelt and stirred the porridge. "By the stars, it must be a wonderful place, your world," she said. "To eat meat every day like a lord, and cinnamon like a queen."

"Why, don't normal people get to eat bacon and eggs and cinnamon and stuff?" Max asked.

Linnet shook her head. "Only the rich eat meat every day, while cinnamon is rare indeed. The queen loves dates flavoured with cinnamon, I know, because Lord Montgomery took her some as a gift earlier this year and it cost him a pretty fortune. Why, we do not even know where cinnamon comes from. The merchants keep it a closely guarded secret."

"Wow," Hannah said. "We can buy it any old place."

"Well, here all we have is what we can grow or catch with our own hands," Linnet said. "So, come eat your porridge while it's hot and let us be on our way. Angus will catch us up when his temper has cooled."

The old man did not join them until late in the afternoon, and then he carried two fat red birds hidden in his plaid. "Let us hope no one sees us till we've eaten every last scrap of them," he said dourly. "I have no desire to lose my ear."

The children winced and did not know what to say, feeling bad that it was their complaints about the food that had led him to poaching.

"I'll cook us up a feast tonight!" Linnet cried, clapping her hands. "And make us some proper soup with the bones. Thank you, Angus!"

"Thank you!" the children echoed.

The roast grouse that night seemed the most delicious thing Hannah and her friends had ever eaten in their lives, and they were lavish in their praise of Angus's hunting and Linnet's cooking, so much that the old man seemed to forgive them their complaints of the morning. The children sucked every last scrap of meat and fat from the bones, and then Linnet put them to boil with the leaves of wild garlic and some carrots so that their broth the next day should taste a little more flavoursome.

At dusk on the following day, they came to Stirling, with its grim grey castle towering over the town and the river. The children were very excited by the sight of it, and began to talk animatedly about inns and fires and hot stew and soft beds, but to their disappointment Angus said he did not have the money for them to live in the lap of luxury, and he marched them past the town and back into the forest for another night shivering on the iron-hard, iron-cold ground.

"But why?" Scarlett raged. "It's so unfair! Why couldn't we have a night inside for once? We could've done the washing-up or sung for them to pay for it!"

"Better no one sees you," Angus said shortly. "I don't want any talk."

"But surely they're used to people travelling by?" Max said. "Why would we cause talk?"

"You're bound to be noticed," Angus said.

"But why?" Scarlett demanded. "We'll all catch pneumonia if we sleep outside every night."

"You don't catch pneumonia from getting cold," Max said. "Pneumonia is caused by bacteria, usually. We could get hypothermia, though."

"I think I've got hypothermia now," Hannah said, huddling her plaid around her. "I am so cold! Please, please, can't we just spend a night in an inn somewhere? I'd wash a hundred plates for a nice soft bed!"

"No," Angus said.

"Why not?" Scarlett demanded. "It's so unfair!"

"Your manners are too bad," Angus snapped, as if goaded beyond all patience.

Scarlett was affronted. "Our manners aren't bad! We say 'please' and 'thank you' and 'excuse me' if we burp!"

Angus pressed his lips together, looking very dour.

"What do you mean?" Hannah demanded, feeling quite as affronted as Scarlett looked. Her mother was always drumming the need for politeness into her, so much so that Hannah felt she was half crippled by the need to always be courteous. Most teenagers were not half as well mannered as she was, she thought.

"Do not be angry, my lambs. Angus does not mean to upset you," Linnet said gently.

"But what does he mean?" Max demanded. "We haven't been rude, have we?"

"You argue with him a lot," she said unwillingly.

"Well, yes," Hannah said, surprised. "But. . ."

"I don't know what children are permitted to do in your day," Angus said huffily, "but in our day children listen to their elders and do what they're told."

"Oh, all that stuff about children being seen and not heard!" Scarlett said scornfully. "That's so old-fashioned!"

There was a little silence, then the four friends exchanged guilty looks.

"We didn't mean to be rude," Hannah said. "That's just how we talk."

"And as a matter of fact," Max said, "your manners aren't so hot either. You wipe your mouth on your sleeve, and blow your nose in your fingers, and then we all have to eat out of the same pot, which must be simply seething with germs. . ."

"You do not raise your hat," Angus said angrily, "or stand and bow when I come by, or say your prayers upon going to bed, and not once have you waited for me and Linnet to finish our meal before you begin yours. Such rudeness would raise eyebrows in any village we stopped by."

"We didn't know," Hannah said. "Why didn't you tell us?"

"I didn't wish to be rude," Angus replied gruffly.

The children laughed at that, and once they began laughing, could not stop. Linnet laughed with them. After a moment Angus's face relaxed and he allowed one corner of his grim mouth to lift in what may have been a smile.

"You'd better give us lessons in manners," Scarlett said. "What a hoot! Maybe you could teach us how to curtsy too, Angus, and flutter our fans."

"Fans?" he asked, puzzled. "What's a fan?"

The next morning, the children were dumbfounded to realize that the main road in Scotland was little more than a muddy cart-track through the forest, so deeply rutted you could have hidden a baby in some of the potholes.

"You should see the M9 now," Max told Angus and Linnet. "It's got three lanes in either direction. Cars and trucks and buses just whiz along. It takes less than an hour to get to Edinburgh from Stirling."

"You're trying to make a fool of me," Angus said suspiciously. "It's just not possible!"

He would not believe any of their stories of the marvels of modern life, though Max was in his element, telling him about landing on the moon and heart transplants and submarines and escalators till the old man was puce in the face.

It took the weary travellers another long day's hard walking to reach Edinburgh from Stirling. Upon its ramparts, the castle glowed like a great golden crown with irregular peaked roofs and windows glittering like diamonds. It seemed a much greater and more magnificent building than Hannah had seen in her own time, surrounded as it was by empty snow-dusted fields and winter-bare woods.

A suspicious-eyed guard let them through the gate in the stout grey wall after Angus told him they were just travellers passing through. Within the wall was a different world, a warren of narrow stinking alleyways and courtyards, stairways and vaults and cobbled squares, with filth pooling in the gaps between the stones and running down the walls from the windows. The streets were crowded with people, some of them dressed in doublets and ruffs and codpieces and pointy shoes, just like people in paintings. Pigs rooted through the rubbish, and a skinny dog chased a squawking chicken down an alley, chased by a barefoot urchin with a grubby face. A huge black rat with a white belly and feet raced between their legs and up a wall, turning to stare at them with beady eyes before swarming along the wall beside them. Max yelped and jumped backwards, and both Scarlett and Hannah screamed, much to the amusement of everyone around them. A fat woman whacked at the rat with a broom, and it disappeared down a drain.

Hannah had found it easy to forget that she was back in the sixteenth century when they had been tramping through the forest, but in Edinburgh the difference between times was all too clear. The streets stank, and even the people looked quite different. They were smaller than Hannah was used to, both shorter and thinner, and many were scarred with pockmarks. Most had lost some or nearly all of their teeth, and she saw one man who had had both his ears carved off, leaving him with ugly stumps.

So little light struck down between the towering buildings that it was dim and shadowy in the alleys. Angus led them up steep cobbled lanes and stairwells, his square, indomitable figure a source of secret comfort to them all. At last he led them to a broad, sunlit street that ran along the bony spine of rock that connected Edinburgh Castle on its high rampart at one end, and the glowing bare rock of Arthur's Seat at the far end.

"Less than a mile from here," Angus said, panting slightly from the climb. "If we hurry, we'll make it before sunset."

By the time they reached Arthur's Seat, it was growing dark. The great hill, shaped like a crouching lion, reared above them, bare and windswept, blocking the light from the setting sun so that Hannah and her friends were climbing into sombre shadow, although behind them the firth blazed scarlet and gold. Hannah's breath was coming sharply, hurting her side. She stopped, and turned to look back on Edinburgh and the palace of Holyrood, glowing golden in the last rays of light. She could see all the way to the river and the firth, and across the grey winter fields. Rooks' nests swung precariously in the delicate tracery of twigs, bare against the pale sky.

On the hill above was a picturesque ruin, its Gothic arches gaping black. Hannah hurried up the path, eager and impatient to reach the fairy well, where Linnet had danced and where maidens came on May Day to wash their faces and make themselves beautiful.

A few more steps and Hannah reached the great boulder from which water gushed down, swirled in the stone basin, and overflowed to be lost in the heather. Hannah bent and drank gratefully, washing her hot, grimy face. The water was crystal clear and icy cold, and utterly delicious.

It was growing almost too dark to see. Hannah plunged

her hands into the basin and let her fingers explore within. She found nothing. She searched all round the roots of the boulder and under the basin. Nothing. More and more frantically she searched. By the time the others scrambled up to meet her, she was lighting one of her candles with shaking fingers. Even by its wan, flickering light, Hannah could find no slender golden loop. There was nothing to find.

"It's not here," she said blankly.

"It's been a while since the ring was broken," Donovan said. "And people would come here, to this little well, wouldn't they? If it's meant to have healing powers. Maybe someone found the ring."

"I'll look through the hag-stone," Hannah said. Disappointment weighed on her heavily. She fumbled in her pocket with cold, numb fingers and brought the hag-stone to her eye.

"Where now is the golden ring, found and taken from this spring?" she asked.

Hannah's gaze was dragged, helter-skelter, down the hill to the beautiful palace that lay at the foot of Arthur's Seat, outside the tall grey walls. She saw through a window into a small, richly decorated room where a group of woman were laughing and dancing to music played by a trio of men with lutes and drums and pipes.

One woman was far taller than the rest, and very richly dressed in black velvet with a great white ruff that framed her long aristocratic face. Her hair blazed golden-red under the candles, and her eyes were a most extraordinary golden colour, almost exactly the same shade as her hair.

Closer and closer Hannah's vision raced, until all she could see was one white, long-fingered hand, gesturing languidly from within its ruff of white lace. On one finger she wore a thin, oddly twisted gold band.

Hannah lowered the hag-stone from her eye.

"The ring is down there, at Holyrood Palace," she said in a low, shaken voice, pointing to the graceful stone building at the foot of the hill, its round turrets topped with pointed roofs. "It's . . . it's on the finger of the queen."

The Queen of Scots

"Och, it's a bad business," Angus said. "The court of the queen is a dangerous place."

Hannah ignored him. "All the books say Mary, Queen of Scots, loved music and singing. We'll pretend to be travelling minstrels. I'm sure she'll want to hear us! Then we can ask her for the ring."

"Tomorrow is the last Sunday before Lent," Angus said gloomily. "No merry-making allowed during Lent."

"Then we'll have to do it tomorrow," Hannah said with determination. "We can't wait forty days."

"So we'll get to sing for the queen!" Scarlett cried, clasping her hands together over her heart. "Glory hallelujah!"

"Maybe," Angus replied stolidly. "It's a good enough plan, I suppose. The queen's known for her open-handedness, and often gives away rings and brooches and suchlike to those who please her." He shook his head disapprovingly.

"I wonder how she got the ring," Max said.

"Probably someone found it and gave it to her," Donovan said. "Maybe trying to win her favour."

"What shall we sing?" Hannah asked.

"Better not to do anything too modern," Donovan said.

"Everything we do is modern compared to these days!" Max cried, running his hands up through his dark hair and scrunching it in despair.

"That makes a nice change," Scarlett said sarcastically.

Hannah was running through songs in her mind. "'Over the Sea to Skye' is no good; it talks about Bonnie Prince Charlie and he isn't even born yet. What else do we know that's really old?"

"How about 'Greensleeves'?" Max suggested.

Everyone's face lit up. It was a favourite song of Lady Wintersloe's and so they often played and sang it for her. Donovan liked it because they let him do a horn solo, and Hannah loved the words and the melody. Scarlett thought it was musty and dusty, like so much of the music they played, but she was used to that, and besides, it suited her high, sweet, ethereal voice.

On Sunday morning they washed themselves and brushed the leaves and mud off their clothes, and went nervously down the hill to Holyrood Palace. This was much smaller than the palace Hannah had visited in her own time, a small stone building with round towers and narrow windows, dwarfed by the Gothic pile of the abbey behind. To their surprise, they were permitted entry at soon as the guards saw their musical instruments.

It seemed there was a wedding that morning, between Queen Mary's favourite valet, Sebastien Pagez, and one of her maidservants. Sebastien was Italian, and a singer and musician as well as a valet. He often designed the queen's masques for her, and so to celebrate his wedding Mary had organized a day of carnival and celebration. The four friends, with a surly Angus towering over them, were taken to see the queen's lute player, John Hulme. He was richly and extravagantly dressed in embroidered silks and velvets, with lace at his wrists and a stiff white ruff. He examined their instruments with interest, particularly Hannah's guitar, exclaiming over how big it was, and how many strings it had.

"Where did you get such an instrument?" he asked. "In Spain? I hear they have big guitars like this there."

"My teacher gave it to me," Hannah replied truthfully. "I do not know where he got it."

"Very well, sing to me then," John Hulme said. "Don't play yet. I just want to hear your voices."

Nervously, the four friends sang. The lute player stroked his pointed beard thoughtfully, then nodded his head.

"We haven't had anything quite like you before. The queen will adore it. You will need some other clothes. Molly! Find some costumes for these performers! All in white, I think, perhaps with roses in their hair. . ."

"At this time of year?" the maidservant said sceptically.

"I'm sure you'll contrive," he replied with a grin.

The maidservant led them away, chattering excitedly

about the wedding, and asking them all sorts of questions they found hard to answer. Luckily, she did not pause to listen. She told them the queen loved a wedding, for it gave her a chance to dance without arousing the ire of the preachers, and that she had given the bride seven ells of the loveliest blue brocade to make her dress. The queen herself, Molly said, was to be dressed all in black and silver, with her famous black pearls about her neck.

She chattered on the whole time she helped the four friends dress. They needed her help, as they did not know how to put on the clothes, which had no zippers or buttons or velcro to fasten. It turned out that formal clothes in Tudor times were pinned on to the body, and then unpinned again at night. It was like being a dressmaker's dummy. Molly laughed at them all and called them foolish bairns as she shoved them this way and that, and pricked them unmercilessly.

"This is more like it!" Scarlett cried, swinging her white brocade skirt from side to side. "Much better than those horrible old brown things."

Hannah saw Angus scowl, and wished Scarlett would remember Angus had spent all his savings on their clothes. She loved her own dress, though, which was also white and gold. The boys looked handsome too, if rather uncomfortable, in tight white tights and padded white and gold doublets. The girls could not help giggling at their codpieces.

Linnet brushed out the girls' hair, as Molly found them

gilded garlands to wear. "Och, you look like angels!" the maid cried.

Max and Donovan cast agonized glances at each other.

The palace was crowded and busy. People rushed everywhere, carrying great trays laden with jugs and cups, or barrels hoisted on to their shoulders. Three maidservants carefully carried a velvet dress heavy with gilt embroidery. Two fat dwarves pushed past, dressed in red and yellow motley, scowling and grumbling about the crowd. A little later a white horse's head ran past, followed soon after by the tail, the man within calling petulantly, "Where have you got to, you clod-pole!"

Molly led them to an antechamber where they were told to wait, holding their instruments and feeling increasingly nervous.

"I need to go to the bathroom," Scarlett whispered to Hannah. "Surely I won't need to go and squat in the bushes here in the queen's own palace?" Of all the discomforts and difficulties of the sixteenth century, the girls had found the lack of toilets the worst. They asked Molly, who took them to a little stone chamber at the end of the hall. Here there was simply a stone shelf with a round hole in it, above a deep stone shaft that fell down to the outside of the palace wall. Straw and dried twigs of herbs had been scattered on the floor, and clothes were hung on hooks above. When Hannah asked Molly why the toilet was also used as a wardrobe, she looked at them in blank surprise. "Why, the smell keeps the moths away, of course!"

The antechamber where the children waited was freezing, and so they were very glad when at last a cranky-looking page came and ushered them into the banqueting hall. It was painted, gilded, crowded and very noisy. A long table ran the length of the hall, filled with people in ornate costumes eating and drinking and talking. Musicians played in a small gallery, elevated at the end of the room, while entertainers roamed the room, telling jokes, tumbling head over heels, walking on stilts. Wide-eyed, Hannah saw the remains of a roast swan being carried away from one table, its neck still lifted proudly, its great feathered wings folded neatly alongside its bony carcass. She winced and looked away, only to see other servants carrying away great platters of roast boar, the massive tusked heads still mostly intact.

Angus took up position by the door, looking around with narrowed eyes for escape routes and possible sources of dangers. Linnet, who had seemed almost invisible since they entered the palace, melted once again into the background.

"Your job is to sing while the musicians have a break and wet their whistle," the page whispered. "Give the servants a chance to clear the tables before the next course."

Hannah nodded, her gaze flying up to the long table at the top of the room. Men and women sat there, reaching for food from the platters before them, laughing at the sallies of a female dwarf who was capering before them, pretending to be a simpering bride preparing for her wedding day.

Queen Mary was delicately washing her fingers in a bowl held for her by a richly dressed young man on bended knee. She was magnificently attired in black velvet and satin, with silver embroidery. Her ruff was small and folded back to show the white skin of her throat and breast. Around her neck hung loops of enormous black pearls, glowing against the pallor of her skin. Her hair shone richly from under its simple snood of pearls.

Hannah stared at her in awe. The queen was not beautiful, exactly. Her nose was too long, and her eyelids were strangely heavy, giving her a brooding look. She was tall, her regal head on its long neck higher than nearly all of the men who clustered round her. Then the man next to her bent his head and said something to her, and she threw back her head and laughed, her topaz eyes flashing. At that moment she seemed the most strikingly lovely woman Hannah had ever seen.

"Is that her husband?" she whispered to the page, for the man beside the queen – a strong, vigorous-looking man with thick black curls and a neat moustache and beard – was also dressed in black and silver.

The page looked at her in scorn. "Him? Of course not! He's Lord Bothwell, you fool, the queen's closest advisor. His Majesty is not here. He is sick still, out at the provost's house at Kirk o' Field. He does not come till the morrow."

The name stirred a faint chord of memory in Hannah. *Kirk o' Field. . .* Where had she heard that before? She had no time to wonder, though, for the page gave her a rough push. "Well, get on with it then!"

Hannah took a deep breath and marched up to the high table, her friends beside her. Hannah carried her guitar and Donovan his flugelhorn, while Max had the old-fashioned flute he had taken from Wintersloe Castle, and Scarlett had her tambourine, newly tied with gold ribbons.

"Your Majesty, lords and ladies, begging your favour, we would like to sing and play for you today," Max said. Since he had hidden his glasses in his pocket, he was squinting in his attempt to see. Queen Mary inclined her head graciously, and the children bowed and curtsied, as Angus had instructed them. "We will sing 'Greensleeves'."

Donovan lifted his flugelhorn to his lips. The familiar music rang out. They waited for his solo – deep, haunting, filled with loss and longing – to finish, then Hannah began to strum her guitar.

To her surprise, everyone stirred and a small hum of shock and displeasure rose. But the sound died away as soon as she and Scarlett began to sing, their voices in perfect harmony.

As the song died away, there was a little pause. Hannah loved that small moment of silence. The greater the pause, the wilder the applause, it seemed to her, and so she was pleased and relieved when the nobles all clapped and shouted out words of praise.

Queen Mary was smiling. She stood and raised her hand,

and the noise died down. "This is a pretty sight indeed, and a pretty sound too. You play very sweetly for ones so young. We have not seen you at court before. . ."

"Surely that is because their mother's milk is still wet on their lips!" Lord Bothwell quipped.

"Where do you come from? You speak French very well. Are you come from Paris?"

Hannah was astonished. She did not speak French at all. She looked at Scarlett and Donovan and Max, and saw the same flustered surprised on their faces. Then she realized it must still be the magic of the hag-stone.

"No, Your Majesty. Though my teacher played there for many years." Hannah smiled at the thought of old Mr Wheeler, who often told her stories about his years playing in the jazz nightclubs of the French capital. He had once played trumpet for Nina Simone there.

"Ah, that explains it. Your teacher, is he here?" Queen Mary looked about her.

"No. He's a long way away." Sadness touched Hannah's face. She did miss her old friend and teacher.

"You are alone? You have no parents, no protector?"

Hannah shook her head. "My father is dead," she said huskily. "Or so we think. My mother too is far away." So far away it was impossible to think of the distance that separated them. Tears started to her eyes, for the fear that she might never be able to find her way back to her own time had weighed on Hannah ever since she had first realized *when* she was.

Pity softened the queen's face. "So you wish to stay here at court?"

"No!" Hannah said hastily. "I mean, I thank Your Majesty, but we must go on just as soon as we can."

"Ah! Travelling troubadours, I see. Well, then, you will want my protection. I will arrange a pass for you." She waved one hand at a soberly clad man standing against the wall, who nodded his head and bowed. "We would not like four such pretty young people to be branded on the cheek for singing in public without a licence." Although the queen smiled, Hannah felt a little shock at her words. She had not realized that travelling musicians needed a licence.

"Will you sing for us again?" the queen asked.

Hannah nodded. She glanced at the others, trying to think what song to perform. Her fingers strayed into "Black is the Colour of my True Love's Hair". Although it was an old Scottish folk song, it was one Nina Simone often sang. The others followed her lead. Again there was that little hum of surprised displeasure as Hannah began to play her guitar, but again the beauty of the song hushed the crowd and they listened quietly. To Hannah's surprise, the words of the song caused a few titters of laughter round the room, with many turning to look at the black-haired Lord Bothwell lying back in his seat beside Queen Mary, a look of sardonic amusement on his strong, dark face.

After they had finished, the four children were accosted by all sorts of men and women, asking them questions, pressing wine and sweetmeats upon them, asking them to come and sing at this party and that. A tall, thin man dressed all in black satin, with a flowing white lace cravat instead of a ruff, and shoes so pointed they looked like weapons, came and bent close to Hannah, smiling and murmuring something she could not hear. She inclined her head, trying to hear him, and suddenly he reached out and viciously plucked a strand of her hair. She cried out in pain and clapped a hand to her head, and the man – smiling still – melted away into the crowd.

"Who was that?" Linnet asked in some agitation.

"I don't know," Hannah cried, her eyes smarting with tears. "He pulled some of my hair right out by the roots!"

Linnet looked grave. "One of the black witch's spies, no doubt. She can find you more easily if she has part of you to hold. Usually she prefers a finger or toe, but a strand of your hair works just as well, particularly if it is pulled out by the roots and so has your blood on it."

"A magpie plucked some of my hair back in my own time," Hannah told her, rubbing her head furiously.

Linnet nodded. "She may not be able to track you here with that, though, for you are out of time. I was hoping she had lost our trail. We were careful to keep out of sight as much as possible. I'm guessing she knew we must come to Edinburgh, and so her spy was waiting for us."

Just then, John Hulme came up to them, drawing Hannah aside and looking at her sternly. "That is a dangerous game you play, strumming with the Devil's hand. You must not do that again. The crowd was merry, and you are very young, and no one wished to spoil the festivities. But if that firebrand Knox should hear of it, there'd be trouble."

Hannah shrank back. She had read of John Knox, the strict and puritanical preacher who had led the Protestant Reformation in Scotland. He had written a pamphlet denouncing the rule of Mary, Queen of Scots, and her cousin Mary Tudor of England, calling it "The First Blast of the Trumpet Against the Monstrous Regiment of Women". He preached such fiery sermons that riots broke out in churches, and he had confronted the young queen and lectured her upon her frivolous ways until she had wept.

"What do you mean, the Devil's hand?" Hannah had never heard the left hand being called that before.

John Hulme stared at her in angry incredulity. "But surely you must know! Why, they will burn you if they see you using the Devil's hand."

"Burn me?"

"Aye. For only a witch would ever use her left hand!"

The World's End

Hannah found it hard to take a breath. Her whole body felt hot and dizzy. She looked down at her left hand in horror. Of course she had heard stories about how, in the olden days, children had been beaten for using their left hand and had had it tied behind their back. She had never heard of anyone being burnt to death for it.

"I didn't know," she managed to say.

"No one has ever told you before? Warned you against using the Devil's hand?" When she shook her head, he went on, in a kinder tone of voice, "Where have you come from? The Outer Hebrides! Well, I tell you now. I wish I had seen you play before you did so before the whole court! You must not do so again."

But I don't know any other way to play, she thought.

"It is a good thing that you are leaving right away," he said.

"But no! Not at all! They must not leave so soon!" A warm, sweet, persuasive voice rang across the room. The queen had risen, her ladies clustering about her. "They are virtuosos! I must hear them sing again. Not now. We're going to dance now, and then I have the ambassador's dinner afterwards. But tonight!"

"They could sing at the masque tonight," John Hulme said. "Sebastien plans a midnight supper, before the putting-to-bed ceremony. It would be a lovely way to end the day, with sweet love songs sung by such angelic voices."

"Wonderful," the queen agreed. "But do you really plan to move on again in the morning, my dears? It is Lent, you know. You cannot play and sing again for forty days."

"We must, Your Majesty," Scarlett said dramatically. "We cannot tarry."

Hannah shot her a warning glance, then turned back to the queen, seeing at last a chance to beg her for the loop of the puzzle ring. But the queen was speaking, and Hannah dared not interrupt her.

"In that case, you must come with me tonight when I visit my husband. I know the king will like to see the new singers the whole court is speaking of. You shall walk to Kirk o' Field with us, and entertain us while the men play at dice!" She nodded and moved away, leaving Hannah with that faint uneasy flicker of memory. Where *had* she heard of Kirk o' Field before?

The moment of puzzling cost Hannah her opportunity. She would have started after the queen, even dropped on her knees to beg her for the golden loop. But it was too late. The queen was dancing with Lord Bothwell, the two tall figures in their matching black and silver sweeping through the crowd of dancing courtiers like an iron scythe. Hannah fell back, troubled and afraid.

As the shadows closed down over the gardens outside, great branches of candles were lit, and the laughing queen retired, taking with her a host of lords and ladies and attendants. Linnet came and took the children to the kitchen, sitting them down in front of a bowl of broken meats and vegetables. The children had not eaten since their porridge that morning. They ate ravenously, finding the clatter and commotion of the kitchen nearly as fascinating as the swirl of dancers above.

"How many people must the cooks have to feed every day?" Max wondered. "It must be hundreds, maybe even a thousand."

"I wish they didn't have to eat the swans," Scarlett said.

"You're probably eating a bit of swan right now," said Donovan.

Scarlett faltered, holding a piece of meat to her mouth, then shrugged and ate it anyway. It was delicious.

Later that evening, a page came to fetch them to join the royal party, heading into Edinburgh town. The queen and her courtiers rode gorgeously caparisoned horses. Everyone else walked through the frosty darkness, the flare of torches sending great banners of smoke up into the night sky, dimming the stars. Everyone was still dressed in their carnival finery, some wearing masks like cats or dragons or terrifying birds. The queen wore a black fur mantle against the cold. Everyone chattered in high shrill voices. Max and Scarlett were running about, scraping up the snow and pelting each other with icy snowballs. Donovan was staring up at the night sky, where a new moon hung among stars, while Angus stumped behind, Linnet a slim shadow by his side.

"Why does the queen's husband not live at the palace too?" Hannah asked John Hulme.

He glanced down at her in surprise. "Well . . . he has been sick . . . and Her Majesty did not want him to return till she was sure he was fully recovered. And of course, they have not been so sweet to each other this past year, not since David Rizzio was killed. . ." His voice trailed away.

Hannah remembered that David Rizzio had been the queen's secretary. He had been stabbed to death in her bedchamber at Holyrood Palace, leaving bloodstains that could never be washed away. The queen's husband had believed Rizzio was her lover, even though he was an ugly little hunchback, and so he and his friends had burst in upon them playing cards one night, and killed him right in front of Mary's horrified eyes. She had been seven months pregnant then, and felt sure that they had meant to murder her too, leaving Lord Darnley – her husband – to inherit the throne. Hannah thought it very strange that the queen could still be married to a man who had murdered her friend and tried to murder her.

"So why does she go to visit him now?" Hannah asked.

John Hulme hesitated a moment, then answered frankly: "They say you should keep your friends close, and your enemies closer. With the king here, under her eye, she can be sure he is not plotting against her again."

Hannah pondered this, more puzzled than ever.

The queen's party went through the massive gateway of Netherbow Port, Lord Bothwell calling greetings to the guards and tossing them a handful of coins. Once again it was like entering a different world. Outside all was dark and peaceful, with the graceful shape of the palace lit up with candles, and the distant sound of music drifting on the wind. Inside, it was noisy and raucous, with people swarming everywhere, drinking ale and singing loud choruses that involved a lot of banging of tankards and shrieking with laughter. Some children were playing with firecrackers in a corner, a dog was chasing a scrawny cat, and six couples were dancing boisterously to the sound of a fiddle.

"They call this the World's End," John Hulme told Hannah. "Many people cannot pay the fee to come in and out through the gate, and so they live and die here, within the city's walls."

"So they never go anywhere else?" Hannah looked around at the dark, smoky streets with pity.

"Why would they want to? Edinburgh is the greatest city in the world!" the lute player boasted.

Donovan and Hannah smiled wryly at each other.

The queen was smiling and waving to the crowd and the earl was throwing more coins, but Hannah noticed some of the crowd scowled in response and shook their fists.

The bells of St Giles rang out noisily, filling the air with their clangour, and at once boys began to walk the streets, banging on drums. Heads appeared at doors and windows high and low, calling out loudly, "Gardyloo! Gardyloo!" Then they emptied out their chamber pots into the street, in foul-smelling deluges that splashed on the heads of those who were not quick enough to draw away from the walls. One of the queen's pages ran on ahead, waving his torch and calling, "Hold your hand!" and the ladies held scented pomanders to their noses, but otherwise no one seemed to notice or mind.

"Ewwww," Scarlett cried, and muffled her face in her plaid. "What a stink!"

"The ancient Romans had sewers two thousand years ago," Max said, screwing up his nose. "No wonder everyone gets so sick these days!"

Through the maze of dark, noisy streets the procession went, Hannah trying hard not to step in any muck. Then they came to a gate in a high wall, which one of the servants unlocked, then stood back to allow the queen to enter. Within were a garden and a house, lit dimly with candles. Hannah and her friends followed the crowd of courtiers up the stairs to a small chamber where a young man of around twenty years of age lay in bed, beneath a purple velvet canopy, all trimmed with cloth of gold.

He was thin and pasty, with a hollow look about his face and fair curls that clung damply to his brow. Although he was undeniably handsome, there was a sulky, petulant cast to his mouth, and his chin was rather slack. He sat up as everyone came in, and complained that they should be so late. Queen Mary went to sit by his side, soothing him and asking someone to pour them some wine.

Hannah carefully laid her guitar against the wall, and then the four of them sang again, racking their brains for songs they all knew that would not seem too strange to these sixteenth-century ears. They could not sing "House of the Rising Sun", with its talk of New Orleans and sin and misery. They could not sing "I Kissed A Girl" or "Bootylicious". They could only imagine how the queen would react to John Lennon's "Imagine".

Let alone John Knox.

Luckily all four of them had sung in school choirs over the years, and so had a fair repertoire of songs that they knew (most of) the words to. So they sang "Amazing Grace", and "Scarborough Fair", and, rather anxiously, "Kumbaya". No one asked them what the words meant, though, and so they relaxed, and sang as sweetly and innocently as they could. For once, not even Max had the desire to ham it up. It was too strange, singing in this crowded, smoky room, with men wearing swords as they played dice, and the queen laughing and drinking wine with a man who had tried to murder her.

The queen asked them to play "Greensleeves" again,

and they would have sung "Black is the Colour of my True Love's Hair" too, if John Hulme had not leant over and surreptitiously shaken his head at the very first chords. Hannah did not understand at first, until he jerked his head slightly at the queen and her fair-haired husband. She remembered Queen Mary laughing and dancing with the black-haired Lord Bothwell, who was now leaning up against the wall, drinking wine and watching the queen broodingly.

So she quickly segued into "Morning Has Broken", and the others followed her lead.

"Morning *has* almost broken," Lord Bothwell said when they finished. "Must be time to be getting these young folk back to bed."

The queen rose quickly to her feet. "Good heavens, the masque! I promised! I must return to the palace too."

The king scowled. "You said you would stay here tonight!"

"But it is Sebastien's wedding supper. I promised I would come. I cannot break my promise, you know that. Besides, I will see you in the morning. Have you not ordered the carriage to bring you to the palace? See, it shall not be so very long before I see you again."

The king was cross and sulky. He muttered something under his breath, and the queen, smiling, drew a gold ring from her finger and pressed it into his hand. "There you are! My lucky ring. You have my pledge that I shall see you bright and early in the morning."

Then, in a whirl of silver-encrusted skirts, and black fur as dense and velvety as a panther's, she was gone. Like a swarm of eels, the crowd of courtiers followed her. Hannah and her friends gathered up their instruments hastily, gazing at each other in agonized dismay. The queen had given the king the loop of the puzzle ring!

Hellfire

Hannah lagged behind, watching as the king petulantly cast the ring on to his bedside table and grabbed once more at his wine glass. Then she had to follow the queen's party out into the frosty night.

The queen was mounting once more upon her horse when a young man climbed up the stairs from the subterranean basement. Although his clothes were fine, they were dishevelled and grubby, and his face was smeared with grime. Hannah recognized the queen's page, who had been in attendance upon her all day.

"Jesu, Paris," the queen said. "How begrimed you are!"

He muttered an apology, bowing low, and said he had just been checking on the king's wine cellar. The queen laughed merrily. "And drinking it too, by the look of you!" she cried, and wheeled her horse about. All the men leapt into their saddles and followed the queen away, leaving the servants and musicians to follow wearily behind on foot. The queen's page hurried after, wiping his face clean.

Hannah and her friends fell behind, out of earshot. "What shall we do?" Hannah whispered. "Did you see? Oh, if only I'd asked her for it before!"

"We'll have to steal it," Scarlett whispered.

"You must be joking," Max cried. "If they brand you on the cheek for singing without a licence, imagine what they'll do to you for stealing a ring from the king!"

"Sssh!" Hannah hissed.

"What choice do we have?" Donovan asked. "That guy's never going to give it to us! He looks like the sort who would hang on to it just to spite us. Besides, it's the perfect opportunity. We could never have stolen it from the queen at the palace, with all those guards and servants and lords and ladies hanging round all the time. But here it'd be easy enough to break into that house; there are no guards, and it's very secluded."

"An odd place for the king to stay, don't you think?" Scarlett said. "I'd have thought he'd be in a castle, if he wasn't going to stay with the queen. Which is odd too, don't you think?"

"I think they're kind of separated," Hannah said.

"Why don't they just get a divorce?" Max demanded.

"Mary, Queen of Scots, was Catholic, remember?" Hannah said. "I don't think she's allowed to get a divorce."

Angus loomed up out of the darkness behind them, looking anxious. He and Linnet had not been permitted into the king's house, and so they had been waiting outside the garden wall, shivering in the cold.

"How's all with you?" Linnet asked anxiously.

"The queen gave the ring to her husband!" Hannah said in a low, urgent whisper. "It's up there, just lying on his bedside table. We're going to sneak back later, when everyone's asleep." Hannah flushed uncomfortably, knowing her mother would not approve. "I mean, it's not like it's stealing. It's our ring – I mean, my family's. I have to get it back!"

"A dangerous ploy," Linnet said. "They are cruel, this court. Quick to condemn and quick to kill. We did not realize, my lady and I, how different a land this was when we first came. But I know now. You do not wish to be caught, I promise you that."

"No," Hannah said. "We'll have to be careful."

"It is too dangerous for bairns," Angus said. "I will get it for you."

Hannah felt a moment of immense relief, but then she shook her head. "Thank you, Angus, thank you so much, but I can't let you do that. They would hang you for sure if you were caught. While I'm just a girl . . . I could say I left something behind."

"Something so important you'd sneak back under cover of darkness to get it?" Donovan said drily.

"My guitar?"

"It's too big, everyone will have seen you carrying it out," Max said.

"My Cairngorm ring," Hannah said. "I can say, truthfully, that my great-grandmother gave it to me and that it is one of the most precious things I own."

"But why not just ask for it in the morning? Why sneak back?"

"I was afraid one of the servants would pocket it and then say it could not be found," Hannah replied.

"No one would believe it," Max said.

"We'll just have to make sure no one catches us, and then we won't have to make up a story to satisfy them," Scarlett said briskly. "Which means, clodhopper, that you're not coming."

"Who, me?" Max said indignantly.

"Yeah, you, Mister Xam Pow Bam! You'd better lurk outside where you can't knock over anything with your elbow, or stamp on anyone's toes."

"I guess you think you'd do a better job," Max said, rather sulkily.

"Sure. After all," Scarlett said, "I am the only one with a purple belt in karate."

Some hours later, the small party hurried through the dark palace garden, their hearts hammering in their chests. It had been much harder than they had imagined creeping out of the palace, for all the servants – a category which included dwarves, fools, fiddlers, singers, stilt-walkers and actors – slept together in the great hall, on thin pallets of straw. It had been agonizing, stepping over huddled snoring forms, tiptoeing down dark corridors patrolled by guards with long halberds, and trying to find a door or window that was unlocked in a palace filled with a thousand unsettled sleepers.

Then they had to get through the gate at Netherbow Port again.

"Isn't there some other way of getting into the town?" Scarlett demanded.

Angus shook his head. "There's a gap in the wall, at Leith Wynd, but it's guarded too."

"Such a sweet, trusting lot round here," Max said sardonically.

Angus scowled at him. "It's only that wall that's kept the English out of Edinburgh in the past. You want us to just leave ourselves open to the south?"

"No, of course not," Donovan said quickly.

"They took for ever to let us through the gate that first time we came," Hannah said. "We're just signalling that we're up to some kind of skulduggery, trying to get in the gate so late."

"We could bribe them, maybe?" Scarlett said.

Angus scowled, and closed his hand protectively over his coin purse, newly heavy with the queen's gold. "We'll need our money," he protested, "if we want to eat tomorrow. Besides, it'll only draw attention to us. We'd be remembered."

"Maybe if we explained that we were in the queen's party," Donovan said.

"No, that's no good! We want them all to think we slept the night peacefully in the palace," Max said.

"We need to go through in disguise," Scarlett said with relish. "Let's wrap our plaids around out heads, and chuck

281

a coin at the guard as we go through and say we're with that other guy, the one who paid when the queen came through. They opened the door fast enough when they heard his name!"

"Lord Bothwell?" Hannah asked. "That's not such a bad idea."

So when the night guard sleepily called, "Who goes there?", Angus shouted back, "My Lord Bothwell's men!" The gate was swung open at once, and they all strode through, keeping their plaids wrapped close about their heads. Pocketing his coin, the guard went back to his little hut, and the companions plunged exultantly into the dark and empty streets, filled with new confidence.

All was quiet at Kirk o' Field. It was after half past one, and clouds had obscured the moon, bringing the occasional flurry of snow. Angus hoisted Hannah and Scarlett up and over the wall, grumbling anxiously into his beard. Donovan had wanted to go too, but at last had agreed that the two girls were the smallest and lightest, and the least likely to be punished if caught.

Nervously, her heart hammering, Hannah crept through the dark garden, Scarlett at her heels. There was a little window ajar into the pantry. No man could have squeezed through, but both the girls were slim and supple. They managed to wriggle through, landing with soft bumps on the tiled floor. Hannah caught her breath, but there was no sound, so she and Scarlett crept up the stairs to the young king's bedroom. Scarlett stayed out on the landing, keeping watch, while Hannah eased the door slowly open and stepped into the stifling-hot closeness of the king's sickroom.

The room had been crowded with chairs and cushions, Hannah remembered, and a low table covered with green velvet where the lords had played cards. So she went cautiously through the darkness, her hands held out, sliding one foot forward, then the other. Her groping fingers found the king's bedside table. Gingerly she felt all over it, and caught her breath with excitement as her fingers found the slender hoop of gold. It was bent and quirked into an odd shape on one side, rather like a whorl of petals. Hannah seized it, but accidentally knocked her hand against the king's wine goblet, which gave a loud clink as it bumped against the candlestick.

"Wha . . . at?" the king murmured.

Hannah backed rapidly away, the golden loop thrust deep inside her pocket. She heard the king sigh heavily, and turn over, and felt behind her for the door. It creaked as she pushed it open.

The king's bedclothes rustled. "Is someone there?" he asked in a trembling voice. "Taylor?"

"Aye, my lord?" a sleepy voice said, right at Hannah's feet. She gasped in shock and backed rapidly out of the room, bumping her hip on a sideboard as she went. She heard an inarticulate cry of alarm from the bedroom, and the sound of someone getting up. Hannah and Scarlett ran as quietly down the stairs as they could and wriggled out the pantry window again.

"There was someone in his room, sleeping on the floor," Hannah gasped. "I almost trod on him!"

"But you got the ring?" Scarlett's voice was shaking.

"Yeah. Come on! Let's get out of here."

The two girls had a great deal more trouble scaling the wall without Angus to lift them up, but both could hear sounds coming from the king's bedroom window and were anxious to get out of sight as quickly as possible. Hannah boosted Scarlett from below, then her friend reached down and hauled her up, and somehow they managed to scramble over, scraping their knees and elbows on the way.

"Come on!" Max cried. Donovan seized Hannah's hand and they broke into a run, Angus pounding before them, his dagger in his hand. Linnet ran lithely and silently behind.

Suddenly an almighty explosion rent the night in two. Flames shot high into the sky, like some vision of hell gaping open. The children were thrown off their feet as debris rained all around them. Foul-smelling smoke billowed into the air. Shakily, everyone scrambled back to their feet, then clutched each other in horror. Behind them, the king's lodging had been reduced to a pile of rubble.

"The house. . . the king. . ." Hannah said stupidly. "That's right, I remember now where I'd heard the name . . . Kirk o' Field is where her husband got murdered. . . "

"It's gone! Blown up!" Max said. "But how? Who?"

"Terrorists?" Donovan whispered. "But . . . now?"

"We were there just seconds ago," Scarlett said numbly.

"Come, bairns! We must get out of here," Angus whispered, and he seized the two girls' hands and drew them quickly away. The boys followed, Linnet hurrying them along. Now they could hear shouts and cries of alarm. Lanterns kindled in windows all about them. "The king! Murder! Murder!" a voice screamed.

"Keep your heads down," Angus whispered. "Here, duck in here."

They took refuge in a stinking alleyway as men in armour went running past, swords drawn.

"Now we're in strife," Angus said. "The king dead, and us on the very scene. How are we to get free of this coil of trouble?"

A Bloodsucking
Mad-Headed Ape

Hannah had little memory of their escape from Edinburgh. No more than a confused impression of running, hiding, creeping, ducking, through a world of flame and shadows. Once they were accosted, but talked their way free. The guards were looking for armed desperadoes, not an old man, a young woman and four scared teenagers.

As they walked, heading west towards the coast, everyone talked about the explosion, wondering and afraid. No one could understand what had happened. Hannah slept badly, waking in the middle of the night with a pounding heart, her dreams reeking of gunpowder. She could see by her friends' pale faces and short tempers that their sleep was disturbed too. Her only consolation was the slender gold loop of the puzzle ring, which she sewed into the hem of her chemise.

A magpie flew overhead as they crossed the Firth of Clyde on a boat Angus begrudgingly hired for the day. It did not return, so that Hannah hoped it was just a bird, and not one of Irata's spies. All four children spat at it, however, and shouted "I defy thee" seven times, just to be sure. Somehow, it made them all feel much better.

A week later, they came to the town of Dumbarton. For once Angus did not lead them in a wide circle around the town, but jerked his broad thumb and said gruffly, "Let's go in and have some hot stew and some ale, and see what news there is."

"Glory hallelujah!" Scarlett said. "I'm about to drop dead from exhaustion."

"And hunger," Max said.

"I never thought I'd get excited at the thought of stew!" Hannah said, and saw Donovan smile.

Angus did not have to remind the children to keep their heads down and their mouths shut. Everyone was still afraid that someone would realize they had been at the king's house the night he died, and the crime would somehow be pinned on them. Hannah could only hope that no one would bother to wonder about their disappearance from the palace. After all, they had said several times they planned to leave early.

Dumbarton was a busy port town, dominated by the twin peaks of Dumbarton Rock, which had been fortified and turned into the rambling mass of Dumbarton Castle, an ancient stone fort which overlooked the river. It was one of the queen's castles, Angus told them. Queen Mary had lived there for a time as a child, leaving when she was six to spend the next decade of her life in France. Because it was a port town, people came and went all the time and so their presence would not occasion any remark.

They slipped into a crowded inn, a white plastered building with great oaken beams stained black from the fire in the middle of the room. Hannah's eyes stung and watered from the smoke in the room, which belched up from the sods of peat in the hearth and rose in billows from the innumerable long clay pipes clenched in the corners of everyone's mouths. The innkeeper brought them haddock soup, thickened with turnips. After a week of nothing but porridge and thin broth, it seemed an unimaginable delicacy. The children were so busy gobbling they did not pay much attention to the crowd. Once Hannah finally pushed her bowl away from her, though, she realized the mood in the inn was tense and ugly.

"They say the king was found in the garden outside the city wall, strangled to death," a brawny waggoner was saying. "He was still wearing nothing but his nightgown."

"But wasn't the house blown up with gunpowder?" a sailor in broad canvas trousers demanded. "Why would they blow up the house?"

"I heard the idea was to kill him while he slept, but then maybe he heard something – or saw something – and tried to escape. So they chased after him and strangled him in the garden," the waggoner said.

"They say the queen is distraught with grief," the young sailor said, wiping his mouth on his sleeve.

A black-clad man snorted. "She's a fine actress, that one!"

"I know she hasn't been on good terms with her husband in recent times, but that doesn't mean she's not upset," a fat woman said belligerently, taking her clay pipe out of her mouth to point it at the man in black. "He is the father of her child, after all."

"I heard she and Lord Bothwell danced the whole night away," a red-faced man said. "Happy as clams at high tide, they were!"

"That's not true!" a merchant in a rich velvet gown cried, banging his fist on the table. "The queen was with the king all evening! She meant to stay the night there, and would have if she hadn't remembered the wedding. The explosion was clearly meant for Her Highness! Who cared about young Darnley? He was just a lazy fool who trod on a few too many toes. It was the queen who was the target!"

"Which is why she so conveniently remembered another engagement elsewhere, at twelve o'clock at night!" the man in black sneered.

Hannah remembered the smiling queen, sweeping out in her black furs, followed by her train of haughty courtiers. She could not believe that Queen Mary could possibly have known about any plot to murder her husband. Could anyone smile so sweetly with such dark knowledge in their heart?

All round the inn, people were arguing. Some were

defending Queen Mary, others were insinuating that she was the chief plotter, others were saying, "No smoke without fire."

"Tell me this," said the man in black, "if our precious queen is so distraught with grief, why did she go to yet another wedding only two days after the explosion? And now I've heard she's gone to Seton, and is playing golf and dilly-dallying with her ladies in the garden!"

"The poor queen can't lie abed all day!" the innkeeper's wife said, though with a shade of uncertainty in her voice.

"If she's well enough to play golf, I can't see why she's not well enough to find out who murdered her husband!" the red-faced man retorted, banging one fist on the table.

"Isn't that the job of the sheriff?" someone enquired, which elicited a bitter laugh from the red-faced man.

"And who, pray tell, is the Sheriff of Edinburgh?" he sneered. "Why, Lord Bothwell, of course, the queen's favourite! And may I add that some of Bothwell's men were let into the city only a scant half-hour before the explosion, their plaids wrapped well about their heads so their faces couldn't be seen!"

Hannah started guiltily, colour surging to her cheeks. She dared not look at Angus, or Linnet, or any of her friends, who were all listening just as intently, turning their faces from speaker to speaker, Max squinting to see without his spectacles.

Cries and exclamations rang out all round the crowded, smoky room.

"You cannot mean . . . I don't believe it!"

"No!"

"Really? But. . ."

"They say Lord Darnley and Lord Bothwell have hated each other for years."

"You can hate a man without deciding to blow him to smithereens!"

"I bet it was those foreigners she keeps hanging round her," someone else said. "All those Frenchies and Italianos, always singing and playing the lute. Faugh! It makes me ill!"

Max scowled and looked like he would like to protest, but Linnet surreptitiously shook her head, laying one hand on the boy's arm.

On and on the discussion raged, growing ever more heated. Angus got up, paid quietly, and led the party outside again.

"But I thought we were going to stay overnight?" Scarlett protested. "In nice, soft, warm beds, with pillows and blankets. . ."

"And bed lice, probably," Max said.

"At least it was warm in there," Donovan said, pulling his sheepskin coat back on. "Though didn't it stink?"

"If there isn't a fight before much longer, my name isn't Angus MacDonnell," the old man responded, hoisting his unstrung bow back over his shoulder. "We're better off out of it."

"Never mind, my lambs," Linnet consoled them. "At least we're not hungry."

"Hag-stone, help us on our quest, where is the ring thrown to the west?" Hannah asked in the cold, frosty dawn, the hag-stone lifted to her eye, as she had done every dawn since leaving Edinburgh.

She saw nothing but a swirl of spinning water. Her heart sank. She thought as she walked, trying out different rhymes, but every time she asked she saw the same vision. That night, as they sat wearily by the campfire, eating their thin broth, she asked: "Angus, do you know of any whirlpool around this way?"

He shook his head, but Linnet said, "There is the Hag's Washtub west of here. It is where the Cailleach Bheur goes to wash her great plaid. When it is all clean and white again, she then flings it across the land so it too is white again."

Hannah remembered Miss Underhill, with her blue-painted face and her orange lantern, intoning, "The ocean's whirlpool is my washtub. . ."

"Where is the Hag's Washtub?" she asked in a leaden voice.

Linnet shrugged. "I'm sorry, my chick, I do not know. I have just heard the old tales. In the western islands somewhere."

"Do you know how many islands there are on the west coast?" Scarlett demanded.

Both Linnet and Hannah shook their heads.

"Hundreds. Maybe even thousands! I don't think anyone knows!" Scarlett spread wide her arms in a dramatic gesture.

"I'm betting there's only one whirlpool," Donovan said drily.

As so often proved to be the case, Donovan was right. The closer they came to the coast, the more stories they heard about the Hag's Washtub. No one had ever managed to navigate across it. It was a ship's graveyard. You could hear its hungry roar more than ten miles away.

Nearly three weeks after leaving Dumbarton, the six footsore travellers came at last to the coast. It had been a slow and arduous journey because of the many lochs and hills and forests that had to be crossed or circumnavigated. The ferryman who took them across Loch Fyne had told them to head towards Port Righ, a small fishing village on Loch Crinan. It was, he said, the closest port to the Gulf of Corryvreckan, the turbulent stretch of water between the islands of Juta and Scarba where the Hag's Washtub was to be found.

Port Righ was a very small village, with only a handful of stone cottages built on the rocky shore of a harbour protected by a steep headland. Small, shabby boats were pulled up on to the mud, and men sat on the rocks smoking long clay pipes and mending nets and sails. They stared in surprise at the small party of travellers who came wearily down the steep goat track, and nudged each other and whispered.

"We're looking for passage through the Gulf of Corryvreckan," Angus said. "Anyone willing to take us?"

The fishermen all shook their heads, frowning and muttering.

"Are you daft?" one said. "No one sails past the Hag's Washtub!"

Unwillingly Angus took out his purse, still heavy with the coins the queen had given them at Holyrood Palace. He hefted it in his hand. "I'm willing to pay good coin," he said.

Scarlett and Hannah, sitting wearily on the rocks behind him, exchanged looks of unholy glee. Angus never parted with good coin if he could possibly help it.

"I'll take you," one of the fishermen said. He was an elderly man, with a shock of silver hair and beard, skin as thick and brown as old leather, and very blue eyes that squinted up at them from deep creases of wrinkles.

"How much?" Angus asked suspiciously. Then, when the fisherman named his price, he roared, "You bloodsucking mad-headed ape! Have you lost your wits? Who would pay such a sum?"

"Only a witless mad-headed ape would want to sail past the Hag," the old fisherman said amiably, sucking on his pipe. "Since it'll be the death of both of us, I might as well make sure I leave a nice bit of coin for my missus. And you sure won't be needing it."

"Surely it's not as impossible as all that," Linnet said gently. "You look like a man who knows the sea. I'm sure if anyone could tame the Hag, it would be you."

The fisherman's blue eyes twinkled up at Linnet. "You think to cozen me with sweet words? It just might have worked if I was forty years younger, and if your father hadn't called me a mad-headed ape."

"Please," Hannah said. "It's really important."

"That you risk your lives to have a look at the Hag? I can't see why."

"Something was lost there," Hannah said. "We've got to get it back."

His blue eyes gleamed with interest. "A treasure hunt? Well, well. Perhaps if I was to have part of the treasure. . ."

"It's of no real value," Hannah said. "Except to me."

He frowned at that, and sucked on his pipe. There was a long silence. Hannah gazed at Angus with pleading eyes.

The old man gave a sigh. "We need to head north afterwards," he said in a long-suffering tone. "If you will take us past the whirlpool, and then up the Firth of Lorne and to the north, then I will pay you the sum you asked for. But you must get us safely north first."

"Where in the north?" the boatman demanded. "As far as Fort William?"

"Maybe," Angus said. "Maybe not."

The boatman frowned more deeply. "I'd want the money now."

"Not a chance," Angus said. "Half now, half when we land safely."

There was another long pause.

"Take it or leave it," Angus said.

"All right, you bloodsucking mad-headed ape, it's a deal," the boatman said, spitting on his hand and holding it out for Angus to shake. Angus shook, and then, looking

295

very dour, counted out a pile of coins into the boatman's leathery brown hand. The boatman weighed each one in his palm, bit it carefully to check it was really gold, then gave Angus an astonishingly sweet smile. "Fergus MacGillivray, at your service, sir. And a pleasure it is to be working for such a generous, open-handed gentleman!"

Angus snorted in disgust.

The Hag

It was midmorning when they employed Fergus, but they could not set out at once, for the old boatman had to finish mending his sails and provisioning his boat. He allowed the six weary travellers to camp in his cow-byre, for an extra fee, which Angus paid begrudgingly, and only because it had begun to rain heavily.

The next morning dawned grey and blustery. Fergus shook his head. "I'm sorry, my bairns, but we're not going anywhere today."

"But we have to," Hannah said.

"Hear that?" Fergus asked. "That's the Hag roaring. Any man with sense knows not to go out when the Hag is angry."

Hannah could indeed hear a low, continuous roaring to the west. She looked at her friends in dismay.

The next day Fergus said the same, and the next day too. By that time, Hannah was sick to death of baked herring, the cottage, the smell of Fergus's pipe, and her companions. "We can't spend the whole winter cooped up here," she said crossly. "We have to keep moving!"

"It's too dangerous," Fergus said. "You may be paying me a king's ransom, but that doesn't mean I want to die in your service."

Linnet looked troubled. She had spent much of the previous day standing in the doorway, staring out at the rain. "Hannah," she said in a low voice. "Why don't you use the hag-stone? Weather magic is one of its powers, didn't you know?"

Hannah turned to her in surprise. She remembered the entry on hag-stones in her father's notebook. It had said something about storms, she remembered now.

"But how?" Hannah instinctively held the hag-stone out to Linnet.

She stared at it with a strange look on her face. "Once you give a hag-stone away, you cannot take it back again," she said softly.

Hannah's fingers closed about the stone and her hand fell down by her side.

Linnet nodded. "I'd like my lady's hag-stone back again one day, to take home with me. It is one of the treasures of my land, always carried by the crown prince or princess. Your father gave it to you, and you must keep it until it is time for you to pass it on too."

My father didn't give it to me, a toad in the witch's pool did, Hannah thought, but she did not say anything. She found the gift of the toad obscurely embarrassing, because it was so very odd.

"Will you tell me how to use it then?" she asked.

Linnet nodded. "If I can. It's wild magic and thus mysterious, a magic of instinct and impulse. It cannot be taught like the words of a spell or a sorcerer's drawing of symbols."

"So what do I do? To drive away the storm, I mean," Hannah said.

"I'd hang the stone on a cord and swing it about your head," Linnet said. "Make sure you keep a tight hold of the cord, though; you do not want to lose it."

"No," Hannah said in heartfelt agreement. She found a long piece of leather cord, strung the hag-stone upon it and hung it about her neck, tucking it inside her bodice. Then she went to the doorway and peered out into the pouring rain. "I'm going to go for a walk," she announced.

"Are you crazy?" Scarlett said. "You'll get soaked."

"I *will* go crazy if I have to spend any more time in this cottage with you lot," Hannah said rudely.

"Well, I hope you get soaking wet and catch pneumonia," Scarlett returned.

"Remember they don't have antibiotics here," Max warned her. "If you do get pneumonia, you'll probably die."

Donovan uttered a groan and jumped to his feet. "I'll come with you, Hannah! I'm going stir-crazy too."

"OK," Hannah said, though the idea of Donovan watching her use the hag-stone made her feel hot and uncomfortable. "Though it's bucketing down!"

299

"I don't melt," Donovan said scornfully. "Not like the sugarplum fairy there."

Scarlett stuck out her tongue at him, and went back to chipping the old polish off her toenails.

After the first few minutes, Hannah and Donovan got used to the rain and even began to enjoy it. The air smelled so fresh, full of salt and seaweed. The mud was damp and cool under their bare feet, for they had taken off their boots and most of their clothes so they had something dry to change into when they got home. Seabirds wheeled in the blustery wind, calling out to each other in their raucous voices.

"What a good idea this was!" Donovan said. "I hate being cooped up inside."

"Me too!"

The wind was so strong it almost blew them over. Donovan spread wide his arms and ran in great swooping curves, like a hawk riding the aerial currents. Hannah swung the hag-stone round and round her head, chanting, "Rain, rain, go away, come back another day!" It seemed as good a rhyme as anything she could come up with on her own.

She raced along the beach, dragging the hag-stone through the tumultuous waters. "Waves, waves, calming down, choose another day to frown," she chanted. She felt amazingly free and light and, for the first time in her life, completely unselfconscious. Donovan seemed to take her chanting and capering for granted. He never did mock her, she realized, not even when she had first begun to talk about fairies and curses and travelling back in time. She felt a smile curve her mouth.

"It's stopped raining," Donovan said.

"I think the sea's calming down as well."

Donovan stared out at the bay, frowning, his eyes as grey as the wind-ruffled water. "So it is," he said slowly, and looked at her sideways.

Hannah slipped the hag-stone back over her head. "Let's go tell Fergus. I think we should set out just as soon as we can."

Donovan was silent on the walk back to the village and glanced at her once or twice, but did not say anything. Hannah was glad. The power of the hag-stone troubled her as much as it thrilled her, and she wanted as little talk about it as possible. They burnt witches here.

"Glory be," Fergus said, pushing his cap to the back of his head and scratching his balding temple. "I thought that storm was here for days. Well now, it's coming up to low tide. I guess if we want to see the Hag at her quietest, we'd best be getting a move on."

"Well done," Linnet said softly. "You have a gift for it, no doubt of that."

Hannah felt warm all through with pleasure.

Despite the magic of the hag-stone, it was still a rough, tumultuous ride out of the loch and into the Sound of Jura, the boat's brown, patched sails billowing in the wind. On the far shore of the loch was a small grey castle; otherwise bare brown hills rose high all around, capped with mist. Scarlett gripped the side of the boat with both hands, the wind whipping her blonde hair across her face, which had lost its roses. Max too had lost as much colour as it was possible for someone with his olive skin to lose. It made him look oddly green.

"Seasickness is . . . caused by . . . the disturbance . . . to the inner ear," he said. "You just need . . . to . . . look . . . at the horizon. . ." His last words disappeared as he vomited violently over the side of the boat. Scarlett clapped her hand over her mouth.

Hannah looked round. "What's wrong?"

"Doctor Death is seasick," Donovan said.

"Just need to . . . trick my brain . . . into thinking . . . we're steady," Max said, and was sick again.

Linnet bent over him, her hand rubbing his back.

"Ewww, yuck," Scarlett cried and scrambled up to the prow of the boat, where Hannah and Donovan clung to the wooden gunwales of the boat, revelling in the fresh wind, which tasted of salt.

They passed a flock of small islands, some no more than bare rocks rising out of the sea, and headed towards the coast of Jura, which lay due west. Its landscape was dominated by three tall snow-capped hills that lay in a row. Seabirds followed the boat, crying raucously. Some made spectacular dives from high in the air, plummeting below the wave and then bursting out minutes later with silver-backed fish wriggling in their long beaks. They were gannets, Donovan told Hannah, and nested in their hundreds of thousands on the islands to the west.

About an hour later, the little wooden boat rounded Jura's northernmost tip. The waves were wild and mackerel-backed with foam, and the boat pitched and swayed and spun so that Max moaned and clutched his stomach, occasionally retching miserably. Hannah could hear the roar of the whirlpool clearly. She leant forward, half excited, half filled with dread.

It was not what she had expected. Somehow she had imagined a perfect whirl, like water being sucked down a plughole. Instead, the water churned about in wild confusion, waves crashing up against other waves with a slap of spray and a swirl of spume.

"The tide's on the ebb," Fergus shouted from the tiller. "The Hag's much calmer now. You should see her when the tide is on the flood! Glory be! That's a sight to chill your soul."

Hannah looked down into the white-frothed, churning water and felt her stomach sink. She pulled out the hag-stone and held it to her left eye. "Magic stone, show my eye, where the puzzle ring does lie."

Her gaze was plunged beneath the water, down, down, down, to the black swirling depths. She could just see, through the murk, a tall pinnacle of rock, encrusted with barnacles. Caught on an upreaching finger of stone was something that glinted, faintly, gold.

She swallowed and tucked away the hag-stone with

fingers that trembled. "Fergus, could you drop anchor here?"

He opened his blue eyes wide. "Here? You must be joking!"

Hannah shook her head. "I have to dive down to the Hag. If you could drop the anchor down on to the rock, I'd have something to hold on to and guide me back up."

"You mad-headed fool!" Angus roared. "You can't dive down there!"

"I have to," Hannah said. "The ring's down there. It'll be all right. I've dived before."

Though in warm, clear, tropical waters, not into a freezing-cold, murky-dark whirlpool, she thought to herself.

"I won't let you!" Angus raged. "You'll be killing yourself!"

"No one's ever dived down to the Hag before," Fergus said.

Linnet knelt down before her and took her hands. "The hag-stone will calm the waters, but not for long," she said in a strained whisper. "And when the waters are released, they will be wilder than ever. You must be quick."

"I'll be as quick as I possibly can." Hannah began to strip off her clothes.

"Oh, Hannah, I don't want you to die!" Scarlett wailed.

"I'm telling you, lass, it's too dangerous! I'd never have brought you out here if I thought you were going to try and swim the whirlpool!" Fergus shouted.

"Don't be a fool," Angus pleaded.

"I wonder how far down it is?" Max said, holding

304

his arms across his aching stomach. "You know you go crazy if you go too far down? They call it 'rapture of the deep'. People pull off their scuba gear and think they see mermaids and stuff."

"I won't be wearing any scuba gear," Hannah said grimly, standing shivering on the deck in her smock.

"Can we tie a rope or something to you?" Donovan was very pale. "So we can pull you back up?"

"That's a good idea. I'll tug on it three times if I need you to haul me up." Hannah's voice sounded far away even to her own ears. Her legs felt rubbery. Donovan and Angus rushed to find a spare coil of rope, while Fergus brought the boat around – a long and difficult process that involved lowering his square sail, lifting it to the other side of the mast, and hoisting it again on new tack. The whole time, the boat dipped and lurched like a bucking bronco, and Max stopped talking about the symptoms of diving too deep and was heartily sick again all over the deck.

"If you see any crabs scuttling for cover, it's time to come back up," Fergus said urgently. "Oh, glory be! Why am I letting you do this?"

"It's not up to you to say what we can and can't do," Angus roared, in a surprising about-face. "We're paying you a bag of gold, so shut your mouth and mind your boat!"

Hannah dived overboard. The cold was like a blow to her lungs. For a moment, she could not persuade her arms and legs to move. Water boiled about her, grey and

305

white and speckled with foam. The hag-stone hung about her neck on its cord. Afraid it would be lost in the water's turbulence, Hannah put it in her mouth, then dived under the surface, following the angle of the anchor rope.

Visibility was very poor. She swam as much by feel as by sight. Soon, the blood was pounding in her ears and still she had seen no sign of the underwater rock formation they called the Hag. She surfaced, panting and dizzy, and clung to the anchor rope. Again she dived and, fuelled by desperation, kicked harder than she had ever kicked before, the hag-stone still clenched between her teeth.

Down she dived, peering through the murk, feeling the cold bite into her very bones. Suddenly something slid past her legs, sleek and fast. Hannah involuntarily gasped with terror. *Shark!* she thought, and recoiled. A moment later she saw more racing past, their bellies flashing white. She curled herself into a ball, gripping the anchor rope with dread-stiffened fingers. They were small whales, she saw, or perhaps large, black-skinned dolphins. As they zoomed past, she relaxed. Only then did she realize that she was breathing, in fast, harsh gasps that burst out of her mouth in a twirl of tiny bubbles. In her surprise, she drew her breath in sharply, past the hag-stone, and tasted pure oxygen. Realization, joy and excitement fizzed together in her blood. In a flash, she uncurled her body and plunged downwards, swimming strongly, into the greenish gloom.

She had never dived so deep. It must have been twenty times her own length. The water was vast and dark and eerie. Currents buffeted her, dragging her away from the anchor rope, but she kept one hand upon it to guide her, and kept on swimming down.

Black and tall and twisted, her feet lost in the abyss, the Hag reached up towards Hannah. Her hair was drifting green seaweed, and she had a thousand tiny blind eyes. Hannah came down lightly by the anchor and felt about with one hand, searching for the loop of the puzzle ring. It was like trying to see through twilight, although above the surface it was midmorning. Everything was soft and vague and hidden, except for the currents tugging at her, pulling Hannah's hair sideways.

She had to let go of the anchor. At once Hannah felt herself dragged towards the abyss. Frantically her hands groped over the rock. She felt a protrusion of stone and, caught firmly upon it, a slender circlet of something smooth. She yanked till it broke free. Clutching it in her hand, Hannah twisted about and tried to swim back towards the anchor, her breath rasping in her throat in her panic. The current was too strong. She was being dragged away. Hannah kicked and kicked, but her legs felt limp and weak.

Suddenly another black and white whale came barrelling out of the abyss, slamming into her and knocking her sideways. She was flung against the stone pillar, tearing her skin on the barnacles. The hag-stone was knocked out of her mouth and would have fallen into the abyss had it not been secured about her neck by the cord. The whale spun about and came racing towards her, its jaws gaping open. Hannah choked back a scream, frantically shoving the hag-stone back in her mouth so she could breathe. She then slipped the golden loop on to her ring finger, clenched her fist about it, and swung round to the other side of the Hag. The whale went past in a stream of bubbles, moving astonishingly fast.

Hannah seized the rope about her waist and yanked it three times. At once she was jerked upwards. The rope about her middle hurt her cruelly as she was dragged, in rough fits and bursts, towards the surface. Hannah could have wept with relief. She tried to help, but her arms and legs were so tired she could barely find the energy to move them. She looked round anxiously for the whale, and saw it swooping towards her. At once she spat out the hag-stone and thrust it towards the whale, shouting silently in her mind, seven times, "I defy thee!"

To her relief, the whale spun away, as if it had slammed into a wall of glass, and disappeared into the black abyss. Hannah was dragged, coughing and choking, out of the water and on to the deck.

"I thought you would've had enough of almost drowning." Donovan's mouth was twisted in a wry half-smile.

Hannah managed to smile back, opening her hand to show him the slim hoop of oddly twisted gold upon her finger.

The Blue Men

"Ahoy port side!" Fergus shouted late the following afternoon, as the small boat sailed up the Firth of Lorne.

"What is it?" Angus shouted back.

"I don't know. It looked like a man, but it can't be."

Hannah stared out across the choppy water. "Gosh, look, there's hundreds of them," she cried.

Men with wild hair and beards were bobbing up and down all around the boat. Their skin was not the blue of a summer sky but rather the clammy, skimmed-milk colour of men who had been submerged in cold water a long time.

"Where's the boat hook?" Angus shouted. "Let's drag the poor souls aboard!"

"No!" Linnet cried. Everyone stared at her in astonishment. "They're Blue Men! Have you not heard of them? They'll wreck the boat for sure!"

"The Blue Men of the Minch?" Angus demanded. "What are they doing so far south?"

"They must serve the black witch!" she cried.

One of the blue men spun a long, stone staff, and the wind roared, rocking the boat dangerously. The sails cracked like whips, and one tore free, flapping wildly. Rain lashed their faces, yet sunshine gleamed on the waters of the bay behind them and glowed on the distant hills of the Isle of Mull.

"If this keeps up, we'll go down for sure," Fergus cried, clinging to the rudder. "What do they want with us?"

"To drown us, of course," Linnet snapped.

"To drown the puzzle ring," said Hannah, fingering the hard bulges in the hem of her chemise, where she had sewed the two golden loops.

"But why? Why does the black witch care about the puzzle ring?" Max demanded, looking greener than ever as the boat rocked wildly from side to side.

"She thrives on chaos and unhappiness, so the last thing she wants is for me to break the curse," Hannah said. "Besides, there's the prophecy. 'The thorn tree shall not bud, the green throne shall not sing, until the child of true blood is crowned the rightful king.' She's afraid the true heir will be found once the curse is broken!"

The wind howled like a banshee, and a great wave washed over the prow of the boat, knocking them all down and almost sweeping them overboard. The Blue Men shouted in triumph, as the sea surged in great grey-green waves around them.

"What can we do?" Scarlett cried. "I don't want to die!"

"The only way to defeat them is to beat them in a rhyming contest," Linnet gasped, wrapping both arms about the mast.

"Hannah's good at rhymes!" Scarlett cried.

"Not that good," Hannah protested. "Doggerel only."

"I don't even know what doggerel means!" Scarlett exclaimed. "Come on, Hannah! If we drown now, you'll never break the curse."

Again the leader whirled his spear above his head, and at once the little boat was spun in a maelstrom of wind and water. The sail came crashing down in a tangle of rope, and Fergus would have been swept overboard if Angus had not lunged forward and caught him by his belt.

"How dare you sail our sacred seas?" the Blue Man roared.

Hannah tried to think. "Bees, keys, wheeze. . . ." she muttered. "Ease. . ."

Again the Blue Man whirled about his white spear. As the boat spun, Hannah shouted: "Why should we not float at our ease, instead of fighting the angry waves?"

The Blue Man uttered a short, harsh laugh. "Why should *we* not show *you* our caves, deep beneath the white foam?"

"Thank you, but I prefer the sky's blue dome," she answered, quick as a flash, "where I can breathe the pure, fresh air."

"Where every day is weighted with care? Let us release you to the fathomless deep."

"I would rather laugh and run and leap," Hannah returned, trying to think of a word that had no rhyme he could match. "Knowing I'll walk again in sunshine."

Without even a blink he answered, "Yet you could be swimming with me in the brine, diving through the great blue sea."

"Please, we would so much rather sail free, we mean you no harm, I promise."

He floated upright in the water, frowning, then bowed his head in agreement. With a flick of their tails, the Blue Men dived beneath the waves and were gone.

"I promise," Hannah breathed. "Of course. That's a hard one to rhyme with."

Scarlett and Max and Donovan leapt up and down, shouting with joy. "I knew you could do it!" Scarlett shrieked.

"Well done, my lamb," Linnet said, hugging her warmly.

"It was just luck," Hannah said. "I didn't have time to think. I just said the first thing that came into my head. I could've said 'I swear' and then he could have said pear, or mare, or square. . ."

"That was amazing," Donovan said. "You were so quick."

"I didn't feel quick," Hannah grinned. "I felt as thick as a brick."

"Oh, God, she can't stop," Donovan said, laughing. Max and Scarlett laughed too, and somehow once they started they couldn't stop. Angus could only shake his head in bewilderment.

They rested that night on the island of Lismore, and the next day Fergus worked to repair the damage wrought on the boat by the Blue Men's storm.

Hannah got up at sunrise and went out alone, taking only her rowan walking stick with her. She found a high outcrop of stone, with early crocuses and daffodils pushing their way through the grass, and drew out the holey stone.

> *"Hag-stone, where is the last loop, the fourth,*
> *that was flung to the north?"*

The landscape raced towards her, forest and mountain and moor, river and waterfall and circles of standing stones. At last it steadied, and Hannah could see a tall, cone-shaped mountain through the hole in the hag-stone. Its peak, perfect as any in a child's drawing, was streaked with snow. Below it stood a tall rock, split right down the middle so that it resembled two hands folded together in prayer. The light of the rising sun struck upon the rock, making the lichen glow, and glittering upon a shard of gold that rested on the very tip of the stone hands.

"It sounds like Schiehallion," Max said when Hannah described the mountain to her friends on her return. "That's the only mountain I know of that looks like a perfect isosceles triangle."

"Schiehallion," Hannah repeated, trying to give it the same thunderous roll over her tongue. "Shee-HALLION!"

"It sounds like some kind of war cry, doesn't it? It means 'hill of the fairies', though," Donovan said. "Not quite so macho."

"It's got to be the right place," Hannah said. "So far the rings have all been found at fairy places, haven't they?"

Linnet nodded. "Schiehallion is a gateway to the Otherworld. I do not know these praying hands, though."

"I guess we'll find them when we get there," Scarlett said.

"If we're quick enough, we can get the last loop and get back to Fairknowe by the spring equinox," Hannah said. "That's the twenty-second of March. I wonder what the date is today? If we don't get back in time, we need to wait till the next thin day, which is not till the first of May."

Scarlett jumped up. "Well, let's get a move on then!"

Within the hour, the little boat was sailing up Loch Linnhe and by early evening had tacked into the mouth of Loch Leven, which lay at the foot of the mighty Glencoe Mountains. Black and grim, with snow on their hunched heads and mist huddled about their bare shoulders, the mountains seemed ancient and impenetrable. Hannah felt a shiver run down her spine. She closed her hand about the hag-stone, which still hung on its ribbon about her neck. For the first time it occurred to her that her hag-stone was made of the same substance as these old mountains, worn by wind and water over centuries to a mere nub she

314

could slide her finger through. She had wondered at its inexplicable powers, which let her see over vast distances, understand strange tongues, and breathe deep beneath the surface of the sea. She wondered no longer.

"So what do we do now?" Scarlett asked when they had made their farewells to Fergus and paid him the money they owed, and watched him tack his little boat away over the shining water.

Angus looked sour. "We start walking."

Glencoe was a long, narrow valley, filled with the shining waters of the loch. On either side the steep mountains soared a thousand metres high. It made Hannah's head spin looking up at them. She looked down, concentrating on the rough ground under her feet. Her arms and legs did not seem to want to work properly. *It's just adapting to solid land again*, she told herself. She crossed her arms over her chest, hugging herself against the chills that racked her. The others were a long way ahead now. Hannah stopped on the top of a slope and bent over, trying to catch her breath, as the others turned, calling to her.

They spent the night in a crofter's cottage, huddled together in the stable on a pile of damp straw. When Hannah woke she knew she was not well. Her head ached, her limbs felt weak and her throat was hot and sore. She said nothing, though. All Hannah wanted to do now was find the last loop of the puzzle ring and go home. It had taken them so much longer than she had expected, and the spring equinox was hurtling towards them. The very thought of not making it back to Fairknowe in time was enough to propel her up off the straw and back on the road.

The six companions reached the top of the mountain range and began to cross Rannoch Moor, a bleak, bare, windswept expanse of peat bogs, heather, long stretches of lonely lochs, and weirdly shaped granite rocks. Clouds raced over the sky, bringing squalls of cold, stinging rain to lash their faces. Hawks called eerily, swinging through the sky. All Hannah could do was put one foot forward after another. She felt as if she had travelled a thousand years back in time, ten hundred thousand years, to a time before humans.

By nightfall, Hannah had fallen far behind the others. The ground was undulating beneath her feet as if her slight weight were irritating the hide of some immense and stony creature. She leant heavily on the rowan walking stick, afraid she might fall.

"Hannah, are you all right? What's wrong?" Donovan came quickly towards her.

"I don't feel so good," she said.

"What's up?"

"My head . . . my throat. . ." She tried to swallow, but it felt as if she had razor blades instead of tonsils.

"Max!" Donovan called.

"What is it?" Max came bounding towards them, thin-legged as a grasshopper. The setting sun glinted off his glasses.

"Hannah feels sick."

"Oh, goody!" Max rubbed his hands together. "A medical emergency. Doctor Max is here." He took Hannah's wrist, pretending to read her pulse in a doctorly manner, but almost immediately his expression sobered. "Your pulse is galloping away. Ouch! You're burning up. You really are sick."

"I don't feel so good," Hannah said, and leant against Donovan.

"We'd better get her some shelter," Max said. "I think she's got the flu."

"I'm not surprised, swimming in the ocean in March," Scarlett said.

"You don't get the flu from getting cold," Max said. "It's a virus. Let's hope it's not a bad one. Hannah won't have any resistance to sixteenth-century viruses."

It took the companions more than an hour, walking slowly, before Angus found a small cottage where he could knock and ask for help. Built in a narrow dip between hills, with a view across Loch Eigheach, it was little more than one room with a low shed attached, where a goat was penned in with lengths of driftwood.

A young woman opened the door a mere crack. She was thin as a stick and white as whey. "Wha' do you want?" she asked in such a strong accent that Hannah could barely understand a word.

"We have a sick lass here," Angus said. "She needs warmth, shelter. . ."

The woman shook her head. Her tangled brown hair hung lankly about her thin face. "I don't want any sickness

317

here. I'm wi' bairn." She opened the door a smidgen wider so they could see she was heavily pregnant, the hard bulge of her belly pushing out her ragged dress.

"Please," Linnet said. "She cannot walk any further. Can we shelter in your shed?"

"I don't want you here," the woman said. "My man's been called up by the laird and I'm here all alone." Her voice quavered with fear.

"If you let us use your shed, we can help you," Angus said. "These lads are strong. They can gather firewood for you, and draw water from the loch. . ."

"We don't go near the loch if we can help it," the woman said with a shudder.

"What is your name, lass?" Linnet said kindly.

"Edie," she said after a moment, her eyes narrowed suspiciously.

"Edie, my name is Linnet. I can help you too. I can clean for you, and sew, and milk the goat, and I can make up some tea for you to help the pains in your belly."

"Very well then, you can stay, but I don't want you or your fever anywhere near the house, and you must help me while my man is gone. Tether the goat out under the trees; he'll come to no harm outdoors for a day or two."

Linnet nodded and gently guided Hannah into the shed, which was filthy and smelled strongly of goat.

"My guess is she'll make us work hard for the privilege of staying in this muck," Linnet said grimly. "Come, my lamb, sit and I'll see if I can clean it up a little."

The Devil's Influence

The next few days were a blur. The fever made the world seem as fragile and transparent as cellophane, another, darker world pressing up close behind. Hannah heard weird laughter and sobbing and a high whining sound, and saw, against her closed eyelids, faces like demons, contorted and coloured like dancing flames.

"Hannah, you must give me the hag-stone," a demon with Linnet's soft voice said. "I can heal you."

"No!" Hannah cried. "It's a trick. Go away!"

"I'll give it back to you," the demon promised.

"You're lying," Hannah sobbed. "Leave me alone."

"Can't you just take it?" some other demon asked.

"Hag-stones can only be found or given," the demon with Linnet's voice said. "If I take it, it will turn against me."

Hannah could not make sense of the words. She felt like she was in the abyss again, fighting hard to swim to the surface, while the black immutable tide dragged her down.

She wanted her mother, and wept at her absence. She wanted Linnet. Not the slim young woman she knew now but the stooped old woman with the lilting voice and cloudy eyes she had known before. She wanted to be at home in her own bed, in crisp sheets smelling of lemon washing powder and her quilt with all its soft velvets and silken patches that she loved to rub between her fingers. She wanted it all so badly she could not help sobbing, which made her headache and sore throat worse.

"It's all right, Hannah." Donovan laid a cool damp cloth on her forehead. She stared at him blankly, then turned her crimson face from side to side, her breath sharp in her throat.

"She's got a high fever," Max said. "We've got to bring her temperature down. I've already given her all the aspirin I brought with me, and there's not exactly a chemist nearby where we can buy more." His voice was bitter rather than sarcastic.

"There's an elder tree down by the loch," Linnet said. "Both elderberries and the flowers are good for fevers. I'll go and see if it's blossoming yet."

She was back a few minutes later, a green flowering branch in her hand, a rueful expression on her face. "That girl Edie saw me praying to the tree," she confessed in a low voice. "We do not cut an elder tree without asking permission first, for it's sacred to the Great Mother, you know. But now she thinks me a witch and has barricaded

320

herself inside her house, weeping and praying. I think we should leave as soon as we can."

"We can't go till Hannah's fever has broken," Max said firmly.

"Is she going to die?" Scarlett asked, clasping her hands together.

"Lots of people died of the flu in the olden days," Max admitted.

"She's not going to die!" Donovan said fiercely.

"Let me make her some tea from the elderflowers," Linnet said, "and maybe she'll be well enough to leave in the morning."

Linnet lifted Hannah up and held a cup of something hot and fragrant to her lips. Hannah drank it down gratefully, then fell back asleep. She woke some time later, to find Linnet kneeling beside her again, holding the steaming cup.

"Hannah, will you dip the hag-stone in the cup?" she whispered. "It will help heal you."

Hannah managed to lean up on one elbow and dangle the hag-stone in the cup, before drawing it out by its cord and letting it hang about her neck once more. She drank down the elderflower tea, and sank back on to the straw. Within seconds she was asleep again, but this time her sleep was sweet. When she woke, the fever had passed.

"Do you know what influenza means?" Max asked when Hannah told them what she had seen and heard while in her fever. "It's from the Spanish for 'influence'.

Spanish doctors called it 'Influenza de Diablo', because they thought only the Devil could cause such a sickness."

"The things you know." Scarlett shook her head in mock amazement. "Where do you get all this stuff from?"

"Books," Max said. "You know, things made from words printed on paper and bound together. I'm sure you must've seen one even if you've never opened one."

"Ha, ha, very funny," Scarlett said.

Hannah found she remembered how to smile.

Her legs were very wobbly when she got up and walked around. She insisted she was well enough to move on, however, for her anxiety about the passing of time was far sharper than her desire to lie down again.

"I'll just go and thank that poor girl," she said. "Angus, do we have any money left? Can't we give her a coin or something?"

"I think the sweat of our brows is payment enough," Angus said grumpily. "Me and the lads have worked mighty hard these last few days." He fished in his purse, though, and brought out a coin, which he gave to Hannah. She went and knocked on the door. It opened a crack, and the young woman looked out suspiciously.

"I just wanted to thank you," Hannah said. "It was kind of you to let us use your shed. I'm much better now."

The young woman grunted and went to shut the door, but Hannah put out her hand and touched her arm. "I have a little something for you, to thank you," she said. To her chagrin the girl screamed and jerked her hand away as if Hannah's fingers had burnt her. "The Devil's hand!" she screamed. "You touched me wi' the Devil's hand!"

Blushing scarlet, Hannah snatched her left hand away and put it behind her back. "I . . . I'm sorry, I didn't mean. . ." she stammered, but the young woman slammed the door shut and Hannah could hear her sobbing inside.

"We'd better get out of here," Scarlett said with a giggle. "Next she'll be waving ropes of garlic at us, or bringing out her cross."

"Not unless she wishes to be burnt for a Catholic," Angus said dourly. "Come on then, let's go."

"She's all alone, and very close to her time," Linnet said sadly. "She must be afraid of strangers, and we brought sickness and fever into her house. I am not surprised she's glad to see us go!"

The path wound away from the little house, heading north. Angus stood on the crest of the hill, shading his eyes and looking east. "The fairy mountain is that way," he said, pointing. "I can just see its peak. The shortest way will be along the loch shore. It's a fair walk, lassie. I could do it in a day, but you're looking rather peaky. I think we'd better take it slow."

"I wonder what day it is," Scarlett said, some hours later. "It's so hard to keep track without a calendar."

"The days are growing longer," Linnet said. "Soon it shall be the equinox, where the day is as long as the night for the first time in months."

"The thin day," Hannah said.

Linnet nodded.

"Can we get back to Fairknowe in time?" Hannah asked.

Linnet gave an expressive shrug. "I don't think so," she said gently. "Not even if we found the missing loop today. It'd take a miracle."

"A miracle like finding a horse to ride?" Scarlett asked in an odd tone of voice.

Hannah looked up. To her surprise and delight, a tall bay horse stood on the shore. It whickered with pleasure at the sight of them and pranced forward a few steps.

"What a beauty!" Donovan cried. He bent and plucked a handful of grass, and the horse lipped at it delicately. Donovan stroked his curved neck admiringly.

"We could take it in turns to ride," Scarlett said. "It could fit two of us on its back, surely? Think how much faster we'd get along then!"

"That's true," Max said. "But surely it must belong to someone? I'm sure they have a nasty punishment for horse-stealing these days."

"Come away, my lambs, you should never try and mount a horse by water."

"Why on earth not?" Scarlett demanded. "A horse is just what we need! Obviously it's lost. We'll ride it into town and they'll reward us for returning it. I'll catch it!"

"Scarlett, don't!" Linnet called, but Scarlett had caught a handful of mane and commanded Donovan to boost her up. In a moment, she was on the horse's back.

"Oh, you beauty," Scarlett whispered, her face alight. "Isn't

324

he good? He's tame as a lamb. Come on up, Hannah."

"Hannah, no!"

But Hannah had already put her boot in Donovan's linked hands and let him lift her up to the horse's back. "There's heaps of room! Come on up, Max."

"It's not safe," Linnet said urgently. "Have you never been taught not to mount a horse near water? It's not safe."

"You're a funny old thing," Scarlett said indulgently as Max scrambled up behind Hannah. "Whyever not?"

"A horse like that, on the shores of a deserted loch, that grows in length to fit each new passenger, it must be a kelpie!" Linnet wrung her hands in dismay. "Oh, why will you not listen to me?"

Hannah had, of course, read about kelpies. At once she tried to slip down from the horse's back, but he began to grow and grow, writhing and rippling horribly. His beautiful, proud head sprang teeth as sharp as daggers; his neck turned long and slippery as an eel; his body elongated and grew black and slimy. Whiskers sprang from his chin and flippers from his crooked legs. He screeched, high and shrill, and undulated swiftly towards the water, Hannah, Scarlett and Max screaming in terror upon his sinuous back.

"Iron!" Linnet screamed. "We can only tame him with iron!"

The words were barely out of her mouth before Donovan whipped off his iron-studded belt and flung it about the monster's neck. The kelpie screeched and thrashed wildly, flinging Donovan off his feet. Angus seized the two ends of the belt and held the water-horse firm. For one minute, for two minutes, the battle raged, while the muscles in Angus's arms stood out with the effort and his face grew red. At last the monster succumbed, though, and changed shape once more into a tall bay horse, his satiny neck burnt black from the touch of the iron studs. Donovan stood up shakily, wincing as he put weight on one foot.

"You may as well get up on his back too," Angus panted. "Since we've caught ourselves a water-horse, we may as well use it!"

The kelpie cantered the rest of the way to Schiehallion, easily carrying the weight of four tall teenagers, his supple back and legs simply stretching to accommodate them. His black mane and tail writhed in the wind, and he flared his blood-red nostrils and tossed his proud head, snorting and neighing ferociously. Angus pounded along beside him, gripping firmly to the end of the iron-studded belt. The kelpie tried many times to jerk him off his feet, or ram him against a rock or a tree, but the old man was surprisingly quick and nimble, and kept the water-horse under tight control.

Linnet ran behind, never seeming to lose breath or grow tired. She ran as easily and naturally as a gazelle, so lightly that Hannah began to think her feet did not even bend the blades of grass or bruise the early flowers.

Schiehallion dominated the skyline. Tall, perfectly

symmetrical in its proportions, and capped with snow, it arrowed into the blue sky. Hannah could not take her eyes from it. *Let us find the last loop of the puzzle ring and then we can just go home*, she thought.

By early evening it towered above them, set ablaze by the light of the setting sun. It was no longer a perfect isosceles triangle, revealing a long spur of land that ran away to the east. Hannah felt a clutch of anxiety in her chest.

Angus came to a halt, his breath wheezing, his furrowed face red. Linnet was not panting at all. She stepped forward lightly and took the end of the leather belt in both hands. The horse fought her touch, yanking his head back, but she clung on grimly.

"Haven't . . . run like that . . . in years," the old man gasped, bending over, his hands on his knees.

Hannah and her friends slid to the ground, landing in a crumpled heap.

"Ow! I hurt all over!" Max got up stiffly and took a few painful steps. "That horse's spine was bony!"

"I think I've got saddle sores," Donovan said. "Max, you do know the cure for saddle sores, don't you?"

"No more horse riding!" Max said, one hand on his bottom.

"We'll have to ride again," Hannah said. "We have to get back to Fairknowe by the spring equinox, remember, if we want to get home again. The water-horse can carry us much faster than we can walk!"

"Well, I suppose we'd better start searching for the loop,"

Scarlett said, getting to her feet and trying to pretend she did not hurt as much as the other three. "We're looking for a tall, split rock that looks like praying hands, right?"

But although all six companions split up and fanned round the base of the mountain, they could find nothing that looked like the rock Hannah had seen through the hag-stone. Hannah looked through it once more, but saw only the vision she had had before, and when she asked it which way, the little twitch it gave was so slight that Hannah could not tell what way it meant.

"It must be close," she said in frustration. "Let's keep on looking."

Angus had tethered the water-horse to a tree, and as darkness fell, everyone made their way back there, all looking very downcast. The water-horse had once again tried to escape, and the ground was dug up all around where it had reared and trampled. Its neck was scarred with black.

"I'm so sorry," Donovan murmured, stroking its shoulder. "We don't want to hurt you. Won't you settle down now, and stop hurting yourself, and we'll promise we'll let you go just as soon as we can."

The water-horse harrumphed as if in disbelief.

Angus built a fire while the children cut bracken for their beds, and then morosely they ate their brose, wrapped themselves in their grubby plaids and lay down.

It was a clear starry night, and the icy peak of the fairy mountain shone faintly in the starlight. Although Hannah was exhausted, she could not sleep. She hurt too much. She lay and stared at Schiehallion, worrying what to do if she could not find the last loop of the puzzle ring. They had been back in the year 1567 for weeks now. If they failed to return to Fairknowe by the spring equinox, they would be trapped until the next thin day, which was May Day.

Pale green fire flickered over the white peak. Hannah stared, then rubbed her eyes. The green fire rippled and wavered.

"It is the merry dancers," Linnet said softly. She was sitting up by the fire, her plaid drawn close about her face. "The northern lights. It is a sign that the spring equinox is near."

"How near?" Hannah asked.

"Tomorrow, I think," Linnet answered.

Hannah's shoulders slumped.

"It may not matter," Linnet said. "Schiehallion is a gateway too, you know. If we find the ring tomorrow, perhaps you could go through it instead of the gate at Fairknowe."

"You mean we can travel back to our own time from here, instead of travelling all the way back to Fairknowe?" Hannah sat up straight. "Really? That would be fantastic! I mean, we'd still be miles from home, but at least we could catch a bus back, or ring Mum to come and pick us up. Oh, what a good idea!"

Linnet was silent a moment. "My only fear is who – or what – will be guarding the gateway."

"What do you mean?"

"Fairknowe is only a small gateway, rather like a back door. Schiehallion is like the front door. It will not be easy to sneak through. And my lady's cousin, that black-hearted murderess, will be watching."

"But why? Why does she care what we do?"

"She wants to be queen of the fairy realm."

"But. . ." began Hannah, who thought Irata already ruled the fairy realm. Then she remembered that they were in 1657, and it was only a few months since Eglantyne had died. Irata had not yet stolen the throne.

"Already she has caused the death of my lady through her wickedness," Linnet said. "I do not doubt that she means to kill the king too, and my lady's sisters."

"That's right. I forgot Eglantyne had sisters."

"Two. She was the eldest, and then there is Maeve and Morgana. The black one can inherit only if the princesses are all dead. I have had a dreadful fear in me ever since I realized what she was plotting. I tried to get a message to the king, but I have had no answer. All these months, since my lady was tricked and betrayed, I've dreaded what may be happening in my homeland. Mayhap the king is already dead. Mayhap the little princesses too. Already I can see signs of *her* influence in this land: the spy in Edinburgh who plucked your hair, the Blue Men of the Minch travelling so far to challenge us, the water-horse waiting for us on the shores of the loch."

"So Ira . . . I mean, the black witch . . . she wants to

stop me joining the puzzle ring to stop the prophecy being fulfilled? To make sure the child of true blood is not found?"

Linnet nodded. "I fear so. It's the only reason why she would've called upon the Blue Men. They're fairies of this world, not the Otherworld. They are not constrained by its boundaries. The black witch lives in the Otherworld, and can only enter this world on the thin days, or sometimes, if her will is strong, at dawn or dusk or midnight, when the moon is dark or full, or when her name is called. . ."

"And that is why she killed my father," Hannah said passionately. "Or did whatever it was she did to him. Do you think he could still be alive, Linnet? A captive in the Otherworld, perhaps?"

"It's possible. It is not unknown for humans to be taken captive, as punishment or even just for amusement. Although I think she took him, or killed him, to stop him rescuing my lady. We thought she was safe. It was a bitter day when we heard your father had failed." Grief thickened Linnet's voice.

They sat in silence for a while, watching the faint flicker of the northern lights dance across the clear sky.

"So how will we cross through the gateway without her seeing us?" Hannah asked.

"I will find some fern seed and make you a spell of invisibility," Linnet answered. She sounded sad. "I know the secret recipe."

"I really, really want to go home, Linnet."

"Aye. I long for home too. Well, the sooner we find that last loop and join the puzzle ring together, the sooner we can all go home."

The Girl From Under the Hill

But the last loop of the puzzle ring could not be found.

"We'll have to ask someone," Donovan said. "There must be someone who knows where the praying hands are."

"Fortingall is not so very far from here, if I remember rightly," Angus said. "A matter of five miles or so."

"Maybe we could see the praying hands if we climbed Schiehallion," Scarlett suggested. "You can see half of Scotland from up there."

"Great," groaned Max. "How about you climb the mountain and I'll see if I can catch us a fish for dinner. I am so sick of porridge!"

"I'll ride to Fortingall," Angus said. "The less folk see of your strange ways, the better."

"I'll climb the mountain," Linnet said. She was carefully making a thick, brown, unpleasant-smelling paste from fern spores and spring water, adding the golden pollen of some newly opened poppies and some other herbs that

Hannah did not recognize. "Hannah should rest some more. She's still very weak after her fever."

"I'll stay and keep her company," Max offered.

"Well, one of you lads should stay with Linnet and keep her safe," Angus said.

"I guess that means me," Donovan said and got up, tossing Hannah a rueful smile. "At least this means I can add Schiehallion to my list of Munros."

"To your list of what?" Hannah asked.

"Munros are mountains in Scotland over nine hundred and fourteen metres," Donovan explained. "There are two hundred and eighty-four of them. I aim to be the first teenager to bag them all."

"I'll go too," Scarlett said. "Not that I care about bagging Munros, but I hate fishing even more than climbing mountains."

Linnet scraped the gritty brown paste into a pot, pushed the cork back in, and gave it to Hannah. "This should do the trick," she said. "You rub it between your eyes and say, 'Things seen and things not seen, let me walk between.' Keep it safe because I harvested the seeds of all the ferns I could find, and so I cannot make any more."

Angus stumped towards the water-horse, which rolled a panicked eye towards him and began again to try to slip his tether. Angus seized the belt and drew it tight about the horse's neck. "I'll see if I can't buy us a bridle while I'm in Fortingall."

"Oh, don't buy a bridle!" Linnet protested. "It'd be so

cruel to put iron in his mouth when iron hurts him so much. He's a fairy creature, remember."

"If he behaves on the ride in, I'll see about buying just a halter, but if he gives me any trouble, it's a bridle with the heaviest iron bit I can find!" Angus gave the water-horse a stern glance, and he at once looked meek and biddable. With a grunt, Angus mounted, waved his hand in farewell, and rode off.

"Does iron hurt you too?" Hannah asked.

Linnet nodded. "I don't understand why you humans love it so much. It puts me on edge just being near you all, with all that iron about you. And it hurts like a brand to be touched by it. Poor kelpie!"

Hannah put her hand in her pocket and fingered the iron key she still carried there. She had not realized iron would affect Linnet that way. She thought about Linnet in modern-day times, and realized suddenly that she had always seen her use copper saucepans and ladles, and old-fashioned wooden spoons.

It was quiet once they had all gone. Hannah lay back under the tree, turning the hag-stone over in her palm. Max went down to the stream and sat by its rushing waters, a line in his hand, but when she looked round a while later she found him asleep in the grass, his tam o'shanter tipped over his eyes.

The shadows grew longer. Hannah felt restless and anxious. She looked constantly for her friends, but there was no sign of them. When the sun was poised just above the mountains to the west, she caught up her walking stick and went in search of them.

At first the ascent was easy enough, and Hannah enjoyed the sight of the purple hills and mountains rolling away in every direction. Soon, though, the way grew steeper and night pressed in. Early stars prickled the sky. Hannah paused, her heart galloping, a stitch slicing her side. She did not know whether to go on or turn back.

Suddenly she heard desperate sobbing from higher up the mountain, and a little girl came hurtling towards her, barefoot and wild-haired. She practically fell into Hannah's arms. "Help me! Help me! After me!"

"Who? Who's after you?"

"Quick! Please! Help me!"

Hannah cast a quick glance up the mountain and heard a deep, throbbing growl that made the hairs on her arms stand upright. She grasped the little girl's hand and began to scramble down the steep slope as fast as she could. A howl rang down the mountain, sounding like something out of a wicked fairy tale. Pulse racing, Hannah lifted the little girl down the rock, then, hand in hand, they raced on again.

"What is it? A wolf?" There had been something so wild and cruel about that howling that Hannah knew it was no ordinary dog.

"A phantom hound," the little girl panted. "It hunted me out of the cave. It'll kill me if it catches me!"

"A phantom hound?" Hannah was puzzled. "What's that?"

Behind them the howl came again. Glancing back, Hannah saw a huge black shaggy dog leaping down the rocks. Its eyes were red as coals, and its sharp claws clattered on the rock. It moved astonishingly fast.

"Come on!" She broke into a run again, but found the little girl could not keep up with her. She was sobbing with exhaustion. Desperately Hannah looked around her. Ahead was a tree, its branches curving down low to the ground. She shoved the little girl up into the tree, then hurriedly clambered up herself, keeping her rowan stick clasped firmly under one arm. As the huge black dog leapt towards her, she whacked it as hard as she could. It howled in pain, but leapt again, so close Hannah recoiled from the stench of its hot breath. Hannah wished she had thought to bring her dagger, but it lay with her guitar back at the camp. Suddenly she remembered what Linnet had told her about her walking stick. *If you're ever in any trouble, twist the handle three times. . .*

Hannah twisted the handle. A long, slim sword sprang free of the stick. As the phantom hound leapt for her once more, its fangs dripping foam, its red eyes glaring, Hannah thrust the sword as deep as she could into its breast. The giant beast tumbled down and lay still.

Hannah struggled to catch her breath. "Who are you? Why is this . . . thing . . . hunting you?"

"My name's Morgana." The little girl was clinging as

337

high up the tree as she could climb. "I come from under the hill." She pointed at Schiehallion.

Morgana. . . Where had Hannah heard that name before? Then she remembered what Linnet had told her of Eglantyne's two younger sisters.

"You're a fairy child!" she exclaimed. "Have you come through the gateway?"

Morgana nodded her head. Her hair was black and wild and very long, hanging to the backs of her knees. Her eyes were a bright and vivid green, the colour of a sunlit forest pool. "My cousin . . . Irata . . . she poisoned my father and my sister! She tried to poison me too . . . only I don't like spiced pomegranate wine, I fed it to my father's hound . . . and he dropped dead as well! My father, my sister, and half the court . . . all dead. . ." Her words were lost in gulping sobs.

"When? Just now?"

The little girl nodded, her face white with horror. "It was the feast to celebrate the spring equinox. It's the first time I was ever allowed to join the feast, and I was so pleased with my cousin for persuading my father. . ." Morgana wiped her eyes on her sleeve. "If I hadn't seen it with my own eyes . . . but she passed the goblet to my father, then laughed as he choked and writhed. All round the room . . . everyone falling, choking . . . I ran and hid, and she called upon her servants to find me. . ."

More howling echoed down the mountainside. Hannah stared out into the darkness with horrified eyes. She saw another huge black shape leaping down into the clearing, its eyes as red as hot coals.

"What are we to do?" Morgana sobbed.

Audacia, Hannah told herself, and gripped her bloody sword with trembling hands. As if scenting her fear, the dog flung back its head and howled.

Suddenly there was a twanging noise. An arrow sprang out of the darkness, taking the phantom hound through its throat. It keeled over and lay still, a shaggy heap in the darkness.

"Lassie?" Angus strode out of the darkness, another arrow cocked to the string. "How are you? What has happened?"

"Those dogs . . . they came out from the hill." Hannah's voice trembled.

Angus kicked one with his boot. "What a brute. A fairy dog, is it? I've heard of them. Lucky I heard it howling. Come on down, lass."

Hannah slipped down, first wiping the sword on her skirt and sliding it back into the stick.

"Is all well? No damage done?"

"No, I'm fine." Hannah hated hearing her voice shake. She took a deep breath and squared her shoulders. "But there's a little fairy girl from under the hill. She's Eglantyne's sister."

"What?" Angus peered up into the dark branches, then held up his arms to the child in white, who was cowering at the very top of the tree. "Come down, sweetling." His voice was the most gentle Hannah had ever heard it.

With a little sob, Morgana slipped and slithered down until she could drop into his arms. He held her close. "Come on, little one, you're safe now. We'll go back to the camp and see if we can find Linnet to make you a hot posset."

"Linnet?" Morgana's voice brightened. "Not my sister's handmaiden? Is she here?"

"Indeed she is. You're safe now."

"No, I'm not. Irata is after me. She'll come with her host and hunt me down."

"Don't say her name!" Hannah cried. Far away, they heard more howling and a strange, high gibbering sound.

"We must get away from here!" Morgana cried.

"We'll get you away from here. Don't fret, little one."

Carrying the fairy child, Angus hurried away from the corpses of the dogs, Hannah close on his heels. At the camp Max was on his knees, hastily gathering together all their belongings. Hannah caught up her guitar and slung the strap over her head so it lay on her back. She still had her stick in her hand. The water-horse was wearing a new halter heavy with iron rings. He shook his head and stamped and strained away from his tether, his hide shivering with fear as the howling came closer and closer. Then Hannah heard the pound of running feet. Scarlett came racing down the slope, skirts clutched in her hands, her fair hair flying. Behind her were Donovan and Linnet, running full pelt.

"The black witch is hunting!" Angus shouted. "Linnet, here is a wee maid from under the hill. I think you know her."

340

"Lady Morgana," Linnet gasped.

"Linnet!" the child squealed, and flung herself into Linnet's arms.

"We need to get away from here! Take the water-horse and ride him as far and as fast as you can. Here!" Angus seized the halter and threw Linnet up on to the horse's back with one brawny arm, passing her the rope reins. Morgana was tossed up behind her, clinging to Linnet's waist. Angus looked round at the other children's anxious faces. "We can't all ride the horse. Lassies, there'll be room for you." He lifted Scarlett up and turned to Hannah.

She shook her head. "I can't go! You and the boys are only here because of me. I can't ride away and leave you here. Scarlett! Take my guitar for me." Hurriedly Hannah passed her guitar up to Scarlett, who slung it over her shoulder, her face pale.

Angus hesitated, then nodded his head sharply. He released the halter, bringing his hand down on the water-horse's rump. The horse reared, whinnying, then took off into the darkness, his tail whipping behind him. In a second he and his riders were out of sight.

The Jester

Hannah felt weak-kneed. She gripped her rowan stick and told herself she had done the right thing.

"Let's find running water to cross. That'll help shake them off our trail. And remember they hate iron."

"What about brass?" Donovan joked weakly as he slung his flugelhorn over his shoulder.

The only answer Angus made was to pull a slender black knife out of his boot, holding it close to his body.

It was so dark now they could barely see each other's faces. A bitter-cold wind shrieked down the mountainside, bringing with it swirls of snow. Mist billowed up from the ground.

"She comes," Angus said. "Let's run."

The four companions ran through the stinging storm, trying not to stumble or turn their ankles on the rough ground. Twigs whipped their faces, and an eerie howling rose high on either side. A huge black dog leapt at Hannah out of the darkness. She smashed her stick over its head and it yowled with pain and fell back. Hannah ran on.

She heard the tumult of water over stones. Angus plunged in and waded downstream, holding his bow high so the string would not get wet. Hannah hitched up her voluminous skirts and followed. Within seconds her boots were filled with water and her feet were numb. She lost her footing and fell, and at once her skirts were like lead weights, dragging her down. Donovan helped haul her up, and Hannah ran on again.

A howl rose close behind them and was answered by another to their left. They heard galloping hooves, and mad gibbering, and the clank of weapons. Angus turned back anxiously, his finger at his lips, then hurried on. Hannah tried her best to be quiet, but her breath came harshly and the water splashed noisily about her knees.

Suddenly eerie green lightning flashed across the sky, illuminating the darkness. Hannah ducked her head, but it was no use. There was a roar of triumph behind them, and the sound of a hundred hooves and a hundred flapping wings.

"Run!" Angus roared. He burst out of the water and bolted across the grass, the children close on his heels. Into the forest they fled, hoping to lose their pursuers among the trees. The flying creatures wheeled away, their riders screaming their frustration, but others came racing through the trees. Hannah caught glimpses of them every time she glanced over her shoulder. In the darkness all she could see were squat shapes that ran with long swinging arms like apes, or scuttled like spiders, or hopped and bounded at great speed. One seized her by the shoulder and flung her to the ground, but she cracked her stick against its snout, and it squealed and cowered away, paws over its eyes. Donovan seized her hand and dragged her up, and clinging to each other, they ran on.

Suddenly one of the giant winged creatures plummeted out of the sky, landing in front of Hannah. She screamed and scrambled backwards, her heart thumping. Green lightning played all round the rider, so Hannah could see her clearly.

It was Irata, the black witch. She was tall and pale and strong-boned, with thin black brows that flared out above slanted eyes and a sulky mouth that was red and swollen as if she had been biting her lips. Her hair was black and writhed about her body in twining tendrils. In one hand she held a long wand of twisted wood. Irata leapt down and, in two quick strides, was towering over Hannah.

"What do I find here? Someone aiding and abetting Morgana's escape? Have you never been warned not to meddle with those of fairykind, human?" Suddenly her eyes sharpened and she leant forward and seized the hag-stone, which hung on its cord around Hannah's neck. "What is this? The royal hag-stone!"

She ripped the hag-stone from Hannah's neck and brought her wand down in a whistling blow that sent Hannah sprawling. Irata raised her arm again, only to find her blow blocked by Angus's long black knife. For a moment they fought, perfectly balanced, then a whip came snaking along the ground, wrapped about Angus's ankles and brought him crashing down to the ground. The whip had been wielded by a small, squat, loathsomely ugly hobgoblin, with only a few wispy silver hairs on his leathery chin. He wore rough furs and skins pinned together with wood, and a tall red-brown cap, which made Hannah shudder. She had heard of Red Caps, who dyed their hats with blood.

Angus rolled and tried to leap up, but Irata nonchalantly waved her wand. Where an old man with burly shoulders and a silver beard had been was now suddenly, horribly, a warty brown toad.

Ribbett, ribbett, the toad croaked.

Donovan had been close behind Angus. He cried out in dismay, then seized a rock from the ground and bowled it overarm, with stunning accuracy, right at Irata. It struck her on the temple, and she fell back. At once the green lightning was extinguished and the scene was plunged once more into darkness.

Donovan ran forward and scooped up the toad from the ground. Hannah raced after him. "Here!" she gasped, holding open the capacious pocket of her apron. Donovan dropped the toad in and together they bolted for the trees, Max trailing behind them, panting and holding his chest as he fought for breath.

Green lightning blazed up again, lighting the forest for miles around. A tornado sprang out of the ground and seized hold of them all. Hannah was flung under a bush,

Donovan was sent sprawling on the ground, but Max was spun higher and higher into the air. Gasping, her hair all over her face, blood running down from a scratch on her cheek, Hannah saw Irata, her wand drawing circles in the air, her face a white mask of fury.

"How dare you think to stand against ME!" Irata screamed. "Poor, pathetic, BREAKABLE human!"

She stopped the gyrations of her wand and the tornado suddenly blew itself out. Max fell out of the sky. Down he came, arms and legs flailing helplessly, then he thudded into the rock and lay still.

"No!" Donovan screamed. He cast one swift, compelling glance at Hannah, jerking his head to one side as if to tell her to go, then scrambled up and ran out into the clearing. Hannah, too shocked to even move, watched in bemusement as Donovan raised his flugelhorn to his lips. He blew a high, shrill note of defiance, then stepped forward to face Irata.

"Leave them alone! I'm the one you want," he said clearly. "I'm Eglantyne's son."

"You?" Irata screamed. "That's not possible! Eglantyne died! I caused the vehicle she was in to spin and crash; I saw it explode with my own eyes."

"She didn't die right away," Donovan said steadily, though his eyes widened with sudden shock. "She had time to give birth to me first."

"But the vehicle went right over the cliff. I saw it burst into flames."

"My father. . ." Donovan's voice faltered, but then he went on. "My father managed to drag her free first. He was badly burnt saving her."

Hannah was transfixed. Donovan grimaced at her, jerking his head to one side. She knew he meant for her to try to escape while he kept Irata occupied, but she could not tear herself away. It was clear to her that Donovan had only said he was Eglantyne's son to distract Irata while she and Max escaped, but it seemed he had spoken more truly than he knew.

"Allan was hurt? Eglantyne died? Oh no!" a voice spoke sharply from the crowd. Hannah turned her head and saw a tall man with copper-coloured curls and a wild beard hurrying forward, his pale face set in a grimace of distress. He looked exactly like Hannah's photo of her father.

He was dressed like a court jester, in a tunic quartered in orange and purple, with orange hose tied with cross-garters of purple. On his feet were ridiculous purple shoes with long, backward-curling toes with a bell at the tip. More bells hung on his dangling ass's ears. He carried a hobby-horse with the face of a devil, a mandolin slung across his back. He put out one hand to Donovan and said hoarsely, "Can you really be her son? But you're so old, so tall! What are you doing here?"

"Who gave you permission to speak?" Irata screamed. "Dance for me, fool!"

The Red Cap cracked his whip at the jester's legs. The jester at once began to play his mandolin and dance, skipping nimbly over the whip. His copper-coloured hair blazed in the green light.

It has to be my father! Hannah thought with a surge of excitement and incredulous joy. *I have to rescue him! But how?*

A low groan caught her attention. Max was moving feebly. One of his legs was bent awkwardly. Hannah bit her lip. She had to get him away somehow. She put her hands in her pockets to touch her key and hag-stone, an action she did unthinkingly now whenever she was troubled, and found two things. One, a large, damp, rather slimy toad. Two, a small ceramic honeypot with a fat cork.

Of course! Linnet's invisibility spell!

Hands shaking in excitement, Hannah drew out the cork and dipped her little finger into the paste. She smeared it on her forehead, trying hard to remember the rhyme Linnet had told her. "Things seen and things not seen, let me walk between," she muttered under her breath, hoping it was right. She then slowly crept towards Max.

No one paid her any attention. The crowd laughed at the jester riding his hobby-horse round and round, pretending to whip it with his hood. It was the strangest sight Hannah had ever seen. The crowd was filled with all manner of extraordinary beasts and creatures – black, horned dogs with eyes that glowed red, grinning dwarves with enormous heads and feet, tiny fluttering fairies with wings like butterflies and stings like wasps, old women dressed in grey rags with eyes all swollen with weeping, hags with blue faces and black claws and squat hobgoblins with single, enormous eyes that glowed like open furnaces. One of the most awful sights was a creature like a centaur, except that it had no skin. Hannah could clearly see the knotted muscles and blue, pumping veins running all over its body. The man-figure upon its back carried a spear in its long, skinless arms, which it beat in time to the jester's song.

There was one tall, elegant man in black satin with a white cravat and pointy shoes who Hannah thought she recognized. He was dancing arm-in-arm with a sneering young woman who wore a cloak made of living larks all chained tightly about the throat, their wings beating frantically. Dancing beside them, laughing and calling mocking comments to each other, were a dozen other couples, all as tall and beautiful as Irata, dressed in extraordinary garments made of jewels and furs and leaves and scales. One had an adder wound about his throat like a poisonous necklace; another wore a giant stag beetle as an ornament in the writhing snakes of her hair.

Hannah reached Max and quickly smeared some of the fern-seed paste on his brow and repeated the spell, then helped him sit up. He winced and repressed a grunt of agony. His leg looked very bad. Hannah did not know what to do.

"Splint it," Max whispered. "To support it while I walk. Find two sticks, as straight as you can."

Hannah nodded and searched the clearing till she found

349

two straight branches. No one saw her, though she pulled one stick right out from under the heel of a squat green bogey-beast. Slowly, trying to be quiet, she tore her petticoat into long strips and used the strips to bind the broken leg to the sticks. Max could not help a sharp cry of pain.

At once some of the goblins glanced round, and a few rose from their haunches, looking round the clearing suspiciously. Hannah shrank back into the shadows under the trees, trying to calm the hurried tempo of her breath. Max was biting his lip to stop himself screaming out in pain. The jester shouted out a loud "Hurrah!" and began to dance a sailor's hornpipe. The goblins turned back to watch, sniggering and nudging each other. Hannah bent over Max again, her hand trembling uncontrollably as she did her best to straighten the broken leg and strap it tight to the sticks. Max was a sickly yellowish-white when at last he stood, leaning heavily on Hannah's rowan stick. They began to move away, step by slow step.

"Enough!" Irata cried. "You need to learn some new tricks, fool. You begin to bore me. Perhaps we should set the Wild Hunt on to you. We have not enjoyed a good chase for a while."

At once the jester stood still, his mandolin clasped to his chest, his hobby-horse drooping from one hand. His face was still and expressionless.

"So, boy." Irata glared down at Donovan. "You claim to be Eglantyne's son. I cannot believe her son would be such a fool. Surely you realize that means I must kill you now?"

Hannah froze in her tracks, turning to look back at Donovan in horror. He stood very still, his fingers white where they gripped his flugelhorn.

"There's no need to kill me," he said. "I don't believe in kings and queens. I won't challenge you for the throne."

Irata laughed. "You expect me to believe that?"

The crowd shrieked and gibbered, leaping up and down.

"He amuses you," the jester spoke out, raising his voice above the din. "You say my tricks are beginning to bore you. Why do you not make him your fool too? Surely it would amuse you to keep the true heir to the throne as a capering fool, instead of simply killing him? He's only a boy. He's no threat to you."

Irata tapped her finger against her mouth, looking Donovan up and down. "Can you play that horn?"

In answer, Donovan lifted his flugelhorn and began to play "Time After Time". Miles Davis playing this song on his trumpet was one of his favourite pieces of music, and Hannah had learnt to play it and sing it with him over the last winter. The sound of it brought a sting of tears to Hannah's eyes. She knew he was playing it for her.

Slowly, slowly, she and Max began to stagger away from the clearing. It was one of the hardest things Hannah had ever done, walking away from Donovan and the father she had never met, leaving them there at the mercy of the black witch and her mob of howling goblins. Six months earlier she would have charged into the clearing, demanding Irata

351

let them go. Hannah knew, however, that their only hope was in stealth and subtlety. She had to get Max and herself safely away. All of the fern-seed ointment was gone, and Hannah could not save Donovan and her father without more. She needed to find Linnet.

Still, even knowing she was doing the right thing, tears flooded down her cheeks as she and Max stumbled away through the trees. He could put no weight on his broken leg, so she supported him as best as she could. He leant heavily on her walking stick, the bound and splinted leg dangling uselessly. The ground began to slope away under their feet, and Hannah's foot slipped, jerking Max cruelly. He cried out in pain. At once the goblin with the red cap swung his snout around, scowling and scanning the clearing with narrow, suspicious eyes. He sniffed the air, his nostrils flaring, then began to shuffle round the crowd, his head low to the ground. He found the spot where Hannah had fallen and sniffed all about, his long pointed nose twitching from side to side.

Hannah swallowed hard, her heart battering against her ribs. She felt sick with terror. She tried to urge Max to hurry, but he was in so much pain he could barely hop along. The goblin with the red cap tracked Hannah's scent across to where Max had been lying, uncoiling his long whip as he went. A few other goblins had noticed him, and began to sniff around as well. A few howls of excitement rose up into the air. Hannah slung her arm under Max's shoulder, taking as much of his weight as she could, and broke into a staggering run. They slipped and crashed down the slope, Max sobbing brokenly, as behind her Irata screamed, "Where are they? Find them!" There was no time to lose.

She urged Max on. His breath came in little whimpers. Behind them they could hear running feet, yelping, a dreadful snuffling noise. Ahead, a river raced down the centre of a narrow valley, foaming white in the darkness. Hannah looked up. She could see the eerie green glow racing towards them above the trees. She lifted Max and half-carried him down the slope, his leg dragging behind. She heard him bite back a scream of agony.

"We need to get into the river. So they don't smell our tracks," she whispered. "Here's a log. If you lean on it, it'll help keep you afloat. I'll kick us along. Can you manage?"

Max nodded, lying down awkwardly on the log. Hannah took off her apron and tied it about her shoulders so the toad in her pocket hung down her back. Then she pushed the log out into the river, kicking as hard as she could. The icy current caught the log and swept them away, just as dark shapes hurtled down the slope towards the river, howling in the chase.

It was a terrifying journey, whirling about, knocking into rocks or piles of driftwood, racing through the darkness. Looking back, Hannah saw the green glow swirl up and soar away towards Schiehallion. Slowly the night faded and a cold, red, angry dawn spread across the sky. Hannah's legs were numb, and her skirts dragged in the foaming water.

She looked across at Max. He was unconscious. She tried to steer the log towards the shore, but the current was too strong. It was not until they were dashed up against a great rock, where the water fell over in a series of foaming cataracts, that Hannah was at last able to drag Max away from the log and on to the shore. It took all her strength, and she was shivering so violently that her arms and legs and hands would not work properly. Hannah could only be grateful that Max was still unconscious and so unaware of his pain and the bitter cold. Hannah lay curled beside him on the stones for a long time. At last she found the strength to heave Max up and drag him away from the river.

Drag. Stop. Drag. Stop. Straighten her aching back. Drag. Stop. Drag.

The hours passed in a daze of exhaustion. At last Hannah found a broad cave under some twisted hazel roots. She lay Max down on the earth and sat beside him, head drooping, panting. Max moaned and rolled his head, but did not wake. Hannah groped for her hag-stone, but it was not hanging about her neck as usual. With a sinking sensation in her stomach, she remembered how Irata had torn it from her neck.

Her hag-stone gone. Donovan a captive. Her father a grinning fool.

Hannah put her head down and wept.

Port Wine Stain

Finally Hannah could cry no more. She wiped her face, blew her nose on her apron, and got Angus out of her pocket.

"I'm so sorry," she said. "This is all my fault. I'll find some way to change you back, I promise."

Ribbett, ribbett, the toad replied.

Hannah took off her wet dress and plaid, and hung them over a rock. She busied herself making Max more comfortable. She took off his shirt and sheepskin jacket, and hung them out to dry. She cut heather and bracken and made a bed for him. She gathered armfuls of dead branches, and tried her best to light a fire by rubbing sticks together. She failed. She went often to look out at the narrow, steep-sided valley, to look for any signs of pursuit, or in the vain hope that Linnet would somehow find them. She looked hopelessly for food.

Much, much later, when the sun was sinking down behind the trees, Hannah called out, in desperation, "Hag-stone, wherever you are, bring me Linnet. I want her now, this very minute!"

She spoke with no true confidence, and got up soon afterwards to tuck Max's plaid around him more securely. Yet when she heard the drumming of hooves on the hard ground, she knew at once that the spell had worked and went running out, laughing with joy, to see the water-horse galloping along the ridge, three riders on its back. Linnet, Morgana and Scarlett. There was a tumultuous reunion, Scarlett and Hannah crying and laughing at once, Morgana leaping around and clapping her hands, and Linnet smiling, her eyes bright with tears.

"I can't believe it worked! You're here! I called you and now you're here!" Hannah flung herself into Linnet's arms.

Linnet hugged her close. "But of course I am here. You called me, didn't you? I am bound to your service and so must always come when you call."

Hannah looked at her in surprise. "But I've lost the hag-stone. The black witch . . . she took it from me."

"A hag-stone can never be stolen or bought, only given with free will," Linnet reminded her. "She will find it refuses to work its magic for her."

"Well, that's something, I suppose." Hannah sighed gustily.

"Where's Max and Donovan? And Angus?" Scarlett looked round eagerly.

"A lot has happened," Hannah said. "Come into the cave and I'll tell you. . ."

The next five weeks were the most miserable of Hannah's life.

They lived in the cave, scrounging for food along the riverbank, looking after Max, who slowly, day by day, began to heal. Linnet searched for comfrey and horsetail in the meadows, to make up potions to help his bones knit, and gathered fern seed whenever she could find it, to make some more of the spell of invisibility. Scarlett and Hannah together raided birds' nests for eggs, rigged up nets with their aprons to try to catch the salmon leaping up the falls – and, amazingly, sometimes got one – and searched for mushrooms and lichen in the woods. They never had enough food, and so, after much discussion, the girls risked riding into Fortingall and singing ballads in return for a few coins with which they could buy supplies.

Morgana was at first extremely difficult, so that Hannah secretly wished that she had never helped the fairy princess escape. Although Morgana was at least seven years old, she expected Linnet, Hannah and Scarlett to dress her as if she were a doll. She wanted to be waited on hand and foot, and broke into stormy tears every time her will was thwarted. Her white dress was in ribbons from her frantic escape, and so she expected them to conjure another for her.

"You must be joking!" Scarlett cried. "Do you have any idea how much new clothes cost?"

Then, hearing herself, she met Hannah's eyes in a rueful glance, missing Angus more than ever.

Until Angus had been turned into a toad, Hannah had not realized how much he had done to make their journey comfortable. He had drawn water, gathered firewood, foraged for food, cooked their meals and guarded their sleep. Now Linnet and the two girls had to do everything. It was exhausting and back-breaking work. At night, Hannah fell on to her bed of dried leaves and branches and slept like the dead.

The water-horse was a great help to them. It meant that Scarlett and Hannah were able to ride deep into the forest in search of food and kindling, or ride to Fortingall. They could never leave the water-horse untethered or take off his halter, but as long as his head was bound with iron and leather, he remained, if not exactly docile, at least controllable. If it were not for the fact that he ate fish – snatching them out of the air as they leapt up the falls – he would have seemed like any other ill-tempered, fiery-natured stallion.

The days grew longer and warmer. Linnet, Max and the two girls spent any free time devising a plan for rescuing Donovan and Hannah's father. They knew that they could not pass through the gateway into the Otherworld until May Day, and so all their energies were bent on keeping themselves safe till Max's leg had healed enough for him to leave the cave. Linnet sprinkled salt and the ashes of the fire before the entrance to the cave, and, with Morgana's

358

help, wrought spells of protection to keep the spies of Irata from discovering their hiding place.

The countryside was in ferment as outrage over the murder of the king continued to grow. Every time Hannah and Scarlett rode to Fortingall, they heard snippets of news and gossip.

Queen Mary's forty days of mourning were over and the queen had come out of seclusion, though she was still ill with grief and shock. Her young son, Prince James, was locked up safe in Stirling in fear of an uprising. Lord Bothwell's wife was desperately ill and some thought he had poisoned her so he could be free to marry the queen. Others scoffed at this idea, saying the queen must surely marry a rich foreign prince who would bring Scotland gold and a well-trained army to defend her.

Hannah could only wonder why everyone seemed in such a hurry for Queen Mary to marry again, when her last husband – her second – had been dead only forty days. It did not take her long to realize that it was because Queen Mary was considered merely a weak woman, incapable of ruling on her own.

"Better a crowing hen than a whistling woman," one man said contemptuously.

In mid-April news came that the queen had allowed Lord Darnley's father to present a private accusation to Parliament, accusing Bothwell as the slayer of his son. Everyone was agog to hear what Parliament would say, but in the end it came to nothing, for the streets of Edinburgh were filled with thousands of Bothwell's supporters and so Lord Lennox, the king's father, was too afraid to present himself, and Bothwell was acquitted.

He sent a town crier round the streets of Edinburgh, loudly proclaiming his innocence, and put up posters offering to fight in single combat with anyone who doubted his word. Although many people muttered behind their hands, no one dared to challenge him.

Although Fortingall was only a tiny hamlet consisting of a few thatched cottages clustered around a church and a huge old yew tree, it was as concerned with the doings in the capital as any other town. Hannah and Scarlett normally rode to the village on market day, when people from the furthest reaches of the glen came to buy and sell supplies, and exchange news. Hannah could never pass the ancient yew tree without thinking of Donovan with a sharp pang, remembering the day he had told her that it was older even than the pyramids.

In late April, the market was humming like a beehive attacked by a bear. No one made any pretence of buying and selling. They all stood in small, agitated clumps, talking and arguing.

Scarlett seized an old woman by the sleeve and asked what was wrong.

"It's the queen!" the old woman cried, her eyes red from weeping. "That devil Bothwell has seized her! He's got her locked up in Dunbar Castle. They've been ringing the alarm bell in Edinburgh and getting together some men to rescue her, but what of our poor queen in the meantime?"

"Hah!" another younger woman said angrily. "They say Queen Mary went with him willingly enough."

"Only to avoid any harm coming to her men," the old woman protested.

"I'd say she knew of the plot from the start," the young one scoffed. "She and that Bothwell have been thick as thieves for months."

"It's not true. Bothwell is her sheriff, a lord sworn to protect her. How could she suspect him of wanting to murder her husband and steal her away?"

"Well, she rode forty miles with him and didn't once call for help," the young woman pointed out. "You'd think she'd have screamed for help if she didn't want to be stolen."

The old woman mopped her eyes with a rough handkerchief. "She would've been frightened. . . Oh, what will happen to her now?"

"She'll have to marry him, that's what," a stern young man said. "She can't spend the night alone with him, without a chaperone, and not marry him."

"I'd say that's what she wanted all along," the young woman replied cynically.

"But isn't he already married?" Hannah asked.

"Wives are easy enough to get rid of when there's a crown to be won," the young woman said.

"I tell you what, though," the old woman said as she turned back to her honeypots, "there'll be bloodshed if Bothwell thinks he can clamber on to the throne over the body of that poor murdered boy."

There was bloodshed, Hannah remembered. A battle that Queen Mary lost. She was taken prisoner, and although she eventually escaped, it was only to find herself kept prisoner by Queen Elizabeth, her cousin, who eventually cut off her head. Hannah's stomach cramped in fear.

We have to get home, she thought. *I'll rescue Donovan and my father, and get back the hag-stone, and find the last loop of the puzzle ring. Then we can go home. . .*

Hannah refused to admit that she might fail in her tasks and be stuck in the sixteenth century for the rest of her life. She could not even let the seed of the thought waft across her mind, in case it took root there and flourished, and sapped all her resolve.

"Let's head back," she muttered to Scarlett.

"But we haven't bought anything yet! And imagine little Princess Morgana's face if we come back empty-handed. She'll throw a right royal tantrum."

"I don't think anyone would like us to sing today. Everyone's too upset."

"But there's fresh bread for sale! And honey and cabbages and blackberries. Linnet could make us bramble crumble again. And look, Hannah!" She pointed to where a butcher had hung a row of freshly slaughtered carcasses from a tree, flies buzzing above the puddles of congealing blood. "Lamb! Oh, I've been dreaming of roast lamb for months. Please, Hannah. Please."

"I don't think we should. . ."

"They'll be glad of something to distract them." Scarlett

jumped up on a stile and called out, "Such long faces you've got! Who'd like a wee song to brighten the day?"

A few people shrugged and gathered round, and Scarlett tapped her tambourine against her hip and mouthed "Greensleeves" to Hannah. Reluctantly Hannah climbed up next to her, and they launched into the song.

A few small coins had been dropped into Hannah's tam o'shanter and she had begun to relax when she saw a young woman standing at the edge of the crowd, staring at her. Wearing a ragged shawl wrapped close about her head and shoulders, the young woman was as thin as a stick and as white as whey. Recognition came – it was Edie, the young woman that had let them sleep in her goat shed while Hannah was sick – and so she smiled and lifted a hand in greeting.

Her left hand.

Even as Hannah remembered and guiltily dropped her hand, Edie started forward. "It's her!" she cried. "The witch-girl. She touched me with her devil's hand and scarred my little boy. Look what she did! Look!"

Edie flung back the shawl to show a small baby nestled in the crook of her arm. An ugly purple-red stain spread over the baby's head, covering almost half of his face. A murmur rose from the crowd.

"She did it! It's her fault. She came and slept in my goat shed. Her friend gathered the flowers of the elder tree, and they drank it together! She's a witch! She touched me with her devil's hand and look what happened."

"Don't be silly!" Scarlett cried. "Of course she's not a witch."

"Where do they live, these lassies?" a man asked, frowning.

"They come down from the fairy hill on their horse," someone cried. "I've seen them come out of the woods."

"Look at them! They're as wild as any fairy bairn."

Scarlett and Hannah glanced at each other. It was true they were ragged and filthy. Although they washed in the river most days, they had no soap, and their hair was matted with knots, for they had lost or broken their combs long ago. Their feet were bare, for their boots had worn through the soles, and their aprons were badly stained from carrying berries and herbs.

"Please, we're not fairy children," Hannah cried. "I had nothing to do with the poor baby's birthmark."

No one listened. Cries and accusations rang out from all sides. Edie shouted and wept and pointed accusingly at Hannah. The baby screamed. The port wine stain turned a deep purple as his skin reddened. Men jostled closer, saying the girls should be seized and taken up before the magistrate. Hannah was pushed roughly, and flung out her left hand to save herself. At the sight, the crowd grew ugly.

"Come on! Let's get out of here!" Scarlett tried to push her way through the crowd, but someone seized her arm. At once she kicked him hard behind his knee. He fell with a grunt. Another man grabbed hold of her, but Scarlett twisted free and kicked him hard in the stomach. He bent over, winded. For a moment, the crowd just stood, goggling in surprise, and Scarlett seized Hannah's hand and raced to where the water-horse stood. His head was up, his nostrils flaring red, his ears laid back against his skull. Scarlett leapt on to his back, and hauled Hannah up after her. A quick slash of Hannah's dagger sliced the rope free. The water-horse reared, trumpeting a challenge and showing his sharp fangs. A woman screamed and flung herself away from his clawed hooves.

Galloping madly through the street, knocking over barrels and carts, trampling fruit under hoof, sending people racing out of his way, the water-horse cut a swathe of destruction through the village. People raced after them, shaking their fists and shouting. The girls could only cling to the water-horse's mane and give him his head.

He followed the River Lyon, heading west along the glen. Tall mountains towered high on either side, still streaked with snow despite the warm spring weather. Behind them came the sound of pursuing hoof beats. Hannah glanced back and saw a few grim-looking men on horseback, spurring their mounts on.

"Stop the witch-girls!" someone shouted. "Stop them!"

A man ran into a cottage and came out with a longbow. Scarlett cursed under her breath and leant forward, trying to seize the trailing rope so she could turn the horse's head. The stallion turned and plunged into the river. Hannah's breath caught in her throat. She was sure he would transform back into his serpentine water shape and drown them both. The power of the iron held strong, however. The stallion swam strongly across the fast-running river, and came out galloping on the far side.

Into the forest and up the hill he went, stones scattering under his hooves, and wound his way along a narrow path between rolling hills. Scarlett and Hannah could only cling on tightly. At last the horse slowed to a walk. Hannah could not see or hear anyone behind them, and so she heaved a great sigh and looked around.

Purple-brown mountains soared into the sky, their lower flanks dark with forest. Directly ahead was a hill shaped like a perfect isosceles triangle. Two tall grey stones reared up before it, like a pinnacle that had been cleaved in two by a giant sword. Hannah stared and could not speak. She tugged at Scarlett's sleeve and pointed.

"The praying hands," Scarlett breathed.

Hannah nodded. She slid down from the water-horse's back, rubbing his damp neck in thanks, and slowly climbed the hill. Her emotions surged so strongly in her that her throat felt thick and her eyes hot. She came to the base of the split stone and laid her hand upon it. The rock was warm beneath her fingers.

She had to climb the rock, grazing her knees and her hands, wedging her body into the split so she could brace herself on either side. At the very top of the left-hand side, she saw a glint of gold. The ring was caught in a crack in the rock. Hannah was only just able to reach for it. She slid it on to her finger, feeling happy and confident for the first time in weeks, and slowly climbed back down to where Scarlett and the water-horse were waiting for her. Hannah was smiling so widely her cheeks hurt, and Scarlett was jumping up and down with joy.

"That's all three loops now," Scarlett said, as they slowly rode north again, looking for a way back through the hills to Schiehallion.

"And we found it without the hag-stone," Hannah said. "When I lost it . . . I thought every chance of finding the last loop was gone."

"The water-horse led us to it," Scarlett said, bending to stroke the weary stallion's neck.

"It's a fairy horse and that was a fairy site," Hannah said. "I wonder. . ."

"What?"

"My father said, in his notebook, that there are lines . . . roads . . . connecting places of power. I wonder if the horse was travelling one of those roads."

"Could be, I guess."

They rode on in silence for a long while, until the sun had set and the stars were sprawled out across the sky.

"You know," Scarlett said, "I really hated you when you first came to Fairknowe."

"Yeah. How come?"

"It's stupid." Scarlett was silent for a while. "You know, there was always this big mystery about you. The little Rose heir, whose father disappeared and whose mother took you away soon after. People often used to wonder what had really happened."

Hannah listened quietly.

"I . . . oh, this is really stupid. I used to pretend that *I* was the missing Rose heir. That Lady Wintersloe was my great-grandmother, and that was why she took such interest in me." Scarlett heaved a big sigh. "I wanted to think I was really adopted, because *my* family was so *ordinary*. So when you came and I had to stop pretending . . . I really hated you."

"I'm sorry," Hannah said.

"Oh, it's not your fault. So then . . . when you told us about Eglantyne being rescued and maybe having had her baby . . . well, I wanted to think that it was me. That it would make me special somehow. But you know what?"

"What?" Hannah spoke softly.

"I can't wait to get home to my ordinary life and my ordinary family. I'm never going to wish I'm someone else again!"

Witch-Hunters

Hannah smelled the smoke of the witch-hunters' torches before she saw the bobbing red lights. The men of Fortingall were searching the lower slopes of Schiehallion, the gusting flames snapping in the wind like forked banners.

The water-horse paused on the ridge of the hill, ears laid back against his skull. "Quietly now," Scarlett whispered, nudging the horse forward. He stepped delicately down the stony slope. In the darkness he was almost invisible, and the two girls drew their plaids close about their faces and tucked their hands out of sight, so the white gleam would not betray them.

They came close to the witch-hunters, close enough to hear their shouts and curses, and for the smoke of the flames to sting their eyes. The men did not see the girls upon the horse, however, or hear a single clink of hoof against stone. Smoothly and silently, the water-horse led them past the gang of witch-hunters and down to the stony banks of the river. He entered the water without a splash, and began to swim swiftly downstream. Hannah was sure she could hear the rhythmic beat of flippers, and every muscle tensed with fear. But the water-horse did not plunge below the water, or seek to roll and drag them under. The iron bound about his head kept him under their control, and so the two girls were able to slip right past the searchers, even when the reflection of their flaming torches rippled right across the water to touch their faces with heat.

"We'll have to leave right away," Hannah whispered in Scarlett's ear. "We cannot risk being caught by them."

"But where shall we go? Back to Fairknowe?"

"Unless we can find another fairy gateway closer," Hannah whispered. "It's almost May Day now. We have the third part of the puzzle ring. If we can just find a gateway, we can rescue Donovan and my father and then go home again."

"I think it's getting a bit hot for us here," Scarlett said wryly.

The girls found Linnet waiting for them anxiously at the mouth of the cave, her plaid wrapped close about her against the early morning chill. Max was awake too, his thin face drawn with pain.

"Where have you been? What's happened?" he cried.

"We'll tell you on the way," Hannah said. "We need to get moving . . . . fast!"

But it was impossible to move quickly through the countryside. News of the fairy bairns and their fiendish horse had spread fast, and anyone who caught sight of

Linnet and the children ran at once to call for help. Time and again the water-horse was forced to gallop from angry villagers, tossing his mane and baring his fanged teeth in rage. Hannah and her friends began to travel only in the early hours of the morning and at dusk, when people had gone home to their cottages and the roads were empty.

When May Day came, they were still far from Fairknowe Hill and so had no chance of getting home for another seven weeks. The next thin day was Midsummer's Eve, on the twenty-second of June. Till then, Hannah and her friends were trapped in sixteenth-century Scotland, with civil war threatening to break out at any moment. Hannah, Max and Scarlett were very quiet that night, sitting with slumped shoulders by the campfire and barely tasting the game soup Linnet had cooked especially for them. Hannah felt as if she would never get home; never see her mother or her great-grandmother again; never go to the movies or watch TV or catch a train wherever she wanted to go; never wear comfortable clothes that could be washed and dried by machines, instead of by her own chapped and chilblained hands; never eat a hamburger or chocolate or ice cream again. No one said a word, just sat staring morosely into the campfire, then wrapped themselves in their plaids and pretended to sleep.

They missed Angus more than ever over the next few days, for the old man had known many secret ways through the forests and hills. Hannah and her friends did not know the secret ways, and found the mountains to the west completely impassable. Again and again they would follow a river or explore a glen, only to find their way blocked by immense brooding pinnacles of stone. The forest on the valley floor was tangled and overgrown, and there were signs that outlaws lived there, rampaging forth to steal what they could.

"I can't risk the puzzle ring being stolen," Hannah said anxiously. "I think we should stick to the road if we can."

"There are outlaws on the roads as well," Linnet said.

"Yes, but at least there aren't any wolves," Hannah said, for they had all been frightened by an unexpected encounter with a shaggy grey wolf the previous evening. It had only stared at them with fierce golden eyes, growling low in its throat, its hackles raised, before loping swiftly away when the kelpie growled back.

As Hannah and her friends came closer to Perth, they began to see bands of men with great two-handled claymores strapped to their backs marching the muddy roads. Max still found it hard to walk, so he and Morgana rode on the water-horse, while Hannah, Scarlett and Linnet hiked alongside, foraging for food as they went. The further south they went, the harder it was to find mushrooms or birds' eggs or fish, as the land was rounded and green and planted with crops. Luckily, blackberries were plentiful, as brambles grew all over the stone walls. Linnet cooked them with a crust of oatmeal and wild honey and, after weeks of plain porridge, Hannah and her friends could not get enough, so that their mouths were stained with purple all day.

They could not live on blackberries and porridge alone, though. At last, Linnet left the four younger ones camping in a small copse of trees and walked to Perth for news and supplies. The town was milling with worried, frightened people, Linnet said when she got back. A few days earlier, Queen Mary had married Lord Bothwell in a rushed ceremony at Holyrood. Bothwell had divorced his wife only a week earlier. Queen Mary wore an old dress, and was said to have wept afterwards. Many people thought she had been forced to wed against her will. Others said she wept for joy.

"But how long has it been since the king died?" Scarlett demanded.

"Thirteen weeks," Linnet replied unhappily.

"No wonder people are upset. Thirteen weeks is not very long!"

"What are we to do?" Hannah wanted to know. "At this rate, we won't get back to Fairknowe by Christmas!"

"I've been thinking," Linnet said. "No one paid me any mind at all in Perth. Either the story of the two wild fairy bairns has not travelled this far south, or everyone's far too worried about what's going on to care."

"So?" Scarlett said.

"Well, we'd have a long, hard journey from here to Fairknowe through the hills. I've never travelled that way myself, and Angus cannot show us the way." As Linnet spoke, she cradled the toad in her hands. He croaked and shot out his long sticky tongue to catch a midge. "There must be a path, but I don't know the way. However, if we stick to the highway it'll take us straight down to Edinburgh. And there are so many people travelling the roads now, no one will notice us."

"But we want to get home," Hannah cried. "What's the point of going to Edinburgh?"

"There's a fairy hill there. Another gateway into the Otherworld. It's only very small, and not much used these days. My lady's cousin may not even have guards on it."

"Really? A fairy hill in Edinburgh? Where?"

"It is called Dow Craig, which means the Black Rock," Linnet said. "It stands just outside the walls, separated from the city by a gorge. I have ridden out the gate there before; I know where it is. If we can get there by Midsummer's Eve, you should be able to pass through."

"But we'll still be miles and miles away from home, or from Schiehallion, where they took Donovan prisoner," Hannah said hopelessly. "How are we meant to find him or my father, or get home?"

"You know that time moves differently in the Otherworld," Linnet said quietly. "Well, space moves differently too. What would take you days to walk in this world would take you a few hours, or maybe even minutes, in the fairy realm."

"Really?" Hannah was filled with new hope. "You mean we could cross into the Otherworld, rescue my father and Donovan, and escape back out the gateway at Fairknowe, all in a matter of hours?"

374

Linnet nodded.

"Then why didn't we just do that in the first place, instead of traipsing all over Scotland?" Scarlett demanded. "We needn't have walked all the way to Edinburgh; we could have just gone through the gateway at Fairknowe Hill and popped up outside the city walls a couple of hours later."

Linnet regarded her gravely. "Do you think I would willingly take you to the black witch's realm? Do you have any idea of how dangerous it will be? I would not suggest it now, if we did not have to brave her in order to rescue poor Lord Fairknowe and Donovan! The very thought of it makes me feel sick to my stomach. But I can think of no other way, if we are to save them."

"We can't just leave them there," Hannah cried. "Of course we have to rescue them!"

"And try to get back the hag-stone," Max said. "Because I really don't want my leg to stay like this." He looked down at the thin, crooked, misshapen limb with a wry twist of his mouth. Linnet had told him, very unhappily, that his only hope of walking properly again was the magic of the hag-stone, which Irata had taken back to the Otherworld with her, and so Hannah and her friends were determined to wrest it back from her, if they could.

"Well, we'd better get moving then," Scarlett said doggedly.

So the travellers set out for Edinburgh, following the narrow, rutted road through rolling green hills where shaggy highland cattle grazed, past fields of oats and barley, and over humpbacked stone bridges that crossed countless stony burns. The days grew warmer, and the girls folded back their sleeves and wished they could strip off their tattered petticoats.

Food was always a problem, and so Hannah, Max and Scarlett once again began to sing for their supper. Linnet took in sewing from the soldiers and, rather to the girls' surprise, Morgana proved she could sew exquisitely. She helped Linnet without complaint, and stopped demanding everyone wait on her hand and foot.

There were many scuffles and outbreaks of violence, as those who supported Queen Mary argued with those who believed her a murderess. On the thirtieth of May, Queen Mary made a call to arms, declaring that some of the nobles were plotting rebellion against her and asking for aid from those still loyal to her. Thousands of men were now marching towards Edinburgh, sometimes in small bands, armed only with daggers and shields, others wearing armour and led by skirling pipers.

A week later, the rebel lords surrounded the castle of Borthwick, where Queen Mary and Lord Bothwell were staying. Bothwell slipped away secretly through a side postern and escaped, leaving Mary to defend the castle herself. When it became clear that the castle would fall, the queen dressed herself in the clothes of a man and escaped under the cover of night, leaving her wardrobe and all her belongings behind. She fled to Dunbar Castle, on the coast to the east of Edinburgh, where she was reunited with her new husband.

A few days later, Hannah, Scarlett, Max, Linnet and Morgana reached the outskirts of Edinburgh, only to find the city gates locked tight and no one permitted to enter. It was here that they learnt Queen Mary had been betrayed by one of her most faithful lords, who had sent her a message telling her Edinburgh would rise on her behalf. Except the lord had secretly turned Edinburgh Castle over to the rebel lords and Queen Mary was caught out in the open, with only a few hundred men to protect her, while the rebel lords prevented those trapped inside Edinburgh from riding out to support her.

"We had better stay well away from the city," Linnet said, looking pale and worried. "We still have several weeks until Midsummer's Eve. Let's find somewhere to hide out."

Yet there was nowhere safe they could go. Battalions of soldiers marched along all the roads and byways and across the fields, crushing the crops underfoot and raising clouds of dust. There were constant skirmishes and retreats, shouts of alarm, and flying rumours. Eventually the little group of travellers took refuge in a roadside inn on the road to Musselburgh, where the innkeeper and his wife were so glad of some extra hands to help that they let Hannah and her friends sleep in the hayloft. It was hard work, and by the end of each long, hot day Hannah could not wait to lie down in the rustling, scratchy straw and sleep.

Early on the morning of the fifteenth of June, she was woken by the rhythmic beat of hundreds of marching feet. She crawled across to the loft door and peeked out. A long procession of soldiers passed down the highway, led by stern-faced men in armour upon prancing horses. Banners flapped in the breeze, showing the crest of family after family. Soldiers from the inn were pulling on their boots, seizing their weapons, shouting with excitement. "We'll show that murdering witch that she can't foist her lover upon us!" one shouted.

Hannah stood for a long time, watching the soldiers march past, a tight knot of anxiety in her belly.

It was a blazing hot day. Luckily there was not much work to do, with the soldiers gone and no one knowing what to expect next. The sun slowly sank down in the west, through clouds of dust that turned scarlet and orange and gold.

In Scotland in midsummer, the light lingers long after the sun has set. It was still bright enough, then, for Hannah to see the faces of the soldiers returning to Edinburgh from the battlefield at around nine o'clock that evening.

They were laughing and shouting. "Kill her, burn her! Hang her from the highest tree!"

"No, let's throw the witch in the mill-pond and see if she floats!"

"No more women ruling the roost!"

In the midst of this noisy, chaotic crowd rode Queen Mary, alone, dressed in the shabby clothes of a commoner, dusty from the road, torn and dishevelled. Her red petticoat showed beneath her bedraggled hem, her bodice was half torn away, and her bright chestnut hair fell out of its pins down her back. She wept as she rode, shrinking away from the jeers and catcalls of the soldiers. Every now and again she held out a hand of entreaty, calling for help.

"Your precious husband has abandoned you!" someone shouted. "Murderess! Jezebel! Burn her, I say!"

Hannah and her friends could only watch in shock and horror. It seemed impossible that this weeping, haggard, forsaken woman could be the same beautiful queen they had seen laughing and dancing only four months earlier.

They watched until the queen was gone from sight, dragged towards the city that had once been her home.

"What happens to her?" Scarlett said shakily. "Doesn't she die?"

"Not for a long time," Hannah said. "They keep her captive first and make her give up her throne to her son, who's only a baby. In the end she escapes, dressed like a servant, and flees to England. Queen Elizabeth keeps her prisoner there for about twenty years, and in the end cuts off her head."

"It doesn't seem fair," Scarlett said.

"No."

"I wish we could rescue her," Max said.

"Lots of people tried, and they all died horribly. There's nothing we can do." Hannah felt a fierce determination rise in her. "We may not be able to save Queen Mary, but we *can* and we *will* rescue Donovan and my father!"

Into the Otherworld

Seven days later, it was finally Midsummer's Eve.

At the base of the steep green hill called Black Rock, Hannah and her friends made their farewells to Linnet, Morgana, Angus the toad, and the water-horse. If all went well, they would be back in their own time before dawn.

Although it was late and the sun had set, the sky was still full of light. Edinburgh lay across the narrow gorge, crouched higgledy-piggledy within its stone walls, a city of spires and towers and slanted roofs and narrow crooked chimneys. Black Rock – better known in Hannah's time as Calton Hill – looked quite different without its crowning monuments and follies.

"I wish that I could go with you, to help you and guard you!" Linnet said. "But you know I cannot. I must keep Lady Morgana safe, for if you fail to rescue Donovan, she is the only child of true blood left. And I cannot exist in both times – it could wrench the whole world awry."

"Yeah, imagine young Linnet running into old Linnet,"

Max said exuberantly. "What do you think would happen?"

Hannah had to swallow a lump in her throat before she could speak, for the idea of leaving Linnet behind filled her with misery and anxiety. "There are two theories, Mum says. The first is that the universe would have to split into a kind of parallel universe. The problem with that idea is that we could have billions and trillions of different universes, all of them with different Linnets in them, and that just seems impossible. The universe would have to split at every single little tiny decision every single one of us made. . ."

Hannah suddenly realized that, in an attempt to keep her grief and fear at bay, she was lecturing her friends, just like Roz always did to her. It gave her a swift keen insight into her mother's heart. Wishing she had been kinder to her mother, Hannah continued in a gentler tone.

"Mum says it's more likely that the universe would just protect itself, making sure that nothing happened that would change the future, or affect the past. So that if Linnet tried to travel back to the twenty-first century with us, something would happen to stop her. Which means something would happen to stop *us* too! And we don't want that."

"So I will stay here, in this time, and look after Angus and Lady Morgana," Linnet said to Hannah. "I'll go back to Wintersloe Castle, and wait for you there."

"It'll be a long time," Hannah said unhappily.

"I know. I'm patient. I will look after the family and try to ease the burden of the curse as best I can."

"I'm so sorry, Linnet. I never meant for this to happen."

Linnet smiled, her green eyes bright with tears. "I know. But those of fairy kind are long-lived anyway, you know that, Hannah. And I swore an oath to my lady Eglantyne, as well as to you, and I should like to see the end of the story."

"What about me?" Morgana demanded, looking frightened.

Linnet drew her close. "I'll take care of you, my chick. You can't go back to our own world, you know that. It's too dangerous. Like it or not, you're in the human world now and you'll have to find some way to live here happily. You'll grow up and make a life for yourself, never you fear."

"So I'll never see my home again?" Morgana asked in a small voice.

"I don't think so," Linnet said. "But maybe, one day, if Hannah succeeds in reuniting the puzzle ring, your children might, or their children. All things are possible in all the worlds."

The little girl drew herself up. Tears were winding down her face, but she did not sob or scream as she might once have done. She took Hannah's hand in her own small, cold one, and said in a trembling voice, "Defeat Irata for me, Hannah, will you?"

"Don't speak her name," Linnet and Hannah said together.

Morgana nodded. "Defeat her. Cast her out of my land for ever. Make sure she never comes back."

"I'll try," Hannah said rather hopelessly. "But I'm only a girl myself, Morgana. How am I meant to do such a thing?"

"You'll find a way," the fairy princess answered. "I know you will!"

Scarlett was saying goodbye to the water-horse. "I wish you could come back with us. I'd love a horse like you! But you belong here, I know. Linnet will let you go just as soon as she's safely away from here. I hope you get back to your loch all right. Just don't try eating any more kids, OK?"

The water-horse shook his head and harrumphed as if he understood what she was saying.

"Come on, girls," Max said. "We'd better get going."

He stood leaning on Hannah's rowan walking stick, his leg still bound with rags to two old sticks.

"When you get the hag-stone back, remember it has healing powers too," Linnet said to Hannah. "You must heal Max before you go back to your own time, else he will be lame all his life."

"But what do I do?"

"The magic of the hag-stone is wild magic, remember, and so is held as deep within your blood and bone as it is within star and stone. If you trust yourself, you will know what to do."

"But. . ." Hannah began, but then grew silent, thinking.

Linnet nodded and kissed her brow. "Keep safe, my lamb. I will wait and watch for you."

"Goodbye!" Scarlett cried, beginning to climb Black Rock. "Wish us luck!"

"Goodbye!" Max called. "Thank you!"

There was time for one last loving embrace with Linnet, then Hannah began the steep climb up to the cave, where the doorway to the Otherworld lay hidden.

The three friends crept quietly into the narrow cave halfway up the hill. Although they wore fern-seed paste on their brows, they did not want to make any noise that might attract attention. It was pitch-black inside the caves, and so they carried candles impaled upon rough wooden holders.

At last Hannah led the way into a much greater chamber. There was a tall, smooth wall, running beyond the reach of the candles' faint light. This, Linnet had told them, was the gateway to the Otherworld. Rather tremulously, Hannah and her friends blew out their candles and waited in the heavy darkness until they could no longer smell any trace of smoke.

Then, holding hands, Hannah, Max and Scarlett began to sing. "Open the door in the green hill, open the door and let us in." Their voices sounded unearthly as they echoed through the caverns.

After a long moment they heard a grating noise, and then a vertical crack of light appeared down the length of the wall. Slowly the crack widened as two immense stone doors were dragged open by two hulking giants, with heads as large as boulders upon thick, crooked torsos. Their long arms hung right down to their knees, for their bowed legs were much shorter than their bodies, with huge, flat feet that turned out like a duck's.

With pounding heart and trembling legs, Hannah hurried invisibly past the giants and through the doorway, Max and Scarlett at her heels. The huge guards scratched their heads, peering out into the darkness. After a while they shrugged their immense shoulders, drew the doors shut again, and went to refresh themselves from tankards as large as buckets.

Hannah and Max and Scarlett tiptoed away down a long stone corridor, hands pressed over their hearts as if that would stop them beating so loudly. The ceiling of the corridor was vaulted like a cathedral's, with stone gargoyles every few paces. These gargoyles, however, were alive, with bright impish eyes and chattering mouths. One of the gargoyles, with a broad flat nose and horns like a goat, snuffled the air and remarked, "Can you smell that? Fee-fie-fo-fum, I smell the blood of a human."

"It's that new jester of the queen's," remarked another; this one had a fat face and ears like a cow. "Ooof, but that boy stinks! I wish the queen would stop cluttering up the place with mortals."

"She likes to think she's queen of both worlds," another said. "I've never known such a one for galloping out into the mortal world."

"No one left here to terrorize," said the next in the line. "They're all too browbeaten."

Tiptoeing past, Hannah did not breathe freely until she and her friends had left the gargoyles far behind them.

The corridor led into a vast and gorgeous palace made of pale stone, every inch of which was carved and gilded. Tapestries and embroidered cloths hung on the walls, and flower petals were scattered over the flagstones. The air was warm and smelled deliciously of roses and apricots. Every room had a wall of tall arched windows that looked over boundless gardens and orchards to a dazzle of sea.

"We need to find the doorway that leads to Fairknowe," Hannah said. "This place is so huge! Can you remember Morgana's directions?"

It took them about forty minutes, walking slowly for the sake of Max's aching leg, to find the little low door Morgana had described to them. It was made of grey rock, and had two stone gargoyles perched on pillars on either side. One was happy and held a branch of flowering blackthorn. The other was doleful, and held a branch of sloe berries.

"This is it!" Hannah cried.

A clamour approached them along the corridor – the sound of voices and cruel laughter and a wild sort of music. Then the stone door was slammed open. Irata strode through, dressed all in green with flowers twined in her hair, with a procession of fairies and bogey-beasts streaming along behind her. She looked furious.

"But how was I meant to know that Lord Montgomery

has ridden to war?" a dwarf was saying piteously, wringing his hands. "He was there when last I looked, I swear, Your Majesty."

"I'll see you swinging by your heels above a pit of snakes," Irata snapped. "How am I meant to win his love when he's a hundred miles away?"

"We can try again at the autumn equinox, Your Majesty," the dwarf suggested.

"I don't want him in autumn, I want him now!" she snapped. "I'll teach him to prefer my whey-faced cousin Eglantyne to me!"

She strode on, snapping her fingers at some guards, who seized the dwarf and dragged him away in the opposite direction. The rest of the procession surged after the queen. Hannah had to stifle a little gasp when she saw her father and Donovan, with ropes around their necks, being tugged along at the rear by the Red Cap. The goblin looked round sharply and flared his broad nostrils, but there was such a stench and a noise in the corridor that he could not sense the three invisible watchers in the shadows, and so he stumped on, his captives stumbling along behind her.

A guard pulled the stone door closed. Hannah quickly ran forward and, taking her eating knife from her belt, drove it into the crack between the two doors so that they did not properly close. The guard did not notice. He was too busy exchanging banter with the gargoyles.

Hannah ran back to the others. "Let's find somewhere you can sit and rest, Max," she whispered.

He was looking white and tired after the long walk. "OK. But don't be long."

"We'll be as quick as we can."

They settled him in a little antechamber with a bed made from their plaids, some food and a leather bottle of water – boiled and cooled. Hannah left her guitar and her walking stick with him, but took her long dagger. Scarlett left her tambourine too. Then the two girls crept back out into the corridor, and went in search of the Unseelie Court. A cacophony of music, singing and roaring could be heard in the distance and the girls followed the sound, down broad marble steps and through immense empty hallways. Hannah was so afraid she felt quite sick.

They reached a banqueting room, crowded with goblins and bogey-beasts of all size and description. They were gnawing on bones and tossing them to the floor, dancing on tables, sending fine crystal crashing everywhere, and swinging on the chandeliers. Harassed-looking fairies hurried everywhere, sweeping up glass and chewed bones, mopping up spilled wine, and bringing in great jugs and platters that were seized upon with roars of approval. Irata herself was seated on a tall wooden throne at the head of the room, with four small elflike boys to serve her wine and sweetmeats, fan her with peacock feathers, massage her scaly feet and buff her long, silver-painted nails.

The throne's headrest had been carved into the semblance of a horned and bearded face, and it had lion's paws for feet and eagle's wings for armrests. The wooden face wailed and moaned incessantly, its features screwed into an expression of anguish. Irata lashed it with a silver-tipped switch, snarling, "Sing, why don't you? Sing! I'm the rightful queen. Stop your caterwauling."

The throne winced and tried to sing, but only a miserable ululation came out of its contorted mouth. Irata lashed it again, shrieking, "Sing!"

Sitting at a tiny child's table nearby was Hannah's father, Robert. His chair was so ridiculously small, his knees were up near his ears. He was still dressed in his jester's motley, with long ass's ears and belled toes. Although she was relieved to have found him so easily, Hannah was very worried to see no sign of Donovan.

Hannah signalled to Scarlett to keep close behind her, and crept along the walls until she was crouched behind her father. He was looking down into a tiny two-handed silver cup – like a baby's christening cup – with an expression of such misery and despair that Hannah's heart went out to him. She forgot the humiliation of his costume, and her angry misery over his absence from her life, and longed to throw her arms about his neck. She dared not do anything that might draw the eyes of the Unseelie Court upon them, however, and so she leant over his shoulder and breathed upon the round silver saucer on the table. Her breath misted the bright silver, and she drew in the condensation her father's symbol, the two Rs looking backwards and forwards like the two-headed god, Janus.

His eyes widened, and his hands trembled so much

he had to put down his cup. "Is someone there?" he whispered, looking around him slowly, so as not to draw any attention. "Who are you?"

Hannah breathed on the saucer again and swiftly wrote her name, in her special way, with the two Ns facing back to front, much like her father's own symbol.

"Hannah? Not my girl?"

Yes, she wrote in the condensation, then breathed on it again and drew a capital D and a question mark, hoping her father would understand she meant Donovan.

He nodded his head almost imperceptibly, then got up, pushing back the tiny chair so it fell over. He stood, smiling inanely, pretending to sway as if he were drunk. Hannah looked anxiously towards Irata, who raised her eyes and studied him for a moment, then went back to examining the newly buffed nails of one hand. Robert stumbled towards the nearest door, Hannah and Scarlett slipping along behind him, trying to avoid being trodden on by a foursome of wildly dancing goblins.

Audacia

"Where do you think you're going, fool?" a squat guard demanded, raising his spear so he could prod Robert in the stomach.

"Gotta go relieve myself," Robert slurred, swaying from foot to ridiculous foot. "Even humans have . . . bodily functions, you know."

The guard grunted and stood aside. "Don't be long. The queen is looking bored. She'll start breaking bones if someone doesn't amuse her soon."

Robert lurched out the doorway, Hannah close by his side. As soon as it shut behind him, Robert ripped off his ass's ears, his unsteady gait turning into a quick stride. Leading the way quickly down the corridor, he said in a low voice, "Hannah?"

"I'm here."

"I can't see you. Is it some kind of invisibility spell?"

"Linnet made it for us. Here, let me put some on you too so no one can see you either." She stopped him with one hand on his arm and daubed some of the fern-seed paste on to his brow. "Things seen and things not seen, let my father walk between," she chanted. He looked down at his arm and hand with a dubious expression. "You still see yourself, but no one else can," she said. "Only those wearing the fern seed can see each other."

He looked up at that and stared at her. "Look at you! So tall! So beautiful. You've got the red hair of the Roses." He held out his arms to her, and rather shyly, she permitted him to embrace her. It felt both very odd and awkward, and yet, somehow, quite blissful.

"Red as any Rose," she quoted with a smile.

"I can't believe you're so grown-up. If I had not met Donovan and seen him so tall, and heard all his stories of you. . . Last time I saw you, you were just a tiny baby."

"And probably hideously ugly," Scarlett put in.

He looked round quickly. "No, no, she was gorgeous. Big grey eyes, and just a few little wisps of red hair. But who are you?"

"I'm Scarlett Shaw."

"Not Bill and Maureen Shaw's baby? You weren't born yet when I . . . was taken . . . but your mother was out to here." He measured a large distance with his hand. Scarlett shot Hannah a rueful glance at this final proof she was indeed her parents' daughter.

"Come on, let's get a move on," Robert said, taking off his long pointed shoes and thrusting them into a painted ceramic jar, along with his ass's ears. "Are you sure no one else can see me?"

"Quite sure," Hannah answered, not quite truthfully.

They hurried on. Robert's arm had fallen away from Hannah's shoulder, but he kept staring at her, and after a while, burst out, "I've been hoping and hoping that somehow . . . one day . . . has it truly been thirteen years since she caught me?"

"In my time," Hannah said. "In Eglantyne's time, it has been six months."

"It feels like only weeks to me," Robert said in a dazed voice. "I did not quite believe the boy. . . Is it true he is Eglantyne's son?"

Hannah nodded. "I think so. He's been brought up by your friend, Allan MacEwan."

"I gave Eglantyne into Allan's care," Robert said. "Eglantyne was ill, exhausted. . . Allan promised to take care of her for me. What happened?"

Hannah felt cold and shaken. "She was going to have the baby . . . to have Donovan. Allan tried to take her to hospital, but it was snowing. The black witch made him crash his van. By the time the ambulance got there, Donovan had been born but Eglantyne was dead."

There was a long silence. Robert pressed one hand against his eyes. "Poor Eglantyne. Poor little sweetbriar rose. I had so hoped. . ."

"So what happened to you?" Hannah demanded. "Why didn't you come home with her?"

Robert gave a deep groan. "If only I had! I was arrogant and impatient. I was so pleased with myself for rescuing

Eglantyne, and so eager to break the curse . . . and it was close to midnight by the time I had got her to Allan's house and explained to him, and asked him to keep her safe. . . I came home past the hill, and thought to myself, *The gate is open; I can go back in time again and find the three other loops of the puzzle ring now. Then the curse would be broken, my family would be safe. . .*"

He did not speak for a long moment, his brow furrowed, his eyes shadowed, then he went on, slowly, "I should have known the gate would be watched. The Unseelie host were waiting for me just inside the passage. I turned and ran for home, but they caught me under the yew tree. I only had time to throw the hag-stone into the witch's pool before I was dragged away. They took me to the Otherworld, and I have been here ever since, playing the fool and waiting for a chance to escape. I cannot believe thirteen years have passed, and that the little newborn baby I left behind is now a teenager. I am so sorry, Hannah."

"I'm just glad we found you," Hannah said gruffly, unable to look at him.

"Me too!" His step had faltered, but now he strode on again. "Well, then, let's get Donovan and get out of here!"

"Where is he? Is he all right?" she asked.

"Yes. I'm taking you to him now. He'll be badly frightened. The queen does not treat her servants well, and he's been defiant. She threw him into the dungeons for a spell, to soften him up."

"We need to get the hag-stone too," Hannah said. Her

father grimaced, but said nothing as he led the two girls deeper and deeper into the bowels of the palace. There were no windows down here, only flaming torches set in the damp stone walls. They passed a guard, engaged in picking his toenails with the tip of his knife, and came through a low archway into a dark and stinking chamber. A row of barred and bolted oaken doors lined the far wall. From behind one came the wistful tones of a flugelhorn, playing a familiar tune.

Hannah raised her voice and softly sang a few lines from "Time After Time".

The flugelhorn faltered. "Hannah?" Donovan cried.

"Shh. I'll have you out in a moment," she whispered, and drew back the bolts and the bars. The door squeaked loudly as she opened it, and she heard the guard's feet hit the ground. "Quick!" she hissed, and grasped Donovan's hand and drew him out of the cell. He was dressed in jester's motley, yellow and blue, with a ridiculous three-peaked hat hung with bells. He stared around, bewildered, at the empty room, clutching his flugelhorn to his chest. "It's all right, I'm here," Hannah whispered. "I'm invisible. Here, take my hand. I'll make you invisible too."

He grasped her hand tightly. "I am so glad to see you! Well, at least *hear* you."

"Sssh," she whispered, daubing him with Linnet's paste. As she spoke the words of the spell, Scarlett quickly shut the door and shot home the bolts again. The guard came hurrying in, looking surly and suspicious, his foul-smelling lantern held high. Hannah and her companions shrank back against the walls. The guard came and checked the door was still shut, then called, "You've finally shut up, hey? Stopped your blasted caterwauling?" He grinned at the silence and said, "You'll learn," and stumped away again.

The four invisible humans tiptoed after him, barely daring to breathe until they were back in the main part of the palace. At once, Donovan turned and grasped Hannah's hands. "I knew you'd come!" he said huskily.

"I'm sorry we took so long," she replied past a hard lump in her throat. "I'm so glad you're all right!"

"To think I once longed to go to the Otherworld," he said wryly. "Now I can't wait to get out of here!" He cast a quick glance round. "Where's Max? Is he all right?"

"His leg hasn't healed right," Hannah said. "We need to get the hag-stone back so we can fix him up properly."

"And Linnet? She's not here?"

"She couldn't come," Scarlett put in. "Something about not meeting herself in the corridors at Wintersloe. You've got to admit that'd be creepy!"

Hannah could hear shouting and caterwauling coming closer and closer. At first, she hoped it was just more of the midsummer celebrations. The noise was spreading through the palace, though, and she was afraid it meant Irata had realized Robert had never come back to the banqueting hall. A look at his pale, thin-lipped face showed Hannah her father feared the same.

"All we have to do now is get the hag-stone and then we can get out of here," Hannah whispered.

"Well, yes," Robert said. "I've been worrying about that. You see, the queen is wearing the hag-stone about her neck. We're going to have to steal it from her."

There was a long silence. The children stared at each other in dismay.

"How?" Donovan cried, looking quite sick at the idea of going anywhere near Irata.

Robert took a deep breath. "My bet is that the time for subtlety is over. She'll have the phantom hounds on our trail. It won't be long before they pick up our scent. I think we'd probably just better go right up to her, snatch the hag-stone and run. If you kids cause some kind of diversion. . ."

"But it's so dangerous!" Scarlett cried.

"Yes," Robert said. "But I see no other way." He smiled at Scarlett. "You know what the motto of the Rose family is?"

"*Audacia*," Hannah said at once.

"Do you know what it means?"

"To be audacious!" Hannah cried.

"Absolutely right."

"Which is just fine if you know what *that* means," Scarlett said caustically.

"To be brave," Robert said. "Come on, kids! *Audacia!*"

So the four of them, stupidly, crazily, ran straight towards the roar of the Unseelie Court. As they ran they knocked over candelabras, tossed vases and glass bowls, pulled hair and tweaked noses. Confusion reigned everywhere. Fist fights broke out, a fire was ignited when a candelabra toppled into a pool of spilled liquor, and fairies tripped and tumbled over each other.

Irata was on her feet, shouting orders, her eyes glittering with rage. Robert sneaked towards her, then flourished his invisible dagger before her eyes. "Draw, O coward!" he shouted. At once Irata froze, her eyes darting from side to side, her stiff hands clawing at the air. Robert laughed, and cut the hag-stone free with Hannah's dagger. As it fell, his invisible hand closed over it and suddenly the hag-stone was invisible too. Then he turned and ran, the children at his heels.

"Find them!" the queen screamed, clutching at her neck.

An eerie howling rose as the black phantom hounds put their noses to the scent. Hannah had thought she was running as fast as she could. The sound gave her fresh speed. Leaping down steps three at a time, she swung herself round the corner, leading the way towards the doorway to Fairknowe Hill. It was a long way, through a maze of seemingly endless stone hallways, and soon all four were panting for breath, stitches in their sides. Still they ran on, as the howling grew closer and closer.

"Max! Max!" Scarlett screamed, bursting into the little chamber. "Come on!"

Max was waiting for them, looking sick and scared. He

held Hannah's guitar and was leaning on her stick. Hannah grabbed the guitar and flung the strap over her shoulder.

"Dad, give me the hag-stone!" she yelled.

He tossed it to her. She caught it in mid-air and bent and scooped up the water bottle. Holding the hag-stone by its leather cord, she quickly dunked it in and out of the leather bottle, crying aloud the first words that came into her head:

> "*Hag-stone, mend the bone!*
> *Make strong what is weak.*
> *Make straight what is bent.*
> *Make swift what is slow.*
> *By star and moon, hag-stone.*"

"Drink!" she ordered. As Max obediently swallowed down a mouthful, she hung the hag-stone about her neck once more. She then drank herself, and passed the bottle along to her friends.

At once the stitch in her side disappeared. New strength and well-being flowed through her. "Come on!" she cried.

Max gave a wild whoop of excitement, flung the walking stick away, and led the way down the corridor, running faster than Hannah had ever seen him move. Scarlett caught up her tambourine and ran with Donovan, shouting with nervous excitement. The guitar bouncing on her back, Hannah raced after, risking a look over her shoulder.

Ten great black hounds loped towards them, eyes glowing red. Hannah sprang forward. Never had she run so fast. The ground whizzed beneath her feet. Her father caught up the old rowan walking stick and followed swiftly.

They reached the doorway where the two gargoyles sat peering around, puzzled to hear shouts and the pound of feet, but seeing nothing except flickering shadows.

"What's going on?" the sad one shouted. "Is it a fire?"

"Oh, it must just be a merry game of hide-and-seek," the happy one said.

Ignoring the gargoyles, Hannah pulled her little eating-knife out of the crack and flung the door open. Max shot inside as if he had rocket-propelled boots, with Donovan a stride behind. The phantom hounds were upon them, though, snarling and slavering with yellow foam. Robert twisted the handle of the walking stick three times, and drew out the slim sword. He drove it straight through the breast of one of the phantom hounds, and cracked another on the head so it yelped and slunk away.

There was a bang, and a crash of cymbals, as Scarlett brought her tambourine down upon the head of another black hound. It sat back on its haunches, shaking its head frantically, trying to get rid of the broken tambourine. Yellow foam splattered the walls. Scarlett ran through the door as Robert whacked another of the hounds with the stick and sliced off the ear of yet another.

"Dad!" Hannah cried. "Come on!"

Robert gave one more swift lunge towards the hounds,

who yelped and cringed back; then he ran towards the doorway. As he leapt through, Hannah slammed it shut.

It was dark on the other side. They hurried down the passageway, hands on either wall, until they came to another doorway. Light burned from a lantern, and a fat old dwarf in leather armour lay sleeping in a comfortable chair, tilted back on its legs so it rested against the stone door. Very carefully they set the chair straight and pulled it away from the door. The dwarf mumbled, but did not wake.

Hannah took down the lantern and they all joined hands, Robert at the end of the chain with the rowan stick clenched in his hand. Hannah laid her hand on the door and sang the words she had composed only yesterday, on the slopes of Black Rock a hundred miles away and four hundred and forty-odd years ago.

> "On this Midsummer's Eve,
> open, hill, and let us leave,
> let us go back to our own time,
> by the power of rhythm and rhyme,
> back to the dawn of the next day,
> after the day we went away.
> Open, open, great door of stone,
> by the magic in my blood and bone."

Howls echoed down the corridor as someone opened the doorway at the other end of the corridor. Hannah took a deep breath, opened the door, and led the way through.

By the light of the lantern she saw a narrow, crooked passageway beyond. She walked out, praying incoherently under her breath. The others followed her, and Robert shut the door behind him. They hurried down a series of rough steps and rocky falls, and came through a familiar graffiti-scrawled cave. Hannah's heart leapt with joy.

Still clutching Donovan's hand, she hurried out into the icy-cold grey dawn. Frost crunched under her bare feet and silvered the roof of Wintersloe Castle below. The light in her lantern was dim now.

Everyone clustered round, cheering and clapping. Suddenly Hannah heard behind them the dreadful howling of the hounds. Her stomach lurched.

"They've followed us through to this time!" Scarlett cried. "What shall we do?"

Hannah's mind moved like lightning. She remembered the first time she had climbed this hill, with Donovan at sunset on her first day at Fairknowe. He had broken off a bare twig from the blackthorn tree and told her some of the stories about its powers. That twig was back in her bedroom, kept in her wooden box with all her other treasures, but the blackthorn still grew on the crown of the hill above them.

"Dad, my dagger!" she cried.

He hesitated, but when she gestured wildly, he passed it to her, hilt first. "Hannah. . .?" he began uneasily.

She wasted no time on explanations. She thrust the knife through her belt and desperately clambered up the rock, grazing her knees and her palms. Panting, her hair all over her face, she reached the hill's crest and swiftly cut another twig from the ancient tangle of thorns. She scrambled back down, sliding half the way on her bottom.

The howls were very close now. Hannah glanced wildly into the cleft in the hillside. Irata was running towards her, her wand glowing green in her hand, a host of malevolent fairies at her heels. Black hounds, eyes glowing madly, raced before her.

"Run!" Hannah shrieked.

Everyone took to their heels. Hannah gulped a deep breath, clutched the hag-stone tight in her left hand and flung the blackthorn twig over her left shoulder. As soon as it touched the ground, an impenetrable hedge of vicious thorns sprang up, barring the entrance to the cave. She heard faint screams of rage and pain from behind the hedge, and howls, and shouts of despair.

Hannah smiled and ran down through the winter-bare trees, her red hair flying. Below her, warm lights spilled from the kitchen windows of Wintersloe Castle and smoke drifted from the chimneys. Her father turned back and waited for her, smiling gladly.

"We're home!" Hannah cried. "We're home at last!"

PART THREE

THE SINGING THRONE

The Rose of the World

The door to the kitchen was still unlocked, just as Hannah had left it, eight hours and four hundred and forty-odd years earlier. Even though Hannah had grown used to the mental flips and cartwheels needed to calculate the differences in time, it still made her feel very strange coming back into the kitchen and knowing little had changed here, in her own time, when so much had happened to change her.

Linnet was sitting by the fire, the toad crouched on her lap. The lines in her old, wrinkled face were driven in deep, and she looked older and smaller than Hannah remembered. She jumped up as Hannah eased open the door, letting the toad spring to the floor, and held out both her hands. "Oh, my lamb, you're safe home again!"

Hannah leapt across the flagstones and into Linnet's arms, her eyes smarting with tears. She had to stoop to embrace the old woman, and felt the tiny hands patting her all over as Linnet said brokenly, "My lamb . . . my chick . . . you're safe . . . you're home again . . . och, I've been worried!"

It felt so strange to see Linnet as a stooped, white-haired old lady when Hannah had grown used to seeing her young and lissome. Hannah hugged her as hard as she dared – for this Linnet seemed so frail and breakable – and managed to say, "We're home, yes, all of us, home again!"

Then Linnet drew herself up, tears running down her face, as she saw the others piling in through the door – Donovan, Max and Scarlett, all filthy, tousled-haired and very oddly dressed – and then behind them, the tall figure of Robert, his red hair and beard wilder than ever, dressed in the motley of a court jester.

"Bobby!" Linnet cried, her voice breaking. "Bobby, you're home!"

In two strides, he was beside her, lifting her up in his strong arms and swinging her round as if she were a child. A babble of voices broke out as Linnet asked questions and demanded explanations, all the time patting Robert's shoulders as if she could not believe he was really there in her kitchen. Then Donovan burst out laughing and pointed to the toad, which was leaping and jumping and croaking with joy underfoot, in grave danger of being squashed. Hannah went down on her knees and gathered the old toad close.

"Angus, Angus, I'm so sorry," she said, nearly as croakily as the toad. "I never realized . . . so long trapped as a toad . . . we missed you so much!"

The toad croaked complacently.

Scarlett was down on her knees too. "We did, we did!" she cried. "We wished you were there the whole time."

"Don't worry," Donovan said in his grave way, bending down to touch the toad's head lightly. "The tale is almost all told; the spell shall soon be undone. We promise."

Angus the toad leapt high on his springy back legs.

"I knew last night was the night," Linnet said, wiping tears away from her cloudy green eyes. "I dared not say anything, unless I changed history somehow. . . Oh, but I watched you sneak out, my chick, and I've stood vigil all night, so afraid for you. . . I knew the whole story, you see, right up until the time you and Max and Scarlett disappeared into Black Rock. But I had no idea what happened after that. More than four hundred and forty years I've had to wait to hear the end of the story. . ."

Helter-skelter they told her, and she gasped and sighed and covered her eyes with terror and laughed out loud. Before the story was done, though, Robert was already looking towards the swinging door.

"You'll be wanting to see your grandmother," Linnet said. "And Roz, of course!"

"She's here?" Robert asked, starting forward, and then casting an anguished eye towards Hannah. "But . . . she must hate me . . . thirteen years gone . . . how can I explain it?"

"Leave that to me!" Hannah cried. "You go see Belle and I'll sort Mum out, don't you worry."

"And I'll whip you all up something to eat," Linnet said, seizing one of her copper pans from the rack. "But you must all wash first, you're filthy!"

"Hot running water!" Scarlett sighed, clasping her hands together above her heart. "Flushing toilets! Oh, it's so good to be home!"

Linnet gurgled with laughter. "I must admit, running water and flushing toilets almost made the long wait worthwhile. Not to mention supermarkets!"

Hannah paused only long enough to avail herself of the running water and flushing toilet, before making her way to her mother's bedroom.

"Mum! Wake up!" Hannah stood at the foot of her mother's bed.

Roz stirred and stretched. "Mmm?"

"Mum. I need you to wake up. Guess what?"

"What?" Her mother sleepily opened her eyes.

"I've got a surprise for you."

"Look at you! You're all in a mess. Look at your hair. You look like you've been dragged backwards through a thicket! Hannah, what have you been doing?"

"Never mind that now. Come on, I've got a surprise for you. You've got to get up."

"But it's still so early . . . what surprise?" Even as she spoke, Roz threw back the bedclothes and sat up, reaching for her shabby old dressing gown.

"You can't wear that," Hannah said. "Here, I've brought an old one of Belle's for you. See, isn't it pretty? All silky, with roses on it. Just let me brush your hair, it's sticking up all over the place."

"Hannah, what's this all about?" Roz submitted to her

daughter's fussing, but with a worried frown between her brows.

"Can I put some powder on you? And some lipstick? Why do you wear such a boring brown? It makes you look old."

"Hannah! What's this all about? Hannah!"

"Oh, you are going to be so surprised. You won't believe what I've found for you. *Who* I've found." Chattering all the way, Hannah led her mother down the stairs.

"Who? Hannah, what do you mean? Is someone here? I don't want to see anyone when I'm in my nightie. . ."

"*He* won't mind," Hannah said and flung open the door to the drawing room.

Robert turned quickly and started forward, his hands held out. He had spent the last ten minutes washing and brushing himself up as best he could, but it was still a rather wild-haired, oddly dressed man who came towards his startled wife.

"Bob!" Roz screamed, and flung herself into his arms. They hugged each other for a few minutes, patting each other, murmuring each other's names. Hannah and her great-grandmother watched happily, holding each other's hands tightly. Lady Wintersloe was not at all her usual elegant, stylish self, sitting in her chair in an old bathrobe with her white hair falling down on to her shoulders and her broken leg sticking out from underneath her flannelette nightgown. She was laughing and clapping her hands together with joy.

411

Roz suddenly drew back. "But . . . Bob! This is unbelievable. You're alive! I thought you were dead, we all thought you were dead. Where have you been?"

Robert took a deep breath and straightened his shoulders. "I know you may find this hard to believe, Roz, but. . ." His words ran dry.

"He's been trapped in the Otherworld, Mum," Hannah cried, dancing about in excitement. "I went there and found him and brought him back!"

"Don't be ridiculous!"

"It's true. All the stories are true. Fairknowe Hill is a gateway to another world, and to other times too. We've been back in time, Mum, back to the time of Mary, Queen of Scots! I met her! She was beautiful. We sang for her. And I swam through a whirlpool, and rode a kelpie, and. . ."

"She's ill," Roz said, feeling her forehead. "Delusional."

"It's all true, Roz," Robert said.

"Don't you dare go filling her head with all your nonsense!" Roz flared. "Where were you all the years I had to raise her alone? Where were you when I. . ."

He seized her hands. "If I could I would've been with you both, you must believe me!"

She snatched her hands away. "Believe you? When you tell me such rubbish? Where were you really, Bob?"

"Oh, Mum," Hannah said. "And you a scientist! Can't you trust the evidence of your eyes? Look at what we're wearing! Are these what people normally wear in the twenty-first century?"

412

"You've been to a fancy-dress party?" Roz said weakly. For the first time, she really stopped and looked at her daughter, and her eyes grew wide with amazement. Hannah was not the same girl she had been yesterday. She was taller, and her body was thin and wiry and strong, as if she had spent days walking and running and riding. Her mass of curly red hair was longer and wilder than ever, and her blue-grey eyes seemed much larger in her thin face. Most surprisingly, her face had lost its sulky defensiveness and was bright with humour and self-assurance.

Hannah laughed. "Come and listen to the others! They'll tell you." She flung open the doors and called her friends in. They had all been waiting in the kitchen with Linnet, drinking hot tea and eating drop scones. They came in, wiping the jam and cream off their chins. Linnet came in too, pushing the laden tea trolley, hunchbacked, cloudy-eyed, and more than four hundred and sixty years old. She smiled fondly at Roz, saying, "Och, now, it's all been too much for you, my lady. Sit you down and I'll pour you a nice hot cup of tea."

The others clustered around Roz, looking as wild and filthy as Hannah. Words flew around the room. Phantom hounds. Fairy princesses. Men turned into toads.

Roz sat and accepted a cup of tea, looking dazed. "Collective madness?" she murmured. "Doesn't bad bread send people mad? Maybe you've all eaten something. . ."

"You only get ergot poisoning from bread made from infected rye," Max said cheerfully. "I read an article about it on the net."

413

"We haven't been eating rye," Hannah said impatiently.

"We haven't eaten much at all for an awfully long time," Donovan said, grabbing another drop scone dripping with honey.

"You all ate dinner here last night," Roz said firmly. "Haddock and potato soup and roast chicken with oatmeal stuffing."

"No rye," Max said. "Though you can get poisoned from eating green potatoes. . ."

"We're not poisoned!" Hannah cried. "We're all quite normal and sane."

"Though very, very hungry," Donovan said, through a mouthful.

"You look so thin, my poor lambs," Linnet said. "I'll have to cook you all a feast to celebrate your safe return."

"They were all here last night!" Roz cried.

They ignored her, bombarding Linnet with requests for their favourite food. Roz sighed, and drank some tea.

"Please believe me," Robert said, taking away her cup so he could hold her hand. "I know it's hard for you. It defies all logic. But some things are illogical! Like love, or faith, or trust, or. . ."

"All right, all right," Roz said wearily. "It doesn't help the fact that you've been gone from our lives for thirteen years!"

"I'd give anything to have those thirteen years back again," Robert said, and kissed Roz's hand. She blushed and snatched her hand away, smoothing her sleep-ruffled hair as she glanced anxiously at herself in the mirror.

414

"You're as beautiful today as the day I met you," Robert said.

Her cheeks reddened. "I'm thirteen years older," she said caustically. "I have grey hair and wrinkles . . . while you! You don't look a day older."

"I'm sorry," he said uncomfortably. "I never meant for this to happen. I love you just as much as I ever did. More, because I thought I had lost you for ever." He seized her hand again, and this time she let it lie in his, though her look of worry and puzzlement did not ease.

"He couldn't help it; he was cursed, you know," Hannah said to her mother. She was feeling rather giddy with relief and excitement and exhaustion. "He tried his best to break the curse. He found one part of the broken ring, and I got the other three!" Her voice rose high in jubilation. "Look!" She lifted her dress to show the bedraggled hem of her linen smock. Taking a knife from the trolley, she ripped apart the seam, and three small loops of gold fell out into her hand.

"You found them!" Robert shouted. "Oh, well done, Hannah!"

"It wasn't easy," she said. "I can't believe I haven't had a chance to tell you yet. Though we have been rather busy."

He put his hands on her shoulders and pulled her close for a warm hug. "Oh, you clever girl, you brilliant girl! I can't believe you found them."

"All we need to know now is where you hid the loop

you found, Dad. I've searched everywhere. But there are so many roses in this place! Ceiling roses, roses on cushions and carpets, hundreds of roses in the garden. I just couldn't figure it out."

Her father laughed. "But I thought it was clear enough. I left it safe with the rose of the world, my *rosa mundi*. . ." He bowed towards Roz, who looked puzzled. "That's one of the meanings of Rosamund," Robert explained. "From the Latin, meaning 'rose of the world'. . ."

"Oh, yeah, I knew that," Max said. "I take Latin at school. You've got to know it if you want to be a doctor."

"Why didn't you tell me?" Hannah demanded. "I practically dug up all of Belle's rose garden!"

"I didn't know you wanted to know," Max said. "You just asked me if I knew anything about double roses. Though you should know I hate gardening."

"Rosamund Rose, my darling double rose," Robert said and smiled at Roz, who sighed and muttered, "Ridiculous name!"

"So you gave the ring to Mum!" Hannah said, torn between exasperation and excitement.

"It was her wedding ring," Robert said. "I do hope you didn't throw it out, darling?"

Roz put her hand to her chest in a familiar gesture, groping for the ring she wore on a chain about her neck. "No, I didn't throw it out," she answered quietly.

"I can't believe it! It was under my nose all the time! Can I have it, Mum? Please?"

Her mother unhooked the chain and let her wedding ring slide off it. Hannah caught it up with a crow of delight. Then she placed the four loops together on the table. Instinctively she laid them at the points of the compass: north, south, east, west. Hannah's voice shook as she clasped the hag-stone next to her heart and said, improvising, "Hag-stone, help me break the bane, make the golden rose whole again."

From the hag-stone whirled a rush of wind, which caught up the four slender loops of gold and dragged them up and around in a spinning vortex. Then the tiny whirlwind retreated back into the hag-stone, leaving a single ring rocking gently on the table. The loops were now intricately woven together, forming delicate leaves and thorns about a simple five-petalled golden flower like a sweetbriar rose.

Robert picked the ring up and turned it in his fingers. "More than four hundred and forty years it took us to find and mend this ring. Four hundred and forty years!"

Hannah was too full of emotion to speak.

"So much sorrow, so much suffering," Lady Wintersloe whispered.

Robert turned to Roz, who was staring at the restored ring with a stunned expression. "Rosamund Rose, I promised you that one day you would have the whole ring to wear on your finger. I had no idea it would take thirteen years, or that it would mean I would miss so much of our lives together. I swear I'll try to make it up to you. Will you

417

let me give this ring to you again, as a token of my true love and my promise to never, ever leave you again?"

Roz hesitated, biting her lip. She looked up at her husband, then at Hannah's pleading face, then at the circle of expectant watchers. Then she laughed, shrugged and jammed the ring on to her left ring finger. "You have a lot of making up to do," she warned, then at last her face broke into a broad smile and she leapt up and cast herself into her husband's arms. He folded them about her, and buried his face in her soft brown hair.

Hannah expelled her breath in a big sigh. Lady Wintersloe dabbed at her eyes, while Scarlett pressed her hands over her heart, turned her eyes up to heaven, and said, "So romantic!"

"I think we deserve that celebratory feast now!" Linnet said, smiling happily. "I'd better start cooking! Why don't you all go and ring your parents and tell them where you are? Then you really all need a long, hot bath, I think. You've brought more than a whiff of the sixteenth century back with you!"

"Bringing back memories, hey?" Donovan grinned.

"And not all of them pleasant," Linnet retorted.

It was a joyful meal. Linnet cooked sizzling-hot bacon, eggs, and sausages, croissants with strawberry jam, warm cinnamon rolls and frothy hot chocolate with marshmallows. Deep happiness radiated from all the members of the Rose family, and everyone else was so

418

relieved to be safely home that jokes and laughter and teasing banter flew from all sides of the long table.

Only Hannah remained quiet and thoughtful.

Donovan leant close and spoke in a low voice. "Are you worrying about . . . you know. The black witch."

Hannah nodded. "She'll find a way through that hedge sooner or later. It was dawn, and so her powers were weak. But some midnight, she'll come back."

"But not for a while, surely? It's seven weeks until the next thin time," Donovan reassured her.

"Linnet said she can come any time, if her will is strong enough. At sunset or sunrise, or midnight or noon, or when the moon is full or new, or when her name is called. . ." Hannah stopped, the thoughtful expression on her face deepening.

"So she might be coming through any time now?" Donovan looked alarmed.

Hannah nodded. "I think I need to go and talk to Miss Underhill."

"Miss Underhill? Why?"

"I think she may know a way that we can trap her."

"Really? OK. Should we go now?"

Hannah smiled. "I'd like to, though I'm really, really tired. I feel that if I go to bed, I might never get up again. So I thought I'd go now, and then I'll be able to sleep easy."

"Yeah. Good idea."

Hannah hesitated. "Donovan. . ."

"Yeah?"

"You know you really are Eglantyne's son? That Allan is not really your father?"

Donovan bent his head so his long black hair fell over his face. "Yeah. I know."

"It means we're cousins, in a weird sort of way. I mean, your real father is Lord Montgomery. He died soon after the battle where Queen Mary was defeated, when the old castle was burnt down. His younger brother inherited the castle and I'm descended from him. That means your uncle was my great-great-great-great-grandfather – with probably about twenty 'greats'. That makes us kin."

Hannah loved the word "kin".

Donovan shook back his hair and smiled at her. His blue-grey eyes were filled with light. "Kin," he repeated softly.

"It means we're both Roses," Hannah said.

"So *I'm* the Black Rose, the one in the old story, that had to be saved by a Red Rose before the curse could be broken?" Donovan asked. For a moment he looked away, his thin cheeks reddening, then he flashed her a smile. "You did save me, and for that I thank you." His words were oddly stilted and formal, as they often were.

"So don't you think we could just call ourselves cousins? I've always wanted a cousin," she said.

"Me too." Donovan flashed a smile at her, but bent his head again so the hair fell over his face, obscuring his expression again.

Hannah knew him well enough now to know what

he was thinking, though. She touched his arm gently. "It was pretty amazing what he did, you know. I mean, my dad turns up out of nowhere with some strange girl, and thrusts her upon him, saying, 'Look after her,' and then he goes and disappears, and the girl has a baby and then dies. Your dad . . . Allan, I mean . . . could've given you away. I mean, for adoption or something. But he didn't. He looked after you all this time, not even knowing who you really were. I think he thinks you're really my dad's baby. I mean, you do look a bit like him. Apart from not having red hair."

Donovan turned and stared at Robert, who was talking earnestly with his wife and grandmother. He noticed Robert's fine pale skin, his expressive blue-grey eyes, his straight patrician nose, his long-fingered hands. Donovan looked down at his own hands. "It explains a lot," he said slowly. "About my dad, I mean. About Allan."

Hannah nodded.

They were silent, lost in their own thoughts.

"It means you're the rightful heir too," Hannah said softly. "To the throne under the hill. You're the lost king."

"I've been worried about that," he said in a burst. "What does it mean? I'm just a kid. I don't want to have to go away by myself and be king of the fairies. It's just ridiculous."

"I don't want you to go away either," Hannah cried, then reddened. "I mean, we've only just found out that we're cousins."

"I don't know anything about being a king. I don't

421

even believe in kings!" Donovan looked at Hannah with troubled eyes. "So do you think I have to go? Is it my duty?" He spoke the last word bitterly. "There were so many things I wanted to do in this world! I wanted to play my horn, and be a famous musician. I wanted to climb all the Munros and go to the Himalayas and see Mount Everest. Maybe even climb it one day, and play my horn up there at the very top of the world. I wanted to see a real live snow leopard and hear a nightingale sing. I wanted . . . oh, I wanted. . ." He fell silent.

Hannah put out one hand and touched his sleeve gently. "There may be a way. . ."

"How?"

"Let's go see Miss Underhill."

The Child of True Blood

Miss Underhill was dusting a shelf of crystals when Hannah, Donovan, Max and Scarlett pressed their faces against the shop window. She looked up and her face suddenly came alive with eager curiosity.

"Come in! What are you doing here so early?"

"We've come to ask your help," Hannah said.

Miss Underhill scrutinized them closely. "You look thin, all of you, and maybe taller too. And all of you – your hair is longer, much longer. You've been there, haven't you?"

"Where?" Scarlett said innocently.

"I watched you go," Miss Underhill said. "Last night, at midnight. Carrying candles and singing. I was standing guard, but instead of someone coming *out* from under the hill, I saw you four go *in* . . . and you didn't come out again."

The four children were silent.

"I followed you into the passageway. I walked through it three, four times. But there was no sign of you. You'd just disappeared. That's when I knew it was true. After all my years of trying, all my study, all my attempts . . . I've never been able to find the doorway through to the Otherworld. Yet you children. . ." Her voice was raw with longing. "How? How did you do it?"

Hannah drew out the hag-stone and held it, dangling from its cord, towards Miss Underhill. She took it wonderingly. "A hag-stone. But . . . where. . .?"

"A toad gave it to me," Hannah said. "At the witch's pool."

"A toad. . ."

"A man who had been transformed into a toad," Hannah said. "He's been waiting there for me for four hundred and forty-odd years. He's a very old toad now."

Miss Underhill sat down suddenly. "Four hundred and forty years. . ."

"Miss Underhill, why are you so interested in fairy lore? Your whole life is devoted to learning about it and trying to keep it alive." Hannah waved her hand about the shop. "How come?"

"There's a story in my family," Miss Underhill said slowly. "Once, a long time ago, one of my ancestors barely escaped from the Otherworld with her life. She was a fairy child, the daughter of the king of the mountain . . . that's where my surname comes from, you know. The child that came from 'under the hill'."

"Her name was Morgana." Hannah heard a faint hiss of breath as her friends suddenly understood, but she did not take her eyes from Miss Underhill's face.

"Yes. I'm named for her. All the eldest girls in my family have been. And we were all told the story. My mother thought it was nothing more than a lovely old story, though she kept her last name, as all the women in my family have done. So we wouldn't forget." Morgana Underhill paused, then took off her glasses and rubbed her eyes. When she looked up, Hannah saw her eyes were the most beautiful clear green, like a sunlit forest pool.

"My grandmother, though, she believed the story, and she taught me to believe. I've been searching all my life to find some way back to the homeland that my ancestor lost. I go to every fairy knowe and hill I can find, I search every cave and passageway, I go round them nine times widdershins. . ." Morgana's voice trailed away. She looked down at the hag-stone. "There was a red-haired witch who helped my ancestor. Or so the story goes. She promised to defeat the evil queen who had killed the king of the mountain and his two eldest daughters, and to help Morgana win back her throne. She had a hag-stone just like this."

"It was the same one," Hannah said. "That red-haired witch was me. We went back in time when we went through the hill, back to the time of Mary, Queen of Scots."

"You helped my ancestor?" Morgana sounded dazed, and she turned incredulous eyes from one face to another.

"Yes. For us it was only yesterday that we said goodbye to her and promised her we would do our best to defeat Irata."

"Don't say her name!" Morgana cried.

"I want to say her name. I want to call her. We can never defeat her as long as she comes with the Wild Hunt at her heels. She turned Angus into a toad. She threw Max high in the air and broke his leg. . ."

Startled, Morgana looked at Max, who was kicking his heels against his stool leg in his usual way.

"It was weeks ago," Max said. "For us, I mean. And Hannah made healing water."

"With the hag-stone," Hannah put in, feeling colour rise in her cheeks as Morgana turned that intense gaze upon her. "I think it's more powerful when it's in the fairy realm."

"Because it worked a treat!" Scarlett cried. "I was so hot and worn out and exhausted, I just wanted to lie down and die, and then we drank the water and I felt like I could fly! It was fantastic!"

Hannah glanced at Donovan, who was looking as pale and sombre as she had ever seen him. He noticed her look and sent her a quick, flashing smile. He had, she saw, seen all the possibilities of the discovery of who Miss Underhill really was.

"Miss Underhill. . ." Donovan began, then stopped.

"Yes?"

"If you are descended from Morgana, Eglantyne's sister. . ."

"Yes?"

"Then that kind of makes you an auntie to me," Donovan

said in a rush. "Because, you see . . . I'm Eglantyne's son. I know it sounds crazy, but. . ."

Hannah and her friends told Morgana Underhill all they had learnt in the past few weeks, and she listened quietly, turning her face from one to the other, emotions flitting over her face. Disbelief, wonder, anger.

"So if you are Eglantyne's son. . ." she said to Donovan, when they had convinced her that their story was true, "that means you are the true heir."

"Not if I don't want the throne," Donovan said in a rush.

"We were thinking . . . we were wondering . . . you're a child of true blood too, aren't you? Couldn't you go and be queen in Irata's place? A good queen?" Hannah asked.

Morgana had a faraway expression in her eyes. "Me? Go and be queen of the realm under the hill? No, no, it's a fantasy. A fairy tale. Things like that don't happen in real life."

"All things are possible in all the worlds," Hannah quoted.

Morgana smiled. Her green eyes were filled with light. "Well, I guess there's no harm in trying. If I had the hag-stone. . ."

"It's yours," Hannah said, speaking past the lump in her throat. "It belongs to the princess royal, doesn't it?"

Morgana looked down at the small, rough stone in her hand. Colour rose up her face. It made her look quite different.

"But first we need to deal with Irata," Hannah said firmly. "As long as she still rules in the fairy realm, none of us will be safe. That's why we need your help."

"But what can you hope to do?" Morgana asked.

"Well, you see, if we call her, she'll have to come alone. We can choose the time and place. We can make sure we're strong and protected. And best of all, she'll think she's coming to face children, not a real, live witch. Because you truly are a witch, aren't you, Miss Underhill?"

"I like to think so," she answered rather shakily.

"So you'll know what to do." Hannah spoke confidently.

Morgana blinked. "I might have to do some reading up on it."

"That's good. Because we've been up all night . . ."

"We are so, so exhausted!" Scarlett said, giving a huge yawn. At once the others yawned too, Max so widely you could practically see his tonsils.

". . . and it'd be really good if we could catch some sleep," Hannah finished. "What time should we get together?"

Morgana gave a sudden grin. "Sunset is a border time, a place between day and night. Let's say sunset. At Fairknowe Hill."

Dusk came early.

It was cold, and Hannah's breath frosted the air as she came quietly through the shadowy garden. Her stomach was tight with nerves, and her ribcage ached as if a boulder rested upon her chest. She had slept all day, though, and eaten another of Linnet's delicious meals, and felt ready for anything.

Her friends were waiting for her by the yew tree. "You nervous?" Donovan asked.

"Very. What happens if we fail?"

"We'll think of something else. Don't worry."

"We're not going to fail," Scarlett said.

They went together through the yew tree, past the gleaming witch's pool and up the pathway to the fairy hill, which rose steep and black against the pale sky. Morgana Underhill was waiting for them by the blackthorn hedge, which barred the entrance to the cave. She was dressed in a soft white woollen robe, knotted about the waist with a black cord. She wore the hag-stone on another black cord about her neck. Her grey hair hung loose on her shoulders. It made her look much younger.

She was sitting cross-legged, with two black candles in holders made from the twisted twigs of the blackthorn. A mirror with an ornate, gilded frame lay between them. In her hands Morgana held a small, dark wand made of blackthorn and a knife with a silver blade and a white handle.

"There are five of us," Morgana said without preamble. "That is perfect. Five for the limbs and head of the body; five for the points of the pentagram and the five elements, earth, fire, water, air and spirit; five for the fingers of the hand; and the five senses; and the fivefold kiss of the Wiccan, feet, knees, womb, breasts, lips."

The children were shaken and afraid. She looked and sounded so different.

"I have drawn a pentagram here in the ground," Morgana said. "Come and sit on the other four points."

Looking down, Hannah saw a five-pointed star carved deeply into the hard ground. Feeling very nervous and rather silly, she sat down as instructed. Morgana rose slowly to her feet and began to walk in a circle around the outside of the star, muttering under her breath: "I consecrate and conjure thee, circle of power. . ." She walked round again, sprinkling salt, and then a third time, trickling water from a small bottle, muttering all the while.

Then she sat again at the top point of the star, which faced east, directly towards the barred cleft in the hill. She lit the two black candles and put them either side of the mirror, which she propped on a black-draped stone so it stood upright. "Hold hands," she instructed. They did as they were told, without any silliness, and waited nervously.

"Hannah, you need to call Irata now. Call her name nine times."

Hannah looked into the mirror. It was almost dark. The sun was slipping away below the horizon and bats were flitting through the trees.

"Irata, I call thee," she said. "Irata, Irata, Irata. . ." Nine times she called the dark queen's name. To her surprise and horror she saw the proud, pale face rushing closer and closer towards her in the mirror, as if it were a window and the queen was running towards her down a long dark hall. Hannah's voice shook. She could barely manage to finish the incantation.

"You fool!" Irata's voice dripped with scorn. "Do you know what you've done?"

"I've called you out of your world into mine," Hannah said, her voice weak as a little girl's.

"I thank you!" Irata replied. "I was searching for a way through. Now you'll be sorry you ever sought to cross wills with me!" She raised her hand, so that the wand filled the mirror with eerie green light. It spilled out of the glass, making the candle flames look wan and turning everyone's faces into demonic masks.

Quickly Morgana snatched up the black cloth and flung it over the mirror. They heard a sudden gasp of surprise from Irata. Morgana took up a coil of black cord and began to wind it round and round the mirror, chanting, "By the power of star and stone and tree and running water, I bind thee, I bind thee, I bind thee! By the power of blood and bone and eye and hand, I bind thee, I bind thee, I bind thee!"

"No, no, no!" Irata screamed. The mirror rocked wildly. Morgana held it steady, winding the cord about it three more times, chanting, "By the power of love and loyalty, faith and friendship, I bind thee, I bind thee, I bind thee! Nine times I bind thee, three times three, that you may never again be free, and so I say and so I will, so mote it be."

431

She stopped, her breath coming fast. The black-bound mirror was still and quiet. "So. It's done."

They stared at the black bundle for a long while, but nothing happened.

"What do we do now?" Hannah said very quietly.

"Throw it in the deepest part of the loch," Morgana suggested. "We don't want it to ever be found again."

"The mirror might break," Donovan said.

"We'll wrap it up well," Morgana said.

So the four friends helped Morgana wrap up the black-bound mirror in a thick, dark blanket which Hannah fetched from the house, and tied it up with rope that Max fetched from the shed, and then they rowed out on to the dark, still loch. Somewhere an owl hooted. The moon was rising and turning the world to silver and black. They went far from shore, in a deep gulf between the islands, and there they heaved the mirror over the side of the boat. It sank in seconds, leaving only a ripple to disturb the silvered water.

"So will you go and take her place in the fairy realm?" Hannah asked.

"I will, the very next time the gate opens," Morgana replied. "The next thin day is the spring equinox, in seven weeks' time. That will give me time to prepare. I can't just leave the shop as it is, it wouldn't be right. Donovan, I thought I would leave it all to you. The shop, my flat, my savings. You're my only kin."

Donovan was wide-eyed and silent with amazement.

"It's not much," Morgana said, "but it's something. It

should mean you're never wanting for anything. If you look after it and don't waste it."

"Mum and Dad will help," Hannah said, feeling a little secret thrill at being able to say those words. *Mum and Dad. . .*

"Max, Scarlett, I thought you could choose something from the shop, whatever you like. And Hannah, I thought you would like my books. And, perhaps, my wand and my dagger."

"I'd love them!" Hannah said.

"Let's go home now," Morgana said. "It's late and your parents will be worrying."

They rowed back to shore and tied the little boat up at the rickety wharf. Wintersloe Castle was warm and welcoming, with lights that streamed across the frosty grass. The forest and the hill and the road that ran down to the town looked cold and dark and lonely.

"Do you want to come back for dinner?" Hannah asked Donovan in a low voice.

He shook his head. "I think I'd better go talk to my dad, don't you? Tell him that I know."

"That'll be hard."

He grinned. "No. It'll be good. He should've explained to me a long time ago. We could go looking for stags in the morning if you want? I'll come chuck some stones at your window, bright and early."

"OK. See you then. Bye, Max! Bye, Scarlett! See you tomorrow. Bye!"

Blowing on her frozen hands, Hannah went up the slope towards the house, which lifted its mismatching turrets against the starry sky. A delicious smell of roast grouse and bramble crumble filled the air. Hannah looked back once at the loch, now hiding another secret in its murky depths, then smiled and ran up the stairs to the house where her family was waiting for her.

Blackthorn Blossoms

Almost seven weeks later, as the sun was rising on the morning of the spring equinox, the green hill opened its secret door and let in a grey-haired, middle-aged woman and an old hunchbacked woman with cloudy green eyes.

Morgana carried a box of books and treasures she could not live without. Linnet carried one large warty toad and a small grey cat, which wriggled desperately, trying to get away.

"Don't cry, my lamb," Linnet said to Hannah. "Och, but it's glad I am to be going home at last. I don't think I could survive another Scottish winter."

"Oh, but Linnet, I don't want you to go!" Hannah sobbed.

"Wheesht! You'll come to visit us, by and by, you and the laddie. You know where the door is."

"But I haven't got the hag-stone any more!" Hannah wiped her eyes and blew her nose, and cast a longing look at Morgana, who wore the hag-stone on a cord about her neck.

"You don't need the hag-stone. You've got the wild magic, in here and in here." Linnet tapped Hannah on the head, between the brows, and then again above her heart. Tears sprang to Hannah's eyes again, and she threw her arms about Linnet and hugged her close.

"Och, you'll be breaking my bones if you keep on so! Now, I need you to be looking after your great-grandmother. She's had me all her life and she'll miss me sorely. Will you do that? I've left you my recipe book. She does love my marmalade cake. Could you be cooking it for her sometimes?"

"I'll try," Hannah said, glancing back down the path to the clearing beside the yew tree, where the rest of the family waited by the witch's pool. Linnet had prepared them all one last feast before leaving them, and it was spread out on a picnic blanket. Roz and Robert leant against each other, feeding each other strawberries, while Genie and Allan were busy cutting the marmalade cake and pouring glasses of home-made lemonade. Lady Wintersloe stood, leaning on the rowan walking stick, waving her handkerchief. A few weeks in hospital, and healing water made with the help of the hag-stone, had seen her broken leg mend, but she was still not nimble enough to climb the steep path to the fairy hill. She was very sad to see Linnet leave, but glad that the old fairy had at last been released from her centuries of service.

Hannah's friends were there too. Scarlett was demonstrating how she had fought off the witch-hunters in Fortingall, and had just thrown Max over her shoulder

436

and flat on to his back. Breathless, his black hair sticking up, his glasses on crooked, Max was protesting loudly, while the adults all laughed.

"And you might want to get her another cat. She loved this bogey-beast, Lord knows why!" Linnet waggled the grey cat, who hissed and spat at the toad. Angus just blinked his imperturbable black eyes.

"I'll find her a lovely little kitten," Donovan promised. "A white one with green eyes to remind her of you."

"Are you sure you'll be able to turn Angus back?" Hannah asked. "I do hate to think of him being a toad for so many years!"

"Sure I will," Linnet answered. "Lucky he was a toad, and was there that night to see your father throw the hagstone into the pool. Else it might have been lost for ever!"

"Strange how things work out," Hannah said.

"I will miss you two," Linnet sighed. "Take care, won't you? Don't go falling off any mountains, Donovan! And look after Hannah for me, won't you?"

"I will," he promised.

"I don't need looking after," Hannah flared. "I'm quite capable of looking after myself."

"Oh, you are, I know it, my lamb," Linnet said, and gave them each a last kiss before following Morgana into the dark cleft of the hill. Morgana had cut a way through the blackthorn with her witch's knife, which Hannah now held in its embossed white leather sheath, along with the twisted wand of shining black wood.

"Hannah! Donovan!" Roz called. "Come and eat."

"One minute!" Hannah called back. She and Donovan pressed their ears to the rock.

"Can you hear anything?" she asked.

"Sssh!" Donovan said.

They listened intently and heard, far away, a high, wild, ethereal song, weaving through the caves and chambers of the knowe. "It's there! Can you hear it? It's the throne, singing for the child of true blood," Donovan cried. "Oh, isn't it beautiful!"

Hannah nodded, unable to speak.

"They've made it. They're home." Donovan dashed his arm across his eyes.

"Come on," Hannah said after a moment. "I want to get a photo of us, all smiling and happy, for the great hall. The first happy snap of the Rose family in more than four hundred and forty years. We don't want to have red eyes and miserable faces! I'll get Scarlett to take it. Max can't keep still long enough to take a decent photo."

They walked back towards the sound of voices and laughter under the ancient spreading branches of the yew tree.

"Look, it's snowing!" Donovan said. "Yet it's such a beautiful sunny day. How can it be snowing?"

Hannah and Donovan stood still, holding up their hands to the shower of sweet-scented white blowing over their faces. "It's petals," Hannah said. "White petals."

Instinctively they both looked back at the green knowe.

The blackthorn tree upon its crown had burst into blossom. Like tiny white stars, the flowers bloomed all over the black twisted twigs, turning the tree into a shining beacon upon the hill. Hannah and Donovan smiled at each other.

"Come on!" Hannah cried. "Let's go tell Belle. Now we know the curse truly is broken. Everything will be all right now."

The cousins grabbed hands and ran down the pathway. A gust of wind sent a spindrift of blackthorn blossom spiralling up around their running bodies and flying hair, before falling down to float upon the dark surface of the witch's pool.